FEVER!

ZOMBIE RULES BOOK 6

DAVID ACHORD

SEVERED PRESS
HOBART

FEVER!

CHAPTER 1 – TRUE - 3 A.Z.

Nimrod Abraxas True. That's me. Named after my father, or so my mother claimed. Truth be told, I had no idea who my father was. He was African American though, which wasn't a good thing for my mother. Her family disowned her the moment I was born, or so she said.

I guess I was around fourteen or so when I told people to stop calling me by my given name. I hated it. Being named after a man who took no interest in me was hard, so I'd tell people just to call me True.

I was the oldest of seven. My momma was what you'd call a wanton woman. Each of my siblings had a different father, so there you have it. Life growing up for me was about what you'd expect under those circumstances, I was constantly doing stupid shit and getting in trouble.

When I was seventeen, I got caught breaking into a home, the home belonging to my history teacher. He was an old, crusty-looking dude. Rumor had it he was a Vietnam veteran and had lots of medals. He visited me in juvie and told me if I enlisted, he wouldn't press charges.

It wasn't a hard decision. I'd been arrested so many times, the District Attorney told my public defender she was going to get me tried as an adult. Make an example of me, she said. She was a big, fat, homely woman who always seemed to be scowling. She made it plain she didn't like me none. Like I said, it wasn't a hard decision.

Besides, the only thing waiting for me back home was an apartment in government housing I shared with my siblings, my mother, and whoever she was sleeping with at the moment. The place had a permanent odor of overcooked food and dirty clothes.

Mister Johnson himself signed me out of juvie and drove me directly to the recruiting office. It was at one of those commercial strip malls. They had the Army, Navy, Air Force, Marines, Coast Guard, and National Guard all jammed together in a row of offices. Everyone had gone home for the day, except for a National Guard sergeant who was playing solitaire on his computer. Mister Johnson had a long, private talk with him and the next thing I knew, I was signing papers as a full-time member of the National Guard.

Basic training was a culture shock, as you might expect. I thought I was tough, but I didn't have anything on those drill sergeants. I did alright though. After I graduated AIT, that's advanced individual training, I spent some time overseas before transferring to Houston Barracks in Nashville, Tennessee.

It seemed like everything in my life was finally going okay, and then, it all went to hell. That was eleven hundred and eight days ago. I kept track of the day the world ended by starting on the day I first saw a zombie. In fact, I saw about five thousand of them. It was a game-changing moment.

It don't matter what all I got into during that time. Not much to tell. Chaos, people going crazy, and the National Guard being called upon to restore order. Hah! What a joke. There wasn't no way to restore order.

Several months later, here I was, standing outside in the middle of the night with three white men who'd become my friends.

"The truck is a good one," Zach said as he handed the keys to me. It was a red dually 4X4 diesel. The man had modified it all kinds of ways. He had those big redneck tires on it, a huge bumper with a winch so you could either push things or drag them out of the way, a light bar on top, and he'd even put some fencing over the windows so the zombies couldn't get to you. We even found a camper top that fit on the back so we always had a place to sleep.

"There's an M60 in the back with five hundred rounds," Zach told us. "It's all I could spare."

"You are awesome, Zach," Blake said.

Zach's full name is Zachariah Gunderson. That name alone screamed, *"White Boy!"* but, he was a good dude. Smart too.

"Are you guys sure I can't talk you into coming with us?" he asked.

I shook my head. Most of them were going to pack up and move to a place called Mount Weather. With us being in the military, it was naturally assumed we'd go too. We'd talked about it many times and a few days ago, we made the decision. Me and my two friends, Blake Mann and Brandon Caswell. We decided we were tired of being in the military and tired of taking orders. We were going to strike out on our own. I wanted us to keep it a secret, but BC, that's what we called Brandon, decided to get advice from Zach.

I was pissed at first. I thought Zach would snitch us out. But, he didn't. The next day, he approached us and opened up a spiral notepad. It was full of ideas and suggestions for us. That boy sure liked to write stuff down.

We sat in the privacy of his barn and read his notes over while he talked. He had things in that notepad that I would've never thought about. I had to admit, talking to Zach was a good idea after all. And he didn't tell anyone of our plans.

Yeah, Zach was a good dude.

We met at midnight the next night. Zach shook our hands and wished us well.

And so, on a warm August night on the eleven hundred and ninth day that I saw my first zombie, the three of us headed out. Our destination was a place called LBL, the Land Between the Lakes. BC had an aunt and uncle who owned a marina and campground somewhere around there, and he seemed to think they were still alive.

It was a life-changing decision. At the time, the three of us were convinced it was the best course of action for us. If I had only known.

If I had known the path we had set for ourselves was going to lead to us becoming murdering marauders, I would have jumped out of that truck right then and there.

CHAPTER 2 — NEW JOHNSONVILLE

We made it to New Johnsonville with little trouble, encountering only a few zombies wandering around. Most of them were out of the roadway, but any of them who were stupid enough to not move were run over by BC. Otherwise, we didn't waste our ammo on them.

New Johnsonville was a small southern town located on Kentucky Lake in the western part of Tennessee. The nearest city was Waverly, eleven miles back to the east, but it wasn't much bigger. BC pointed.

"Kentucky Lake is up ahead. It's really the Tennessee River, but they dammed it up; now they call it a lake. I have no idea why they didn't call it Tennessee Lake. It's always been a small town, only about two thousand people lived here the last time I visited." He turned onto a side road off State Route 1 onto Nell Beard Road. "The marina is at the dead end. I hope it's still intact. It was pretty impressive, back before."

"I hope your people are still alive," Blake said.

"Yeah, me too," BC replied.

I could hear some tenseness in his tone of voice and he was looking around as he drove. It was a long rural road, with lots of trees and bushes on both sides. But, there was something a little different about this road.

"Ain't no trees lying across the road," I mentioned. BC and Blake looked around. Blake then pointed.

"I see a lot of tree stumps and cut up trees," he said.

BC slowed to a stop. "Yeah, somebody's been working to keep the road clear. That's a good sign, right?" he asked.

"Well, someone's doing the work," Blake replied.

"Yeah," BC muttered and started the truck moving.

He got quiet now. He was trying to hide it, but I could see he was tense. I guess the not knowing of what awaited us at the marina, whether or not his kin were alive, was getting to him.

He had been holding steady at twenty-miles-per-hour, but as we rounded a slight curve, he slowed to a crawl. There was some barbed-wire fencing and a heavy gate that was currently open.

"I don't remember this," BC muttered.

"It's new, huh?" Blake asked. "That's got to be a good sign."

He was trying to be optimistic, but I wasn't so sure it was helping BC.

"Well, here we go," BC said and eased the truck through the entrance. There were several campers to our right, and each of them had been fortified with barbed wire and sandbags. We eyed them as BC proceeded forward, and soon we were in a decent-sized parking lot. Ahead of us was a cove and a boat dock with multiple piers and slips. A lot of the slips had a boat tied off.

"There are some nice boats out there," Blake said. "Someone's been taking care of them."

BC put the truck in park and killed the engine. I could hear a dog barking from somewhere, but otherwise, it seemed quiet. I opened the door to the truck, got out, and stretched. I then slowly, nonchalantly, turned back toward the truck as Blake opened the passenger door.

"We got company," I whispered.

They emerged from some trees that lined two sides of the parking lot. I counted nine of them and they were all armed with various firearms. I was holding an assault rifle, but I held still and did not try anything.

"Holy moly, hold up, fellas," BC said and ran over to an older woman. Her jaw dropped as he grabbed her in a bear hug. Thankfully, she recognized him immediately, so nobody was shot. He motioned us to walk over. I wasn't so sure, but I trusted my friend. She looked to be in her late fifties, with long gray braided hair and a face that looked like she'd seen a lot in her lifetime.

"This is my Aunt Leslie," he said with a big grin. "She's the best aunt you could ever have."

While we said our hellos, a man separated himself from the others and walked over to BC. He looked meaner than a Tennessee cur with a biker's beard and long gray hair also braided. He looked like he was in his sixties with a whipcord lean physique. That didn't fool me though; he looked as strong as any thirty year old.

When BC saw him, his face widened in surprise.

"Boy, you sure have grown," he said. The two men approached each other, shook hands, and then hugged tightly.

"Guys, this is my Uncle Gavin," BC said.

We introduced ourselves, and when he shook my hand, he squeezed it a little tighter than normal and gave me an unfriendly stare with shrewd gray eyes, silently letting me know what he thought of me, which I assumed meant he didn't care much for blacks. The tattered rebel flag fluttering on the pole nearby was another clue. I met his stare, letting him know I didn't give a shit. He responded with a small smile.

"So, you boys are friends with my nephew?" he asked, although the answer seemed obvious to me.

"They're my best friends, Uncle Gavin," BC replied. "You can count on them to have your back."

He looked us over again. "Is that right?"

"Yes, sir," BC replied.

"Oh, it is so good to see you, Brandon!" Aunt Leslie exclaimed and hugged him so tight I thought he was going to piss himself. Uncle Gavin joined in and gave BC what I suppose was a friendly slap on the shoulder.

I looked over the other seven people. All of them were giving me some other curious looks, nothing hateful, but curious. BC's aunt and uncle were the only old ones. The rest of them were all younger. They were mostly a scraggly looking lot. Except for one. She was a blue-eyed blonde who was built like a brick shithouse, and when she saw me looking, she gave me a slight smile. If I didn't know any better, I'd call it a friendly smile, maybe even a little bit flirty.

It'd been a while since a woman looked at me like that. I smiled back. It'd been so long since I actually smiled, it felt strange and uncomfortable.

CHAPTER 3 – ACCEPTANCE

"So, you boys are soldiers too, huh?" Gavin asked.

We were sitting at some picnic tables overlooking the marina. Aunt Leslie doted over us like we were her own long-lost kin and had plates of fried fish sitting in front of us before our butts could warm up the chairs.

I watched quietly and tried to remember the names of everyone. There was Aunt Leslie and Uncle Gavin, of course. The beautiful blonde's name was Sandy. She had a brother named Shane, who had the same ashy blond hair and blue eyes. I found out later they're fraternal twins. He was a cocky shit who looked like he used to work out with the weights a lot.

The rest were Lee, Jinni, Jolene, Big Bear, and Kathy Ann. Jolene saw Blake staring at her.

"Heterochromatic," she said.

"What's that?" Blake asked.

"My eyes, they're heterochromatic. Very rare. I was promised a job with a prestigious modeling agency in New York. The agent said he'd never seen eyes like mine before." She looked off wistfully, and then gave a languid smile.

"Now she's all mine," Shane declared, reached over and gave her a slap on the behind. She let out an embarrassed yelp which caused Shane to guffaw like an adolescent kid.

"Mind yourself," Sandy admonished and looked at me. "So, is True your first name or last name?"

"Yeah, or is it a nickname, like mine?" Big Bear asked. The man was a big one, well over six feet tall. He was wide and barrel-chested, with big gnarly hands. He was also covered in thick, coarse hair.

"We just call him True," BC said. "He doesn't talk much, but anything that comes out of his mouth is always the truth, you can count on it."

"You got the right," Blake added.

I caught Gavin staring again. He nodded slowly and looked like he was thinking something over. He then gave a grin that didn't reach his eyes and waved a hand at the food.

"Dig in, boys, the women here are damn good cooks."

We talked as we ate. After we'd finished eating, the man they called Lee went inside an RV that was parked nearby and emerged a moment later with a bottle of Jack Daniels. "Let's have some dessert."

"Now you're talking," Blake said with a grin.

"Our reserve stock," he replied with his own grin. He was missing a tooth or two, and the ones still left looked like they were barely hanging on. I guessed him to be in his mid-twenties, wiry, brown hair and eyes, and a scruffy beard that had some bare spots. His hair and clothes were clean though, so that was saying something.

Sandy brought some glasses over and Lee poured us all a shot. By the time he'd filled twelve glasses, the bottle was almost empty.

"Here's to our nephew and his friends," Gavin said.

We all raised our glasses and drank. I don't think I'd had a drink since way back in Manchester, so I'd forgotten how whiskey would sneak up and burn your throat. I kept from coughing and making a face though and put the glass back down on the table slowly. I caught Sandy out of the corner of my eye staring at me again.

"Any of you see any action?" Lee asked. "Besides killing stinkers?"

BC laughed. "Stinkers, marauders, we've had plenty of both." He then pointed at me. "True served a tour in Iraq. He saw a little old-fashioned combat action with those ISIS motherfuckers."

Lee looked over at me. "How many of them damn ragheads did you kill?" he asked.

"Hard to say," I replied, which was true enough. Sometimes you saw your target, sometimes you were putting rounds downrange so fast you didn't know if you were hitting anything or not.

"Lee, damn it, don't you know real soldiers don't brag about who all they killed," Gavin declared. I looked over and he continued staring. I didn't see any warmth those eyes.

He glanced at BC. "Isn't that right, nephew?"

"That's right, Uncle Gavin," he replied and looked over at Lee. "True is rock steady in a fire fight though, you can count on it."

Gavin laughed, finished the dregs from his glass, and poured himself another shot.

"Well now, my nephew seems to think a lot of you, Soldier True."

"We're friends," I said.

"That's good. A man needs friends he can depend on." He gestured around. "These are my friends. They always have my back too."

"All white folks," I said levelly. "Don't you have any black friends?"

He gave a slight smirk. "Now, I'm not saying folks around here have any qualms about blacks, but we ain't exactly fond of them either."

"True is my friend, Uncle Gavin," BC said.

"We're a package deal," Blake quickly added. "If True is not welcome here, just say so and we'll move on."

Gavin's expression was like a block of ice, cold and unemotional. Only his eyes held any emotion, and they weren't showing any hints of kindness. He looked over at BC. "What about you, nephew, how do you feel about it?"

BC's expression was different from his uncle's. There was a lot of what you'd call conflicted emotions. I was about to save him the trouble of making what was a hard choice for him.

"Listen, I…"

BC stopped me with an upraised hand. He then squared his shoulders and faced his uncle.

"Like Blake said, we're a package deal. If True isn't welcome here, well, we haven't even unpacked the truck yet. I'll give Aunt Leslie a hug and we'll be on our way."

Gavin sat silently. I guess we had our answer. The three of us stood at the same time, but Gavin flicked a hand.

"Sit down, fellas," he said and reached for the bottle. "Welcome to the family."

BC picked up his glass but held off from drinking. "I appreciate this, Uncle Gavin, but what about the rest of you people?"

Now Gavin smiled, but there wasn't much warmth to it. "They do what I tell them. Don't worry though, we need you boys for the kind of work we do."

I waited all of three seconds before asking. "What kind of work do you do, Mister Gavin?"

He looked at me with those gray eyes. "We do what we have to in order to survive. You can understand that, can't you, soldier?"

"If you want cold air, you'll need to start the generators, but I haven't run them in a while and the gas might be bad," Lee said.

While BC got reacquainted with his aunt and uncle, Lee volunteered to show Blake and me around. It was a nice marina with several boats still in good shape. There was also the campground section with several RVs and campers.

"You can live in one if you want, or pick you out one of the empty houseboats." He pointed. "Me and Jinni live in one, Gavin and Leslie live in another. Shane and Jolene share another one. Big Bear and Kathy Ann live in that RV over there," he said as he pointed.

"Now, I've got to warn you, some of them had dead people in them, and a couple had zombies. We pulled them all out maybe a year ago, but there might still be some smell. So, y'all pick whichever one you want to call home. You can all live in one, or each of you pick one for your own. It don't matter to me, there's plenty of empty ones. Oh, none of them have any water in them. We have drinking water over there." He pointed to the main office. "But, if you want to take a bath, you need to go down there on the bank and clean yourselves up with the river water. It ain't too dirty," he said with a grin.

"Do you have much of a problem with zombies?" Blake asked.

9

Lee scratched his head. The question seemed to confuse him, though I didn't know why.

"Well, we've killed off a bunch, but every once in a while, one or two or three or four will come around. Gavin says they're like bears. Bears don't have good eyesight, but they sure can smell food."

"Blood too," Blake said.

"Oh yeah, especially blood, and they can hear decent, so we try to keep quiet. When we hunt close, we use compound bows instead of guns. We only use guns when we, uh, well, when we go on huntin' trips."

He looked a mite nervous when he said that and I wondered why.

"What about fishing?" I asked.

"Trolling motors only," Lee said. "A charged-up battery can last all day. We have to use a jenny to charge them, but you can't have everything. Oh, by the way, Gavin's already told me I need to do some fishing tomorrow. We ain't got all that much food. So, maybe one or two or three of you will go with me," he said with a big grin, revealing a few missing teeth. "I know where all the best fishing holes are."

We opted to share an RV for the night, both for convenience and security purposes. It also allowed us to talk in private.

"What do you think?" BC asked. After the sun went down, BC joined us. We walked over to a semiprivate area and washed down while standing in ankle-deep water. We were now sitting in our new RV, wearing nothing but underwear, trying to stay cool and not break a sweat.

"It's a pretty good set up," he said.

"Yeah," Blake replied. "There are some improvements they could do; their defense works are awful, and with this readily available water supply, they should be able to produce at least a hundred gallons of clean water a day, but we can help out with that." He then turned to me. "You haven't said much."

"Your uncle doesn't seem to like the color of my skin," I said to BC.

"Yeah, he's an old Tennessee redneck, but while you two were walking around with Lee, I set him straight. He'll be alright, you'll see."

We talked about it for a few more minutes. Finally, Blake looked pointedly at the two of us.

"Alright, let's not beat around the bush here. BC, I know you want to live here with your aunt and uncle, and I'm willing to live here as well. But, True, if you aren't comfortable here, BC can stay here and the two of us can leave in the morning."

To tell the truth, I was what you'd call conflicted. A couple of them seemed like decent people, but I got a bad vibe from Gavin. I guess what decided it for me was that smile from Sandy. She was a fine-looking woman and I couldn't stop thinking about her.

"I guess we could stay here a while and see how it works out," I found myself saying.

BC gave a whoop. "Awesome!" he said in nearly a shout.

CHAPTER 4 – HUMBOLDT

"You see 'em?" Lee whispered. I was sitting back beside a triple loader, watching them through binoculars. There were four of them, but the rest of their group a couple of miles up the road. That's where they lived. Lee and I were sitting in an abandoned laundromat, watching the four of them load up their truck.

"You see 'em, right?" Lee asked again.

"Yeah," I answered, handed him the binocs, and retrieved my rifle.

The stench was horrible in this place, a combination of zombie stench and old, backed-up sewage, but it offered the best view. When we set up in it, we had to kill two zombies that had been nesting in it for some time. We couldn't make a lot of noise by shooting them, but that was no problem. Lee got their attention and held them off with an old mop while I snuck up behind them and bashed their brains in with a crowbar.

"Don't get too close to the window," I admonished in a whisper. It wasn't really a window anymore, more like a window opening with shards of glass around the edges. Lee stepped back until he was once again hidden in the shadows.

We were on the outskirts of a town called Humboldt. We'd been on the road for three days before we found this group and started stalking them.

Our job was to cover them in case it all went bad. The plan was for Gavin and a few others to wait for them to finish loading their trucks, bum-rush them, and convince them at gunpoint to give it up or else. We'd done it once before on a group of survivors outside of Jackson, Tennessee and got a pretty good reward out of it.

I sometimes wondered how these little groups of people had survived for so long. When you stepped out beyond your little hidey-holes or your fortified encampments, you always had to have a plan and needed to have people posted up to guard your sorry ass from zombies or marauders when you're scavenging. Just because you haven't seen either one in weeks didn't mean they weren't around. This group, like the group in Jackson, had no lookouts and had lingered around a little too long. If they'd been quicker, we probably couldn't have been able to set up on them.

Anyway, it went off without a hitch, up to a point, and then it went bad. I don't know what. I was watching them through a rifle scope and I didn't see nothing but those boys raising their hands. Gavin shot first, which caused the rest of them to open fire. Like I said, there was only four of them and they didn't stand a chance. I heard Lee inhale sharply and glanced over at him. He had been watching them through the binocs.

12

"Oh shit, not again," he muttered.

"This shit happened before?"

Lee stared a moment longer before lowering the binoculars and looking at me. "Well, sometimes people don't want to go along with the game plan."

I didn't respond. Wasn't no need to. Any false beliefs about the people we'd hooked up with, this right here cleared it all up. These folks were marauders, murderers. I found BC and looked at his face through the scope. He was smiling and laughing with the rest of them. All of 'em were.

I didn't say nothing when they came and picked us up. What could I say? You people are nothing more than cold-blooded killers? Maybe once we got home, I'd pack up and sneak away. That sounded pretty good. I did the same thing back in Manchester and I could do the same thing now.

"You ain't saying much, brother," Lee said.

It was dark in the cab of the Chevy Suburban. Blake and BC were chatting away up front. It sounded like they were bragging about our haul, but I wasn't paying much attention. I couldn't see Lee's expression, but I could tell by his tone he was worried what I was thinking.

"Ain't got nothing to say," I replied.

"Are you okay?" he asked after a moment.

"Why wouldn't I be?" I asked, although I didn't want him to answer. In fact, I didn't want to talk to any of them.

It was an eighty-mile drive and by the time we got home, there was only a smudge of moonlight left in the sky, and since we were the last vehicle in the convoy, it was our responsibility to make sure nobody followed us. Lee and I jumped out of the Suburban five hundred yards from the entrance to our little compound. We took up positions on either side of the road, rifles at the ready, and waited while BC drove away. Aside from crickets and cicadas, there was nothing.

"They must have done something," Lee whispered, referring to the people back at Humboldt. He waited for me to answer, but I didn't. "They must have, right?"

He wanted to talk about it, he wanted me to speak my mind. And, more importantly, he wanted me to say something to make it seem okay that we murdered some people.

"What's done is done," I replied.

He probably wasn't through talking, but realized I had nothing more to say. We stayed there for a solid ten minutes before I stood. "We ain't being followed, let's go."

They'd left the gate open for us. We closed it in silence and pulled the barbed-wire barricades across before rejoining the rest of them. There was supposed to be a guard on duty, but I imagine whoever it was wanted to join the group and admire our spoils. I could hear them laughing and joking, like they'd done something worthy enough to celebrate.

"See you tomorrow," I said to Lee and peeled away from him, heading to the RV I was now living in.

"You don't want to look over all of the stuff?" he asked.

"Tomorrow," I replied and kept walking.

I stopped long enough to start the generator I shared with a couple of others and flipped the circuit breaker to the little water heater in my RV.

I sat on the steps in front of the door and fished out a pack of cigarettes I had hidden in a crack between the steps. Cigarettes were hard to find these days and even when you were lucky enough to find a pack, the tobacco was stale. Didn't matter to me though, I needed a cigarette to help me think. I lit one in the dark and waited for the water to heat.

I'll leave tomorrow night. Not tonight though. Tonight, I wanted a hot shower and a good night's sleep. Tomorrow, I'd act like everything was normal, eat a couple of big meals, and claim my share of the loot. After it got dark and everyone was asleep, I'd take one of those trucks we'd stolen and head out. My two friends would understand. Or not, I didn't care.

I finished the cigarette, flicked the butt off into the dark, and went inside. All of the lights were off, but that didn't matter, I knew every square inch by memory. I made my way back to the bathroom, turned a solitary light on, stripped, and got in the shower.

I washed four days' worth of grime off me in less than three minutes. After drying, I wrapped the towel around me and brushed my teeth. I then went outside and turned the generator off before heading to my bedroom. I probably should've turned on more lights, because when I crawled into bed, I realized I wasn't alone.

"Took you long enough," she said. I jumped.

"Damn, girl, you scared the shit out of me."

She pulled me down onto the bed and kissed me passionately.

"Where's Blake?" she asked.

"He's probably wondering where the hell you are about now." There was a moment of silence which told me my answer wasn't good enough. "He's out in the parking lot with the rest of them, talking and bragging about what we did."

"That means we have fifteen minutes. Twenty tops," she said and pulled me on top of her.

I knew better. I really did. She'd been hooked up with Blake for over a month now. But, my will was weak.

It was hurried, intense, feverish. We held each other in our arms after we'd climaxed, but it only lasted a minute before she slipped out of the bed, gathered her clothes, and went into the bathroom. A minute later, she emerged and gave me a kiss on the cheek.

"We can't keep doing this," I said. That smudge of moonlight was peeking through my window blinds now and it made her look like an angel standing over me. She stood there, staring at me for I don't know how long before kissing me and slipping out of the door.

Despite my fatigue, I lay there a long while, staring up at the ceiling before I finally fell asleep. When the sun came up, I did everything I told myself I was going to do, but when midnight of the next night rolled around, I was sitting there on my steps, smoking my last cigarette. When I'd finished it, instead of getting up and walking to the truck, I went inside my RV and straight to bed. When I sat across from Sandy the next morning at breakfast and she flashed me that smile of hers, I knew I was never going to leave.

CHAPTER 5 – PRAIRIE

And that's how it went for the next three years. Sandy and Blake were a couple, but we'd find ways to see each other on the sly. Sometimes, we'd go for months, and during those times, I would convince myself that it was over. But, then she'd sneak out late at night and softly tap on my door. And, I always let her in.

I don't know why I did it. I'm a grown-ass man, but I acted like a teenage boy sniffing around his first piece of tail. The truth was, I was lonely, and I was in love. If I was to discuss it with one of those therapists, they'd probably say something like I allowed myself to be treated like this because I had self-esteem issues, or something like that, and they'd probably be right.

I knew what the cure was. All I had to do was leave. I'd thought it over hundreds of times. I had my packing list memorized. I had the plan memorized. In fact, I had two plans. One was with our truck and the other was with a boat. I'd often thought about going up to Kentucky Dam. Gavin once let it slip there were some people living up there. That was a hydroelectric dam, which meant they probably had power.

I'd actually packed the truck a couple of times. I waited until after breakfast, told BC I was going hunting, and took off. I got as far as the city of McEwen, which was almost halfway to Nashville. But, I stopped. I stopped in the middle of the damn road and sat there, unable to force myself to go any further.

I parked the truck and killed the engine, right there on the oldest state road in Tennessee, State Route One, and got out. I started walking around through the neighborhood. I had no idea why; it was like I was in a daze.

I eventually found myself walking through the parking lot of self-storage units. A zombie charged at me from around the corner. I pulled out my bayonet and stabbed him through the mouth. I knew I'd stabbed the brain stem when he dropped like a lead balloon. It was then I realized two of the storage units still had undamaged padlocks on them.

Retrieving some bolt cutters, I popped both locks. The units contained your standard household items. Furniture, mostly, but there was also bedding and cookware. There were even some sheets still packaged. I let out a long sigh and began loading up the things we could use.

I got back home later that afternoon. Gavin chuckled when I told him I hadn't bagged a deer, but Leslie was overjoyed with the items from the storage units. When we sat down for dinner, Blake thumped his glass with his spoon, silencing the room.

"We're going to have a kid," he said with the biggest shit-eating grin I'd ever seen. Everyone congratulated them, including me. I guess I was really happy for him. During all of this, I caught a look from Sandy. I couldn't decipher her expression, but it didn't matter. The moment Blake announced he was going to be a daddy did something to me and I knew I would never be with her again.

Dinner was filled with happiness. Everyone was laughing, and smiling, and congratulating the two expecting parents. Of course, they'd seemed to have forgotten all about those people they'd murdered back in Humboldt.

After dinner, I took a pair of those new sheets and tossed them into my RV before heading down to the boat docks. I grabbed a Coleman lantern, fishing pole and a tackle box, and then went to the dock the furthest away from everyone. I didn't want company, I wanted to be alone with my thoughts, but within minutes, I heard somebody walking down the wooden dock. I turned to see Lee heading my way. He had a couple of poles and a bait bucket. When he got close, I could see a friendly grin.

"Great minds think alike," he said. "I told Jinni I was going to do some night fishing, and here you are."

He started to sit down, but must have seen something on my face. "You don't mind some company, do you?" he asked.

"Did you bring anything to drink?" I asked, figuring he probably didn't. To my surprise, he pulled out a pint of sour mash whiskey from his waistband and gave me a grin. It looked like he'd lost another tooth, although I couldn't be certain. I nodded at the empty chair sitting a few feet away.

"What are you fishing with?" he asked me.

"Grub worms," I said.

"Real ones or fake ones?"

"Fake," I answered.

He nodded. "I got a bunch of live worms here. Let's experiment and see what they hit on. We're fishing for crappie, right?"

I nodded.

"Good."

He got himself situated, baited a hook, and dropped his line. He then settled back, took the top off of the bottle, and took a pull before handing it to me.

"I thought you was going hunting today," he said.

"I lost the mood and ended up finding some storage units."

"Ah," he said. "I know you can take care of yourself, but the next time you get the urge to go out, let me know. I'll go with you and watch your back."

"Okay," I said, and took another sip of the whiskey before handing it back to him.

Lee was naturally a talker and the whiskey loosened his lips even further. He couldn't help himself. If someone were to tape his mouth shut, he would've farted himself to death. I guess that's why he took a liking to me. He believed my silence meant I was listening intently to everything he had to say. I knew he was going to talk all night.

"You know, back when all this shit started, you had to be careful coming to fish out here," he said as I hooked up a trolling motor to a battery and we headed out of the cove.

He threw the line out and waited for me to take the bait. Sometimes, I'd intentionally ignore him, which gave him fits, but today I decided to play along.

"Why's that?" I asked.

"Back when everything went bad, and maybe even for a year or so after, this river had zombies in it," he said with his mostly toothless grin. "You see, zombies can't swim. They'd somehow get in the river, I don't know how, I guess because they're stupid, and they'd float around until they'd swallowed a shit ton of water, and then they'd sink like a rock."

"Oh, yeah?"

"Yep. They didn't die right away though. They don't need to breathe for some reason. They'd slog around underwater and sometimes when you were fishing you'd hook one. Boy howdy, you do that and you had problems."

"Humph." Most of the time that's all you needed to do with Lee, grunt or something and he believed you were deeply interested.

"Yep. But, you know what?"

"What's that?" I asked.

"Rivers and lakes are bad for zombies. Think about it. They get waterlogged and sink. Then, the fish and turtles come along and start nibbling on them. Before they know it, they're mostly eaten up." He chuckled. "So, all of the fish and turtles in here have been living off zombie meat. It took us a minute for us to realize that, but by then, we'd eaten so many fish, if it was going to kill us, we would've already been dead. Or infected. But, the digestive system of them fish and turtles somehow neutralized that infection. Ain't that something?"

I nodded at his profound wisdom. He grinned.

"Every once in a while, you'll see a body floating by, but they're mostly gone now." Eventually, he ran out of things to talk about, and so we fished in silence for almost an hour before he cleared his throat.

"Me and Jinni know," he said.

Jinni, Lee's girlfriend, was a pale redhead with a bunch of freckles and a few missing teeth of her own. I'd seen some good-looking redheads in my time, but she wasn't one of them. She was nice, but she was a talker too, even more so than Lee. Get those two in the room and you may as well shut up and make yourself comfortable.

"You know what?" I asked.

"We know about you and Sandy."

The words hit me like a kick in the nads, but I acted like I didn't hear him. He wasn't fooled though.

"Don't worry, nobody else knows and we ain't telling."

"Alright," I said. Lee felt the need to explain.

"It goes like this: back when all of this shit started happening, I was married. Her name was Babette and she had the nicest set of titties you ever saw and a big sexy tattoo of a rose right above her cooter. That rose turned my crank like you wouldn't believe. But anyway, we lived in a trailer about five miles from here and we had a meth operation. Not to brag or nothing, but I'm one of the best meth cooks around these parts."

He stopped talking when his line went taught. After he'd reeled it in, he decided it was too small and threw it back before resetting his hook.

"So, anyway, there we were, out in the country, away from them zombies, and there wasn't any law to be afraid of anymore." He wiggled his line a little bit. "Gavin found us one day, him and Shane. We were starving to death, but we were smoking so much of our product we didn't even care. Gavin took us in and got us back on our feet. Jinni was already living here. For some reason, I took an instant liking to her and she liked me too. I took her fishing one day. I got us in a boat and took it over to the channel. I dropped anchor and we smoked a joint. Before you know it, the two of us were naked and going at it. After that, we started seeing each other on the sly."

"Did Babette ever find out?" I asked.

"Ah, no. About three months after we moved here, she overdosed and died. Now, don't get me wrong, when she died, I was sad, but on the other side of the coin, it meant that Jinni and me could be together out in the open. No more sneaking around."

"So, you and Jinni have been together ever since," I said.

"Yep. She got me off the meth too. All we do is drink and smoke weed now. She's been good to me. So, what I'm saying is, there for a little while me and Jinni were in the same predicament you're in now."

"I ain't in no predicament," I spouted.

Lee chuckled. "Yeah, okay. That's probably what I would've said if Babs hadn't of died. If she lived, she would have caught us eventually. People don't think they'll ever get caught, but they do."

We fished in silence for several more minutes before Lee spoke again.

"So, you didn't ask, but I'm going to tell you anyway; me and Jinni don't think it'd be a good idea for you to see her anymore."

"You don't, huh?"

"Don't take it the wrong way, we just think if you don't give her up, you're in for a lot of heartache." He looked over at me. "Me and Jinni like you, True. You're a good dude and she's using you. Jinni said it best. She said Sandy has an itch she can't scratch, so she uses you."

"She ain't using me," I said.

"If that were true, True, why is she with Blake, huh? She met both of you at the same time. If she was in love with you, why didn't she dump Blake for you? Why is she pregnant with Blake's child? She may tell you she loves you, but she don't know what love is, bro." He took a deep breath. "I'm the first to admit I've been a racist most of my life, but Jinni and me are proud to call you a friend and we don't like to see you hurtin' over a woman who ain't never going to do you right."

It took a minute or so before I glanced over at him. He was looking back expectantly.

"Feel free to tell me what you think," he said. "If you're mad at me, just don't hit me. I ain't got that many teeth left."

He grinned in hopes I really wasn't about to hit him.

"Well," I finally said. "You and Jinni don't have anything to worry about. We're done."

Lee nodded. "Good for you, brother."

We fished through the night. We finished the bottle. Lee even brought out some smoke, which he shared and I was appreciative.

We fished until sun up and caught enough crappie to feed everyone for lunch and dinner. I skipped breakfast and went straight to bed. I wasn't surprised to see the new sheets had been put on my bed.

"It ain't going to happen, girl. It's done," I mumbled to myself before nodding off into a deep slumber.

Sandy gave birth to a little girl seven months later. She was a little thing with a wisp of blonde hair and her momma's bright blue eyes. I didn't have to be a DNA expert to know I wasn't the father.

They named her Prairie. They said they named her that because of her hair. I reminded myself this was as good a reason as any to pack up and leave, and even though we didn't get back together after, I still stuck around, and I was a willing participant in Gavin's marauding activities.

If someone were to confront me about it, I might've said I was an unwilling participant and never murdered or robbed anyone, but that would've been a lie. I wasn't a religious man, but I seemed to remember some scripture saying something about if you dig the pit, you're going to fall in.

My pit was about as deep as you could dig it.

CHAPTER 6 — MOUNT WEATHER — 8 A.Z.

I thought I had lost it, or someone had stolen it. At first appearance, it looked like nothing more than a well-used, spiral-bound notebook. A thick one, the kind a college student might have. But, all you had to do was read the first few pages to realize it's much more than that. It's my history, in a manner of speaking. I found it in the flexible document holder behind the passenger seat of our semi.

Since the last entry was a few years ago, I'll try to bring this journal up to date. Here are some summations of various significant events.

February, 3 A.Z.: We had a short warm spell, and then a big ice storm. Lots of trees fell, including one on the main guard post, injuring the sole guard on duty, Bret Conway. Luckily, he only sustained a mild concussion and a broken arm. It was a huge mess, but maybe it was an omen. We rebuilt the guard post to modern-day requirements, using lots of steel and concrete.

July, 3 A.Z.: In an effort to secure the area within the one-hundred-mile radius of Mount Weather, we once again attempted to make a foray into the District of Columbia. It was bloody. We expended a lot of ammunition, and in addition, lost two of our own. He was a young guy, nineteen and full of juice. The truck he was riding in got stuck, the driver tried to simply run over the dead zeds, but even with a four-wheel-drive, you can get hung up. He got out and attempted to work one of the bodies loose. One of them was still alive and grabbed him in a death grip. Before he could get loose, he was waylaid by other zeds. His buddy jumped out and tried to save him, but he too was mobbed. The rest of the team could not rescue either of them in time.

December, 4 A.Z.: We lost three more in a boating accident. They were fishing on the Shenandoah River and somehow their boat capsized. For some reason, none of them were wearing life preservers. We emphasize safety, but unfortunately, some people don't listen. But, there is good news, we had four new births, including one on Christmas Day. I guess there was something special in the Mount Weather water back in March.

May, 4 A.Z.: The entire month of May was filled with beautiful weather. One of our main goals is to expand our farms. This year, we expanded our crop acreage by five hundred acres. In addition, we remodeled 12 houses. This included fixing the plumbing, restoring power, and fortifying them to withstand attacks by zeds and small arms fire. Whenever we got a house ready, we'd move people into them. Two things draw people to us: the vaccine and electricity. Some of them bristle at the rules they have to abide by, but so far, it is working out.

July, 4 A.Z.: We were having a good summer. Four new families moved in back in June and we got them set up in houses. Unfortunately, they weren't pulling their weight. A meeting was held to discuss how to resolve the issue. There was a lot of, shall we say, spirited debate. That's the euphemism the politicians used whenever they had a shouting match. After that much-spirited debate, nothing was resolved. So, Fred and I resolved the matter in our own special way and we had a little chat with them. One family moved on and the other three straightened up. After that, the president would come to us from time to time with special situations that could not be resolved hospitably.

October, 4, A.Z.: We found a family that'd been slaughtered by zeds. There were six of them living in a house near Manassas. It was a fortified house, but somehow the zeds had caught all of them outdoors. The scout team tracked them down and killed them, but it gave us all a harsh reminder that one had to always be vigilant.

April, 5 A.Z.: The previous winter was cold and uneventful. We had suspended long-range scout operations due to a lack of fuel, but then, one sunny day, two men drove up to the main gate driving a tanker truck full of diesel. They went by the names of Johnny G and Roscoe Sidebottom. Roscoe, I swear that's his real name, was the brains behind a group of survivors who lived in Marcus Hook, Pennsylvania. Roscoe was in his sixties with a shock of gray hair and thick bifocals. Johnny G was a plain-looking, nondescript man in his forties. One of the amazing things they had accomplished was to get a gas power plant back online and then they used the power plant to get an oil refinery operational.

Their generous gift came with a price though. He sat us down and proceeded to talk us through a presentation of the Marcus Hook operation and concluded by telling us they were in desperate need of manpower and food. The food was not a problem for us, but manpower was another issue entirely. Nobody wanted to leave the comfort of Mount Weather or the surrounding houses.

May, 5 A.Z.: The satellite feeds are monitored constantly by two siblings, Garret and Grace Anderson, and they discovered a large wildfire in the upper Michigan peninsula. It had been a rather dry winter and somehow a fire started. Whether or not it was by human hands is a mystery. The result was not good. The sky was hazy and overcast throughout June and had a sooty smell to it. It was hard on our crops, which resulted in a diminished harvest that year.

October 30th – the present: We are now in the 8th year of the apocalypse. Mount Weather still uses the Gregorian calendar, but long ago, back in Tennessee, we'd decided to reset the calendar and use November as the starting month for year zero of the zombie apocalypse.

Tomorrow is Kelly's 28th birthday. As her birthday approached, she got it in her head she wanted to have a child, which was a total reversal from the previous five years. I did not argue and gave it the good old American effort whenever I got the opportunity. We were successful and now she's expecting.

Officially, my job title is Assistant Director of Operations. The Director of Ops is my mentor and boss, Parvis Anderson, Grace and Garret's father. In layman's terms, I'm his lackey. There is no clear job description. In fact, I take care of whatever Parvis deems necessary. We have multiple ongoing projects, and I'm often tasked with making sure they proceed in a proper manner, which means I'm constantly putting out fires.

This journal would not be complete if I fail to mention President Abraham "Abe" Stark. He was originally the Secretary of Defense back when it all went bad. When President Richmond was murdered by his lover's jealous husband, Abe moved quickly. He executed what amounted to a bloodless coup and became the de facto president. There has been no election since, so suffice it to say, democracy has been stuck in a closet and it is unknown if it will ever be brought out again.

I can't say I particularly like the man, but I have a grudging respect for him. He is a no-nonsense man, smart, driven, overbearing at times to the point of dictatorial, but he has a clear mission; rebuild America. For him, the end always justified the means. Having said that, every decision he has made has been for the betterment of Mount Weather, and for the betterment of America.

Now, even though our research and logistics team keep fastidious records of events, incidents, and facts, I am going to memorialize some of those statistics in this journal which I believe are important.

1. The population of Mount Weather is capped at one hundred forty people, with another four hundred people living within a hundred-mile radius. Weather can sustain far more than this, but we consider new arrivals who need to be housed until we find a place for them and, of course, newborns. Residents of Weather who have babies are not required to relocate, unless they request it or if they are troublemakers. So, the permanent population consists of only select people.

2. 87% of the Virginia population are under the age of sixty. 15% are under the age of twenty. Our birth mortality rate is slightly under 20%, which is excellent, considering the extreme shortage of modern medical care. Having children is encouraged at Mount Weather, but even so, our medical abilities have limitations.

3. Speaking of power, we now have a second hydroelectric dam operational. Captain Seth Kitchens is heading up this project. Even though he was a military lawyer back before, he has found his niche in hydroelectric energy.
4. We have four major communities outside of Virginia who have joined us: Oak Ridge in Tennessee, Marcus Hook in Pennsylvania, and two Ohio communities, one in Dayton, one in Cincinnati. There are other, smaller communities here and there. We have friendly relations with most of them.
5. Our resident computer experts, Garret and Grace, have spent numerous hours over the years compiling data from satellite surveillance. They have located what they believe are fifty-seven significant survival settlements across the United States.
6. The original mathematical projections, compiled during the first year of the apocalypse, put the surviving American population at thirty million, with a loss of twenty million during the next five years, for a net figure of ten million. We have since revised that number downward to between two and four million. Our surveillance of other nations has not been as detailed, but we've spotted multiple settlements throughout the world.

We've made significant strides these last five years, but it always seems to come down to zombies, the infected, the zeds. Whatever you want to call them. We kill them, and kill them, and kill them, and yet, we never can seem to kill them all. They've gotten sneaky too; not as easy to trap and kill them as they once were. They now know when they're outnumbered and will flee. They know how to mass an attack. They know how to flank an opponent. And, of course, since their bodies have started healing again, they are stronger now. Not as strong as a healthy adult, but strong enough. Plus, they don't feel pain.

In spite of them, or perhaps because of them, we've become a people of survivors. It hasn't been easy, and there are setbacks, sometimes perilous setbacks, but we have survived.

CHAPTER 7 – PITTSBURGH

Jorge Garcia walked into the cafeteria and sat beside me as I wrote. He and his family came up with us from Tennessee. "What's that?" he asked, pointing at the spiral binder.

"It's a journal that one of my friends started long ago. After she died, I've been sort of keeping up with it."

Jorge looked at it closely. "Oh, yeah, I remember that thing. That thing's going to be an important history book one day."

I chuckled. "Yeah, maybe. How're you doing?"

"I've been reading up on Pittsburgh," he said. "Did you know the city only had three hundred thousand people living there? It shouldn't be too difficult."

"The surrounding metropolitan area boosted the population to over two million," I said. "It won't be easy."

Jorge's expression went from pleasant to crestfallen. "Holy hell, man," he muttered.

"It'll work out. You don't normally get up so early," I observed.

"Couldn't sleep. Last night's chili did a number on both me and Brenda. We farted all night long. I'm telling you, man, it was awful."

I laughed again. Brenda was a pretty Hispanic girl who showed up at the front gate a couple of years ago along with her little brother. Jorge was working guard duty at the gate and was immediately smitten. Her parents and five brothers had been attacked on the road by a horde of zeds. She and her little brother were the only ones who had survived. They'd almost starved to death before one of the outlying families found them and brought them to Weather.

"She doesn't want me to go, but I told her it was my duty," Jorge said.

I gave him a small knowing smile. He confided to me once that he liked going on away missions.

"I like scavenging," he once told me. "It's like treasure hunting."

I agreed with that sentiment also. I loved poking around abandoned places and finding neat stuff.

"Are we still leaving at eight?" he asked.

"Yes indeed."

"Alright. I'm going to make a pot of tea."

"That sounds wonderful," I said. "Make it the black blend. Strong. I need the caffeine."

Tea was our replacement for coffee. Except for the little freeze-dried packages found in MREs, we had finally run out. To make matters worse, we could not find coffee beans anywhere. However, the green thumbs around here had no problem cultivating tea. They had an entire greenhouse dedicated to growing different varieties, and ginseng grew in abundance in the countryside. So, all of us coffee drinkers had to settle for tea. Once, a few years ago, I came close to dying of thirst, so I didn't complain.

Our muster formation was promptly at eight in the parking lot in front of the motor pool. Our vehicles were all lined up, gassed up, and ready to go. They consisted of a mixture of four-wheel-drive trucks, Humvees, and two armored vehicles known as Strykers. We had all of them running on diesel and all had been modified, except for the Strykers, which needed no modifications, but there were several jerry cans of fuel strapped to them.

It goes without saying fuel is a precious commodity these days. We had diesel, but regular gasoline was virtually nonexistent now. Years before, the EPA mandated cleaner fuel. The oil companies began adding ethyl alcohol, derivatives of methyl alcohol, and oxygenate additives. While this helped create cleaner-burning gasoline, the additives evaporated quickly. The result was, the shelf life of gas was only about a year, and we were into the eighth year of this shit.

Diesel lasted a little longer, but not by much. The bottom line; we had no fuel and the only working vehicle was Melvin's biofuel truck and some electric cars. The trouble with the electric cars was that they were designed for city use. They weren't built for today's rough roads. Plus, the only power ports were here and Fort Detrick, so we only used them for short distance travel.

Then, Roscoe and Johnny G arrived with their tanker of fresh diesel. It was like a Godsend, and it allowed us to resume our scouting and scavenging missions.

It was two hundred miles to Pittsburgh. Once we got there, we were more than likely going to do a lot of driving around, searching and scavenging, and then a two-hundred-mile ride back home. Therefore, each vehicle had several jerry cans full of diesel.

I stood in the back of the formation of people while my friend, Captain Justin Smithson, gave the mission briefing and watched. Justin repeated the purpose of the mission and then described how we were going to travel along I-68, which we had cleared earlier last summer, and then venture into Pittsburgh along I-79.

It was risky. The big cities were still filled with zeds, but we'd been seeing stuff on the satellites. Garret and Grace would work the satellites at night, searching for glimmers of artificial lighting. Lights did not automatically activate anymore, so when nighttime lighting was spotted, we'd try to investigate.

Due to the shortage of fuel, the distances we traveled were limited. Three years ago, it was decided to concentrate in our own backyard, so to speak, until we got matters firmly in our control. When the weather permitted, we'd go on expeditions, looking for survivors, scavenging for resources, and killing zeds.

It's been hard work, but we'd gone on multiple scouting and scavenging missions within the hundred-mile radius. Now, thanks to the group of survivors in Marcus Hook, we had the fuel to venture out further. The reason to visit Pittsburgh came about due to Garret discovering artificial lighting from a satellite fly-over.

There were twenty-four of us in five vehicles. Everyone knew everyone, which included everyone's strengths as well as flaws. We were a tight-knit group. It wasn't always that way, but with a lot of hard work and training, we'd become adept at scavenging, fighting zeds, fighting marauders, you name it.

But, our primary mission, like the one we were on today, was to find survivors who had not turned to a life of raping and murdering. These people who had lived through the worst of the worst were of the toughest mettle, the kind of people we needed to rebuild America. Hence the reason to burn over four-hundred-miles-worth of precious fuel. Whoever was out there in Pittsburgh was worthy of it.

Justin reiterated our radio procedures and code words before assigning teams and giving the command to load up. I was riding in the Stryker, which was the designated command vehicle. Joker, Justin, and Bob Duckworth were with me.

"Remind me again where this supposed sign of life was spotted, specifically?" Bob asked me as we exited the main gate.

"An area known as Mount Oliver," I said.

He gestured at my laptop. "Do we have any satellite intel?" he asked.

I nodded and opened it up. I'd had it on sleep mode, so the screen lit up instantly. A couple of clicks and I handed it over. The pictures did not show a great deal, only some artificial lighting in the neighborhood we were heading to. I sat silently and watched him as he scrolled through the photographs and the map.

Bob was a handsome man in his fifties, with a fit body he developed with a personal trainer, back before. He was a smart and charismatic man, and married to a woman named Angela. She was a pretty woman, ten years younger than Bob. She was a friendly yet reserved woman.

"Have you ever been to Pittsburgh, Zach?" he asked.

"Nope." In fact, I'd never been outside of Tennessee until I went to Mount Weather.

"I've only visited a couple of times. Once to a political fundraiser and once to a Steeler's football game. I don't have any unpleasant memories of the city, but then again, I was limited in what I saw and experienced."

I looked around as we rode. The neighborhoods I could see all seemed old. Years of neglect had taken its toll, not unlike any other suburban neighborhood these days. A lot of buildings had both old and fresh graffiti. I reached for the microphone.

"All Teams, this is Team One-Bravo, give me any sighting of zeds."

"Team Two, negative zed count, over."

"Team Three, negative zed count, over."

"Team Four, we saw three zeds off in a field, west of I-79. They appeared to be huddling together under a tree, but not doing anything. Perhaps they were playing stump poker, over."

Joker chuckled. I probably would have laughed as well, but I was concerned. A city the size of Pittsburgh, and we'd only seen three infected. It seemed odd.

We exited the interstate and started moving along the secondary roads. There was nothing new, but I saw a lot of old structures, older houses built close together, and a lot of old graffiti.

"This is interesting," Joker commented. He was referring to all the numerous side streets that were blocked off by derelict cars. "It's like we're being funneled."

I noticed the same thing. "I don't like it."

Justin didn't like it either. "All stop," he quickly ordered. Joker brought the armored vehicle to a stop.

Justin got on the radio and called Jeremiah, the rear vehicle. "Team Five, Team One-Actual. Anything?" he asked.

"Negative contact," he replied.

"Alright, we're getting bottled up. Back it out to that last big intersection."

"Roger that," Jeremiah said.

We had wide intervals between each vehicle, which allowed each to turn around without much issue.

"Take us back to Phase Line Blue," Justin said to Jeremiah, whose Stryker was now leading the procession. We started moving back to Saw Mill Run Boulevard, but we'd only gotten a half a block when Jeremiah spoke calmly on the radio.

"Contact dead ahead. Looks like about a hundred zeds, coming at us down the street."

I'd wondered where they'd been. Pittsburgh was not a small town, and even though it's been eight years, I knew all of them had not died off.

The problem was we were on a narrow road and could only put the vehicles two abreast. Although the people in the first two vehicles had killed several of them, there were other zeds that had gotten through and had surrounded the next two vehicles. There was little we could do without risking shooting our team members. Justin was on the radio, keeping everyone calm.

"Alright now, remember your sectors of fire and be mindful of your crossfire. They can't get to us as long as we're in our vehicles. First Sergeant, let's move out."

"Ah, small problem up here," Jeremiah replied. "Team Four has a couple of zeds caught in their undercarriage. They're temporarily stuck."

Justin held the microphone to his chest a moment as he shook his head. "We've discussed this at every training meeting," he muttered. After a couple of more invectives under his breath, he brought the mike back up to his mouth.

"Alright, everyone, stay in your vehicles. Make absolutely certain of what's behind your target before you shoot. We can pick them off, it's just going to take a little patience. Team Four, start rocking your van, but don't break anything."

Gunfire soon dropped to nothing, with only a sporadic shot every couple of minutes. From our end, we could not see anything and could only provide rear security while listening to an occasional gunshot. We were there for twenty minutes and there were still a substantial number of zeds when the radio crackled.

"Ah, all Teams, this is Team Five, SITREP follows."

"A SITREP?" Joker asked.

He knew what a SITREP meant; it was military jargon for a situation report. He, along with the rest of us, were wondering what the first sergeant was about to tell us. Justin was probably as confused as I was. We listened intently as Jeremiah spoke.

"We've got zeds dropping from headshots, only we ain't the ones shooting, and we ain't hearing anything."

"Silenced weapons?" Justin asked.

"That's affirmative," he replied. "So far, they're only killing zeds."

Justin turned to me. "We either have some new best friends, or somebody is killing the zeds only to get to us."

The radio crackled to life again. "All zeds are down," Jeremiah said. "We have two armed men approaching on bicycles."

"Alright, Joker, maintain rear security," Justin ordered. "I've got to get out of this can and see what the hell is going on."

I got out with Justin, along with Bob, and the three of us walked up to Jeremiah's Stryker. He had also exited his Stryker and was talking to two men. Both were similar in appearance, each of them six feet tall, full, thick beards, long dark scraggly hair, and hazel eyes. They were both muscular and looked like at one time they spent lots of time pumping iron.

Their facial features were so alike I guessed them to be brothers. Both were dressed in some rough-looking black tactical clothing, along with tac-vests. They were also armed with what appeared to be Glocks in thigh holsters and were cradling assault rifles that looked like AR-15s, but were heavily modified. The two things that jumped out were the scopes and suppressors.

"Thanks for the assist. I'm Captain Justin Smithson."

"Liam and Logan O'Malley," one of them said while pointing his thumb, first at himself and then at the other. "You people owe us some ammunition."

The other one, Logan, gestured at the corpses. "Forty-seven rounds of three hundred blackout," he said. "Now, my big brother here will claim he had the most kills, but he would be mistaken. I clearly had twenty-four kills and he only had twenty-three."

"Au contraire monsieur fuck-face," the other man said. He pronounced monsieur as mon-sewer. "We both know who the superior marksman is. Why are you blatantly attempting to mislead these people and steal my glory?"

This quickly became an argument between the two of them in which they seemed to have totally forgotten we were even there.

"You men are Pittsburgh natives, I take it?" I asked, interrupting their argument. They both immediately stopped and refocused on us.

"Yes, we are," Liam said. "In fact, we were once members of the Pittsburgh Police Department. The SWAT team, to be specific. I, of course, was a far superior officer than my dimwitted brother, but everyone has a cross to bear."

The other brother, Logan, gave Liam a disgusted look. "You keep lying to these people." He turned and looked at us. "He doesn't know the difference between a habeas corpus and a penis delecti. By the way, we still need that ammo."

The other brother, Liam, I think, cleared his throat. "If my idiot brother is through bullshitting, we can have a nice long discussion about why you're here, but we might want to relocate. The gunfire will draw additional unwanted attention."

With all of us helping, we got Team Four's van untangled and free. The two brothers motioned for us to follow them on their bicycles. I thought it would be too slow, but those guys could really move. They made several turns, cut through a park, and eventually, they signaled us to stop on Brownsville Road near a golf course.

"Alright, a couple of you come with us, the rest should probably keep guard," Logan said, and then led us through an overgrown backyard of a shitty-looking house and we emerged in the back of a church. The back door led down into a basement. It was clean, but looked more like a storage room rather than living quarters.

"We had more people at one time, but there is a street gang that we've been at war with for a couple of years now," Liam said. He motioned around. "We're the only two left. Everyone else is either dead or they moved away."

"Are you losing?" Justin asked.

Liam's expression turned cold. "At one time, there were over five hundred of them. Now, there are probably only a dozen left. What do you think?"

"There's no fuel left around here, and they've eaten up everything," Logan said. "They had the numbers on their side, but they're undisciplined and stupid. Even so, we've been talking lately about how futile this is. We were scouting around when we heard you people's gunfire."

"Unfortunately for you guys, you fell right into our trap," Liam said.

"You mean how we were being funneled by the abandoned cars?"

"Yeah, back when the fuel was still good, we'd trap the gangbangers this way. They call themselves the D-I Boys. We just call them dicks. They'd come riding around, looking for someone to rape or kill, so we set up several side roads where they'd become bottlenecked and we'd kill them."

"Were they always around?" I asked.

Liam shrugged. "Back in the day, they were a local street gang that held a piece of turf over near Frankstown Avenue, which is a little north of here, across the river. After it went bad, they somehow managed to get the other gangs to form up with them and virtually took over Pittsburgh."

"Did you say you two were once on the Pittsburgh SWAT team?" I asked.

"That we were," Liam said. "We loved our job, but when everyone started getting sick, Pittsburgh descended into total chaos within a week. It wasn't long before it was every man for himself. A group of fellow officers took over one of the zone stations. It was a living hell, but I don't have to tell you guys that."

"So, in addition to the zeds, you had this gang to contend with?" Bob asked.

"There were several gangs at first," Logan said. "But they were constantly at war with each other before the D-I Boys got what was left of them to align together. At some point, we crossed paths with them. They've killed a few of us, we've killed a bunch of them."

"So, what's next for the O'Malley brothers?" Bob asked with a politician's smile.

"What else is there?" Logan asked. "Food and water are always a day-to-day challenge, we have a reloading station." He pointed over to a rectangular wooden bench for emphasis. "But still, it's not an unlimited resource. Things aren't easy. Say, you never said where exactly you people come from?"

"Virginia," Bob said.

"That's quite a drive. What brings you to our fair city?" he asked. "And, oh, by the way, how in the hell do you people have good gas?"

Bob glanced over at us. Justin and I exchanged a glance. I gave a casual tap on the chin with my finger. Justin nodded in agreement. Bob smiled and turned his attention back to the O'Malley brothers.

"Have you ever heard of a place called Mount Weather?" he asked.

This was the beginning of his recruitment pitch, and his oratory skills were superb. He painted a picture with his words that were so enticing I sometimes found myself wondering if I were living in a different Mount Weather than the one he described. Liam and Logan listened attentively. When Bob had finished, he ended by looking at the two men with a hopeful expression.

"You men are made of strong stuff, that's obvious," he said with a wave of his hand. "Let me ask you two something. What do you foresee in your future? If you two survive this war against this gang, do you plan on continuing to live here?"

Liam and Logan looked at each other. "Honestly, we haven't planned that far ahead," Liam said.

"There's not much left for us here," Logan added. "We've convinced ourselves we need to kill all of them, but, I mean, we've been fighting with them for years now, and I don't even see the point anymore. I'd like to find a nice location for us, but…"

Logan didn't finish his sentence. The two brothers looked at each other somberly. I got the impression they'd had this discussion between themselves many times. Bob sensed it as well and matched their somber expressions.

"We at Mount Weather are always looking for people of your caliber, would you agree, Captain Smithson?"

"Indeed, we are, Senator," Justin responded.

Bob gave a slow, serious nod, like a monumental decision had been reached. "Gentlemen, I am formally extending an invitation for the two of you to join us at Mount Weather."

The two brothers looked at each other before Liam fixed Bob with a pointed, serious stare. "I have one question, well maybe a lot of questions, but right now I've got one important one."

"What's that, Liam?" Bob asked.

"Are there any single women at Mount Weather?"

Priss spoke up. "There might be one or two."

CHAPTER 8 – COIN TOSS

Getting back to Mount Weather was interesting. And what I mean is, we did not see one, single, godforsaken zed. Not in the entire two hundred miles. We did, however, see some more post-apocalyptic graffiti along the sides of the overpasses and other spots of opportunity. Joker gave a running commentary.

"Oh, look, that one blames the infection on gays," he said.

"The one we saw five miles ago blamed the Jews," Bob said. "They can't seem to make up their minds."

"Why aren't we seeing any of the stinking zeds?" Joker asked. "I mean, I know the cold messes them up, but where are they, hibernating or something? What do you think, Zach?"

"They're hibernating or they've migrated south for the winter, but that's only speculation," I said.

"You know, it's almost like they're human again," Flash remarked.

Bob looked at him questioningly. "How so, Flash?"

"They can run again. That one zed that jumped on Conway, there's only one way he got on top of that stack of pallets; he had to climb up there. And, the fact that he climbed up there meant he thought it out, he didn't just mindlessly start climbing."

"Those were freshly infected," I said. "They haven't yet experienced any advanced decomposition. But, I like your powers of observation. What else have you noticed?"

Flash looked at me, trying to decide if I was messing with him.

"I'm serious, keep going."

"Alright. If they're hibernating, how do they know how to do that? I remember enough of high school biology to know that ain't a natural human trait. It's not, um…"

"It's not innate behavior," I said.

"Yeah, it's not innate behavior, and all behavior is either innate or learned, right?"

"That's true," I agreed.

"What if they simply migrated south for the winter?" Joker asked.

"That's a learned behavior too, am I right?" Flash asked.

I nodded in agreement. "The old ones are thinking again. They've proven that several times now." I thought a moment. "Alright, let me throw this at you and see what you think."

"Oh, this ought to be good," Justin said. He glanced at Flash. "He does this all the time. Get used to it."

I ignored him. "Back before, they experimented with teaching apes sign language. Some of them became fairly proficient and built up a decent-sized vocabulary, but even though they could communicate, they never asked questions. Some of the scientists who were in the study groups hypothesized this is what separated them from the human species, because they simply could not think at a level to ask questions."

"So, what's your question?" Justin asked.

"If, somehow, they were able to start communicating again…wait, let me rephrase that. They are able to communicate with each other again, that's a given, but what if they were able to communicate with normal humans again, would they ask questions?"

Justin looked over at me. "What kind of question is that?"

I shrugged. "It's one of those questions that entice a thoughtful, philosophical debate."

The men got a chuckle out of my response, and we idly chatted about it for the next hour before switching to another subject.

"Aren't there any people who live around here?" Flash asked.

I hooked a thumb to my right. "Over that way is a community called Saltlick Township. There's ten to fifteen people living there. We made contact with them last year. They weren't very receptive of us, so we let them be." I then gestured around. "There's a national forest around here. If you stare out of the hatch, you can probably see some trails of smoke, but we haven't made any contact. Those people live deep in the woods; they don't want anything to do with other people."

"They've become isolationists," Bob said. "It's a good way to avoid hostile humans, but it will ultimately be their undoing."

"How so?" Flash asked.

"Simple," Bob said. "Procreation. Eventually, they'll start inbreeding. It's happened before with people who find themselves isolated from others, like the Appalachian people." He chuckled. "Lots of banjo playing and inbreeding."

We laughed some more, and Flash changed topics again. He was full of questions.

"What's up with that Priss girl?" he asked.

Joker and Bob laughed. "You should ask Zach," Joker said. "He knows her better than most of us."

Flash looked over at me. "Have you and her hooked up?" he asked. This elicited more laughter. Even from Justin, who had been rather serious most of the mission.

"No, nothing like that," I said.

Flash listened in fascination as I told him the story of how I met Priscila Rhinehart.

"And you whipped their asses with a switch?" he asked incredulously. I nodded. "Holy shit, I wish I saw that."

"Zach and I bumped into her in the weight room a couple of days after that," Justin said. "I swear to God, I think the ass whipping Zach gave her actually turned her on. She practically begged him for an encore."

They all laughed again, at my expense.

"Believe it or not, we've become friends, and no, we haven't slept together," I said. "Why do you ask? Do you have your eye on her?"

"Dude, it's been two years since I've been laid. I've had my eye on every single woman in the place."

"Well, all I can say with her is think long and hard on it before messing with her. She's...different," I said.

"It doesn't matter, it looks like she's got her eye on one of those O'Malley brothers," he said.

"Yeah, I wonder which one," I said.

"Probably both of them," Justin said. Joker howled in laughter.

When we arrived at Weather, we toiled through the decontamination process, parked the vehicles, and turned in our weapons. Everyone had learned to take turns cleaning their weapons on the ride back, otherwise they'd be stuck for another hour before being excused.

I noticed Priss had been paying extra attention to the O'Malley brothers and volunteered to stay with them while they had their blood drawn. I caught Joker looking at me and rolled his eyes. I grinned.

By the time we made it to the cafeteria, dinner was winding down, but a lot of people lingered. They wanted to hear all about Pittsburgh. When I sat down at our table, the questions quickly started. I filled them in while I ate.

Later, after we'd gotten the kids to bed, Kelly and I shared some much-needed intimacy. I had to be gentle because of her pregnancy, but I didn't mind. After, we snuggled together.

"I think I want you to stay home for the rest of the winter," she said. "I want you close while I'm pregnant. It would mean a lot to me."

I looked at her in the dark. She knew I liked to get out and go traveling. She was content to live within the confines of Mount Weather, only occasionally going out to visit people who lived nearby.

"Yeah, sure, okay," I said.

She turned to me in the dark. "Are you sure?"

"It'll cost you lots of sex though," I said, reached over, and began caressing her breasts. She let out a light moan, which was all I needed for round two.

The next morning at breakfast, I couldn't help but notice Liam and Priss were sitting extra close.

"I wonder how it was decided which brother she ended up with," Kelly mused.

"Hell, they probably flipped a coin," I said.

"Yeah, but which brother lost?" Rachel questioned.

The entire table erupted in laughter. Even Fred smiled a little.

CHAPTER 9 - HORSE RIDE

Sammy and Fred met up with Zoe and me promptly at six. They were dressed alike; jeans, flannel shirts, duster jackets, and boots. I must admit, I was dressed pretty much the same, but instead of a Resistol hat, I had on an Army jacket and a wool-knit watch cap.

"Good morning," I greeted.

The two of them responded with a micro nod. I smiled at Sammy's mimicking of Fred and gestured at my backpack. It was a smaller one, much like school students would use. I had another, larger rucksack, but it was too big to be carrying on horseback for nothing more than a morning ride.

"I've got my breakfast and hot tea. What about you two?" I asked.

Sammy and Fred had saddlebags draped across their left shoulders. Fred handed his to Sammy, who took off toward the kitchen.

"It's thirty degrees out. Are you sure you don't want to take a Humvee?"

Fred gave me one of his looks. "It wouldn't be a morning horse ride without horses."

I stifled a groan and instead gave him a nod. Fred had a notion that a great way to start off my birthday would be to go on an early morning horseback ride. He decided to rationalize his logic.

"The cool air will be invigorating," he said. "By the way, happy birthday."

I grunted. "Thanks." When Sammy came back, I pointed at the door. "Let's get going then."

"How old are you now, Zach?" Sammy asked as we saddled up.

"Twenty-five," I answered. "Nine years older than you and a hundred and thirty years younger than Fred."

Sammy laughed. Fred gave me a sour look.

"Are you two coming to the party?" I asked as we rode out of the main gate.

"Yep," Sammy said.

Fred gave a grunt, which I interpreted as meaning yes.

Kelly and her group of friends were the social butterflies of Mount Weather. They looked for any reason they could to create a social event. My idea of a nice birthday was to play with my kids, get them good and worn out so they'd go to bed early, and then play around with my wife. But, Kelly had other ideas.

Everyone was always invited, which meant if a party was being thrown, you could expect most of the one hundred and some odd people who lived at Mount Weather to attend. Fred was the exception. He rarely attended any function, so, I happened to know Kelly made a point of inviting him and told him he better not miss it, or else.

She was one of the few people who could talk to him that way. Ever since I'd known him, Fred had been a rather stoic man. After Sarah was murdered, and then his buddy Burt Cartwright died of a heart attack, he'd become even more withdrawn. Although he did not show it, I knew the two deaths had hit him hard.

So, Fred kept mostly to himself these days. After repeatedly ignoring work assignments, I convinced everyone to let him be. He cared for the horses and helped with the livestock, but sometimes he'd saddle up and ride off, not returning for days at a time. He confided to me once he felt out of place at Mount Weather and if not for us, he'd ride out into the sunset one day and not come back.

He was good to us though and the kids adored him. Sammy especially. Fred had decided to help me out, took young Sam under his wing, and was patiently teaching him everything about being a man that they did not teach in the Mount Weather school.

After a quarter-mile, I broke the silence. "Any particular destination?"

"We need to pay Harold and Maude a visit," Fred said. "And then I'd thought we'd do a wide, lazy circle around Weather. See what we see."

He was referring to our resident pig farmers. Harold, or Hog-Head Harold as we fondly called him, was a big friendly guy who had a house built on stilts in the middle of a pig sty. He was mostly a solitary soul, but one day he came to Weather with a woman nobody had ever seen before. When asked, he said she showed up one day and he had no idea where she'd come from. She was a homely woman of about forty or fifty, and only spoke in gibberish. Harold called her Maude, after the movie, Harold and Maude. We reached the gate off of Morgan's Mill Road ten minutes later.

They must have seen us coming and met us at the gate. Both smiled and waved, but Harold was always the one who did the talking.

"Howdy, boys," Harold greeted. "Y'all want to come in and warm up?" He pointed back at his house. "You can take a look at my new stove. I rigged it up so it can burn pig shit. It smells a little, but it keeps the house warm."

"Appreciate the offer," I said. "But, we're only staying a few minutes."

Harold gazed past me. "You get used to the smell, son," he said.

I looked back to see that Sammy had pulled out a bandanna and was holding it over his face. I couldn't help but laugh. When the outbreak occurred, Harold had reconfigured his pigpen so that it surrounded his house. It was great protection; zombies didn't stand a chance against pigs. But, as one might imagine, it stunk to high heaven.

"How've you been, Harold?" Fred asked.

"Oh, can't complain. If I do, Maude starts spoutin' off and damned if I know what she's sayin'."

Maude grinned and giggled. That was about the most intelligent thing I'd ever heard out of her.

"Do you two need anything?" I asked.

"Well, I'd surely appreciate it if you would do something about my deliveries. They've been late almost every day for the past week, and my pigs sure do get cantankerous when they don't get fed on time. I feed 'em on a schedule, you know?"

He was referring to the barrels of food waste from Weather, which we brought to him. It was an efficient disposal method, and it supplemented the feed corn we kept him supplied with. We had some good people at Weather, but we also had some lazy ones. When it was cold outside, a work crew with lazy people would conveniently forget to make the delivery and leave it for the next crew. The result was, Harold's pigs didn't get their slop in a timely manner, which upset both the pigs and Harold. Maude never had much to say about it, but I assumed it upset her as well.

"I'll see what I can do," I said. I didn't want to chew anyone's ass out on my birthday, but this was going to be my first order of business when we got back.

"Oh, and that man who makes moonshine, tell him we're out. We're getting low on weed too. Momma needs her nightly smoke," he said. Maude giggled again.

"You got it," I said. "Alright, give us a report. Have you seen any strangers or zeds?"

"Nah," he said as he scratched his beard. He pulled something out and looked at it thoughtfully before rubbing his fingers together.

"The traps got a couple of coydogs the day before last. I fed 'em to the hogs, but there's a few more wandering around. I heard at least one of them barking last night." He scratched again and then rubbed the top of his big bald head. "If you can spare a few more traps, I'll set 'em out."

"You got it," I said.

"Oh, when the weather gets warm, would you fellas help me build a new smokehouse?" He pointed at the existing smokehouse. "That one's seen better days."

"Absolutely," Fred said. "It'll be a good project for some of these boys we got, right, Sammy?"

"Yes, sir," Sammy replied.

We talked a few more minutes before bidding them goodbye and heading back to Weather.

"Man, that farm stinks," Sammy said once we'd gotten out of earshot.

"Don't disrespect that man," Fred admonished. "He was out here by himself while those Mount Weather people were tucked away down in that bunker. When they finally decided to come out and take a peek, Harold was there. When he heard they'd been living off of freeze dried food, he came riding up one day with over three hundred pounds of butchered pork in the back of his truck."

"And he's been supplying us with pork ever since," I added. "Harold deserves our respect, no matter what he smells like."

"Yes, sir," Sammy said, duly chastened.

We rode quietly the rest of the way back. That's the way Fred liked it. No unnecessary chatter, he'd say. You can't hear if you're not listening.

"I haven't seen any zed tracks," I mentioned.

Fred said nothing, which I assumed meant he agreed. The zeds often wandered out from the big cities, presumably to hunt for food. That was a guess, of course. I don't think anybody was an expert on how they thought.

Even so, they'd become fairly proficient hunters, and when they could not find humans, they would kill wildlife. Rodents, cats, dogs, coyotes, even cows sometimes, but they seemed to take great enjoyment in killing humans, and in spite of our caution, they'd killed more than a few of us over the years. So, we had to be constantly on guard.

I thought about them as we rode. In some respects, they were downright amazing and as clever as any normal human, but the infection did something to their brains. Now, they were nothing more than evil sonsofbitches and I killed as many as I could.

Speaking of coyotes, those rascals were irksome. And black bears. The population of both species had been steadily increasing over the years. We had donkeys to protect the cows, but sometimes they'd still get one or two.

I brought along a computer tablet as well. The reason? We had game trail cameras surreptitiously placed at various locations around Mount Weather, so instead of going on an aimless ride, I suggested we check on them. Fred did not answer, but he led the way and a couple of minutes later, we stopped at an old oak tree near the intersection of Morgan's Mill and Horseshoe Lane.

Over the years, our scavenging efforts had yielded a collection of game trail cameras and we put them to use. They were of various brands and levels of complexity, but most of them were battery operated, which, fortunately, we had thousands of the rechargeable kind, thanks to Parvis and a lavish government budget for such things back when all of this was nothing more than a worst-case scenario game.

All of our cameras had USB ports. So, it was a simple matter of plugging them up to my laptop and having a look-see. Over the morning, we checked eight cameras. There was the usual wildlife and five or six vehicles, all of them belonging to us, but no zeds, which was always a good thing.

After we got back, I walked with them to the barn.

"If you two would take care of the horses, I want to go to the kitchen and figure out what's going on with the food waste."

Fred nodded, knowing I needed to address the issue immediately.

"Alright, I'll see you two in a little while," I said. I then made a beeline to the kitchen and found out who the work crew was. There were four of them.

"You guys have been the dayshift cleanup crew for the last three days, correct?"

"That's right, who's asking?" one of them said.

His name was Charlie Mac. He and another man by the name of Kass were found by a scout team a couple of years ago on I-81 in a broken-down RV. When they were brought to Weather, they were emaciated and pitiful looking. Now, they looked like the kind of guys who spent their weekends drinking beer and watching TV.

"The dayshift cleanup crew is responsible for hauling the waste barrels to Harold. You haven't been doing it," I said.

"We've been overloaded with work," he retorted. "There's no reason the evening shift can't handle it."

"Because, we don't want people going out at night." I pointed to three barrels sitting in the corner. "Stop what you're doing and two of you get those barrels over to Harold right now."

"We'll get to it if we get to it," Charlie Mac said with a scowl. "And you ain't the one to tell us any different."

I made pointed eye contact with Charlie Mac, who acted like I was an irritating pest, and then the rest of them. The other three refused to meet my gaze, but I could see a little concern on one of them, Becky Hardin. She used to be exempt from work crews back when she was an aide for Senator Conrad Nelson, but after the good senator impregnated her, they parted ways. Now, Becky was a single mom who had nowhere else to go.

"Do you like living here, Charlie?" I asked.

His scowl deepened. "What's that supposed to mean?"

"It means, Mount Weather is a small community of people who depend on each other, and everyone knows who shirks their duties and makes it harder on everyone else. If you don't want to pull your weight around here, I'm going to put you out."

Charlie Mac barked out a short laugh. "If you think you have that kind of power, big boy, you just go ahead and try it."

I looked again at the rest of them. "Charlie may not realize it yet, but he has made his decision. If the rest of you don't want to join him, get those barrels to Harold's place, and don't make me have this conversation with you again. It won't be as pleasant next time."

"You got it, Zach," Becky said.

As I walked out, I heard Becky call Charlie Mac a dumbass. I let out a deep breath in an attempt to dispel my anger. There was a time when my anger would have gotten the better of me and I would have smashed a fist into that smart mouth. I actually paused a moment and thought about going back into the kitchen and doing it anyway, but decided now was not the time and headed to the elevator. I guess I was maturing and controlling my temper better these days.

My job today was to check the main heating system and service it. I thought about Charlie Mac as the elevator descended. I'd decided to get my work done, enjoy my birthday, and take care of it in the morning.

I stopped off at the office and picked up my tool belt before heading down to the bowels of Mount Weather. The coils of the heating unit were unusually dusty and it took a solid two hours before I got them clean. By then, it was time for lunch. I grabbed a plate and instead of sitting with everyone, I headed to the office. Parvis, who was absent during my earlier visit, was now sitting at his desk.

Parvis Anderson was the Director of Operations. When I'd arrived at Mount Weather, some five years ago, Parvis took me under his wing and acted as my mentor. Eventually, I took on the role as his assistant, the president giving me the official title of Assistant Director of Operations. It entailed much more than simply making sure Mount Weather hummed along smoothly. We were also tasked with the creation of a new United States of America. It was a lot of work.

"You need to eat," I chided as I dropped my tool belt and headed toward the restroom.

"My stomach is disagreeing with me at the moment. I'll grab something later," he said. "How's your day been?"

I finished washing my hands and then filled him in as I ate, including the incident with Charlie Mac.

"There have been other complaints on him lately," Parvis said. "Are you going to evict him?"

"Damn right I am, but not on my birthday. I'll do it tomorrow."

"Don't forget about Ohio," he said.

I frowned. "No problem. I'll take care of it before breakfast."

Parvis nodded thoughtfully and got on the phone. There were only two people who called the president by his nickname and Parvis was one of them.

"Hey, Abe. We have a small issue that's come up and I wanted to give you a heads up." He went on to explain about Charlie Mac. After a minute, he hung up.

"He agreed and said for you to take care of it."

I nodded. I didn't think President Stark would disagree. Like I said to Charlie Mac, everyone knows who is who and who does what around here, including President Stark. I finished lunch, pushed the tray aside, and logged on my computer. I had a lot of work to do. After an hour, Parvis slid back in his chair.

"I think I'm going to try to eat something."

"Good," I said. "Would you take my dirty dishes back for me?"

"Of course. Why don't you take the rest of the day off? It's your birthday after all."

I smiled. "I'm almost finished. I was thinking about getting in a workout before Kelly and the kids got home."

He smiled, as if remembering a time when he had the energy for heavy physical exertion. "I think I'm going to eat and then, if I can hold it down, take a nap."

"Sounds good, buddy," I said. "I'll see you this evening."

A few minutes after Parvis left, he walked back in. I looked up in puzzlement.

"There are a couple of people at the elevators who would like to talk to you."

"Who?

"Charlie Mac and Becky," he said.

I nodded. "Let them come down," I said. "And then you go eat. I have a feeling I'm about to have a come-to-Jesus meeting with Charlie."

Parvis nodded. "Do you want me to stick around? You know, just in case?"

I shook my head. "Nah, I can take care of him if he shows his ass."

"Okay. Good luck with him."

Certain areas of Mount Weather were restricted, and Charlie Mac did not have authorization to come down into the lower levels. So, Parvis had to use his key card to allow them access. A minute after Parvis left, I heard the ding of the elevator bell.

"Come on in," I said loudly.

I heard the approaching footsteps, and a moment later, Charlie stuck his head in. I motioned him to come inside. Becky was close behind him, looking anxious. I always thought she was a rather plain-looking woman. Over the years, she'd put on weight, another side effect of a good food supply here. She had given birth to a son a year after Mount Weather went on lock-down. It was Senator Conrad Nelson's son, even though it was supposed to be a secret and he never acknowledged the son as his.

Charlie was rather plain-looking as well; average build, brown hair that was starting to thin out on top, and a moderate pot belly. I had no doubt what precipitated this visit. Someone, Becky probably, explained to him how he'd stepped on his dick when he smarted off to me. The main question was how he planned on proceeding. I had a gun in my desk drawer, and another one in the crotch of my pants, but I didn't think I'd need either. If it came to fists, Charlie didn't stand a chance against me, but I wondered if he knew that.

"Do you have a minute?" he asked tentatively.

"I do," I said. "In fact, I'm glad you're here. I suppose there is no reason to surprise you, so I'll go ahead and let you know now. We'll be escorting you off of Mount Weather premises first thing in the morning."

His face paled and Becky gasped. "Uh, I was hoping to talk to you about that," he said.

I purposely waited a long moment before speaking. "Alright, I'm listening."

"First, I want to apologize for earlier. I wasn't in a good mood and you caught me at the wrong time."

"I would not have caught you at all if you'd been doing your job. I don't know if you are aware of it, but there have been other complaints on you over the past few months."

"There have?" he asked, as if this were news to him.

"Yes, it's noted in your personnel file. Your work ethic and your interaction with other people here leaves a lot to be desired."

He grumbled and I could see he wanted to say something negative, but Becky grabbed his hand and squeezed. He held his tongue. I continued.

"Your file says you're forty-four now, and back before you worked in the insurance business. Is that correct?"

"Yes, my primary job was a bond underwriter," he said, and then shrugged. "It was decent money, but it seems like a rather worthless occupation now."

"And there are no other specialties listed."

"I was a scratch golfer, but it doesn't do me much good these days."

I looked at his bio on my laptop. "A graduate of Western Kentucky with a degree in business, correct?"

"That's right," he said. "What's with the questions?"

"I'm trying to find something here, but you're not fitting in here, Charlie," I said. "You're not getting along with people, and I'm thinking you're too old to change your ways."

He grumbled some more under his breath and Becky squeezed his hand tighter. The two of them exchanged a glance before he looked directly at me. "Well, anyway, I apologize for my behavior."

He turned to walk out. There were tears in Becky's eyes and she gave me a silent, plaintive look. I did not know Charlie Mac all that well, but I knew Becky. She was a nice woman with a pleasant personality and she adored her son, who often played with Frederick. She must see something special in Charlie Mac, even though all I saw was a lazy smart ass. I made a split decision.

"Have a look at this," I said as I stood. He stopped in his tracks and turned back toward me. I motioned him over to one of our dry erase boards.

"This is a list of pending projects for Mount Weather," I said as I waved a hand at the board. "Oh, that reminds me." I grabbed a dry erase pen and wrote down Harold's request for a new smokehouse.

"I suppose this is our Mount Weather business model, in a manner of speaking. Has anyone ever told you what our goal is?"

"To rebuild America," he said. "Yeah, everyone knows that."

"Yeah, silly question, I know, but what I'm trying to get at is this is the base of Mount Weather business model. We have to keep it running at peak efficiency before we can even concentrate on the rest of America." I gestured at the board. "Here is a small part of what we do. The purpose of these projects is to not only keep Mount Weather strong, but to improve our quality of life. For every project we accomplish, there's always two or three more that pop up," I said. "It's a lot of work making these plans a reality, and this doesn't even cover the day-to-day chores, like hauling barrels of food waste to a smelly pig farm when it's cold and wet outside."

Charlie gazed over the board and the others for a long minute before speaking. "What's wrong with Harold's smokehouse?" he asked.

"It's falling apart. He wants a hand building a new one. I personally think the best course of action is to build one that's larger and more efficient so he can accommodate us better. I honestly don't know why, but Harold goes out of his way to take care of us. He doesn't ask for much in return."

He nodded slightly. "That's a lot of work," he said, almost in a whisper. He turned and focused on one of the maps.

"What's this all about?" he asked.

"It's our houses in the area," I said and pointed at the various houses. "These are the ones that are occupied. As I'm sure you know, there are houses everywhere, but they need to be repaired and hardened. You helped with one of the houses last fall, didn't you?"

"Yeah, me and Kass," he said. He then turned to face me again and looked me over. "How did you get so dirty? You weren't so dirty when you were in the cafeteria."

"My work assignment today was to clean and service the main heating unit. Somehow, it'd been overlooked for over a year, so it was pretty dirty."

He looked surprised now. "I didn't think you higher echelon people did any grunt work."

I shrugged. "While that is certainly true for some of them, I am not immune to being given work assignments, nor do I want to be." I did not tell him I chose my own assignments now, but he didn't need to know that.

He nodded thoughtfully and then gestured at Becky. "Becky said you have more power here than anyone realizes."

I shrugged again. "I suppose it would depend on who you ask." I gestured at the whiteboards with a hand. "Here is my primary job. I work for Parvis, who is the Director of Operations."

"And Parvis works directly for the president," Becky said to him. I think he understood the implication.

Charlie Mac nodded again and continued staring at the boards and the map.

"Zach," Becky said. "We've known each other ever since you came here."

"Yes, we have," I acknowledged.

"Am I a bad person?" she asked.

"Not at all. I think highly of you," I replied.

"If you'll give Charlie Mac a second chance, I'll promise you he'll straighten up."

She continued gazing at me, silently pleading. I looked over at the man in question, who was staring back hopefully.

"What about it, Charlie?" I asked.

He looked at Becky and cleared his throat. "I would appreciate a second chance."

CHAPTER 10 – HAPPY 25TH

My birthday party took place after dinner and was held in the designated recreation room. There'd been more than a few wild wing-dings in the room over the years, which always amazed me. We had an entertainment committee, which Kelly was a member of, who did a great job of creating all kinds of recreational activities to keep the Mount Weather community occupied, but even so, people seemed to have an insatiable desire for wild, decadent parties. I admit, Kelly and I had been to a few, but we had never engaged in any of the rowdier activities that some of them loved so much.

Many of our friends were already present when we arrived. They greeted us with smiles, birthday wishes, and all of the other silly birthday clichés. Macie and Frederick ran over to join the other kids, who were at the far end of the room playing some type of game.

I made my rounds, saying hello to everyone and thanking them for their birthday wishes. Some were old friends, some were new. Some of them were sincere in their flattery, others were duplicitous. But, this evening, they were all smiles. I reciprocated in kind.

Most of our Nolensville group was congregated at one table. After spending thirty minutes or so speaking with everyone else, I headed over to them. It was funny, we didn't always like each other, but we'd mostly stuck together all this time. I sat down in between Janet and Kelly.

"The birthday boy finally decided to join us," Janet said.

I glanced over and noticed she had a tea glass almost full of wine. "Oh, don't get started," I said. "You know I have to be hospitable to everyone."

"He's an important member of the community, Janet," Grant said from the seat on the other side of her.

Grant Parsons was originally a Major in the Marines and part of the Chemical Biological Incident Response Force, or CBIRF. He was an average-sized man in his fifties, and over the years, his salt and pepper hair had segued to a mostly salty gray. He and Janet had a brief affair, back several years ago when they were both at the CDC, but it ended when she left him for that psycho, Colonel Almose Coltrane. They started back up again not too long after arriving at Mount Weather and had been together ever since. I have no idea how or why he'd put up with her for so long.

I hated him at one time and came close to killing him. But, time has proven to me that I would have made a terrible mistake had I followed through, and now I called him a friend. For that matter, I hated Janet at one time as well. I don't think I ever considered killing her, but you better believe I came close several times to taking her out in the country and dumping her on the side of the road, like an unwanted cur dog. Grant interrupted my thoughts.

"He's expected to be polite and gracious," he added and smiled at me.

Janet took a liberal swallow. "Well, happy birthday. You've certainly come a long way from the skinny kid I met way back when."

I put my arm around her and gave her a hug. I knew it would make her feel wanted and would, hopefully, keep her in a good mood. Nobody was fond of Janet, with the possible exception of Grant, but, I've come to tolerate her. She was a good grandmother to my children and we'd worked out most our differences over the years.

"The president did not see fit to attend," Janet said. She was one of those people who always looked for the negative. A real Debbie Downer.

"Don't be so sure," Rachel said and pointed at the door.

And, wouldn't you know it, you mention his name and he appears. He walked through the doors with his small entourage of the Anderson family and Kate Redbank. The Andersons, Parvis, Garret, and Grace, were an integral part of the president's team. Kate was his mistress.

Fifty-seven years old now, President Stark was still fit-looking with sharp features, alert blue eyes, and steel gray hair. And, wouldn't you know it, he was wearing a starched white button-down shirt and a pair of gray slacks that looked like they'd been bought a couple of hours ago. He said hello to various people, forgoing handshakes—he never shook hands—and slowly made his way over to our table while Parvis and his two children went in the opposite direction and joined his girlfriend. I stood as he approached.

"Happy birthday, Mister Gunderson," he said with a small, seemingly warm smile.

"Thank you, sir."

He made a generic motion with his hand. "You've become a popular man these past few years."

I nodded, but didn't answer. As far as I was concerned, with a couple of exceptions, my only true friends were the people sitting at this table.

"Won't you sit down, sir?" Rachel asked. She patted the chair next to her while smiling sweetly. She wasn't necessarily being flirtatious, she only wanted to get a rise out of Kate. Kate Redbank had come to Tennessee along with her sister, Sammy, and Sarah. From there, she traveled with us to Mount Weather. I'd never seen eye-to-eye with Kate. There was no overt animosity, but I guess it was a simple clash of personalities.

She'd hooked up with Shooter while still in Tennessee but had left him almost two years ago and had hooked up with Stark. She was called the

First Mistress by everyone and she didn't like it. Currently, she was standing beside Stark and shooting daggers with her eyes at Rachel, who acted like she didn't notice.

"I'd be delighted," Stark said with a smile bordering on lecherous.

Rachel Benoit was the same age as Kelly. Cute, lots of freckles, she had a dry, often whacky sense of humor which was always preceded with a mischievous grin.

We chatted about inconsequential things for several minutes. I caught Fred looking at me a couple of times. He didn't like stuff like this, but suffered in silence. I sympathized with him. I didn't care much for this stuff either.

Eventually, President Stark stated he had other duties to attend to and stood. "I hope you don't overdo it tonight, Zach," he said. "We have a lot to go over tomorrow."

"Roger that, sir."

"Walk with me to the door," he directed. We walked outside into the hallway before he spoke.

"Ohio has gone dark," he said.

"I've heard," I said. "No radio contact whatsoever."

"Correct. We'll discuss it in more detail in the morning. Enjoy your party."

After he left, I returned to the table. I glanced over at Fred, who looked downright miserable. I decided to throw him a lifeline.

"Hey, Fred. The president said he was outside earlier and thought he heard some kind of disturbance in the horse barn."

He stood, almost a little too quickly. "I better go check on it."

Rachel stood too. "I'll go with you," she said, and then flashed her usual grin. "You might need protection."

Fred frowned and Kelly giggled as the two of them walked out. They were an unlikely pair. Both of them had a relationship with Sarah at one time. After her death, they'd formed a deeper friendship. We suspected the two of them were occasional lovers, but if they were, they weren't telling.

"What did the president say?" Kelly asked.

I leaned over to her and spoke quietly. "Big meeting in the morning. We might be going on a road trip in the next day or so, depending on what the president says." I started to explain, but she cut me off.

"Yeah, the rumor mill is already churning. Ohio has gone dark. No comms from them for five days now, right?" she asked.

"Yeah," I said with a grunt. The Mount Weather grapevine ensured there were no secrets around here.

"How long, do you think?" she asked.

I shrugged. "Depends on what we find."

She gave me a look, so I modified my answer. "No more than three days, I'm thinking."

She sighed, but after a moment she reached under the table, found my hand, and gave a squeeze.

Because so many people had young children, the party did not last long, thankfully. Almost everyone had left by ten. Janet and Grant surprised me by telling us they'd take care of cleaning up and shooed everyone off.

I looked over at Kelly as we walked back to our suite. She returned a small, knowing smile because she knew exactly what I was thinking. All we needed to do was to get the kids to bed.

CHAPTER 11 – LIFE IS A MEETING

Sex. All I wanted was peace and harmony in the Mount Weather universe, and sex. But, Murphy's Law always seemed to intercede on both fronts. Last night was a good example. Kelly had teased me throughout the day with little hints of what awaited me after the party, but, the little hellions overdid it with the sweets at the party and ended up getting sick.

Honestly, it was our fault, we should have kept a closer eye on them. Even so, I was frustrated, both emotionally and sexually. I took pity on my beautiful pregnant wife and let her sleep while I dealt with their aching stomachs. Macie puked first, which caused Frederick to puke, which caused Kelly to jump out of bed and run into the bathroom puking, which almost caused me to puke. Fortunately, Macie went to sleep almost immediately after I got her cleaned up, as did Kelly. My son was another matter. He moaned and complained, convinced there was a miniature zombie running around in his tummy. He finally fell asleep a little after two in the morning.

So, yours truly only got four hours of sleep, and no special birthday present. I suffered in silence and gave Kelly a smile when the alarm clock went off.

"Did you sleep okay?" I asked.

"Yeah, once the odor went away, or maybe I just got used to it," she answered. "How about you?"

"Oh, okay, I guess."

I hopped in the shower first, bathed quickly, and then swapped with Kelly. I watched her as I toweled off, which was stupid. Watching her did nothing but get me aroused. She noticed when she stepped out.

"Wow, look at you," she teased.

"Pregnant women are sexy," I said as I dried off her back. She faced the mirror and ran a hand along her stomach.

"I'm going to get stretch marks," she lamented.

I reached around and began rubbing her belly. She moaned in appreciation.

"Your boobs are getting bigger," I murmured in her ear as I worked my hands upward and started nibbling on her earlobe.

She moaned again. I started to bend her over the sink counter when we were interrupted by the bathroom door being thrown open. The two little monsters burst in, causing me to hurriedly turn my back to them and cover myself with a towel.

"Daddy, I'm hungry!" Frederick shouted.

"Yeah, Daddy, I'm hungry too!" Macie shouted.

Kelly gave me a look as she wrapped the towel around herself. "I guess they're not sick anymore."

I stifled a sigh and smiled. "Alright, kids. Let's go eat."

"Put some clothes on first, Daddy," Macie admonished.

Breakfast was subdued; a lot of people were hung over. No doubt there was an "adults only" party after my birthday party.

"We need car parts," Josue informed me as we ate.

"What kind?" I asked.

"The kind that wears out, especially tires."

That didn't help me much, but in Josue's own way, he made sense, I guess. I started to ask him to write me up a list and email it to me, but Josue did not care for computers and seldom wrote anything down. He kept it all in his head.

"Alright, I'll add it to the list," I said. After all, we had a complete inventory of everything in Mount Weather on spreadsheets, including all of our vehicles. I could extrapolate what parts we needed from it.

An hour later, I was sitting in the office I shared with Parvis. If one wanted to be technical, he shared his office with me, but he'd been sharing it for the past five years, so I guess it was mine as well. Normally, it was large enough for two or more people, but Parvis was a collector of sorts. The office was a conglomerated mess of organized chaos. In addition to two desks, there were books, technical manuals, scattered files, various pictures of the area around Mount Weather, and of course, there were the dry erase boards. We had four and they were filled with notes detailing the progress of all of our ongoing projects.

In one corner was a table with a hotplate. Parvis stood when I walked in. "Tea?" he asked. "I've got some fresh ginseng."

One thing about Virginia, ginseng grew in abundance in the hills and Parvis loved it.

"Yeah, sounds good," I replied and looked at him. He'd never been a big man, but now he was down to probably a hundred and thirty pounds. "Did you eat breakfast?" I asked.

He grunted. "You sound like Kendra. I managed to get down a piece of toast that I'd sopped up with bacon grease."

He'd told me the grease settled his stomach somehow. Priss had suggested marijuana to help with his digestion, but Parvis was firmly opposed to it.

"Did you enjoy yourself last night?" he asked.

"Immensely," I lied. "How about you?"

He smiled ruefully. "Yes indeed. I apologize for not joining you and Kelly, but I wanted to spend some time with my family, and you and I see each other so much, I didn't think you'd mind. Time is precious to me nowadays, you understand."

"Of course," I said.

I watched as he took the teapot into the restroom and heard him fill it from the sink. He then put it on the hotplate and prepared two tea balls before sitting.

"So, Ohio. What are we going to tell Stark?" he asked again.

He liked doing this before the weekly meetings, going through question-and-answer scenarios. It worked though, so I didn't complain. We talked about it for several minutes while we drank our tea. Our conversation soon segued to the topic of Marcus Hook.

"Have we heard any word from the esteemed Roscoe Sidebottom?" he asked and then snickered. "Every time I say his name, I laugh."

I had to admit, it sometimes brought a smile to my face as well. "We received a radio report from the crew we sent out there. They've repaired some equipment and upgraded their water treatment system."

"Excellent, but we need those people back as soon as possible. We need them."

"They are due back by the end of the week," I said.

Parvis nodded. "Excellent."

"Even so, they need more people living there permanently."

Parvis nodded in agreement with a slight smile.

At the beginning of our second year of living here, Parvis sat three books in front of me one morning. "I expect you to be an expert on the topic," he said with a grin.

I can't say I became an expert, but I learned a lot about the wonders of petroleum. Petroleum was also used in rubber products, cleaning products, bath oils, lotions, toothpaste, lipstick, anything made of plastic, pesticides, preservatives, food and candy flavorings, paint, asphalt, anesthetics, fertilizers, the list seemed endless. All it took was crude oil and refineries.

"Perhaps we should require any newcomers to immediately relocate to Marcus Hook," he suggested.

"We'd need to provide incentives to encourage them, I think."

Parvis nodded at my idea. "Yes, we'll need to think that one over and come up with something."

"It won't be so easy with the ones already living here. They know this is probably the best thing out there."

Parvis chuckled. "I guess we have ourselves to blame."

He was right, in a manner of speaking. We had crops, livestock, some degree of medical care, a secure facility, electricity, potable water, and a sanitary sewer system, almost all of the amenities of what people took for granted, back before.

There were still issues. We had many shortages and we were limited in advanced medical procedures. We had no means to produce pharmaceuticals on a large scale. Our manufacturing facilities consisted of a woodshop, a blacksmith shop, a machine shop, a couple of sewing machines, and a loom.

No, we still had a long way to go, but it was certainly better than living in a farmhouse where you had to depend on batteries and solar energy for power and had to barricade the doors and shutter your windows every night.

"So, more people. We'll get the scouting missions going again as soon as the weather breaks and try to recruit some survivors. We need to start working out way further west." I looked at my watch and stood. "The meeting is in fifteen minutes, we better get going or we'll be locked out."

Parvis chuckled as he stood. "Oh, there is one more thing."

"What's that?" I asked.

"Abe has directed us not to mention the POL report in this morning's meeting."

POL was a military acronym we used for Petroleum, Oils, and Lubricants. We had everything measured down to the ounce and we usually read it out. I looked at him questioningly.

"Okay, but why not?" I asked.

"People may see our surplus in that area as a good reason to take vehicles out on frivolous joyrides."

I guess it made sense. "Whatever you say, boss." I glanced at my watch again and motioned toward the door.

We relocated to the president's conference room. I took my usual seat beside Parvis, booted up my laptop, and sat back. My mind drifted as other people began filtering in and engaging in small talk. Life at Mount Weather was punctuated with meetings. Every decision had to be discussed. Hell, it took hours of debate before we finally decided to use the word "zed" in our records to describe the infected instead of all of the other descriptors that were used.

Senator Rhinehart and Lydia were discussing what kind of work projects they could assign to the scout teams. For safety purposes, we pulled the teams in every winter, with the exception of Melvin and Savannah, who seldom listened to directives. Senator Rhinehart was the head of the logistics team, and they believed in the adage about idle hands are the devil's workshop. I doubted either one knew the origin of the phrase because neither of them had ever read the Bible. Lydia saw me looking.

"What do you think, Zach?" she asked.

"There's always plenty to do around here," I said in agreement. "But, don't forget about our commitment to Marcus Hook. Maybe some of them would be willing to live there for the winter and help them out."

Lydia nodded thoughtfully. Rhinehart scowled at me, probably because he did not think of it first. As we talked, I thought of our scout teams. They had become skillful over the years. Whenever they found pockets of survivors, they'd vet them and extend an offer for them to be inoculated. We had some limited successes, but we were perpetually in desperate need of skilled tradesmen and tradeswomen. Medical people, engineers, electricians, carpenters, plumbers, scientists, farmers, gunsmiths, blacksmiths, farriers, heavy equipment operators, tailors, you name it. The list was endless.

For those who were willing to relocate, we put them up in fortified houses in the area surrounding Weather. It was not a perfect system, but over the years, we'd substantially increased our population within the hundred-mile radius and had made alliances with other groups, but only east of the Mississippi. Hopefully, with the help of Roscoe Sidebottom and his Marcus Hook people, we'd be able to expand our scout teams west of the big river.

I opened a file and was typing some notes when the president walked in promptly at eight. Ruth and Raymond walked in immediately behind, shut the doors, and locked them, a reminder that he had no tolerance for tardiness. They bid everyone good morning and took their seats. He got right down to business.

"Alright, we have a full agenda for this morning, let's get to it. Parvis?"

Parvis started to stand but then he began coughing. I quickly poured him a glass of water. He nodded gratefully and then slid his laptop toward me.

"Mister President, if I may?" I asked.

"Proceed, Mister Gunderson."

I stood as Parvis took a seat and coughed a few more times before taking a tentative sip.

"I'll start with the easy stuff. Our water production is operating at peak efficiency. Our fall harvest was excellent and our greenhouses are going strong. The same with our livestock." I pointed at the screen. "There are the raw numbers for those of you who are interested. In summation, we are well prepared for the winter and even though we've given a sizeable amount to Marcus Hook, we're expecting a surplus."

"Here, here," somebody said.

"As far as our other commodities, we have a severe shortage of sugar, salt, and other various spices."

"Like coffee," someone said.

"Yes, definitely coffee. It is an ongoing concern with no solution in sight at the moment. We'll work on this in the spring when we can renew our scavenging.

"Second, our wastewater treatment plant. The annual cleaning and flushing of the sediment tanks for our waste water facility has been completed. The personnel who undertook this thankless job wanted us to strongly remind everyone that certain things should not be flushed down the toilet."

There were some guffaws of laughter along with some murmurings of consent.

"Second, our Marines, along with our Navy man, Ensign Boner, have been diligently working on reloads. In the past month, they've cranked out eleven hundred rounds of five-five-six and eight hundred rounds of nine-millimeter."

"Impressive," someone commented.

"Our count is still down by over three thousand of each caliber from this time last year," Justin said. Grace had put the numbers up on the projection screen, to which Justin pointed at.

I nodded in his direction. "You are correct, Captain, and in addition, we have a severe shortage of other calibers. At some point, we are going to need to conduct a long-range mission to one of the known arsenals or we get lucky and find the home of a dedicated prepper who died before he used up all of those thousands of rounds of ammo he hoarded."

There was more murmuring. I waited until it died down before proceeding.

"Moving on to our scouting report. Gunnery Sergeant Conway and his team returned yesterday. He reported a successful contact with a group of eighteen survivors living outside of Greenville, North Carolina. They have agreed in principle to join our alliance."

"Here, here," someone once again said.

"Alright, now for our zed report. Our community in Leesburg report contact with twenty-three zeds, possibly coming out of one of the larger cities. They are now requesting a resupply of ammo, five hundred rounds."

There was at least one derisive snort. I had to agree. They killed twenty-three zeds, and in return, they wanted five hundred rounds of precious ammo.

"Those people need to learn how to be self-sufficient," someone said. While I did not disagree, the same thing could have been said about several people who lived here.

"That brings our total count for the year at four hundred, eighty-nine.

"And finally, our scout teams are done for the winter. Gunnery Sergeant Conway and his team just returned from Greenville, North

Carolina where they successfully made contact with a group of a dozen survivors. They have tentatively agreed in principle to join us."

"Excellent, Gunderson. Any questions?" President Stark asked and then changed the subject before anyone could pose a question. "Now, let's move on to Ohio."

I looked at Parvis, who gave me a reassuring smile and motioned for me to continue.

"Okay, I'll start with a brief recap. As you all know, over the years, we have been systematically exploring the territory surrounding us in one-hundred-mile radius increments. It is a slow process, perhaps a little too slow for some of you, but it has been both effective and successful. We are currently at the three-hundred-mile radius." I gestured at Garret, who looked like a younger, healthier version of his father. He worked his laptop, and soon the projection screens lit up with a geographic map of the United States. There were four circles of increasing diameter with Mount Weather being the center. The third circle pulsated, indicating the three-hundred-mile radius to which he referred.

"Now, eight months ago, we had a chance encounter with a similar group of explorers on the outskirts of Columbus, Ohio."

One of the screens instantly changed to a picture of Columbus similar to a Google Earth photo. There was a small code visible. Garret hovered the mouse pointer over it and it became a hyperlink. He clicked on it and the screen changed to show the information recorded by the scout team.

"A friendly dialogue was established with this group of survivors. They informed us they were from Cincinnati."

The screen changed again. Now it showed the Eastgate Shopping Center, located a few miles east of downtown Cincinnati.

"They told of at least one other survivor encampment near the Dayton International Airport."

Before I finished the sentence, Garret had changed the second screen to Dayton.

"Wasn't it you who led the scout team, Gunderson?"

It was Conrad Nelson who asked the question. He was once a senator from Florida and a notorious womanizer. He took over the role of the administrative secretary when one of the prior secretaries died. He had the audacity to hit on Kelly once. I guess he thought I would not do anything about it, but he was dead wrong. I caught up with him the day after Kelly had told me.

"Kelly would never mess around with you," I said to him. "But, if she did, I'd wish her well and we'd go our separate ways. In the meantime, I think, on pure principle, I would feel the overwhelming need to beat the ever-loving hell out you."

"Don't be absurd," he said, with a condescending laugh. I was amused at first, but now he pissed me off. My voice lowered an octave.

"Well, it looks like you think I'm all talk, so let's go ahead and get to it." I squared off and cocked a fist back. His face paled and he quickly threw his hands in the air.

"Whoa, hold on, Zach. There's no need for violence."

I had his full, frightened attention now as I lectured him about proper behavior regarding other people's wives and the consequences that awaited him if he disregarded this friendly warning. And, I reminded him what had happened to the late President Richmond. He never made a pass at Kelly again and the matter was forgotten.

"I was," I answered. "We came upon them while they were getting equipment out of a restaurant." I glanced over at Parvis, who was looking a little pale. He saw me looking and encouraged me to continue. I leaned down and whispered to him.

"Why don't you go lie down?" I suggested.

"I'm fine, keep going," he whispered back.

"It was a friendly encounter," I said. "We had a long, amicable talk. They advised us they had an operational shortwave radio, so we worked out frequencies and call signs. There were multiple radio conversations after that and they finally agreed to meet and discuss a more formal arrangement." I turned to Garret. "Would you put up the pictures of Schmucker and Brumley?"

He did so within seconds and the pictures of two men appeared, each filling a screen.

I pointed at one of the pictures. "The one on the left is Josea Schmucker. He runs the Eastgate group in Cincinnati."

The picture showed an older, square-jawed, stalwart man who looked like he'd been eating persimmons prior to the picture being taken.

"Schmucker is a Mennonite. When the plague spread through his community, he and his family literally fled for their lives. Somehow, they ended up near Cincinnati where they encountered a small group of survivors who had taken refuge in the Eastgate Shopping Mall. They turned it into the fortress that you saw in Garret's pictures. It's an impressive sight. Schmucker eventually emerged as their leader and frankly, they're doing okay for themselves."

I then pointed at the picture on the right, an older, jowly man with black-dyed hair and matching black goatee.

"That is Jackson T. Brumley. When you speak to him, he tends to refer to himself in the third person and that's always how he addresses himself, Jackson T. Brumley. He was a union president, back before. He's a braggart and egotist. He said when the plague broke out, he saw the writing on the wall. He rounded up some union goons and took over a

Proctor and Gamble distribution center in Dayton at gunpoint. They kicked out all of the management personnel and anyone else who did not conform."

"That must have been quite an undertaking," Conrad said.

"Yeah, I'd say so. The building is about a million square feet in size. It has an inventory that'd make your mouth water. Think of all of the products Proctor and Gamble used to sell. That warehouse is full of those products."

"And he took it over?"

"He and his people," I said. "They then converted it into one hell of a trading post. Their bartering system is ingenious. They assign a point value to every individual item in their inventory, and then when somebody shows up looking to trade, they'll inspect their wares and utilize the same point value system. That's how they barter. Of course, the point value differs from day to day, depending on what they need, and it's always to their advantage."

"Remind me again how many of them there are?" Stark asked.

"Approximately one hundred in Eastgate, thirty-four in Dayton," I said. "There are more people living in the surrounding area, but we're not sure of the exact number."

I waited to see if there were any other questions before continuing. "As all of you know, we reached an alliance with both groups. As part of the terms of the alliance, we vaccinated everyone in both groups."

I paused again, but President Stark made a motion with his hand, indicating I needed to continue.

"Parvis and I are unaware of any issues or problems. Nevertheless, we have lost radio contact with them. Our last radio transmission with both groups was at eighteen hundred hours, five days ago. I personally handled both communications. There were no indications of any issues, hostile behavior, nothing. Since then, all attempts to reestablish communications have been unsuccessful."

I gestured at Garret. "Garret has been monitoring satellite feeds of both locations. Garret?"

Garret stood and I handed over the laser. Grace took over the computer and worked her mouse, changing the images to overheads of the shopping mall for her brother.

"This is a live feed. As you can see, there is no human activity. Now, let me direct your attention to all of the vehicles. I can do playbacks if anyone needs to see it, but I can save you the time and trouble. None of those vehicles have moved in at least four days."

Grace then changed the image to the Dayton facility.

"Same here," Garret said as he pointed the laser at the various parked vehicles. He then nodded at Grace, who changed the image again.

"This was three days ago. The various still-shots show people walking out of the front entrance of the warehouse and out of the encampment." The image changed again. Now, it was once again devoid of life.

"This is what it looks like currently. There is some lighting, but there is no movement or any other discernible activity."

"Where did those people go?" someone asked.

"Unknown," Garret replied. He did not offer an explanation as to why he did not follow them with the satellite. I didn't ask. There could've been many reasons, none of which mattered.

Stark took a sip of steaming tea before speaking. "Speculation, Parvis?"

"I believe something significant has occurred at both locations," Parvis said, not bothering to stand.

President Stark directed his attention to Bob Duckworth. "Senator, you and Zach had more than one meeting with each of them, I believe."

"Yes, we did. They are both stubborn and headstrong, but Schmucker is the more reasonable of the two." He nodded at me and I stood again.

"Senator Duckworth is correct. Deacon Schmucker is obstinate, but level-headed. Mister Brumley has a vastly different personality, but we managed to broker a win-win deal with both groups. I don't think they would simply ignore us."

"Perhaps they have radio trouble," someone suggested.

"Each group has a radio station that is independent of the other," I said. "It's possible both of them broke down at the same time, but for both of them to be offline for five consecutive days makes it highly improbable."

Stark nodded thoughtfully and looked up as Ruth whispered into his ear. He waved her off in irritation. "Parvis, what is the best course of action here?" he asked.

Parvis managed a weak grin. "I will once again defer to my worthy assistant," he said.

All eyes once again turned toward me. Some looked at me expectantly. This was the part I was looking forward to, but I was also dreading it, to a small extent.

"A mission team should be assembled, go to Ohio, and get a hands-on assessment." I looked over at Justin. "I think Captain Smithson would agree."

Justin stood. "I do agree. If I may be excused, I will start the process of issuing a warning order and mustering personnel. I should have a task force put together first thing in the morning."

"You don't have that long," Stark said. "Grace, would you explain the urgency of the situation?"

Grace straightened and pushed a stray lock of brown hair behind an ear before speaking.

"There is a high-pressure cell moving up from the gulf," she said and then used a stylus on her laptop to draw several arrows showing the direction of travel of the cell.

"As you can see, it's traveling in a northerly direction up the Mississippi valley." She circled another mass of clouds over what was once Manitoba. "This is a low-pressure cell and it is moving south by southeast. These two fronts will collide with each other in the Ohio valley area." That stray lock of hair escaped confinement and she once again pushed it behind her ear. "Garret and I think it is going to happen in approximately twenty-four hours. We're not meteorologists though."

"It's going to be a big one," Garret warned. "It'll probably start with rain, then sleet and ice, and then a buttload of snow. If you wait and leave tomorrow, you're going to get caught in the middle of that before you get halfway there."

"Parvis?" Stark asked.

"If we're going to send people there, we either need to move quickly, or wait until the bad weather passes," he said. Parvis then turned his attention to me.

"Zach, what do you think?"

I kept my emotions hidden, but I mean, what the hell? If he already knew about this impending storm front moving in, why did he let me ramble on for thirty minutes about trivia that everyone in this room could have looked up and read on their own?

"I think we should treat this matter with a sense of urgency," I said. "The sooner the task force gets going, the better."

Stark then looked at Justin. "Captain Smithson?"

Justin looked at his watch and looked again at the satellite images. "If I may be excused, I'll get everyone kick-started. With any luck, we'll be ready in two hours."

President Stark looked down momentarily at some notes he had jotted. He used notebook paper, even though it was in short supply. "Alright, but before you get started, let's give this a mission designation. Suggestions, Captain Smithson?"

"That's simple, Task Force Ohio," Ruth said.

Justin shook his head. "We've already used it. We all know how Parvis and Zach chide us about how each mission we execute is unique and historical in significance and all of that stuff, so we can't use the same name twice."

This touched off several people speaking at once, and after a minute, a couple of conversations segued into discussions about past missions. I could see growing irritation on President Stark's face and he noticed me looking at him.

"Gunderson, call it," he said.

"Task Force Dark Ohio," I replied.

Stark thought it over for all of two seconds and nodded. "I like it. Mister Gunderson, you'll be going as well, I take it?"

Here was the part I was dreading. On one hand, I loved going on missions, but on the other hand, I felt obligated to Kelly and the kids to stay with them. "Well, sir. I was thinking of sitting out this mission."

He nodded in seeming understanding. "With Kelly being pregnant, you want to spend more time with her. How far along is she?"

"Almost six months."

He nodded again. "Well, it's your call of course, but I can't help but think of the remarkable success you had with those two gentlemen whose personalities were problematic from the start."

I felt myself gritting my teeth. I knew Kelly was going to be disappointed, but…

"If you think I'm needed, sir, I'll go."

He gave a small smile, like I'd called a bet in which he was certain he had the upper hand. "I think you'd once again be an important and valued member of the team," he said. "So, it's decided. Captain, get to work."

Justin stood, came to attention for a one-second count, and hurried out. I jumped up and was right behind him. I stopped him in the hallway.

"I need to make a stop to tell Kelly the news and then I'll head to the motor pool," I said.

"Roger that," he said. "I'll get the Marines together and go from there." He took off in a jog and I was about to do the same when I heard someone call out to me.

"Hold up, Zach."

I turned to see Senator Bob Duckworth hurrying to catch up.

"All of that work for naught," I said as he walked with me.

"Yeah," he agreed. "I counted Ohio as a major success."

"Are you going with us?" I asked.

He grinned. "Of course, I'm going."

"This one might get dirty, I'm thinking."

"I think you may be right," he said. "We'll be on the same team, I trust?"

"I wouldn't have it any other way," I answered.

He grinned again. "I'll see you in a few," he said and trotted off.

I watched him disappear around the corner and grinned myself. When Abe Stark took over, Duckworth, along with the other politicians, suddenly realized they were no long prima donnas in the Mount Weather community. But Duckworth was a rather unique individual. He reassessed the Mount Weather dynamic and found a niche. He developed a training regimen for recruiting survivors into our fold and actively participated in multiple scouting missions. The Ohio mission would have possibly failed if not for him.

I thought back to last summer when we visited Cincinnati and Dayton. Our first stop was the Eastgate Shopping Mall. Josea Schmucker met us at the gate. He was in his late sixties, tall and broad-shouldered, a bit stodgy, but polite and well-mannered. He invited us to dinner and afterward bluntly informed us he and his people considered themselves an autonomous entity and had no desire to join us, even when we told them about the vaccine.

Bob had done most of the talking and at one point appealed to Schmucker's Christian faith. It was a mistake on Bob's part. Schmucker started quoting scripture and the good senator was lost at sea. Fortunately, my grandmother had used the family Bible to teach me to read, and during her later years, when her eyesight wasn't so good, I often read aloud to her. My inherent memory allowed me to keep up with Schmucker's quotes and interpretations, and even threw in one or two of my own. I managed to impress him, which led to more dialogue. Eventually, we worked out an agreement.

Jackson T. Brumley was another story. Schmucker called him a blasphemous dipsomaniac, which was an accurate appraisal. He was in his mid-fifties, fat, pompous, and vain. He drank like a fish out of water and once in his cups would often proclaim God was a sonofabitch. Even so, his people were proud of him and readily accepted him as their leader.

The senator and I coddled him for two days. We listened in mock fascination to his many self-aggrandizing stories. Late into the second night, he launched into a blubbering rant on how us common folk at Mount Weather were doing things all wrong and perhaps he should even come up and take over. Bob prodded him for advice and I took voracious notes as he ranted on and on. The more of our moonshine he drank, the looser his tongue became. At one point, he questioned us about our scouting activities and what kind of success we had in locating survivors.

"We've had numerous successes," Bob said. "The American spirit is still alive and strong."

This seemed to trigger something. He asked a slew of questions about who we found and what we did with them. Finally, he suggested the only way we were going to get any cooperation from him is if we procured him one or two young girls for his personal pleasure.

"What age range did you have in mind?" I asked. We had no intention of pimping for him, but there was an ulterior motive behind my question.

"Just old enough where her hair will tickle my nose, if you know what I mean," he said with a wink and a cackle.

"I'll look into it," Bob said solemnly, keeping his expression neutral. He knew what I was doing. I had my laptop open, the little camera was pointed directly at Brumley, and I was recording the entire conversation. Jackson T. Brumley was oblivious. Hell, he probably didn't even know a laptop had that capability.

The next morning, Brumley met us at the Stryker. Bob and I pulled him aside and handed him a flash drive.

"What the hell is this?" he asked.

I carefully explained everything and even smiled when I saw the color drain out of his face as I told him I'd already emailed it to the president, which wasn't exactly true, but he didn't know that.

Suffice it to say, we reached an agreement and a new understanding of what was expected from him and the good people of Dayton. To be frank, we blackmailed him. We had a good laugh as we told Joker everything on the ride back to Weather.

The bottom line, Senator Bob Duckworth had adapted. He was an integral member of Mount Weather, and if we ever reinstituted the electoral process, I had no doubt he'd run for president.

Hell, I'd vote for him.

CHAPTER 12 – TASK FORCE DARK OHIO

After leaving the meeting, I went directly to the section of Mount Weather where the classrooms were located. Kelly taught grades one through six and also taught mathematics to the older students. The kids loved her. I waited patiently while she gave a lesson on English grammar, gave them a writing assignment, and then joined me in the hall.

"Tell me again why you have to go?" she asked.

"Stark did one of his roundabout moves of urging me to go," I replied.

"He manipulates you," she said quietly.

I reached and grabbed her hands. "I know he does," I said. "But, all in all, he's treated me well. He's treated all of us well."

"I know he does, and I know it's necessary, but it's always in the back of my mind. I always wonder if one day you won't come back," she said. "I mean, it's almost December and we always get ice and snowstorms in December. All of you might get caught in a snowstorm." She stopped when she saw the expression on my face. "What?"

"Um, there's a front moving in, so we're going to have to hustle if we don't want to get stuck in it."

Her eyes narrowed, but instead of giving me an earful, she remained quiet.

I pulled her toward me and gave her a kiss. "I'll always come back."

She gave me a reluctant smile and returned the kiss. "I worry is all, I always worry."

She and I talked some more and I made additional reassurances of how careful I would be before leaving her and going to our suite. When I walked in, I paused and looked around, thinking about Kelly's concerns. I wondered if indeed I'd return safe and sound. It was always something to consider. I'd lost count of the number of times I'd gone out on missions and had close encounters with zombies or evil humans. Anytime I walked out of those gates, I could be caught and overwhelmed by a horde, bested in a fight, or I could be shot by a sniper. There was always a risk, a level of uncertainty. I knew it and she knew it.

But, there was one thing I was certain of. Whatever happened to me, my wife and my children had a safe future at Mount Weather. It somehow always made me feel better.

Our lodgings were messier than I liked, but having two kids would do that. Especially when one of those kids had the energy of a Tasmanian devil on Red Bull. And, I had to admit, lately I'd let the burden of house cleaning fall upon Kelly, which was wrong of me. I thought, now is a good time to earn some brownie points and hastily straightened the place up before packing a rucksack.

First Sergeant Jeremiah Crumby had beaten me to the motor pool. Standing at slightly over six feet, dark-skinned and a perpetually shaved head, he had a lean, runner's physique and could've been a poster boy for the Marines. He was thirty-two now and in the prime of his life.

"How's it going?" I asked.

"Slow. Burns is in the armory and I was about to get us some vehicles," he said.

"How many you need?" Josue asked. Between him and his son, they could fix any vehicle made, so he was a natural choice to be in charge of the motor pool.

"At least ten," Jeremiah said. "And the Strykers."

Josue shook his head. "Only two Strykers working right now. I need time to fix the other two." He made a head motion toward Jorge, who was bent over, under the hood of a car. "My help is no bueno," he whispered.

"I heard that," Jorge said, which elicited some chuckles.

"We're going to need four-wheel-drive vehicles," I said. "And we're going to take the semi. Leave the trailer off of it."

"You got it," Josue said.

"What do we need the semi for?" Jeremiah asked.

"I strongly suspect the Dayton people are dead, and if I'm right, we're not coming back empty-handed. They have several trailers. We'll take one and load it up."

A slow smile creeped across the first sergeant's face. "I like the way you think, Zach. We'll have enough toothpaste and shampoo for the next ten years."

"Yep."

"What's this I hear about Ohio?"

I turned at the voice. It was Cutter, or Theodore Smith as he was known back before. He'd been living at Fort Detrick up until recently, but two weeks ago, he showed up back at Weather with all of his belongings and asked if he could move back home.

He had not changed much over the years. He no longer kept a scruffy beard, preferring a clean-shaven face these days, and he kept his hair cut military short, but otherwise, he looked no different. At the moment, he was standing there, staring at us expectantly.

"You've heard about Ohio?" Jeremiah asked.

I scoffed. "The Mount Weather grapevine travels fast."

"Yeah, but what's going on with them?" Cutter rejoined. "Are they all dead or something?"

I nodded. "It's a distinct possibility."

He looked around. "You guys are going there to investigate, aren't you?"

"Yes, we are," I said. "We need to find out what happened."

"Count me in," Cutter said immediately. "Lydia keeps putting me on maintenance duty. I'm telling you, man, I'm going stir crazy around here. So, what about it?"

I gestured at Jeremiah. "It's up to the first sergeant."

The first sergeant stepped closer to Cutter and looked him over. "Can I depend on you?"

"You know you can, First Sergeant," Cutter said.

"Alright, you're going to be a team leader. Round up some people we can count on. We'll be gone anywhere from one to three days. Tell them not to expect any sleep the entire time. Oh, and it's your responsibility to get everyone squared away on rations and water."

"Roger that," Cutter said. He flashed me a grin before jogging out of the motor pool.

"I seem to recall a time when you didn't care too much for him," I said, even though at one time I felt the same way.

"Yeah, well, he's come a long way," he said.

"Yep," I added in agreement. I walked over and put my gear in one of the Strykers. Thanks to Jeremiah's help, it only took us thirty minutes to get the vehicles squared away.

"Alright, I'm going to spend a little quality time with my kids," I said. "I'll be back here in one hour."

I found my brood in the cafeteria. They were sitting with Janet, Sammy, Fred, and Rachel.

"Can I go with you guys, Zach?" Sammy asked as soon as I sat down.

I caught Fred giving me a silent stare. I knew the man long enough to understand what he was thinking.

"You'd be a welcome addition," I said to him. "But, you've got some other obligations, don't you?"

Sammy's mouth worked in an effort to figure out a way to talk me into letting him go. I cut him off before he spoke.

"You've got school, and I believe you agreed to help Fred get Harold squared away, and then you're about to begin your, what did Fred call it, your master's phase of pistol training, right?

Sammy looked at Fred and hung his head slightly. "Yes, sir," he said. He didn't argue, but I could see the disappointment in his face.

"Next time, we'll see what we can work out, okay, buddy?"

He nodded. I felt for him. When I was his age, I was getting up close and personal with zombies and bad guys. Sammy knew this and wanted to be like me. Still, I worried. Obviously, I did not want him to be hurt, but I also didn't want him to have the nightmares, or the mercurial mood swings I used to have and sometimes still did, thanks to that little demon known as PTSD.

I'd gotten better over the years. Oh, I still had the occasional nightmare, but I'd not had one of those blind-rage episodes in a long time. Like the time at the police department's property room, back in Nashville. We'd gone there to scavenge. It was full of valuable stuff. We'd been loading up when three men drove up in a van. They declared themselves police officers and accused us of stealing from them. One of them, he told us his name was Detective McElroy, made a lot of disparaging remarks and threats. Fred had decked him, but that wasn't good enough. Once he regained his wits, he tried to attack me. I went into a rage and bashed his skull in with my handgun.

There were one or two other times, and Fred had his own moments. Hell, he probably had several moments that nobody knew of. One thing both of us agreed on, Sammy had a good soul and neither of us wanted him to ever suffer like we had.

"Young Sam is progressing well with his firearms training," Fred said, and then he surprised me. "But, his talents lie elsewhere."

"Oh yeah?" I asked. I glanced over at Kelly, who was grinning. "Have I missed something?"

"Yes, you have," Kelly said. "We've recently discovered Sammy has a knack for advanced math. Geometry, trigonometry, calculus, he's a natural with all of them. Fred believes he would be an excellent engineer."

"Just like Fred is," Sammy said with his own grin.

I smiled as I thought about it and held my fist out. Sammy responded and we shared a fist bump. Even Fred got in on the action. As we talked about it, I saw Cutter walk through the cafeteria doors. He spotted me and walked over.

"I've got six volunteers," he said.

I nodded, duly impressed, and looked at my watch.

"Alright, it looks like we've got forty-five minutes before muster. Have them help you with the rations and then herd them over to the armory. Joker's there with arms and ammo."

"Um, can I drive the Raptor?" he asked.

He was referring to my truck, a Ford Raptor. I loved that truck. It was a metallic green, four-door, beautiful piece of automotive equipment I'd found back during the first year of the apocalypse with a good friend, a man by the name of Howard Allen. He was a mechanic, and with his help, we'd made many post-apocalyptic modifications to it and it had never let me down.

"I would, but there's a problem. It only runs on gas and all we have at the moment is diesel. Besides, I need someone to drive the semi."

He pointed out a middle-aged man who'd not shaved in a while. He was scarfing down food like it was going to be his last meal. When he saw us staring, he gave us a thumbs up and spooned another big helping of eggs in his mouth.

"That's Troy. He's a truck driver from Richmond. He said he can drive a truck better than anyone."

I remembered his arrival, a little over a month ago. He showed up at the debriefing drunk and high. I'll have to say though, it was one of the most humorous debriefings I'd ever been a part of. Troy was a damn funny man.

"Alright, put him on your team," I said. "He'll keep you entertained."

Cutter grinned. "You hear that, Troy? We're partners." He then looked back at me. "Alright, I'll see you in a few."

As he walked off, I found myself thinking back to the first time I met him and his brother, Shooter. They showed up at the school near Brentwood one day during the third year of the outbreak. I took an instant disliking to them both and did not trust them as far as I could throw them. But, we'd mostly worked out our differences over the last five years. Shooter was still the same, always walking around with that fake smile plastered on his face, but Cutter had changed for the better, and I had to admit I counted on him as a friend.

I stretched and stood. "I guess I better make myself useful," I said. I hugged my kids and then had Kelly walk with me to the cafeteria's exit.

"We're planning on three days, but I'm going to push them. We'll drive all night and if everything works out, we'll be back sometime tomorrow."

"Barring any unforeseen complications," she said.

"Yeah," I agreed. We did not put into words what the implication of unforeseen complications meant. I hugged her tightly and gave her a kiss before doing the same to my kids.

CHAPTER 13 – THE OHIO MISSION

Eight years without manufacturing had taken its toll. As such, jury-rigging and improvising has become a fine art. We did not have a corner on the market. In fact, when we came across Deacon Schmucker's people, they had disassembled parts out of a restaurant's freezer to repair one of theirs.

We did the same, especially with our vehicles, which saw plenty of hard use. Josue and Jorge were masters of the art. Scout teams would routinely bring home auto parts—it looked like a salvage yard behind the motor pool—and the two men found ways to fit parts together that weren't meant to go together. And now that we had a source of viable fuel, the importance of our fleet of vehicles was higher than ever.

They were lining up the vehicles as I walked over to the motor pool. I knew our vehicles were squared away, although their appearance belied that fact. There were quarter panels of mismatched colors, handmade parts, fenders modified so oversized tires could fit, it all looked like a mess, but looks were deceiving. I stopped a few feet away and watched everyone hurrying about. I counted thirty-eight people with nine vehicles, including the two Strykers and the semi.

I admit, I had not been as hands-on as I normally was when prepping a mission, but hey, rank had its privileges sometimes. I heard Justin barking orders and found him inside the motor pool.

"How goes it?" I asked.

"We're almost ready. I'm about to give the briefing, Crumby and Burns will do the inspections, and then we'll move out." He glanced at his watch. "We're only running an hour behind."

I nodded. "Alright, let's get to it."

We walked outside and the first sergeant gave the command for everyone to form up. When everyone was assembled, Justin moved and stood to the front of the formation. As Justin listened to each sergeant report the names of the people in their individual teams, I stood off in the back with Jeremiah and looked over the people in the task force. I knew all of them. Some better than others, like Joker. When he and Maria fell in love with each other, we became good friends. We often socialized with the Garcia family and Joker fit right in.

The Marines made up the brunt of the military branch at Mount Weather, with Justin the commanding officer. When we'd first arrived here, a little over five years ago now, Ruth and Justin joined the ranks of the Marines. Two of them drowned in a boating accident and three were currently posted at Fort Detrick. One had moved on.

In the ensuing years, Justin had taken the original Marines and promoted them all to gunnery sergeants, and promoted Jeremiah to his first sergeant. They then created a training program that every able-bodied adult was required to successfully complete. Then, whenever there was a mission, each gunnery sergeant created teams from the populace. Most of the time, we had ample volunteers. It wasn't perfect, but we did not have the manpower for a standing army. Not yet.

Justin stood in front of them with squared shoulders. When the roll call was completed, he made eye contact with each of them before speaking.

"First, I want to thank you for volunteering for this mission. Hopefully, we'll be back here by tomorrow, but it may take a couple of days longer, depending on what we run into. So, let me start by going over the specifics of the mission."

He recited the mission in the standard military five-paragraph format. Most of them listened attentively, which was good. After, he had them stand in formation while the two NCOs inspected everyone's weapons.

The entire mission briefing took a little over thirty minutes, and we were rolling out of the gate promptly at eleven hundred hours. Team One led out with a Stryker and Jeremiah brought up the rear with the second Stryker. Those vehicles were awesome, but they were finicky and temperamental, so we only drove them on roadways and always kept them at well below their top speed.

I was in the lead Stryker with Justin, Joker, Bob, and a new guy, whom everyone called Flash. He was twenty or twenty-one, almost as tall as me, a slender, sinewy build, and medium-skinned. Melvin and Savannah found him and a couple of his friends living out of the hotels on Virginia Beach. Melvin convinced them to come live at Weather. Justin had dictated splitting up the rookies with the veterans and put him in the vehicle with us.

"I've never been to Ohio," Flash said. "How far is it?"

"A little over four hundred miles," Joker answered.

"And, we're driving nonstop?"

"That's right," Justin said.

"That's why each vehicle has jerry cans. Captain Smithson told you that during the mission briefing, weren't you listening?" Joker asked. "Dude, in the training class, we emphasized the importance of listening to the mission briefing. Shit like that's important."

Flash clenched his teeth together and stared at the floor of the Stryker. Joker noticed and took pity on him.

"The answer is yes, we're driving nonstop," he said. "Except for a five-minute stop where we'll change over drivers and get to take a leak, if needed. Remember that?"

"Yeah, man," Flash replied.

Justin gave him a look. "When we are on mission status, you address your superior officer by rank."

Flash was stung at the rebuke. Joker saw and tried to lighten the mood. He glanced over at Flash and grinned.

"The captain is a hard ass when we're on missions, but he has to be. You'll get used to it," he said. "We have a certain way of doing things. If we ever get into the doo-doo, you'll all of a sudden understand why we have certain protocols."

"Roger that, Sergeant," Flash said after a moment. "I didn't mean to be disrespectful."

Joker smiled. "No problem, my man." He hooked a thumb over toward Justin. "Captain Smithson will always do us right, and Zach there has a natural talent for this stuff, even though he ain't a Marine."

If Flash had gotten his feelings hurt by Justin's rebuke, he was over it now and laughed at Joker's jibe at me.

"This is your first mission with us, right?" Joker asked.

"Yes, Sergeant," Flash answered.

"Well, you're lucky to be on my team. Just stick with me, listen to orders, watch my six, and don't accidentally shoot me."

"Or anyone else," Justin added.

"Yes, sir."

"It's going to be dark by the time we get there and we don't have enough night vision gear for everyone," I said. "So, stick close."

"Are you on our team?" Flash asked.

I kept myself from rolling my eyes. Justin had read out team assignments during the briefing. I waved my hand around. "Yes. You, me, Bob, and Sergeant Joker."

"It's a damn good team," Bob said.

Flash nodded. "I've heard stories about all of you." He pointed at me. "You especially."

"Well, don't believe everything you've heard." I stood. "I think I'm going to try to get a nap in. If you can keep from hitting every pothole in the road, I'd appreciate it."

There wasn't room to fully stretch out, so, I positioned my ruck in a corner, leaned back, and pulled my hat down over my eyes. I didn't want to get into any storytelling about myself. I knew he was simply trying to get to know me a little better, but I wasn't inclined to tell stories about myself.

The Stryker was not designed for comfort, and I wasn't sure I'd be able to get any shuteye, but the lack of sleep from last night was catching up with me. I made myself as comfortable as possible and was asleep within a minute.

CHAPTER 14 – EASTGATE

We reached objective Alpha, otherwise known as Eastgate Shopping Mall, at 2100 hours, or as civilians preferred to say, nine p.m. It was located in Cincinnati near I-275 and Cincinnati Batavia Pike. There were multiple roads that led to a four-lane asphalt loop that circled around the mall. Deacon Schmucker and his people had made use of the loop and stacked up various types of items to form an eight-foot-tall defensive barrier around the entire mall. It was an impressive sight of crushed cars, concrete blocks, construction debris, you name it. It would have taken a tank to blast through it.

All entrances had been blocked off by the barricade, save one, and it was blocked by a heavily fortified gate with two guard towers on either side. They even had surveillance cameras.

When we stopped, the occupants of all vehicles, with the exception of the drivers, got out and formed a defensive perimeter. I smiled to myself as I watched everyone moving with a sense of purpose. The rigorous training program was showing.

The headlights of the Stryker shone on the gate and towers. All was quiet and there was no movement whatsoever. I tried several times to raise them on the radio, but there was no response.

"Team One to all teams, kill your engines and headlights," Justin ordered and then nodded to Joker, who used the Stryker's optics to scan.

"I'm not seeing anything, and I'm only getting residual heat signatures," he said.

"It's too quiet," Flash whispered.

He was right; once the noise from the engines abated, it was dead quiet, and, there were no lights emanating from inside the mall. I looked over at Justin.

"We need a recon," I suggested. Justin nodded and keyed the microphone.

"Team One to Team Three and Four, recon the perimeter with your vehicles."

Both teams replied in the affirmative and started their vehicles. They moved slowly, and after a minute, the radio crackled to life. "Team One, this is Team Four. All is quiet and dark, over."

Justin acknowledged and ordered them to return to the main group. Growing frustrated, I grabbed Bob.

"Let's knock on the door," I suggested. I got a look from Justin, and although it was dark, I could sense he was frowning at me.

I already had my gear on and quickly checked my assault rifle. As soon as I exited the Stryker, I thumbed the safety to the fire position and approached the gate. I sensed a little bit of nervousness with Bob, but he followed close behind me while keeping his weapon pointed away from me.

"Hello!" I shouted out as I rapped on the metal. Again, no response. The flashlight I carried was small, but I tried it out anyway. Peering through a gap in the gate, I could see cars and various types of machinery in the parking lot, but that was it. I stepped back and turned my flashlight off, but then quickly turned it back on again.

"What is it, Zach?" Bob asked.

"Look at the sign. Notice anything different?"

When the senator and I first visited the place, we watched one of the men mount a metal "No Trespassing" sign on the gate. He said he did it to point out the irony, and then laughed at his own joke. I wasn't sure what he meant, but did not bother asking. I pointed at it now.

"Look at the sign. It's been altered since the last time we were here."

Indeed, someone had taken a sharpie and wrote, "FEVER!" several times.

"Is it a warning?" he asked.

I shrugged. "Possibly."

The two of us shouted out a couple of more times before walking back to the Stryker. I told them about the sign. Justin rubbed his face in puzzlement.

"Why don't we get a drone up?" I suggested.

"Let's get a drone up," he said, like he thought of it first.

We walked back to the third vehicle, which was a Ford Expedition occupied by Kirby Jenkins and his girlfriend. Her name was Erin, and she'd been with the same group of people Flash was with in Virginia Beach. She was an average-looking twenty-something who kept her brown hair cut extremely short. I thought it looked butch, but the first day Kirby saw her, he told she was a sexy looking woman. They'd been together ever since.

He was a pro with our drones and he'd been teaching Erin how to fly them as well. They worked as a team as they unpacked the drone and the control pack. This one was a smaller surveillance model with four rotors and a camera on the bottom of it. They had two of them, and while Kirby got the first one airborne, Erin prepped the second one.

We watched the dull luminescent green of the screen as Kirby maneuvered the drone over the wall and into the compound. Kirby kept the drone at a height of twenty feet as he slowly flew it completely around the mall.

"Whoa, hold on," I said, pointing at the screen. "Go back twenty feet, drop your altitude and point the camera through those plate glass windows."

Kirby did so, and after a few seconds, we saw several faces looking out. Kirby moved the drone as close to the windows as he dared and panned back and forth across the width of the windows.

Suddenly, one of the windows shattered due to the people on the other side pushing against it. They rushed out by the dozens, only it was obvious now they were no longer normal people.

"Shit," Kirby growled as a couple of them lunged for the drone. He expertly maneuvered it to gain altitude, barely escaping their outstretched hands.

"Look at those things," he remarked as he shifted the camera. "They're all infected."

We watched as the occupants of the mall began pouring out of the broken window. Some of them ran directly toward the gate. The fortified perimeter which was designed to keep the zeds out was now keeping them prisoner in their domain. But, it was still unnerving and I found myself gripping my rifle tightly.

"I've got three minutes of charge left," Kirby advised.

"Alright, bring it in," Justin directed.

"Are all of them really infected?" Erin asked.

"It would appear so," Bob answered.

"But, weren't they vaccinated?" she asked, and looked at me specifically.

"Yes, they were," I replied.

"So, the vaccine's no good," Flash said.

"If that were true, we'd all be zombies by now," Kirby said. "But, something definitely went sideways."

We watched as the drone appeared over the wall and landed a mere two feet from us. Jenkins made it look easy.

"Do you want to put the second one up?" he asked.

"No need," Justin answered. "We've seen everything we need to see. Alright, pack it all up, we're moving out."

"Wait, we're leaving?" Erin asked.

"Affirmative," Justin answered, ignoring her lack of protocol, and turned to walk back to the Stryker.

"But, there might be people in there who aren't infected. Shouldn't we try to rescue them?"

There was no hesitation in Justin's response. "Negative. We're moving out."

Erin started to argue, but Kirby intervened. "Sweetie, any survivors have already gotten out. Somebody had to have written that warning on the sign."

"But..."

Kirby interrupted. "Why don't you go get in the truck and review the video recording?" he suggested. "If you spot anything, we'll present it to these men and they'll decide the best course of action." He then focused on Justin. "We'll be ready in a minute, sir."

Erin wanted to say more, but realized the decision was final and gave a curt nod to Kirby. We walked back to the Stryker. Justin got on the radio and ordered everyone to prepare to move out.

"There aren't any survivors in there, is there?" Flash asked quietly.

Nobody answered.

CHAPTER 15 – DAYTON

We always tried to keep things simple. Since Eastgate was designated Objective Alpha, Objective Bravo was the designation we gave the Dayton distribution center. All of those cleaning and hygiene products had been manufactured overseas for several years, hence the need for distribution centers in the United States. The company had several of them all over the nation which distributed their products to wholesalers and retail stores.

"Alright, listen up," I said in almost a shout to be heard over the noise of the engine. "Dayton is going to be more of the same."

"How do you know, Zach?" Bob asked.

"I just know," I replied. "So, we're not going to leave it behind the way we did with Eastgate."

Joker glanced over at me as he drove. "What're we going to do?"

"This is why we brought the semi," I said. "We're going to load up with everything we can."

I saw the confusion in Flash's face. "They have a lot of stuff we can use, and since they're all dead or infected, we're going to take it."

"You're certain they're dead?" Bob asked again.

"Dead or infected," I repeated.

I saw the senator exchange a brief glance with Justin. "You're the boss."

Bob Duckworth and the other senators had lost a considerable amount of their perceived power when Abe Stark took control. Some of them tried their own little rebellion, but they weren't fighters. It resulted in them being banished, which put the others in line.

Bob was once a dot-com entrepreneur who'd made millions before the political bug bit him. He was actually a decent guy, for a politician that is. He and his wife were in D.C when the balloon went up and the rest of his Mormon family were in Utah. He assumed they were all dead, or worse. However, he always had a pleasant smile, never balked at job assignments, and still attempted to contribute to the overall goals of Weather.

"Does it matter?" Flash asked. Bob glanced at him briefly, and then looked down at the floor. I spoke up.

"Senator Duckworth and I worked hard at securing an alliance with the Ohio people. I know he feels frustrated at this turn of events."

He looked up. "Yes, I do," he said. "A lot of good people are gone. Perished to this plague. It is a sad day."

"Oh, man, all that work for nothing," Flash said.

"Indeed," Bob replied.

I had to hand it to him. He was a smooth politician.

"So, what's so important in there?" Flash asked.

"Have you ever heard of the Proctor and Gamble Company?" Bob asked him.

"Uh, yeah, they make toothpaste and stuff," Flash said.

Bob gave a patient smile. "Much more than toothpaste. That building is over a million square feet in size, packed to the brim with toothpaste, mouthwash, dental floss, toilet paper, feminine products, manly products, baby products, cleaning products, you name it."

Flash's eyes widened. "Even four-ply toilet paper?"

Bob laughed. "I imagine so."

"Oh, man, sounds like heaven," he said.

"We're going to load up as much as we can and take it back to Mount Weather," I said.

Flash looked at me in puzzlement a moment before realization came over him. "You already knew this is what we were going to do from the get-go. That's why you had us bring trucks and why you brought the semi."

"Yep," I answered.

"But, how did you know?"

I gave Flash a noncommittal shrug. The truth was, I had dreamed of it. I didn't like Brumley, but the rest of them were good people. Schmucker was a Mennonite, and even though they used electricity and modern technology, Mennonites were natural survivalists. Schmucker could do anything from butchering a cow to building a house with nothing more than hand tools. He and his people were going to be sorely missed.

It was a seventy-mile trek from the Eastgate Mall to Dayton. This route was in far better condition than the route from Weather and two hours later, we were exiting I-70 onto the Dayton International Airport Access Road. Justin called a halt at the West National Road and ordered everyone to suit up.

We'd made improvements over the years with our fighting personnel. The Marines created a training program for all of the newbies, and everyone had to pass, including me. We'd created a cohesive fighting force, but in the past whenever we rolled out, we were dressed like a bunch of ragtag rejects from a Mad Max movie. That is, until we paid a visit to Fort Lee, Virginia.

Fort Lee is one hundred fifty-two miles south of Mount Weather in Prince George. Gunnery Sergeant Merritt Burns led a scout team down there three years ago when we were exploring out past the one-hundred-mile radius. He checked in with the satellite radio and told us to bring the semi. The quartermaster office was full of equipment, including Army Combat Uniforms, or ACUs. Much to the chagrin of the Marines, all of the ACUs were the Army pattern. Even the TAC vests. They didn't like it, but their ACUs were so worn out they had no choice throw them away and start looking like Army men. They got the last laugh though. They'd cut off their old USMC insignias and sewed them onto their new ACUs.

The end result, we had a uniform look now, almost like a professional army. Oh, everyone seemed to like their accessories. Some people wore shin guards. Some people went with the Kevlar helmets, others refused to wear them. I had kneepads, and during the summer months, I wore a padded sleeve on my left forearm. If a zed got too close, I'd simply ram my forearm in their face. They'd instinctively bite down on it, which gave me time to either shoot them or introduce them to my machete. Currently, I had on a heavy jacket, as did almost everyone else, which would also do the trick.

Our weapons were also an amalgamation of different brands and models of firearms, but all of the rifles were 5.56 caliber and all of the handguns were 9mm. Even though we had excellent reloading equipment, our capabilities were limited by our dwindling inventory of primers and cartridge casings. Mount Weather had an ample amount for 5.56 and 9mm, not so much with other calibers. So, until we happened upon fresh brass, we were limited.

We still had ammunition in different sizes, but only in limited supply. It was the same with other munitions. We had a total of sixty Claymores, twenty-three hand grenades, and a hundred and forty rounds of M203 ammo in various configurations. The Marines had the grenades and were under strict orders to only use them in dire circumstances.

We stopped a couple of hundred yards away. Joker utilized the optic sights on the Stryker.

"The main gate is partially open," he said. "They still have heat, but I can't tell anything else. I think I'm picking up infrared signatures of people, but it's hard to tell. There's nobody manning their guard towers though."

The four of us exited the armored vehicle and took up positions. Bob was supposed to take the passenger-side flank, but his attention was fixed on the mall. Joker had the forethought to keep an eye on our opposite flank. Our lights only did a fair job of illuminating the place. I took out my binoculars. The defensive fortifications were not as impressive as Eastgate, but they still had a wall around the warehouse consisting of fencing and concrete barricades. The first drop of sleet hit my cheek while we were back at Eastgate, and now it was thicker. There was no way we could utilize a drone in this weather. I handed the binoculars to Justin. He tried them and then sighed in frustration.

"I can't see shit in this weather," he growled. "Alright, back in the vehicles."

Once he was back in, he grabbed the microphone. "We're moving a hundred yards closer. Everyone stay alert."

"Take it slow," Justin said before sticking his head out of the hatch. Joker moved the vehicle closer and the rest dutifully followed. When he stopped again, Justin ducked his head in from the open hatch.

"Zach," he said.

I joined him and stuck my head out. He pointed. The headlights were shining on no less than a dozen corpses strewn along the road. All of them had been eaten on extensively.

"Holy shit," Flash said. I looked over to see he'd stuck his head up beside Joker. Bob somehow forced himself up between Justin and me.

"Yeah, ain't that some shit," Joker remarked.

Justin let out yet another long sigh, ducked back down, and got on the radio.

"Team One to all Teams, we're going in. Prepare for hostile action."

"Yeehaw," Joker muttered and took his foot off of the brake.

We turned onto Jackson Road, which led to the main entrance. Joker accelerated, and with a rebel yell busted through the fence.

By prearranged plan, our people were divided into two main groups. The first group, led by Justin, was the entry group. The second team, led by First Sergeant Crumby, acted as our rear security.

The convoy halted and Justin ordered the teams to dismount. Everyone exited with a sense of purpose and formed up into their individual squads. It was only a matter of seconds before the doors burst open and several zeds came charging out.

These were freshly infected zombies. Therefore, their muscles were still intact for the most part. They were as strong as a normal human, maybe more so, and with the infection raging through them, they were fast as all get out.

We laid down disciplined fire, but the first thing I noticed was that some of them weren't going down easily, even the ones sustaining headshots. Several times, one of them got to within a foot of one of us before finally going down.

"Double-taps to the head!" I shouted. "Shoot them twice!"

It took longer than it should have to kill them. When the last one went down, we took the time to check everyone and reloaded.

"Well, that was some shit, wasn't it?" Joker said.

I caught Justin looking at me questioningly. "These seem to be a little tougher to kill."

"You think?" Flash said.

Justin hastened a harsh glance at him. "How many are left?"

I did a quick count. "Twenty-one, but I don't think we can rely on that number anymore."

Justin turned toward everyone. "Alright, listen up. We're going in. Stay tight, kill everything, and don't stop with one headshot. Any questions?"

Everyone stared back in grim determination, but there were no questions. Justin gave the order and we moved into the building.

The place was huge and the lighting was barely adequate. There were pallets of products stacked everywhere, which made for a lot of hidey-holes for the zeds. When we first made entry, five of them immediately charged us. Everybody was overly hyped now, so we expended probably a hundred rounds of ammo needlessly.

"Alright, everyone, stay frosty," Justin admonished. "Remember your fire discipline."

It was a textbook room-clearing procedure, slow and steady. The zombies were playing games with us now. One or two would charge out from wherever they were hiding and while we were focused on them, five or six would charge from the opposite side of the building. And, there were far more than twenty-one.

They were fast. Faster than any zed I'd ever encountered. I heard a loud scream and looked over to see that one of them had successfully clamped down on Flash's arm. Apparently, Flash was out of ammo. He started punching it in the face repeatedly, but nothing seemed to dissuade the monster from letting go.

"Hold still!" I yelled as I hurried to him. I grabbed a handful of the zed's hair, aimed carefully, and put two rounds into its head. Only then did it let go and slumped to the floor.

"Thanks," he said breathlessly. "It got me while I was reloading."

We stood beside each other and chose our targets for another couple of minutes before there was a slight lull in action. I reloaded quickly and then motioned for him.

"Pull that jacket off and let me look at that arm," I ordered.

He hesitated a moment, but laid down his assault rifle and worked his jacket off. I pulled his sleeve up and inspected it closely. I could see some indentions, but the skin wasn't broken.

"He clamped down like a bulldog," he said.

"Move your arm around, see if it's broke."

He did so and shook his head, indicating no breakage.

"You were lucky," I said.

"Yeah," he muttered, tugged his sleeve down, and hastily put his jacket back on.

"I've been vaccinated," he declared. "Isn't that enough?"

"They went over this in the training class. You get bit, you get put in quarantine. In this case, we handcuff you and strap a motorcycle helmet on you."

"I know that," he retorted.

I gave him a skeptical stare.

"Well, I'd forgotten that part, but I remember it now," he replied with a little less arrogance now.

We resumed clearing out every little nook and cranny in between the pallets. They'd hide there, and as soon as we'd get close, they'd charge. Some of them were even hiding on top of pallets and would try to jump on top of us. Justin and I were constantly barking orders to keep our overly enthusiastic soldiers from charging ahead and separating themselves from the covering fire of their teams. When we reached the far end of the warehouse, we regrouped and assessed the damage.

"Conway's injured," Merritt reported. "He hasn't been bit, but it looks like his collarbone may be broken."

Justin and I hustled over to where Conway was sitting. He looked up as we approached.

"A big, overgrown zed was up on a stack of pallets and jumped on me," he said.

"How is it?" I asked.

He tried to move his right arm and grimaced in pain. "Feels broke. I have terrible luck." He pointed. "This is the arm that got broke a couple of years back."

Justin pointed at one of the newer guys. "Get him back in his vehicle and guard him."

"You got it," he said.

"You got it, *sir*," I admonished. "Captain Smithson worked hard for that rank, give him the respect he deserves."

"Uh, yes, sir," he said, duly chastened, and then helped Conway walk off.

While Justin was checking the troops, I grabbed Bob.

"We need to find Brumley. Walk with me and cover my back," I said. I walked around the ground floor of the warehouse, pausing only long enough to look at the dead males. "Alright, c'mon," I said and jogged back over to Justin. He saw me approaching and waited.

"Brumley isn't among the dead," I said, thought a moment, and pointed up.

The living quarters were upstairs. We'd not yet cleared any of the rooms. Justin nodded in understanding, radioed First Sergeant Crumby, and advised him to get the vehicle refueled and then start loading up with the goodies.

The living quarters used to be offices for the administrative personnel, with the last one being the president's suite. That was Brumley's personal quarters. Justin called a couple of teams over.

"We're going to clear the living quarters," he explained. "If they look like a zed, kill it, but we're looking for survivors, especially Brumley."

"Another thing," I said. "If there is anyone up there all alone, and you can do it, take them alive."

Justin looked over at me, wondering what I was thinking. "We need to somehow figure out how they became infected."

He nodded. "Any questions?"

There was none and we headed up the steps, our boots clanging on each metal step, announcing our arrival. Our teams split off, Justin, Bob and I provided cover as each room was entered, and then we went to the end of the hall where Brumley's suite was located.

The entrance was a heavy oak door and it was locked. I swapped weapons with Bob and started kicking. The door held firmly. The only thing being damaged was my foot. I stopped and caught my breath.

"Can you pick the lock?" Bob asked.

"I probably could, but my lock-picking tools are back at Mount Weather."

He nodded in understanding. Justin scoffed and pointed at the walls on either side of the door.

"Looks like nothing more than drywall to me," he said.

Before Bob or I could respond, Justin stepped back and launched a kick. The drywall was no match for his heavy boot and gave way easily. The problem was, the force of his kick propelled him forward. Not only did his boot go through the outer wall, it continued past the four inches of insulation and through the inner wall. It resulted in his leg getting hung up. Justin was stuck there, one leg stuck in the wall, struggling to maintain balance. I started laughing, which caused Bob to laugh as well.

"Are you two going to help me or what?" he growled.

Bob and I grabbed him and pulled him out. I bent down slightly and peered in. Justin squatted down beside me.

"No movement," I said. "If there were any zeds in there, I think they would've attacked your foot."

Justin nodded in agreement. We reached inside the hole he had created and started pulling the drywall apart. We made short work of the outer wall and took turns kicking in the rest of the inner wall until it was large enough to walk through at a crouch.

Our noses were immediately assailed by the odor. The place was filthy, with trash and plates of rotten, half-eaten food lying around.

Joker grunted. "It smells worse than a whore's ass on a hot Saturday night in here."

I glanced at him. Although I'd never taken a sniff of a whore's ass, I did not doubt his assessment. We found Jackson T. Brumley cowering under his desk.

CHAPTER 16 – JACKSON T. BRUMLEY

"Get out from there!" I shouted.

Brumley gave me a deer-in-the-headlights look before he slowly crawled out. Once clear of the desk, he sat there on his fat behind, staring blankly. Everyone was quiet as they stared at him. He looked shell-shocked. He'd lost probably twenty or thirty pounds, and I don't think he'd bathed in several days either. I squatted down in front of him.

"Yo, Brumley," I said, snapping my fingers in his face. It took him several seconds before he recognized me. Sort of.

"Senator?" he asked.

"I'm Zach," I said, correcting him, and then pointed at Bob. "He's the senator."

He looked back and forth at the both of us, and then focused on Flash. He pointed.

"Who the hell are you?"

"Oh, sure, point out the black guy," Flash quipped.

It took several minutes and some soothing conversation before he finally came to his senses.

He looked accusingly at both Bob and me. "My people started getting sick within hours of being inoculated."

"Could you describe the symptoms?" I asked.

"Fever, profuse sweating, disorientation, oh and did I mention the fuckers went crazy and started attacking each other?"

"Why aren't you sick?" Bob asked.

"I don't do needles and I don't do vaccinations," he retorted. "Everyone knows all of those childhood vaccinations caused kids to have autism."

I started to correct him, but realized it was futile. The man had lost his wits.

"Where is your nephew?" I asked. Jackson's number two in command was his nephew. He was a quiet, diminutive little man who looked like a younger twin of Brumley, but he was an intelligent man who ran the day-to-day operations of Dayton. He told me once he was a CPA in his past life, which made perfect sense.

Brumley answered my question by waving a hand around ambiguously. "He's out there, somewhere."

We tried to get more information out of him, but like I said, he'd lost his wits and mostly babbled. After several frustrating minutes, I gave up.

I started to give him a sympathetic pat on the back before standing, but then I remembered our previous conversation and his request for us to procure young girls for his sexual pleasure. I remembered my friend, Andie, and of the abuse she'd suffered at the hands of her uncle. I also remembered that time when I had guard duty with Savannah and the look of anguish on her face when those pieces of shit showed up. They'd degraded her, abused her, and robbed her of her dignity. I wondered how many girls Jackson T. Brumley had done that to.

I looked around as my fingers tickled the lock-blade knife sticking out of my pocket. Alas, too many witnesses.

"We're done here," I said to Justin.

We went downstairs and found First Sergeant Crumby barking orders at everyone and there was a sort of a chaotic symphony taking place. Someone had the forethought to hook a trailer up to the semi and it was being loaded with a forklift at one of the loading docks. Everyone else was hand-loading boxes of everything they could find like they'd discovered a lost treasure. I had to admit, I was impressed. When the first sergeant spotted us, he jogged over.

"All vehicles have been gassed up. I'd say another hour and we'll be loaded up and ready to go."

"Alright, when every vehicle is filled to the brim, we're getting the hell out of here," Justin said.

"Yeah, absolutely," I said in agreement.

"What are we going to do with Brumley?" Bob asked.

I gave him a hard look. "Do you really want that pedophile living anywhere near Mount Weather?"

His jaw tightened, but after a moment he gave a grim, silent nod. While we were standing there, Cutter came jogging up.

"First Sergeant, we've found the arms room. There were only a few weapons left in there, but there's a shitload of ammo. Maybe a thousand rounds of various calibers," he said.

"Outstanding," Jeremiah replied. "Get the word to everyone. Load up and make sure the vehicles are lined up in their proper order."

I was about to add my two cents worth, but then I saw those two cop brothers walking up, and they were dragging a bound woman along the floor. She was nude from the waist up and it was obvious she was infected. She was wrapped securely in tape, including her mouth. One of the brothers, Liam, held up a roll of duct tape and gave a big grin.

"You said you wanted a live specimen, man, so here you go," he said.

"What the hell?" Cutter drawled out slowly.

"We found her hiding in the damn mop closet," Liam said with a laugh.

She was in her twenties, and even though she was infected, it was obvious she was once an attractive woman. She glared angrily at us all with blue eyes that the blackness had not yet overtaken.

"You did want one, right?" Liam asked again.

"Yes, absolutely," I replied and looked around. "Okay, load her up in the Stryker." I then motioned to First Sergeant Crumby, who stopped what he was doing and walked over to us.

"There's a change of plans, guys. Sergeant Crumby, lead the caravan back to Mount Weather." I then gestured at us. "We're taking that woman to Fort Detrick."

The first sergeant looked at me and then gave Justin a questioning stare. "Are you sure, sir? We don't know the condition of that route and there may or may not be hostiles about."

Justin gave me a look, looked out of the open bay doors at the falling sleet, and looked back at me.

"Zach, we need to stick to the plan." He pointed outside. "Look at that sleet coming down, we don't need to make any detours."

"Normally, I would agree, but there is something more going on here. These people were infected after being given the vaccine. It is imperative we find out why."

Justin did not respond immediately, but looked outside again and shook his head. I spoke before he could.

"This is not an option, Captain," I said. "If we kill her or let her go, our evidence is gone. If we carry her back to Mount Weather, the delay in getting her to Fort Detrick may be detrimental to finding out what went wrong."

Both Jeremiah and Justin were giving me hard stares. Technically, there was a gray area in the chain-of-command. I did not outrank either of them, but they both knew I had the ear of the president and could make a stink of it if they went against me. I could see from their expressions they were thinking exactly that. But, I could also see both of them getting angry. Other people had stopped what they were doing and were now listening to our conversation. I knew what they were thinking. I was usurping their authority and I was doing it in front of everyone. I was not doing it intentionally, but I was growing impatient.

"Let's take a walk," I said to Justin under my breath. He followed me outside. It'd gotten colder, it seemed like. The sleet stung when it hit my face.

"Are we friends or not?" I asked him.

"I'd like to think so," he replied evenly. "But, I'm in charge of this mission."

"Yes, you are. You're in charge of the military and tactical aspect. But, you have to understand how important this is."

He put his hands on his hips, stared off into the dark, and let out a long, exasperated sigh. I tried another tact.

"Look, I'll make this easy. I'll take her to Detrick. The rest of you get on back to Weather."

"Zach, you need to stick with the group," Justin said.

"I'm taking the woman to Detrick," I said with the tone in my voice belying my growing anger. "That's not open for debate."

"I'll go with Zach."

We turned toward the voice. It was Joker. He decided our conversation was not private and came outside with us. "Yeah, I said it. He'll need someone to drive while he keeps an eye on her. We can take the Stryker." He hooked a thumb back inside. "Flash will go with us. That'll make three of us. Watch." He turned toward the open bay doors. "Hey, Flash! Come over here!"

Flash came jogging up. "What's up, Sergeant?"

"Zach and I are going to carry that infected bitch to Fort Detrick. You want to go with us?"

He looked back and forth at the three of us. "Yeah, sure."

Justin eyed the two men. He thought about it for several seconds before speaking.

"Alright, but you guys better be careful," he said. "It goes without saying if you encounter problems, abort, kill the woman, and link back up with us. This is on you, Zach."

"You got it," I said.

Justin nodded at Jeremiah, who'd been standing inside the doorway, watching and listening. He had good hearing and was even better at yelling. When Justin gave him a tacit nod, he acted.

"Sergeant Jenkins!" Justin shouted. Kirby hurriedly jogged up.

"Get the prick set up and send in a SITREP to Weather. Update our mission status as follows; both locations compromised. One survivor. No friendly deaths but one injury. And those three," he said pointing at Joker, Flash, and myself, "are proceeding to Fort Detrick with a captive zed."

Kirby arched his eyebrows in surprise at the last part of the message. "Aye, sir," he said and jogged over to his vehicle.

"What's a prick?" Flash whispered to me. "I mean, I know what a prick is, but is he talking about something else?"

I pointed as Kirby exited his vehicle. "PRC-155. It's a military radio. We just call it a prick."

Flash watched as Kirby attached a collapsible satellite dish and then worked to get it pointed in the correct position. Within moments, he had a signal and was speaking into the microphone.

"All right, everyone!" he shouted. "Mount up, we're leaving in five minutes! Anybody not loaded up and ready to go will get left behind!"

CHAPTER 17 – FORT DETRICK

We followed the convoy until Cumberland before we split off. The sleet changed to snow about an hour into our drive, which caused all of the vehicles to slow to a crawl. I asked Joker multiple times if he wanted me to spell him, but he refused.

"I got this man, just don't let that woman get loose and bite us," he said as he stared intently at the screen.

I watched from the command seat. Joker took no chances and maintained a slow speed. Normally, this was not tactically sound, but it wasn't like anyone was stupid enough to set up an ambush in this weather. Josue and Jorge had installed LED light bars on all of our vehicles and Joker had this one lit up. Unfortunately, the thick snowfall reflected the light back at us, which diminished visibility even more.

It was cold, butt cold. The Stryker had a heater, but it was a living testament to that old maxim, military equipment is manufactured by the company who submitted the lowest bid. The heater only put out a fraction of the heat needed to warm the interior of the vehicle. I looked over at the woman. She'd stopped fighting shortly after we'd thrown her on the floor of the Stryker and instead lay there, staring at us malevolently for the entire trip.

The roads continued to deteriorate and the journey was slow and arduous, but Joker was an excellent driver and we arrived at Detrick an hour after sunup. It took more than a few hails on the radio before someone finally answered.

"Finally," Flash said.

"At least they're not infected," Joker muttered. I could hear the fatigue in his voice. We'd swapped off driving, allowing each of us to get an hour's worth of sleep. It wasn't much.

I stretched my legs and looked around while we waited for someone to unlock the gate. It was Stretch who finally walked outside.

"Good morning," I said.

She gave a halfhearted wave as she yawned and then fumbled with the padlock. I helped her with the gate and then pointed toward the decontamination station.

"Oh, don't worry about it. It's all frozen up."

I looked at her with a frown. "You guys don't use it anymore?"

She shrugged apathetically. "They don't seem to feel the need for it." She saw me staring and shrugged again. "It's not my call. C'mon, hurry up, it's cold out here."

General Fosswell walked outside and stood under the awning of the entrance, dressed in ACUs and a coat. When he caught my eye, he motioned me over. I cleared my throat. "Alright, guys, wait here and I'll explain everything to him."

"I was not advised of any scheduled visit by the Mount Weather contingent," Fosswell said when I had walked up.

He used to be a part of the Mount Weather contingent, but last year, President Stark directed him to take over Fort Detrick. Since taking over, it was almost like he had become something of a prima donna.

"You're correct, sir," I said. "We were originally scheduled to return home from Ohio, but we managed to capture a freshly turned zombie."

He stared at me a moment before speaking. "Explain, Gunderson."

"The Ohio people became infected after they were vaccinated. We need to find out why. I figure Smeltzer and Kincaid need something to work with. So, we've brought them a live one."

"You brought a live what?" he asked.

"We captured a freshly infected person."

He continued staring with a cold, emotionless expression. "Where is this so-called specimen?" he finally asked.

"In the Stryker," I replied.

He gazed at the military vehicle, mentally debating on whether or not he wanted to walk over in the sleet and have a look, and then pointed toward the NBAC building, which was located at the far end of the post. "Have your men carry her to those so-called scientists. Gunderson, you're with me," he ordered.

"He probably wants a more detailed briefing about what happened in Ohio," I said to Joker and Flash. "Joker, you know where the labs are. You two carry her over there and lock her in one of the labs. The docs should be awake by now, but if they're not, find a room to lock her up in."

"You got it," Joker said. "We'll meet you in the mess hall. Maybe they have something good to eat."

I gave him a grateful nod and began quickstepping to the building the general had disappeared into.

Fosswell's office was also his living quarters, equipped with a desk, some chairs, a couch, and a single bed located against the back wall. It was utilitarian in decoration, mirroring his personality. The only personal effects I noted was a framed family photo and a Bible sitting on his desk. The photo was of him, his wife, and Junior, who looked like he was only about ten at the time the picture was taken. All three were smiling. They looked happy.

"Let's hear it," he ordered.

I spent the next fifteen minutes bringing him up to speed, starting with Ohio going dark, the decision to go investigate, what we discovered, and how we caught the woman and ended up at Fort Detrick. He did not take notes. Instead, he sat there, staring at me the entire time.

"Don't you think it to be in our best interests for you to go back to Eastgate and ensure there are no survivors?"

"We'll definitely need to go back and make an assessment at a later time, but not in this weather."

"Yes, the weather. How long do you intend to stay here?" he asked.

I hid my emotions. It was an odd question. I mean, why was he concerned with how long we stayed? They had plenty of food, yours truly had made sure of that, and at one time, the man was not so unsociable. If we weren't running on only a couple of hours of sleep, I would've agreed to leave immediately.

"I'd like for us to be able to stay here for the night, it that's not too much of a burden, sir," I said.

The two of us locked eyes. For some reason, the general was apprehensive about us staying. I thought for a moment he was going to order us to leave, which was going to be problematic, because Detrick did not belong to him, whatever he thought. After a couple of tense seconds, he smiled.

"You know you're welcome to stay here, Gunderson," he said.

"Thank you, sir," I said and stood. "If there is nothing else, I'm going to get a bite to eat and then check in with those so-called scientists."

When I entered the mess hall, or the cafeteria, whatever you wanted to call it, Flash and Joker were standing at the entrance, waiting on me.

"C'mon, dude," Joker said. "Let's eat. I'm starving."

The kitchen crew called it beef stew, but they should've called it mystery stew. It tasted overcooked and bland, with an overabundance of salt.

"What'd the general want?" Joker asked as we ate.

"About what you'd expect; he wanted the details of what we found at Cincinnati and Dayton. He then suggested we go back to Eastgate and make sure everyone was indeed infected."

"We ain't going anywhere," Joker said. "Not unless they've got some spare parts for the Stryker."

I stopped in mid-bite and looked at him. "What's wrong?"

"It won't start," he said. "I should've left it running, but I'm so damn tired I'm not thinking straight."

"Wonderful," I muttered. "Do you have any idea what's wrong with it?"

Joker shrugged. "Let me get some sleep and I'll see if I can get it towed over to their motor pool and check it out. Besides, the weather hasn't got any better."

"Alright," I said in a hushed voice. "This is actually going to work out to our advantage."

"How?" Flash asked.

"I want to get the scoop on what happened with the vaccinations, not wait for some watered-down report that's been edited by Fosswell."

"It sounds like you guys are having problems with Fosswell," Flash said, his voice barely above a whisper now.

Joker and I exchanged a glance. He was right. Ever since moving to Detrick, General Fosswell had become aloof toward the Mount Weather command staff. It didn't happen overnight. There were small incidences, nothing major, but there were times when it seemed like he was becoming openly defiant.

"Yeah, but keep it under your hat," I said. "He's always been a complex man, but he was a soldier and followed the orders of his commander-in-chief. Now, he can be downright difficult at times."

I finished my glass of water and pushed my plate away. "Alright, I'm going to head over to the labs and see what the docs think of our present to them."

Joker pushed his plate away too. "Well shit. Sleep can wait. I'm going to get on the Stryker. Flash, why don't you lend me a hand?"

"Sure," he replied.

CHAPTER 18 – PATIENT ZERO

The National Biodefense Analysis and Countermeasures facility, commonly called the NBAC, is an oddly shaped building located on the northeast end of Fort Detrick. This is where Doctors Smeltzer and Kincaid had set up shop, along with a couple of other scientists from John Hopkins found by our scout teams a couple of years ago.

Their names were Douglas Throneberry and Jere Washington. They were microbiologists, which was a nice asset and a welcome addition, but, they weren't what you called sociable people. In their defense, they'd been virtual prisoners in the basement of one of the buildings on campus for over three years. They'd survived by eating canned goods stored in the basement, but when the scout team had found them, they'd resorted to eating mice and other rodents that'd fallen victim to their makeshift traps. The isolation had done a number on them. Their personalities were detached, and they had a difficult time fitting into our quaint little society. Eventually, we moved them to Detrick where their skills could be put to better use.

The snow was still falling as I walked over to the building and there was already over an inch on the ground. I made a point of spotting the guards and making sure they recognized me so they wouldn't shoot me by mistake. Still, I carried my assault rifle at the ready and kept a sharp eye out. Even though we'd mostly eradicated every zed in the area, one still had to be vigilant, the bastards had become sneaky and we hadn't gotten them all.

I found the docs in one of the containment labs. They had the infected woman strapped down to a stainless-steel operating table. They'd cut off what little clothing she had on and now she was completely nude. I looked her over. She appeared to be close to my age with a slender yet athletic body, taut and muscular. She had shoulder-length brown hair which was tangled and greasy.

Her vitals were being monitored and displayed on a screen. They were all noticeably higher than normal, even her blood pressure. The docs were in their bio-containment suits and were staring at her curiously, discussing something about her skin tone. One of them bent forward at the waist to take a photograph of the bite mark, only to jerk back in fright when the woman lunged at her and gnashed her teeth. Only the restraints kept her at bay. I watched them for a moment through the protective glass and then activated the microphone on the desk.

"Hello, guys," I said, and gave a small wave when they looked over.

"Ah, hello, Zach," one of them replied in a tinny voice over the speaker. It sounded like Smeltzer.

"We were just admiring this fine specimen you brought to us," he said.

I glanced at the infected woman. She had an athletic body, taut and muscular, but with a slightly distended belly. Her fingernails were broken or torn off, there appeared to be several small scratches on her arms, like she'd been playing with an aggressive cat, and there was a deep bite mark on her upper right forearm in which flesh was actually torn out. Her head was immobilized, but her dark eyes flitted back and forth like a cornered animal.

"How are the tests coming along?" I asked.

"We've already drawn blood and collected tissue samples," Smeltzer said.

I gave a thoughtful nod. They had jumped right on this, which reaffirmed my decision to bring her directly here. "What's next on the agenda?"

The four of them glanced at each other before focusing back on me. "We were just discussing what information we could discover by performing a vivisection."

"A vivisection?" I asked in surprise.

They nodded in unison. A vivisection was a catchall word used by scientists when they performed experiments on a live specimen, usually an animal. Now, they were discussing doing the same thing on the infected woman.

It reminded me of a man by the name of Harold "Boom-Boom" Walsh, whom I had never actually met. He was a correctional officer at the Davidson County Jail when everything went bad. Suddenly, he had a bunch of infected inmates sitting in cells and a lot of time on his hands. He and a female guard conducted experiments on the infected inmates and recorded everything in a journal.

It also reminded me of a conversation I'd had with Major Grant Parsons back about six years ago. When he was at the CDC, they'd capture zombies and perform experiments on them, including vivisections. I said as much to them.

After a few minutes of talking through the intercom, they agreed to come out. Almost as an afterthought, one of them found a plain white sheet and put it over her, leaving only her head exposed. I doubted if she appreciated the act.

I watched as they exited the lab into the decontamination room. They stood under the showers, letting the fine mist rinse them down. They then stripped out of the biocontainment suits and hung them up to dry before coming out to join me in the observation room.

"Alright, guys, I have to ask. Why the biohazard procedures?"

Doctor Smeltzer gave a good-natured smile. "We're sticklers for protocol, Zach. Even though we've been vaccinated, we were drawing blood and tissue samples. No need taking unnecessary risks. Besides, we may be looking at a new strain of the virus."

I suppose it made sense, which made me start to second-guess putting her in the Stryker with us and possibly exposing ourselves. "Any preliminary thoughts?" I asked.

"She's infected," Doctor Kincaid said with a grin. He was sarcastic at times. Occasionally, it was humorous, but mostly it was annoying.

"Freshly infected," Doctor Smeltzer added. "Within the timeline you provided us. There are no outward signs of trauma, other than the singular bite mark, and there is no epidermal presentation of decomposition."

"Did she get infected from the bite or from the bad vaccination?" I asked.

They swapped a glance. "We should learn more once the blood work is complete."

"Are you really going to cut her apart while she's still alive?" I asked.

Doctor Washington looked at me through her thick, horn-rimmed glasses. "Do you find that offensive?"

"I'm not sure what to think of it," I replied. "But, you've not read any of Grant's notes. He was at the CDC for a short period of time and watched as they experimented on zeds, including performing vivisections. They didn't learn much."

"Perhaps they didn't know what they were looking for," she said.

I gazed at her curiously. She was not an attractive woman. Her skin tone was a pasty pallor. The years spent hiding in that basement probably did it, or maybe she'd never been attractive. She'd always seemed cold, dispassionate.

"You don't believe we should do it," she said.

"Honestly, I'm not sure," I replied.

"But you have no trepidations in killing someone who is infected, correct?" she pressed.

I gave a one syllable chuckle. "I see your point, but torturing and killing are two distinctly different."

"The answer to your question is, we are not sure if it would be beneficial or not," Smeltzer said. "The decision has not yet been made, and yes, we've read Major Parson's notes extensively."

Our conversation stopped when the door opened and General Fosswell walked in. He looked around. There were no chairs available. In an attempt to be courteous, I stood.

"Sit here, General," I said.

"Thank you, Gunderson, but why don't we relocate to the main floor?"

He turned and exited the room. We dutifully followed and ended up in a conference room that adjoined several offices, most of them unused. It was cold in here, like the rest of the buildings.

"Are you guys having problems with your heat or lack of power?" I asked.

"Not at all, but there seems to be this air of indifference regarding the use of electricity around here," Fosswell replied and took a seat. "All structures except the living quarters are kept at sixty degrees, upon my order."

I took another seat, glad I was still wearing my jacket. The others did the same.

Fosswell started the show. "Doctor Kincaid?"

Kincaid cleared his throat.

"The patient, or specimen if you will, is a Caucasian female in her twenties. Prior to the infection, she appeared to be have been in remarkable physical shape with no overt congenital issues. There is a singular bite to her upper right forearm, which may be the reason for her to become infected."

"You don't know?" Fosswell asked. "Mister Gunderson here believes you people cooked up a bad batch of vaccines."

Kincaid and Smeltzer exchanged glances. "At this time, it is too early to tell exactly how she may have become infected. Wouldn't you agree, Zach?" Kincaid asked.

"The entire population of both communities was infected," I replied. "The only person in Dayton who was not infected was a person who did not receive the vaccination."

"That's a strong case of circumstantial evidence," Doctor Smeltzer said. "But, I would prefer to wait until the testing on the patient's blood has been completed before rendering a verdict."

"Perhaps we should capture a few subjects who are infected but who not have been bitten or injured," Doctor Washington suggested.

"Sure thing. I'll drive you guys over to the Eastgate encampment and you can go in there where there are somewhere around a hundred zeds and snatch up whoever you want," I said.

Doctor Washington narrowed her eyes at me. "We are scientists, young man, not soldiers, or are you too stupid to understand the difference?"

I was quick with a retort. "And soldiers do not take orders from arrogant, pasty-faced scientists, nor do I, or are you too stupid to understand that?"

Her eyes, which were magnified by her glasses, burned into me. I was tired and cranky and I felt my blood rising. I returned her stare, waiting for her to throw out another insult.

"Alright, at ease, you two," Fosswell said. He then looked at Kincaid. "When will we have definitive results?" he asked.

Kincaid frowned as he pondered the answer. He then looked over at Smeltzer, who got the hint and stood.

"I'll get started on it right away," he said. "Doctor Washington, would you assist me?"

"Certainly," she said, and stood along with him. When they left, General Fosswell looked pointedly at Doctor Throneberry.

"Why don't you give them a hand," he suggested, his tone leaving no doubt he was dismissing the man.

"Of course," he replied, stood, and shuffled out.

I started to stand, but Fosswell held up a hand. I slowly sat back down, wondering what he was up to. He looked over at Kincaid.

"Has Gunderson seen Patient Zero?" he asked.

Kincaid glanced over at me. "I don't believe he has."

"Uh, yeah. No, I've not seen Patient Zero," I said, wondering who they were talking about.

Fosswell gave Kincaid a nod.

"Excuse me a moment," he said, stood, and hurried out of the room. A moment later, he reentered, carrying a laptop. He pulled a chair over beside me, sat, and booted it up. After a few clicks, he turned the screen where I could see it.

The screen showed what looked like a video taken by somebody with a cellphone. The person taking it was obviously nervous or something because the camera was shaky. It showed an older man, perhaps in his fifties, strapped down to a gurney. He was violently struggling against the restraints, and he kept gnashing his teeth. Not unlike the woman currently strapped down in the lab.

"Who is he?" I asked.

"He is believed to be Patient Zero," Kincaid answered. "His name is Omar Amir, a sixty-three-year-old Egyptologist. He headed a team performing an excavation of a tomb near a location known as Sharm El-Sheikh."

He tapped a button and another image came up. It was a picture of a rocky cliff in a barren desert landscape. There appeared to be a rough opening on the side of the cliff.

"This is the cave where the tomb was found. If the photographer were to turn around, there would be a magnificent view of the Red Sea."

Another click and another photo. The photographer was standing at the mouth of the cave.

"At first blush, the inner area of the cave was vacant, uninteresting," Kincaid said, and then he clicked to a new photo. This was a closer shot of the far wall of the cave.

"Have you heard of the Multinational Force and Observers?" he asked.

"Yes," I said. "It's a peacekeeping force stationed in the Sinai Peninsula, right?"

"That's correct," Fosswell said. "They were tasked with keeping watch and ensuring the terms of peace between Egypt and Israel. There is, or was, an encampment near this location known as South Camp Seven, or South Camp. There was a contingent of American soldiers stationed there, usually battalion strength. As you can imagine, when these young soldiers had free time on their hands, their curiosity led them to explore. Some Bedouins showed them this cave and the hieroglyphs."

Another picture was a close-up of hieroglyphs engraved on the wall.

"Do we know what it says?" I asked.

Kincaid nodded. "The rough interpretation declares the cave to be cursed."

He clicked on a couple of pictures, showing various angles and close-ups of the wall.

"The wall was handmade and disguised to look like a natural rock formation," he said, and narrated as he clicked on photos of the wall in various stages of excavation. When it was finished, a hidden room was revealed. There was something else inside.

"Is that a sarcophagus?" I asked.

"Yes," Kincaid answered. He brought another picture up. It was a close-up of the stone crypt.

"As you can see from the roughness and coarse chisel marks in the stone, it appears to be hastily made, unfinished."

He went through another series of pictures, showing the sarcophagus from various angles. The final picture was of Amir standing there, looking down it. The next series of photos was more of the same, with various people looking at it. The next photos showed some more hieroglyphs on the lid.

"According to the Supreme Council of Antiquities, this series of hieroglyphs tells of an unknown stranger from far away arriving in Cairo. He is either sick when he arrives or becomes sick soon thereafter. He then dies."

"Wait," I said with an upheld hand. "Cairo? How far is Cairo from Sharm El Sheikh?"

"Approximately three hundred miles," General Fosswell said. "It's somewhat of a mystery why they transported this person so far."

"Indeed," Kincaid said. "The mystery deepens with the interpretation of the last part of the hieroglyphs." He made a head gesture toward the picture. "It is something of a warning. It warns of calamity and death to anyone who comes into contact with the dead person interred within."

"Not unlike the fourth seal of the book of Revelations," Fosswell, said quietly. "Then I looked and saw a pale horse. Its rider's name was Death, and Hell followed close behind. And they were given authority over a fourth of the earth, to kill by sword, by famine, by plague, and by the beasts of the earth..."

I glanced at him momentarily before looking back at the laptop and stared at the hieroglyphs. I was keeping my face devoid of emotion, but frankly, the man was starting to concern me. I reached out and hit the page down button. The next picture showed the lid of the sarcophagus being opened and a solitary corpse inside.

"Notice, the corpse has not been mummified," Kincaid said.

I felt myself frowning. "I'm not well-versed in archaeology, but I thought the standard procedure was to move a sarcophagus to a controlled environment before opening it."

Now Kincaid frowned. "You know, I believe you're right. I don't know the answer either. But, have a look at this." He tapped the page down button. It was a picture of the inside of the lid.

"Those look like scratch marks," I said.

Kincaid nodded. "Doctor Amir thought the same." He tapped the button again and there was a close-up of the corpse's fingernails. They were decomposed, but even so, you could see definite signs of damage.

"Do the glyphs tell anything specific about the stranger? Like who he was and where he came from? Anything like that?" I asked.

"If they ever completed the interpretation, that information has been lost," Kincaid said.

"So, they became infected when they opened it up and came into contact with the corpse," I surmised.

"That would appear to be the case," Kincaid said. "Doctor Amir was the first one to complain of flu-like symptoms. He went back to Cairo the next morning. His wife took him to the emergency room. The archaeology team consisted of twenty-six people, including Doctor Amir."

He shook his head ruefully. "The entire team became sick. By the time anyone realized something was seriously wrong, many other people had visited the tomb. While Doctor Amir was being seen by a doctor, he suddenly attacked the doctor and four nurses. A security guard shot him multiple times in the chest and stomach. It weakened him long enough for them to restrain him, but the damage was done. As we've previously discussed, the time of exposure to infection varied from minutes to hours."

"So, the infection spread exponentially, starting in a cave overlooking the Red Sea," I said.

"Yes, it would appear so," Kincaid said.

"Has President Stark seen this?" I asked.

"He has a copy of the file," Fosswell said.

I nodded, wondering why it took five years before I finally got a chance to see this. I went through each jpeg again, memorizing them. Finally, I looked at the two men.

"It's fascinating, I'll grant you that, but I believe you two are using this as a deflection."

They both gazed at me steadily, betraying no emotion.

"Come on, you two, spill the beans. What the hell happened to the vaccines?"

Kincaid cleared his throat. "Zach, we're not certain the Ohio batch was compromised. We…"

"I am," I said, cutting him off in mid-sentence. "Gentlemen, all of those people became infected *after* being vaccinated. Apply some statistical analysis to your sample base, and you'll come up with a statistically significant correlation. Tell me I'm wrong."

Doctor Kincaid cleared his voice yet again. "You can't be certain everyone at Eastgate is infected and if I heard you correctly earlier, not everyone at Dayton was infected."

"Brumley was not infected because he did not get vaccinated. But you are correct in one respect, we are not absolutely certain. So, I'll need to see your vaccination records whereupon I can compare them to the census reports." I pointed at my backpack. "I happen to have a copy of those files downloaded into my laptop."

I could see a little bit of tenseness form in Kincaid's jawline. He glanced over at the general, who gave a slight nod of his head. Kincaid worked the keyboard as I got my laptop and booted it up. After a moment, he turned the screen toward me. The list was on an excel spreadsheet format, as was the census data. Mine was in alphabetical order, the vaccination roster was not, but it was a simple change and made it easier to compare names. Kincaid spoke while I went down the list.

"Zach, we've tested the control batch. There's nothing wrong with it."

"If the batch of vaccines taken to Ohio were contaminated somehow, will it show up in the woman's blood work?"

He pursed his lips. "Possibly," he said. "Or, there might have been some other way the vaccines were contaminated."

"Like how?" I asked.

"Any number of ways," he replied.

I looked back and forth at both of them. "You two would agree, would you not, that one possible explanation is the vaccinations were deliberately sabotaged?"

"There is no proof of that," Fosswell said, almost a little too quickly. "And I'll caution you not to spread such a rumor when you get back to Weather."

"What should I tell them, General?" I asked.

He leaned forward in his chair. "Tell them we are investigating all possibilities."

"Alright, I will, but, if it is sabotage, who do you suspect may be responsible?" I asked. "What about those two John Hopkins scientists? They are viable suspects, are they not?"

There was a long moment of silence before Kincaid spoke. "If you think about it, Doctor Smeltzer and I are viable suspects as well."

"Are you going to put that in your report, Gunderson?" Fosswell asked with a hard stare.

"I don't want to sound arrogant, but I have no doubt that someone, perhaps President Stark or someone else, will ask for my opinion. I'm not going to obfuscate my report."

"And your opinion is that it's sabotage?" Fosswell pressed.

I cleared my throat before answering. "Yes. Now, before you say it, I'm perfectly aware that my opinion means I am accusing one of you of doing it."

"Yes, you are," Fosswell said.

"I will make it clear that I do not know the true answer and it is only my opinion. I'll also say I've spoken to the two of you and told you of my opinion." I pointed at the two laptops. "This data will be included as well."

Fosswell apparently had nothing else to discuss and left without a word. Kincaid watched me in silence and waited for me to finish.

"Well?" he asked.

"Of the names on the census and the vaccination records, only the Brumleys did not receive the inoculation."

"Jackson and his nephew, Jeb," he said.

"Correct."

"Remind me again how old they are?"

I blinked and glanced down at the census records. "Sixty and thirty-nine, respectively. Why? Is that important?"

"Oh, I was simply curious. What happened to them?"

"We left Jackson back in Cincinnati, no idea where Jeb is. Probably zombie food by now."

Kincaid leaned back in his chair, folded his arms, and rubbed his chin, like I'd told him something profound.

"Interesting," he said.

I frowned at him. "I don't know if I'd call it interesting. Back before, people were always refusing to get their flu shots because they were convinced there was some massive government conspiracy afoot to poison the population. But," I said as I turned a palm up, "in this case, he was right."

Flash, Joker, and I ate dinner with everyone who was present at Fort Detrick, a total of twenty-eight personnel. Well, with the exception of Harlan Fosswell Jr. I had yet to see him.

"The ignition module is bad," Joker said. "And they don't have any replacement parts here. In fact, there aren't any replacement parts at Weather either. We're going to have to raid some Army bases soon." He looked over at Flash. "Where'd you wander off to? I looked up and you were gone."

"You didn't need me, so I wandered around a little bit and talked to a few people," Flash said. He smiled and waved at an older black man sitting alone. "That's Andre," he said under his breath. "He and I got acquainted. He said I looked like one of his sons."

I knew Andre and gave him a wave as well. Andre was in his mid-fifties now. He was living in Baltimore with his family during the outbreak. He broke his leg jumping out of a second-story window and had to run/hobble for several miles in an effort to escape a horde of zombies. He set the break by himself, which went about like you'd expect if you set a broken leg by yourself, and he walked with a permanent limp now. I could see why Andre liked Flash. Sure, he had a friendly personality, but frankly, our population of African Americans was small, so it was like they were instant kindred spirits.

"Did he have anything interesting to say?" I asked in the same low tone.

"He said there seems to be lots of secret stuff going on and there's an air of paranoia. When we showed up, it got everyone stirred up."

"What do they think is going on?" I asked.

"There's lots of rumors, but Andre thinks Fosswell is up to something no good."

"Does he know anything specific?" I asked.

Flash shook his head. "He either doesn't know for sure, or he's not saying."

"Humph," Joker said as he washed down some food and then looked at me. "Did you get what you needed?"

"As much as I can, for now," I said. I watched as doctors Kincaid and Smeltzer walked in. They did not acknowledge us and walked to the serving line. I can't say why I felt the way I did, but I was certain those two were holding back on me. Somehow, I needed to find out the truth.

I looked over at another table, where Shooter was seated with a couple of people, including Stretch. Stretch was a tall, long-legged, light-skinned African American woman who had been dating Cutter for the past year. Until recently. Currently, she was sitting close to Shooter. Closer than normal. Joker must have been reading my mind.

"I found out why Cutter packed up and came back to Weather," he said.

"Does it have something to do with Stretch and Shooter?"

"Yep. Cutter caught them doing the nasty."

"Ouch," I said.

"Who's Shooter?" Flash whispered.

I looked around and saw Shooter looking at me. I gave him a small head nod. He seemed to think about it for a second before responding in kind. He hadn't changed much over the years. He was six feet, average build, and a slight dimple in his chin. He'd tell anyone who'd listen it made him look like Kirk Douglas.

"And that's Cutter's brother?"

"Yeah," I answered. "Their real names are Simon and Theodore Smith, but they like to call themselves Shooter and Cutter, like they're some kind of badasses."

"Yep," Joker said. He looked at Flash. "What's your real name?"

Flash chuckled. "I think I'm going to let that little bit of information stay with me. As far as everyone is concerned, I'm the Flash."

He finished his glass of water. "How long are staying here?" he asked.

"I was thinking we'd bunk down here for the night and head out in the morning, unless you guys had something else in mind."

"Yeah, sure," Joker said. "I can use the sleep."

I looked up to see Shooter walking over. He stood over me with his usual half-smile, like he was in on an inside joke. I hated that smile.

"How's it going?" I asked.

"Can't complain," he answered. "How's my idiot brother?"

"He's doing great. He was one of the team leaders on our mission to Ohio. Even the first sergeant was impressed with him. Is there anything you want me to tell him when we get back?"

His little smile faltered for a second. "Nah. When are you guys leaving?"

"We're going to spend the night and then see what tomorrow looks like," I said.

"But our vehicle is broken down," Joker said. "We're going to need to borrow something."

"Yeah, well, if you want transportation, Captain Fosswell is the man to speak to. Good luck with that."

"Why's that?" I asked.

"Hell, Zach, you know he's an oddball. In fact, I haven't seen him in a day or two. Maybe he moved to Florida or something." He laughed at his own joke.

"Alright, if you see him, tell him we need to talk to him." I paused for a moment. "If you want to send a letter or anything to your brother, I'll make sure he gets it."

I saw a microsecond of an expression. He missed his brother, but he wasn't going to admit to it. His smile then widened.

"Pfft, I don't have anything to say. I'll see you boys later." He then walked back over to the table with Stretch and his other friends. Stretch gave me a look as Shooter sat down beside her and whispered something in her ear.

Andre led us to an unused dorm room. "You boys sleep good," he said and walked off before any of us could engage him in any other conversation.

The dorm room, living quarters, whatever you wanted to call them, had obviously not been used in a while. Everything was covered in a layer of dust and it felt like it was even colder than everywhere else in Fort Detrick.

Fortunately, there were several bunks, all made, so we stripped off some extra wool blankets and made do as best we could.

"How are we going to get back if the Stryker is broken down?" Flash asked.

"We'll borrow or steal something," I replied. "By the way, you should consider moving here."

"Why's that?" Flash asked.

"Mount Weather's permanent population is capped at one hundred and forty. You're part of our temporary population. Eventually, we'll need to move you out to somewhere like this or one of the neighboring communities."

Before Flash could respond, Joker spoke up.

"For the love of God, take it outside or go to sleep already," he grumbled. I could hear the fatigue in his voice, and honestly, I felt the same way. I turned off the lights before crawling under the heavy wool blankets.

I didn't remember falling asleep, but I was awakened by someone wiggling my foot. I instantly reached for the Kimber under my pillow until my brain activated and I realized it was Stretch standing at the foot of my bed. She put a finger over her lips and motioned for me to follow her out into the hallway.

I dressed quickly and found her standing beside a window. I could see her breath in the cold air.

"Hey," she said.

"Hey, it's cold in here."

She made a face. "Fosswell acts like the electric bill comes out of his own wallet."

I gave a small laugh. "How've you been?"

She responded with a noncommittal shrug.

"Okay, I've got to ask you, what the hell is going on here? It hadn't always been this way."

"I don't know, Zach. We're kept in the dark around here, or in the cold, however you want to put it."

"Is anything wrong with the general?" I asked.

She shrugged again. "Outwardly, he's the same, but he's more aloof now. We don't see him for a day or two, and then he shows up to breakfast one morning and is acting like everything is normal." She shrugged yet again. "It's weird up here, Zach. All we do is our daily duties, but it's a weird vibe. Shooter is on the inside, he's Fosswell's aide, but he doesn't tell anything."

I paused a moment, reminding myself that other people's relationships didn't concern me, but then jumped in. "How's it going with you and Shooter?"

"It's okay," she said. "Good and bad, I'd guess you'd say. How's Cutter?"

"He's really coming into his own," I said. "I think he misses you, but he's not admitting it."

I wanted to ask her why she chose Shooter over his brother. Theodore was far better in character, but I decided to keep my opinion to myself.

"Is there anything you want me to tell him for you?" I asked.

She looked up and down the hallway before pulling some papers from her jacket pocket. They were folded twice and held closed by a singular staple.

"Give him this, okay?" she asked.

"Sure," I said and took the papers. She gestured at them.

"I couldn't find an envelope anywhere. I'd appreciate it if you didn't read it."

"I won't. You have my word."

"Thank you, Zach," she said. "Well, breakfast will be ready in about thirty minutes."

"Okay."

I watched as she quickly walked down the hallway, disappearing from sight, and then hearing a door. I admit, I was curious what she'd written. How do you explain to a man you were supposed to be in love with chose his brother over him? It didn't matter how curious I was though, I'd given my word. I folded it up into a small square and stuffed it into my pants pocket.

CHAPTER 19 – THE ROAD BACK

I woke my two companions and we cleaned up before enjoying a hot breakfast consisting of two strips of bacon each and all of the runny porridge we could stomach. At least they had tea.

It'd stopped snowing, but the temperature stayed at the freezing mark, which did not allow the ice and snow on the ground to melt. But, the three of us were ready to get the hell out of Detrick.

"I'm willing to risk it, I miss my girls," Joker lamented. "Besides, the weather ain't going to get any better. I'll walk it if I have to."

I couldn't help but smile. I don't know how the two of them became enamored with each other, but they hooked up five years ago and now had a young daughter. I nodded in understanding. I missed Kelly and my kids as well.

"Well, I don't have anyone waiting for me, but I'm ready too," Flash said.

When General Fosswell walked in the cafeteria, I went to his table and declared our intentions of leaving. Unsurprisingly, he encouraged me to do so.

"I'll have my son expedite you getting a vehicle. Safe travels," he said and summarily dismissed me.

I walked back to my companions. "Yeah, we're definitely out of here. Let's grab our gear and find something to ride back in."

Captain Harlan Fosswell Junior joined us at the motor pool. I'd not seen him in several months and he'd been strangely absent the entire time we'd been here. He'd lost weight and had a sallow complexion, like he'd been sick recently. I would've asked about his health, if I cared.

"The general said you three are heading back to Weather," he said.

"That's right."

"I guess I'd be anxious to get home too if I had a wife and kids waiting on me," he said and looked over at the Stryker. "I take it you couldn't fix it."

"No, sir, we couldn't," Joker said. "It needs an ignition module."

"Hmm, well, maybe we can spare a vehicle," he said.

"Yeah," I said. "The roads aren't looking good, so we're going to need something in four-wheel-drive."

"No doubt," he said and then gave me a quizzical look. "Do you still have your dog?" he asked.

"What? Zoe? Yeah, we still have her. Why?" It seemed like an odd question and I had no idea why he'd asked.

He nodded and looked off into the distance. "I bet your kids love that dog. Every kid should have a dog. I had a dog when I was a kid. He was a German Shepherd. His name was Roggenwolf. Roggenwolf 1199, to be exact."

I looked at him, trying to subdue my exasperation. All I wanted was to sign out a vehicle and go home, not stand around and listen to a story about his childhood. Fortunately, he seemed to sense my state.

"Ah, well, you need a vehicle." He looked around and pointed at a drab olive truck with six wheels. "Take the deuce and a half. It has six-wheel drive and a heater. As long as you take your time and drive slowly, you should have no problem getting home with that beast."

I'd driven one before. It was a beast alright, but it was also loud and uncomfortable. I didn't complain though. Out of all of the vehicles in the motor pool, this one could drive over almost any terrain. If we ran off into a ditch, the six-wheel drive, the multiple gears, and the added heavy-duty winch would ensure we'd get unstuck.

"Alright, that sounds good," I said.

He walked with us to the truck and watched as we put our gear in.

"You people never cared much for me," he suddenly said.

I was about to get in but stopped and looked at him. "I can't speak for everyone, but when we first arrived at Mount Weather, you didn't exactly make us feel welcome, now did you?"

He stared down at the ground. "I've always lived in my father's shadow. I've never been my own man. I was never allowed to."

Before I could respond, he changed the subject. "If you ever get another dog, consider naming him Roggenwolf 1199. Or, maybe you might want to use the name for something else." He turned and walked off, leaving the three of us standing there in confusion.

"What was that all about?" Flash asked.

I shrugged. "Who the hell knows? Get in. Joker, you driving?"

"Absolutely."

The good news was that the thick powder of snow had not been driven on, which would have compacted it into ice, so we had better traction than I would have thought. Joker drove slowly and had little problem keeping it out of the ditches. I was restless, and said as much to Joker.

"Why don't you school my young protégé about our expressway between Detrick and Weather?" he suggested with a grin.

"That's a great idea," I said and turned to Flash. "We're forty-four miles from Weather. We spent two years repairing the roadway, fixing all of the potholes, and clearing away any trees that may fall and block the road. So, now we can travel back and forth in under an hour. That's when the weather is on our side. But, we can't drive a normal speed today so it'll probably take us three or four hours."

"Yeah, someone said Melvin broke the record," Flash said.

Joker laughed. "He damn sure did. That crazy bastard made it from Detrick to Weather in under twenty minutes one day on a motorcycle."

"What'd he do that for?" he asked.

"Ah, that's a story best told by Melvin," I said.

"Where is he?"

"He and his girl, Savannah, are spending the winter in Oak Ridge, Tennessee," I said. "It turns out there's an old Special Forces soldier living down there that Melvin served with, so he stays there frequently. They'll be back in the spring though. Alright, enough about Melvin. I want you to pay attention to this route so you'll have every curve and bump memorized."

"Alright, why?" Flash asked.

"Melvin said you were the reason your friends survived for so long, so that means you're smart and resourceful. We're always looking for people like you, and Joker has taken a special interest in you. So, we need you to start learning things about Mount Weather and everything around it."

"Besides, we need to improve our racial diversity," Joker deadpanned.

Flash glowered at him a moment before focusing back on me. "Alright, but don't count on Melvin's assessment of me like it's the gospel. The truth be told, I was scared shitless and spent most of my waking hours hiding or running. Erin's a badass though, and man can she shoot a gun."

I glanced at him a second in mild surprise. I'd never interacted with Erin all that much, she didn't seem like some kind of Lara Croft badass type, but I suppose she was an example of never judging a book by its cover. I made a mental note to get to know her better.

"Merritt, that's Gunnery Sergeant Burns to you, also said you've got potential if you can keep your head out of your ass long enough to learn."

"I thought he didn't like me," he said.

I smiled and didn't answer.

"What about Fred?" he asked.

"He's one of my best friends. What about him?"

"Everybody seems to think he's something like Doc Holliday or something. They say he's lightning fast with a pistol."

"He's even faster than you can imagine," I said. "And he can be surly. The best thing to do is give him a lot of space."

"Damn right," Joker said in agreement.

"Why is that?"

I chuckled and hooked a thumb back behind us. "Junior Fosswell made the mistake of smarting off to him one day."

"What happened?" Flash asked.

"Fred jabbed him in the throat."

Joker chuckled. "Everyone thought for a minute Fred killed him. Oh, tell him about Stanley."

"Stanley? Who's he?" Flash asked.

"He's a young man, about your age, cocky as hell and had a smart mouth on him. One day, we were conducting a training exercise and Fred admonished him about not keeping the barrel of his rifle pointed in a safe direction. Young Stanley told Fred to fuck off. Stanley learned the hard way smarting off to Fred was not a good idea."

"Why, what happened?"

I chuckled. "Fred drew his pistol and fired twice in the blink of an eye. The result was, he'd shot little pieces of meat off of the top of both of Stanley's ears."

Flash's eyes widened. "Really?"

"Yep. There was no permanent damage to speak of, but there was a lot of blood, and the way Stanley was screaming, it must have hurt like hell."

Flash snorted. "Bullshit."

"No, it's true, I was there when it happened," Joker said.

"Holy shit," Flash said. "Did Fred like, get in trouble or anything?"

"Oh, it was discussed during the next staff meeting, but, in the end, everyone agreed Stanley was lucky Fred was in a good mood and that was that," I said.

"Wow," Flash said. "Okay, what happened to Stanley?"

"He and his people moved into one of the fortified houses over near Bluemont," I said. "He's doing okay."

"So, are all of these stories I hear about you true?" he asked.

I glanced over and saw a smile creep across Joker's face.

"Probably not. What've you heard?" I asked.

"Let's see. They say you're totally immune or something."

"Yeah, that's what the docs say," I replied.

"They also say you a stone-cold killer and that you're as good with a gun as Fred is, maybe better."

I scoffed. "I'm nowhere near as good as Fred."

"And they say you're as smart as Albert Einstein."

Now, I chuckled. "I'm definitely no Einstein."

"But, you've got to be. You're like the number four man at Mount Weather and you're only twenty-five."

"The hierarchy of command is a little more convoluted than that. There are several senators who'd be quick to tell you I do not outrank them."

"But, you have the ear of the president; he listens to you."

"Sometimes he does," I said and changed the subject. "You did okay back in Ohio, Detrick too."

"Thanks."

"When we get back to Weather, you'll want to record your actions," I said. "I'll see about getting you an account set up on the Mount Weather Intranet."

"Cool," he replied.

I was about to say something else, but I suddenly spotted several figures darting across the road and into the wood line a couple of hundred yards ahead of us. Joker saw them too.

"What the hell was that?" he asked.

"Zeds, maybe. Stop where they crossed the road and we'll check it out," I directed.

He did so and set the brake. The tracks could be plainly seen in the snow. We grabbed our assault rifles before exiting the truck. Flash got out too. He watched as I looked toward the wood line where we'd seen the figures running and then crouched down beside the tracks.

"I'm guessing about a dozen of them," I said after studying the tracks.

"Are they zeds?" Flash asked.

"Yeah, I'd say so," I said. "All of them are running at a pretty good clip too. They're chasing something, or someone."

I looked up at the wood line again. "Alright, you guys stay with the truck. I'll be back in a little while."

Now Flash gave me a wide-eyed stare. "You're going after them?"

"Yep."

CHAPTER 20 – THE HUNT

"Now hold on, big guy, you can't have all of the fun," Joker said with a grin and set the brake. "I'm coming too."

"Suit yourself," I replied. We traded a knowing look. We'd been on several missions together and shared guard duty more than once. During those long, boring nights, we'd had many long conversations and had confided in each other how much we enjoyed hunting and killing zeds. It was a thrill. We shared a few stories of our best kills and our scariest moments, and we also knew we couldn't tell these stories openly, lest someone label us as psychopathic killers.

"Well, I ain't staying here by myself," Flash said.

"You'll be fine," I said. "Keep the truck running and you'll be nice and warm."

"Oh, hell no. I'm coming with."

"You sure?" I asked and gestured at Joker. "We've done this a few times. We're going to be running hard and we're not taking prisoners."

"Damn right I'm sure," he replied.

I looked momentarily at Joker and gave a small grin. "They tell me they call you Flash because you can run fast."

"Fast like Flash Gordon, baby," he said.

I shrugged, got my machete, and strapped it across my back.

"Alright, stay close, but don't get too close and jam us up," I said and made a head nod to Joker. We took off running before Flash had a chance to respond.

We jogged through the snow and woods for several minutes before I stopped and dropped to a crouch. Flash and Joker caught up and dropped down beside me. I'll give him credit, he wasn't breathing any harder than Joker or me. Joker faced back the way we came, scanning with the ACOG on his assault rifle. Flash looked at me questioningly. I pointed to my ear and then toward the direction where I believed they were heading. Soon, we heard the distant crack of a tree limb breaking.

"Got 'em," I whispered and the three of us took off. We were close now.

We soon came to a clearing which was the backyard of an abandoned house. There were two dead zeds with a crossbow bolt sticking out of their eye sockets. There were additional tracks circling around to the front. Before we could follow, the air was pierced with a series of pained screams.

"Watch my back," I whispered and ran toward the side of the house. When I peeked around, I saw ten of them ravaging a person like a pack of rabid dogs. One of them had managed to pull up the person's jacket. The sight of exposed skin worked them into a frenzy and they were butting heads as they all dived in to take a bite. I took aim and began firing. I killed three of them instantly. Joker joined in and killed two more. Flash shot the sixth one before I stopped him.

"Hold your fire!" I ordered. He looked at me questioningly, but to his credit, he immediately stopped shooting. I leaned my rifle up against the house and pulled my machete out.

Joker grinned. "Here we go," he said.

"What?" Flash asked in confusion.

The remaining six zombies were too involved in the feeding frenzy to even hear the gunshots or notice their friends being killed. All except one of them. He stood and charged me. I sidestepped and whipped out a short kick to his knee. He was oblivious to any pain, but it did cause him to stumble. When he turned back toward me, he glowered at me with eyes as black as his leathered skin.

I feinted right, ducked back left, and brought the machete upward. The blade's impact snapped his head back and took his lower jaw off. I pulled it free and his jaw fell slack. Only a couple of pieces of sinew kept it from coming completely off.

I delivered another kick, to the back of his knee this time. He stumbled and fell to his back, his hands reaching toward me as he snarled. I took a baseball swing and the blade dug into both hands at the wrists. Working it free, I swung a few more times until I successfully cut his hands off.

I then turned my attention to the final five. I quickly brought the machete down on the backs of the necks of three of them. Joker couldn't stand it any longer. He took his Bowie knife and stabbed the last two through the eye sockets. It was over in under ten seconds.

"Damn," Flash muttered.

"Good stuff," Joker said.

Flash stood there in a mixture of anxiety and bemusement as we cleaned the obsidian-colored blood off of our blades with snow. I wiped my blade dry on one of the dead zed's pants and squatted down beside the victim. He was chewed up, and I thought he was dead, but then he coughed.

"Oh my God, he's still alive," Flash said.

The two of them walked over and squatted beside me. The hapless victim was a teenage boy, from what I could tell. His face had been badly mauled and they'd bitten out massive chunks of meat from his abdominal area and had practically disemboweled him before we could intervene. Surprisingly, he was still alive. His eyes fluttered and he looked up at me.

"Zach?" the boy said. It took a moment, but then I realized I recognized him.

"Eugene, right?" I asked.

He nodded and coughed up some frothy blood. I glanced over at Joker and Flash. Joker knew, I could see it in his eyes.

"Eugene, I'm going to make sure you get back to your family, okay?"

He looked at me in desperation, but there was no hope for him. I put one hand over his eyes and pulled my handgun with my other. The roar of the 45 was deafening and left a sizeable hole in his forehead. I used some more snow to wipe the spray of blood off of my hands and holstered up before standing. Flash's confusion had deepened.

"There was no hope for him," I explained. "I could have saved a bullet and stabbed him through the eye, but I wanted to put him out as painlessly as possible."

"You knew him?" he asked.

"Yeah, he's with a group that lives nearby. We'll carry him back to the truck and take him home."

Flash slowly nodded in understanding. The zed I left alive emitted a snarl and began trying to crawl toward us. When Flash saw him, he became enraged.

"You piece of shit," he growled, walked over, and started stomping on his head. He continued stomping until it was obvious he was now truly dead, but Flash put in a couple of additional stomps for good measure. He then looked at me in a mixture of rage and confusion.

"Why didn't you kill him?" he asked.

"I wanted him to suffer," I said.

Flash stared back down at the lifeless zombie. "Oh."

He then looked around, probably wondering if there were any others around. Spotting something in the snow several feet away, he walked over and picked it up. He held it up and rejoined us.

"A crossbow," he said. "That kid must have been out hunting and got jumped by those zombies."

"Yeah, I'd say you're right on the money."

Eugene couldn't have been more than twelve or thirteen. I'd spoken to him and his father a couple of times. He seemed like a good kid. I could only imagine why he was out hunting by himself. I pulled his shirt and jacket down and hoisted him onto my shoulders in a fireman's carry.

"Grab my rifle and keep an eye out," I said. Flash quickly complied.

It took us several minutes of backtracking. I had not realized how far we'd traveled, and by the time we got within eyesight of the truck, I was winded and had worked up a good sweat.

"Heads up," Joker said under his breath as we walked through the field toward the truck.

There were three men waiting on us. I recognized them all. They had lived at Weather for a short time before we relocated them to a couple of fortified houses near the community once known as Petersville. We walked up and, as gently as I could, I put the boy down on the roadway. Eugene's father emitted an anguished wail.

"Where'd you find him, Zach?" one of them asked. Everyone knew him as Slick, on account of back before, he was a slick used car salesman.

I pointed at the tracks, which were now trampled, and explained how we spotted them running across the road and gave chase. Slick furrowed his brow and bit his lower lip.

"We were supposed to go hunting together, but he got up early and took off on his own," he said, his voice breaking.

Suddenly, the third man cursed. He'd been looking over Eugene and stood suddenly. "He's got a bullet hole in his head," he said, like he was accusing us of murder.

"That's right, he does. He was bitten several times. It was the humane thing to do."

"Bullshit," he said and pointed at the kid's face. "There's only a couple of bites and he's been vaccinated. He would've lived."

I glanced at Flash, who was once again looking anxious, before fixing the man with a cold stare. "Lift his jacket up," I directed.

Eugene's father, who had been sitting in the road sobbing in anguish, lifted up his son's jacket. At the sight of the carnage done, he was wracked with a fresh wave of grief.

The man who was so ready to accuse us of murder was now dumbfounded. He forgot about us, sat beside Eugene's father, and tried to console him. I got Slick's attention and motioned for him toward the front of our truck away from the other two.

"There's nothing we could've done," I said.

"I know, Zach. Frankly, I'm surprised you stopped and followed them. Say, what brings you out on a shitty day like this anyway?"

"It looks like we've lost Ohio," I said and explained, but I left out the part about the possibly tainted vaccines.

"Man, that sucks," he said.

"Yeah. How're things going with your people?" I asked.

"We're doing okay, except for this. Stu's wife gave birth last week to a healthy boy. We're a little short on supplies, but otherwise, we're okay."

I nodded. "I imagine Johnny will be wanting to get home and bury him, so we won't keep you guys. When things get settled, either me or somebody from Weather will bring some supplies up."

"I appreciate that, Zach. Oh, and please don't take offense at Stu, he didn't mean anything by it."

"Forget about it, I understand. Well, we've got to go. You men be careful."

"Same to you, Zach," Slick said.

"You know what I think," Flash said a few minutes after we'd gotten back on the road.

"What's that?" I asked.

"I think all of those stories I've heard about you are true."

Joker let out a belly laugh as he drove.

CHAPTER 21 - TAINTED

"And you believe the vaccines were tainted somehow?" Senator William Rhinehart asked for the third time.

"Yes, that is my belief," I answered for the third time. When we had returned to Mount Weather, we'd no sooner gotten the truck put away when a runner was sent to inform me the president wanted to meet. So, there I was, once again sitting in the conference room. I'd not even had time to clean up and still had zed goo on me. It was a closed meeting this time. Top secret and all that shit. Only a few people were present; the president, a couple of senators whom the president trusted, and of course, Parvis.

"Alright, let me go over this again. The docs are adamant they are baffled how the two batches became tainted. They are also adamant they adhered to strict protocols to prevent something like this from happening. The results of the blood tests from the infected female were inconclusive. Before anyone asks, I have no evidence that indicates they are lying."

"So, logic would dictate..." Senator Rhinehart said, leaving the sentence unfinished.

"I know what you're implying, Senator. Someone sabotaged the batch."

"Both batches," Rhinehart corrected. "There were actually two batches, made separately, correct?"

"Correct," I said in agreement. I honestly don't know how the man was still alive. He was in his late sixties now and I'd heard rumors the state of his health was in question, but I had to admit his mental acuity was still as sharp as ever.

"Sabotage," he repeated. "One tainted batch is possible. Two tainted batches, highly improbable. So, we're looking at a deliberate act of sabotage."

"I believe so, yes."

Senator Rhinehart, William to his friends, but he had none, shifted in his seat and leaned forward. "President Stark favors you for a reason, Mister Gunderson. Not only are you an intelligent and resourceful young man, you know how to fix problems. Am I right, Mister President?"

I looked over at President Stark who made direct eye contact with me.

"Indeed," he answered.

"So, Mister Gunderson, I'm curious. Who do you think the culprit is?" Rhinehart asked.

"That's the question of the day," I responded. "I don't know who exactly, but let me ask you guys something; do any of you know how to sabotage a batch of vaccines where the recipient instead becomes infected?" I paused only a moment. "I don't, unless I had access to a sample of the plague."

"They have samples at Fort Detrick, do they not?" Senator Nelson asked. He'd been unusually quiet during the meeting, not even taking notes, but instead staring intently at me the entire time.

"They do and they are in a secured area. There are only four people who have access." I counted with my fingers. "General Harlan Fosswell, Captain Harlan Fosswell Junior, Doctor Stephen Kincaid, and Doctor Hiram Smeltzer. It is my understanding that General Fosswell specifically forbade those two new doctors from having access."

"Interesting," Senator Nelson said. It was only then he finally stopped staring at me and started fooling with his laptop.

"What are we going to do about this?" Senator Rhinehart asked.

I felt like fixing him with a scowl and asking him, "What's this we shit?" I never liked Rhinehart. The day after we'd arrived at Weather, I caught his two adult children breaking into our semi-trailer. I ended up whipping their asses, literally. I put a beating on both of them and then whipped their asses with a switch from a tree. He took grave offense and ever since considered me the bad guy.

His son, Paul, was later attacked and killed by zombies. Priss, his daughter, was still here, and still finding new and interesting ways to piss people off. However, the years had tempered any animosity she and I had toward each other. In fact, we had actually become friends, and while her father rarely lifted a finger to perform manual labor, he had a sharp mind and was an integral member of the brain trust of Mount Weather. There would always be a level of animosity between us, but we'd put aside our personal issues for the betterment of our beleaguered society.

"Zach, I've read your report, but I think you're leaving something out," President Stark said.

"Okay, sir. What do you think I left out?"

"The tone of your report seems to indicate General Fosswell is rather ambivalent to this turn of events," Rhinehart added.

"He is," I said. "Or he appears to be. He is either in complete denial or he's playing his cards close until he can identify the suspect. Frankly, I'm not sure which, but I would like to believe he's working on it."

"Do you think Fosswell is a party to the sabotage?" Senator Rhinehart suddenly asked. There seemed to be a silent, collective intake of air. I glanced at Stark, who was staring back. I'd already anticipated this question and had a prepared answer.

"At this time, there is no evidence to either confirm or eliminate either of them as a suspect," I said.

Rhinehart leaned back in his chair and a small smile worked its way onto his old, wrinkled lips. "Spoken like a true politician," he said.

I didn't know if he intended that remark to be a compliment or an insult. I chose not to respond and waited for the next question.

Thirty minutes later, I walked out of the meeting with Parvis. No words were exchanged until we reached his office. He immediately went to his hotplate and put a teapot on the burner.

"Tea?" he asked.

"Yeah, that black blend, if you have it," I said. It had more caffeine than coffee, a lot more, and it was not all that flavorful, but I liked it for some reason.

Parvis prepared two tea balls and waited for the water to boil. I leaned back in my chair, pondering what we knew about the vaccines, but I found my mind wandering. The office was a mass of organized chaos. Parvis had stacks of files both on his desk and the floor, as did I. There were also multiple dry erase boards which we used to track the progress of all of our ongoing projects. They were full of notes. Parvis observed me looking at them.

"As if we didn't have enough problems," he remarked.

"Any thoughts on who may have done it?" I asked.

He stared at the teapot, not making eye contact. "Well, if not Kincaid or Smeltzer, then who? What about those two other scientists? What are their names?"

"Doctors Douglas Throneberry and Jere Washington," I said. "I suppose it's possible they're the culprits, but what would be their motivation?"

"What indeed?" Parvis responded.

I frowned at him. "You know, I always hate when you answer a question with a question."

Parvis smiled as he poured the boiling water into each of our mugs. The tea balls bobbed up and down. "Let it steep," he admonished and sat.

"Alright, without answering my question with a question, how do you think we're going to be able to find out who did it?"

Parvis took a sip of tea before answering. "You will have to become a detective. At some point, you will need to go back to Detrick and interrogate each scientist. And, dare I say it? Conventional methods may not be effective," he said.

"You're not going to be involved in this?" I asked with a small hint of sarcasm.

Parvis sipped some more tea and avoided my question. The implication was clear. When the situation called for harsh measures, it always came down to me. And Fred. He was tacitly telling me we needed to pay another visit to the scientists and get the truth out of them, even if it meant putting a couple of knots in their heads. Rhinehart was probably suggesting the same thing during the meeting.

"In any event, we're at an impasse until the weather gets better," he said. "That could be a month or two."

"Nonsense. That deuce-and-a-half is a beast. We had no problem driving on the roads with it, as long as you drive slowly and don't be stupid." In fact, I wondered why it had been so long before I actually discovered the versatility of the lowly Army truck. "We can drive up there anytime we need to," I added.

I caught Parvis frowning. That seemed odd, or maybe I was simply reading too much into it. He focused on whatever he had on his laptop and seemed lost in thoughts. It was a long, uncomfortable silence before he spoke.

"Are you going to?"

I looked directly at him. "Eventually, it'll have to be done, right?"

"Yes, it will," he said quietly.

I stood and stretched. "Okay, I'm going to go visit Bret and then I have rat patrol."

"Bret?" Parvis asked.

"Bret Conway," I said. "After the surgery, he picked up an infection and your sweetie put him back in the hospital."

Parvis nodded. "Oh, yes. Tell him hello," I said.

"Sure," I said and stood.

Bret was in the same room I'd been in years ago. It had not changed any. I gave a short knock on the open door.

"Hi, guys," I said.

Kerry, Bret's significant other, was sitting in a chair beside Bret, who had raised his bed so he was sitting upright. His arm was in one of those shoulder casts.

"Hey, Zach," they replied.

Both men were of similar age and lean physiques, and both shared boyish good looks and kept the rugged, unshaved look. The single women at Mount Weather occasionally expressed their disappointment the two men were gay, usually during one of the women's group activities which often involved an ample amount of wine and weed consumption.

"How's it going?" I asked.

"A low-grade infection," Bret replied. "They've got me on some antibiotics that probably expired two years ago." He gestured at his immobilized arm with his free hand. "It's the same arm I broke a couple years back. Sometimes I feel like I'm jinxed."

I smiled appreciatively. "I can certainly understand," I said and waved a finger at the scars on my head. "I've felt that way too, once or twice."

"You know, I always wondered about those scars," Bret said.

"This one was from a knife, and this one is from a bullet," I said, pointing to each one. I didn't elaborate though; this visit wasn't about me talking about myself.

"I'm sure the antibiotics will do the trick," I said. "Is there anything you guys need?"

Kerry cleared his throat. "Is there any way to get out of work detail for the next couple of days?" he asked. "Bret is having a hard time doing little things, like showering and things."

"Oh, I'm okay," Bret protested.

I smiled in understanding and pulled out my handheld radio. "Come in, Lydia," I said. When she answered, I asked her to call me and gave her the three-digit extension for the landline in the medical unit. I heard it ring and walked out of the room to answer it. After a minute, I walked back in the room.

"Alright, you have hospital duty for the next five days. That means you're Bret's personal nurse."

Kerry grinned. "That sounds like fun."

Bret groaned. We talked for a few more minutes before I wished him a speedy recovery and left.

Next on my list was rat patrol, and yes, it was one of those detested work assignments. There were maybe one or two people who did not mind rat patrol. I guess I was one of them. It gave me a chance to wander around Mount Weather and check on things. Grabbing the rat bucket, gloves, and a resupply of bait, I set out, making the rounds.

Sometime during the first or second year, the population of mice and rats increased exponentially. Mount Weather was not immune and was inundated with them. So, war was declared. We started with a dozen mouse and rat traps, but through our scavenging missions, we now had almost a hundred and had them set all over the place.

We had a list of where every trap was set, but I didn't need it; I had each location memorized. I went through each room, starting at the bottom level. One would think there was no way a rat or a mouse could get down to the bottom level, but the little bastards somehow figured it out and so we had several placed in different areas.

On this occasion, the only trap containing a rodent was not found until the habitat level. This was a tricky area, because it required me to venture into the female locker room. I announced myself loudly before I'd venture in so as not to offend anyone.

The main level of Mount Weather contained the school, the recreation areas, and the cafeteria. This is where most of the traps held dead rodents.

I dutifully dropped each one into my bucket, rebaited and reset the trap before moving on to the next one.

It only took me an hour to check all of the traps. I didn't see anything out of the ordinary while walking around, which was good. I headed to the front gate and checked in at the guard house. To my surprise, it was Slim and Priss on duty. I had a sneaking suspicion that when Lydia was scheduling guard duty, she paired them together on purpose. After all, she'd done it in the past. I wondered if it was because she didn't like Liam.

"How many?" Slim asked.

"Eight. Two rats and six mice," I answered and held the bucket for him to see. Both of them looked in.

"That's good, right?" Slim asked. I nodded. "I remember a couple of years ago we were catching fifty or sixty a day."

He wasn't exaggerating. The rodent population exploded after the apocalypse, but now the numbers were tapering off. We'd never be completely rid of them, but we'd made significant gains.

"What are you going to do with them? Take them to Harold?" he asked.

I shook my head. "I know he'd like them, but I'm going to burn them." I was referring to the dumpsters located three hundred yards down Blue Ridge Mountain Road.

Slim nodded in understanding. "How long are you going to be gone before I should get worried and send people looking for you?" he asked with a grin.

"Two hours, I guess," I said. "If there's any unburned trash, I'll go ahead and tend to it."

"Do you mind if I tag along?" Priss asked.

"Well…" I said, but Slim interrupted me.

"Sure, y'all go ahead," he said. "It's always better to go out beyond the fence with two or more."

I shrugged. "Alright, come on then. Bring your radio and rifle."

As we walked, I pointed. "We still have a fair amount of black ice here and there."

Priss offered no comment and deftly stepped around a patch. When we got to within a hundred yards, Priss wrinkled her nose. "It's especially bad today."

"The first condition of understanding a foreign country is to smell it," I said.

Priss looked at me in confusion for a moment. "Faulkner?" she guessed.

"Kipling," I said.

She scoffed. "I should have known. You love Kipling."

"He's a man's poet," I said. She scoffed again.

We carefully approached the dumpsters, watching for any zeds, bears, or anything else that might have been attracted by the odors, but we were alone. Two of the dumpsters had tendrils of smoke lazily drifting out. There was a step ladder leaning against one of them. I chose the dumpster with the most smoke coming out of it and dumped the rodents in it. We had a jerry can of diesel nearby, along with a trashcan full of diesel-soaked pine needles. Priss brought it over and helped me through some in. I then used a rusty length of pipe to stoke the fire back to life.

Stepping down from the ladder, I stood by Priss and watched as the smoke increased. Priss pulled a one-hitter out of her pocket, lit it, and inhaled deeply. She then offered it to me. I shook my head.

"Oh, I forgot, you like to keep your head clear," she said.

I smiled. "Yep."

She took another hit. "Well, I need it just to tolerate this place."

I smiled. "So, how's it going with you and Liam?"

"Pretty good, actually," she said and gestured at her one-hitter. "He doesn't smoke either, but he can sure put away the shine."

"Do you think you have a future with him?" I asked.

She shrugged. "I think so. We seem to click, but you never know these days."

"True enough," I replied.

There was a minute of silence before she spoke again. "It'll never get back to the way it was, will it, Zach?"

"Not in our lifetime," I said. "But, you've got to admit, it's a lot better than it was eight years ago."

"Yeah," she said quietly. She tried another hit off of her little ceramic pipe, but she was out.

I'd been looking around, keeping a sharp eye out, and saw some movement down the road. "Look," I whispered. It was three deer, maybe fifty yards from us.

"They look hungry," she said.

"Yeah, probably. We can put some feed corn out for them," I said.

"Would you?"

I nodded. "Sure. Let's head back."

I know she was looking at the deer like they were Bambi's sisters, but I was planning on getting them fattened up and then later harvesting them for a nice venison dinner, but I didn't tell her that.

CHAPTER 22 – SUICIDE

"GM, Reusen," I keyed after we'd given the authentication codes, GM being shorthand for good morning.

"GM, Weather," Seth replied in Morse code, which was much faster than mine. "How's the weather?"

It was a corny pun, but he couldn't help himself. Seth Kitchens was a JAG Captain in the Army and was serving on General Fosswell's staff when it all went bad.

I thought out the words before tapping. "Sunny and 38. Minimal melting."

"Same," he instantly responded. "Progress is slow."

There were three hydroelectric dams on the James River which we were working on to get back online. Seth was the leader of the work crew which had our only two electricians, a couple of men named Briscoe and Stallings. They were currently at Reusen's Dam, which was a couple of miles outside of Lynchburg and a hundred and seventy miles from Mount Weather. It was going to be a long project, but we needed the power for a couple of manufacturing plants we wanted to get operational.

We tapped out code to each other for several more minutes before signing off. Garret watched in silence while he did his own tapping on his computer keyboard.

"Why do you guys use Morse code?" he asked. "The satellite uplink is better and more secure."

"It's fun," I replied.

"Heh, yeah, fun. How's the landline project going?" he asked. He was referring to our project of restoring telephone operations. We'd gotten the telephone system operational within the Mount Weather compound, but we'd not yet been entirely successful with reestablishing phone lines to any of our fortified houses or to Fort Detrick.

"It's not," I replied. "Everything is in place, the switching stations have power and seem to be working properly, but we can't get it working. There's some kind of glitch we can't seem to identify."

"It's a shame we don't have any phone techs here," Garret said.

"Rachel is the closest thing to it. She had a communications MOS when she was in the Army, but she can't figure it out either."

He shook his head. "They must all be dead."

"Yeah, or out on the west coast," I said. "I think it's something in one of the switching stations, or maybe a router is bad, or maybe it's in the programming. It's perplexing."

Garret pondered it while he rubbed his chin in thought. "Speaking of the west coast, we've tried off and on for the last year to make radio contact with anyone on the west coast without success. We've had contact with multiple settlements in the midwestern states, but nothing on the coastal states. I tell you, it's strange."

There was a sudden beep from the radio. It was a signal indicating an incoming coded burst transmission. Garret sat up quickly and punched the appropriate buttons. We then listened in rapt attention to the voice message.

"Wow," I muttered. I admit, I didn't see it coming, but looking back to my last conversation with the man, all of the clues were there. I simply didn't see it.

"Do you want to do the honors of informing the president?" he asked.

"Yeah, I may as well. I have to see him anyway." I looked at my wristwatch. "In fact, I have to be there in five minutes. I better get going."

I hustled out of the TOC and took the stairs two at a time. I made it to the conference room with two minutes to spare. Even so, I was the last one other than Stark to come in. When I walked in, Ruth gave a curt nod and left the room, soon returning with Stark. When he sat, I stood.

"I have some priority news from Detrick," I said and recounted the radio transmission from General Fosswell. As I spoke, I heard a faint chime emanating from Grace's laptop. She started reading something on her screen and her eyes widened, much like her brother did a few minutes ago. When I'd finished, she raised her hand.

"Yes, Grace?" the president asked.

"Garret forwarded a follow-up communication from Detrick. It says Captain Fosswell was found last night after someone heard a single gunshot. He apparently shot himself in the head. When General Fosswell was informed, he ordered an immediate cremation. Since then, he has been incommunicado in his suite."

"Who sent the radio communication?"

I looked to see who asked the question. It was Senator William Rhinehart. It amazed me that he was still alive and hadn't died of constipation, or something similar.

"General Fosswell," Grace answered. "He also stated he does not want any kind of delegation to come to Fort Detrick and when he has recovered emotionally, he will come to Mount Weather."

"He's telling us to keep our nose out of it," Rhinehart muttered loud enough for everyone to hear. I had to agree. Fosswell definitely wanted us to stay away.

"Mister Gunderson," President Stark said.

"Sir?"

"You had a conversation with Captain Fosswell when you were at Detrick, correct?" he asked.

"Yes, sir, I did," I replied.

Everyone was staring at me now, obviously wanting me to elaborate. "Frankly, he looked different and acted oddly."

"How so?" Bob Duckworth asked.

"He'd lost a significant amount of weight," I said. "His paunch was gone and his face was thinner. I would've said maybe he was watching his diet, but his complexion was pasty-looking, like he'd been ill recently. Or he was hungover."

"What do you mean by acting oddly?" one of the other senators asked.

"Well, this may sound funny, but he engaged me in a casual, friendly conversation. That normally wouldn't seem odd except for the fact we'd never really gotten along and had hardly spoken to each other for the past three or four years. On the day we left, he met us at the motor pool, and like I said, he engaged in a light, friendly conversation. He then fixed us up with a deuce without even making a fuss about it."

"A deuce?" Senator Rhinehart asked.

"A two-and-a-half-ton truck," I explained. "It has six-wheel drive and can drive across almost all types of terrain."

Rhinehart nodded in seeming understanding. "No cross words were exchanged between the two of you?" he asked with a healthy tone of skepticism.

"None whatsoever," I said. "Flash and Joker were present during the conversation. They can corroborate this."

"Can you tell us what specifically the two of you talked about?" the senator asked.

"He asked about my kids, he asked about my dog, and then talked about a dog he had during his childhood." I stopped suddenly. A thought had formed in my head. Rhinehart must have seen the change in my expression.

"What?" he asked.

"Oh, nothing," I replied. "I was just thinking about his demeanor. It was like he'd already reached his decision at that time. He never gave any overt indicators of his emotional state though."

There was absolutely no way I was going to tell Rhinehart what I'd suddenly realized. I caught Grace staring at me. I liked Grace. She was horribly introverted, but she was also one of the sweetest people I knew, and extremely intelligent, like her brother and father, but she was the more intuitive of them. So, she knew I was holding back but, that wasn't a problem; I was going to talk to her about it at a later time.

The meeting droned on and on. I was convinced one night this little so-called elite group got together one night and conspired to make every meeting last until exactly fifteen minutes before lunch, so as not to be assigned to any morning work details by Lydia. I waited in silence until the meeting was formally adjourned. I glanced at my watch. Yep, in fifteen minutes lunch was going to be served. Time enough for them to amble down the hallway from their chairs in here to their chairs in the cafeteria.

As everyone shuffled out of the conference room, I lingered behind. I caught a glance from Grace and made a tacit sign for her to stick around. She responded with her own tacit nod and then worked on shutting down the projector screen.

CHAPTER 23 – ROGGENWOLF 1199

"I need to talk to you," I said to Grace in a hushed voice.

She gave me a questioning look and glanced around to see if anyone was lingering and listening in.

"What's wrong?" she asked.

"I need for you to do something and I need for you to keep it a secret."

She listened intently as I explained the conversation with Junior in far more detail.

"I'm convinced he was trying to tell me his password. So, I don't know how simple or hard it'll be, to open up his personal files. I'm hoping you might have some thoughts," I said.

"Let's find out," she said and rebooted her laptop.

After a moment, she'd entered a couple of typed commands and the screen lit up with the individual files of everyone who had an intranet account.

"Administrative access," she said to my unasked question.

"You have access to everyone's account?" I asked.

"Not like you think," she said and pointed. "I can see the last time you accessed your account and if you modified it, like entering new data, but unless I have the password, I can't actually access it."

"Not unless you hack into it," I said.

She gave me a startled look, like I had discovered her secret. I ignored it, for now, and scanned down the list of names. Finding Fosswell's, I looked at the date.

"Alright, look at that. Junior accessed his account the same evening he was found dead."

She looked at me with her mouth open in a silent O. "He must have written something before he killed himself," she said.

"There's one way to find out, open his account," I said.

"I can't without his password," she said.

I pointed at the keyboard. "Roggenwolf 1199," I said. "I don't know if it's all one word, or cap sensitive, or what, but give it a try."

She opened it and when the screen came up with the password prompt, she typed. Her first attempt failed, but her second try opened it up. I saw several files, but suddenly the door to the conference room opened and Senator Rhinehart walked in. He walked over to where he habitually sat to retrieve a Yeti cup he'd forgotten, paused a moment to look at us like he'd caught us talking about him, and then walked out. His demeanor did not bother me, but Grace was another story. You could see the guilt written on her face. She nervously closed her laptop.

"We can't do this here," she said.

I agreed. "Yeah, let's go somewhere private."

She shook her head. "You promised Josue you were going to help him out in the motor pool today. I'll work on it and get back to you."

She hurried out before I could respond. I knew her well enough to know she was heading straight for her office, which was deep down in the bowels of the bunker. Nobody was going to see her for the rest of the day.

My walkie squawked as I walked toward the motor pool. The guard at the front gate advised there were newcomers at the gate. I was curious and diverted course. I mean, who in the world would be traveling in this weather?

There were eight of them, four men, two women, and two children, one of which could not have been any older than four or five. All of them were on horseback. It took me a moment before I recognized three of them; after all, I'd not seen them in five years.

"We can see about rounding up some snacks and hot beverages for you folks while you wait, but we have to follow protocol," I heard the guard tell them. The older man, Joe was his name, nodded in understanding before he saw me. It took him maybe a second before he recognized me. A big grin crossed his face as I walked through the gate.

"Well, I'll be damned. Look at who's come to greet us," he said.

"This is certainly a pleasant surprise," I said. I waited for them to dismount and opted to give them each a fist bump.

Trader Joe did not look any different than when we'd first encountered them back in Bristol. His hair and beard were grayer, but otherwise, he looked as fit as ever.

His son, Little Joe, was only an inch or so shorter than me. I believed he was twenty-three now, and his long brown hair was tied back with what looked like a long strip of leather. He was wearing a thick jacket, but it looked like he was broader in the shoulders than the last time we'd seen each other. He had also picked up a couple of little scars on his face. It looked like he'd caught some shrapnel somehow.

His daughter was standing beside her brother. When I'd first met Riley, she was a skinny, wild-looking girl of seventeen. That made her twenty-two now. Her face was wind-burned and her lips were badly chapped, as were all of them, and although she still had a little bit of a feral look to her, she'd turned into a real looker. She gave me a fist bump while staring at me with a look that could've been interpreted as either she wanted to fuck me silly or rip my heart out and eat it. I'd forgotten about those fiery hazel green eyes. I must admit, I had to force myself to focus. All of them were dressed for the cold weather, and it looked like they'd ridden all the way here on horseback. The adults were wearing backpacks and they had a pack mule, but that looked like the extent of their belongings.

"What brings you to Mount Weather?" I asked. "Have you come to live here?"

"We thought we'd try it out, if we're welcome," Trader Joe replied.

"More than welcome," I replied. "Once you guys go through the testing protocols, we'll get you set up in the dorms and then we'll work on setting you up in one of our fortified houses."

"That would be nice," Joe said. "Oh, where are my manners? This here is Zach. We met him and his people a few years back when they decided to leave Tennessee and come live here." He pointed around.

"That there is Ned, his son Collin, and his daughter, Abby, who is also my daughter-in-law. Those two kids belong to Little Joe and Abby." His wind-burned face darkened. "This is all that's left of us," he said.

I thought back to when we encountered Joe and his kids. That was when we were on our way here from Tennessee, five years ago. One of us had asked him how many survivors were in his group and he had declined to answer.

When we had rebuilt the main guard post, we built a parking area outside of the gate with a canopy and picnic tables. We called it the visitor's area. I motioned for them to follow and led them to one of the tables.

"The guard called it in. The doctor or one of the nurses will be out here shortly. They'll want to take blood samples from all of you and test it before allowing you to enter the compound. It's standard protocol. Also, you guys must be debriefed and you have to have a full physical taken. I can take care of part of the debriefing right now, if you're willing."

Everyone looked immediately to Trader Joe, which reaffirmed he was the leader of the group. He gave a small nod.

"Ask away," he said.

"What happened in Bristol?" I asked.

He bit his lower lip and inhaled before answering. "Two things. Zombies and disease. There were fifteen of us. I suppose the story is the same for everyone else who survived this stuff. It was tough at first, but we managed to adapt, improvise, overcome, and all that shit. Zach, when you and your people rolled through, we were holding our own. I know that's a subjective term in this day and age, but we were doing okay. Up until last year that is, and then we had a series of setbacks."

Little Joe snorted. "That's putting it mildly."

"What happened?" I asked again.

"Oh, gosh, where to start. First, we had some kind of blight wipe out our entire potato crop, and then there was a wildfire that took out most of our corn crop. If that wasn't bad enough, during the middle of all of this, our encampment was besieged by a horde of zombies. We think the fire somehow pushed them in our direction."

"Two of our people died that day," Ned said. He was already crying, even though we'd only been talking about it for a minute. I guessed him to be a sensitive type. He was a small-framed man in his early fifties, and I did not sense any athleticism to him. Nevertheless, here he was, eight years after the apocalypse, still alive and well. His son, Collin, looked like a thirty-something version of him. He reached over and rubbed his father's arm as tears started welling up in his eyes as well.

"It was my mom and little brother," Collin said. "They were in one of our gardens trying to salvage potatoes and a horde of about a hundred attacked them. They put up a good fight, but they were overwhelmed before we could help them."

"And during all of this, people were getting sick," Trader Joe said. "That fire released some kind of airborne toxin, we think. Damned if I know what it was, but a few of our older people and children came down with breathing problems and didn't make it. We had a doctor at one time, but damned if he didn't drop dead of a heart attack about a year before all of this."

He took another breath and sighed heavily. "Between the toxin and the horde, we lost seven people in three days. Our gardens were lost, and the cattle we had were either killed by the fire or scattered."

"So, you decided to move up here?" I asked.

Trader Joe gave a small chuckle and hooked a thumb at Riley. "She met two of your people about six months ago. Who were they?"

"A man and woman," Riley said. "Melvin and Savannah."

I couldn't help but smile. "Ah, yes. They're our people alright."

"They told us a lot of nice things about this place," Trader Joe said. "They even said you people have a vaccine. Is that true?"

"It is," I replied.

"Well, there you go. We made the decision, grabbed what we could, and headed this way. By the way, I see a lot of vehicles. Do you people still have fuel?"

I answered and explained. Our conversation paused when Doctor Salisbury arrived in a golf cart, along with another man, who had a tray of various snacks. She stuck each one without emotion, including the two little kids who didn't like having their blood drawn. She knew Parvis was dying of cancer and it affected her. She tried to keep a strong emotional front, but knowing you're going to lose a loved one was hard on a person.

"Our testing procedure only takes a few minutes per sample," she said. "But, all of you will also be required to undergo a complete physical. We'll get started on that after breakfast tomorrow."

She then looked at me.

"Once they're cleared, make sure they're deloused; they look the type." She did not wait for any type of response, got back on the golf cart, and rode away.

"Nice lady," Abby quipped.

"Yeah, she doesn't make friends with anyone until she's satisfied she can give them a clean bill of health."

"What happens to people who don't pass?" Abby asked.

"We get their information, about like what we're doing now, and then we'll set them up in a house, but we don't let them inside Mount Weather. If they resist, we resort to harsher measures."

"That's hardcore," Little Joe said.

"Tough times," I replied. "At one time, we just sent people on their way, but now we have houses we've fixed up. Some of them even have power. If people qualify, we put them in one of the houses."

Ned perked up. "Power? As in, electricity?"

"Yes indeed," I answered. "So, let's continue with the vetting process."

Since I did not have my laptop or a notepad, I listened intently to each of them. I was going to, at some point before bed, type all of it up and email it out to everyone. Trader Joe was once a lawyer, confirming what I suspected. Ned and his adult children were horticulturists and once had a flower shop. The good thing about it, they knew how to grow stuff. Little Joe and Riley were teenagers when it all went bad, like me. They'd learned how to survive though, so I felt all of them would make good additions to the community.

Doctor Salisbury called the guardhouse an hour later and gave the all clear. I had the guard call Lydia and informed her we had eight new guests.

Sammy and his girlfriend, Serena, joined us and readily agreed to take care of the horses. I led the rest of them to the dorms.

"We call this the dorm," I said as I pointed into the large open room with cots and lockers. "At the moment, there isn't anyone else living here, so you have it all to yourself. But, we could have new arrivals come in tomorrow and they'll be put in here with you."

I pointed down the hallway. "Male and female locker rooms are that way. Not to be rude, but you guys really need to clean up and put some clean clothes on. There's lice shampoo and soap on a shelf by the showers and the laundry room is at the end of the hall. I won't watch, but please take the time to use the shampoo and comb your hair out with the lice combs. Any questions?"

"Will we be able to get something to eat?" Abby asked. "The kids are hungry."

"Yeah, we're all hungry," Collin added.

I looked at my watch. "They start serving chow at seventeen hundred hours. Y'all get yourselves cleaned up and situated and then mosey on down to the cafeteria. Ask anybody where it is, or just follow them."

"You got it, Zach," Joe said and headed over to a bed before dropping his backpack to the floor. The others did the same. I watched a moment as they took their jackets off and looked around at their new temporary home.

"Okay, I've got some things to do, so I'll see y'all at dinner," I said.

I got about halfway down the hall when someone called out to me. It was Riley. I waited for her to catch up. She had stripped out of her jacket, hat, and outer shirt. Now, she was only wearing jeans and a black Under Armour long-sleeve shirt, sans bra. She wasn't the skinny girl I remembered; she had filled out in all of the right places. I focused on her face.

"Are you still married?" she asked.

"Yep. Kelly is about six months pregnant currently. What about you? I figured you would've found somebody by now."

"I did, but he got caught by zombies," she said.

"Oh, sorry to hear that."

"Yeah. Are there any single men here?"

"A few," I replied and grinned. "Why, are you on a manhunt?"

"Yeah," she answered.

I was kidding with her, but quickly realized she was serious. Another thing I remembered about her, she was blunt.

"I need a real man, not some sissy boy. Are there any of those around here? Age doesn't matter, I'll take an older man, if he's decent looking and can still get it up."

I couldn't help but laugh a little. "Yeah, there's a few single men here, some are of better character than others. I'm sure you'll find one you like."

She was staring at me with those fiery green eyes again. "Would you mind helping me?" she asked. "You know who the good guys are around here and who are the losers."

I gave her a nod. "I'll talk it over with Kelly and we'll come up with a list of candidates."

She stared a moment longer. "Thanks, Zach. I prefer a man with muscles and nice teeth, like you. Oh, and disease free. I don't want an STD."

I gave her a shrug. "I have no idea who has STDs. I'd guess only the doctors would know something like that."

She thought for a moment. "How many single men are there?"

"There's a few that live here in the compound and a few more who live in the surrounding area," I said. "The living situation these days tend to encourage people to form relationships, but currently we have more single men than single women."

She thought for a moment longer. "Okay, we'll get started after dinner."

I chuckled again. "I'm going to call Kelly and get her to bring you girls some lotion and stuff."

"That'd be wonderful," she said.

I found Kelly sitting with some of her friends in a room near the classroom and filled her in.

"How are they?" she asked.

"A little rough looking, but they seem to be okay. There's Riley and Little Joe's wife, Abby and two kids. I'd say they'd need some clean clothes and stuff."

She glanced over at Maria and Brenda. "We'll take care of it."

"Thank you, beautiful," I said and gave her a sloppy kiss. "I've got to go bring Parvis and Stark up to speed. I'll see you at dinner."

When new people arrived, it tended to get the Mount Weather community both excited and annoyed. There were some people here who acted like eighty-year-old men with a perpetual case of constipation. They didn't like newcomers and weren't shy about telling people how they felt.

When I walked into the cafeteria, the Bristol people were standing awkwardly while being peppered with questions by a couple of our resident busybodies.

"Hey, guys, you're certainly looking better," I said.

"A hot shower does wonders," Trader Joe said. His hair was damp and tied back. He still liked his long ponytail. "But I have to tell you, that locker room smells like a dirty jockstrap."

"Yeah, it's overdue for a deep cleaning with a pressure washer." I looked at Abby and Riley. Their lips were glossy with petroleum jelly and their wind-burned faces looked far better.

"How are you ladies doing?" I asked.

"Some women brought us some stuff and fresh clothes," Abby said.

I smiled. "That was Kelly, my wife, and her friends," I said and waved off the busybodies. "There will be time enough for the Q and A later. Let's get these people properly fed."

I led them to the food line. "We use the buffet-style system. The kitchen staff puts out these big pans, and there is heated water underneath them. We have a few simple rules. Rule one, no taste testing, it's a health standard. Rule two, only put the amount of food on your plate that you're going to eat. You can go back for seconds, but only after everyone has gotten a plate." I looked at the trays of food.

"Ah, this evening we have ground beef steak, mashed potatoes, green beans, corn, and Jell-O. I can speak from firsthand knowledge, we have a limited amount of green beans, but we have a boatload of potatoes. You'll see. On Sundays, we have baked potatoes, Monday is scalloped potatoes, and so it goes. Are any of you diabetic?"

"No, I don't believe so," Joe said.

"Good, because we serve corn and potatoes with almost every meal. Oh, and I don't know if you guys are aware, but Jell-O is made by boiling down the skin and bones of cows and pigs. We don't have it quite perfected yet, so don't expect it to taste like you remember."

"Gross," Abby said.

"I'll try it," Little Joe said and put a serving spoonful on his plate.

"You'll eat anything," Riley said. Her brother retaliated by putting a spoonful on her plate as well.

"We're a little short of salt, so it's kept in the kitchen for cooking. Same with pepper and sugar."

"Any other rules?" Trader Joe asked as we filled our plates.

"Some," I answered. "You are expected to clean up after yourselves and your kids. You'll be called out really quick if you leave a mess." I pointed at a barrel in the corner. "Put your food scraps in there. Next to it is where you put your tray and utensils, next to that is a bucket where you put your napkins. Simple, right?"

"Got it," Joe said. "Right, guys?" Everyone muttered their agreement.

"Alright, there are a few other little rules regarding the cafeteria, but the next one is going to seem silly."

"What's that?" Abby asked.

"Everyone has their own preferred table. I know, it sounds juvenile, but that's how it is. If you sit at any table that's already spoken for, people get in a snit." I pointed out the various tables and who sat at them, and led them to a table that was only used sporadically. I stood before it and made the sign of the cross.

"I hereby dub this the Bristol table," I said and motioned for them to sit down. About the time I got seated, I saw Cutter sitting at my table, staring curiously. What the hell, I thought and waved him over.

"Do you guys remember Cutter?" I asked them while pointedly looking at Riley. "He's a pain in the ass sometimes, but he's a good dude."

"Hello, everyone," Cutter said.

"Alright, so listen up because I'm going to recite their names only once. This is Joe, his son Little Joe, Little Joe's wife, Abby, their two snot-nosed kids who I don't even know the names of, Abby's father Ned, and her brother, Collin." I purposely paused a second. "And last but certainly not least is Riley."

Cutter gave Riley a grin. Riley stared back at him, giving him the once over up and down. "I remember you," she said.

"I hope I left a good impression," Cutter said hopefully. Riley didn't answer.

I motioned toward an empty seat beside Riley. "Why don't you join us? I'm trying to fill them in about Mount Weather."

Cutter did not need to be asked twice. He readily sat, and for the next hour, we conversed and attempted to bring them up to speed on Mount Weather and our mission to rebuild America.

I excused myself after dinner and headed back to our suite with Kelly and the kids. My workday sometimes lasted sixteen hours, and that was when I wasn't gone on missions. So, when I had free time, I tried to spend as much time with my kids as possible.

I had played with them for a couple of hours and had them in bed reading a Harry Potter book to them when there was a knock on the door. I glanced at my watch.

"Okay, kids. It's sleepy time," I said, gave them both a kiss, tucking them in, and closed their bedroom door. Kelly had answered the door and was talking to both Joes.

"Is there something wrong?" I asked.

"I hope it's not too late," Joe Senior said. "But, we've been talking and we want to know what to expect from this meeting tomorrow."

"Sure." I started to ask them in, but then Frederick started calling for me from the closed bedroom door.

"I'll take care of it," Kelly said and disappeared into the bedroom. I motioned for the men to step out in the hallway.

"It looks like we caught you at a bad time," Joe said. "I apologize. We can talk in the morning."

"No, it's okay. Let me fill you in. After breakfast, we'll all meet in the main conference room. The debriefing will be conducted by the people who used to be the politicians of America. Most of them were evacuated when the balloon went up. Oh, and there are people who are called the secretaries. There were originally eleven of them, but there's only three left."

"What'd they do, take memos?" Little Joe asked.

"They ran Mount Weather, which was a part of FEMA. One of the many things they did was create doomsday scenarios and then create models on how to properly respond to them."

"So, they run the place?" Little Joe asked.

"Not exactly. Abe Stark is the president. The various day-to-day operations are delegated to the politicians, but make no mistake, Stark is in charge."

"So, back to the original question," Joe said.

"You will be debriefed. Most likely, you will be chosen to speak for the rest of you. They're going to ask a lot of personal questions."

"Like what?" Joe asked.

"What kind of life did all of you have before, how you were able to survive, what you did in order to survive. What kind of exposure you had with zeds. If you engaged in any nefarious activity, have you ever killed anyone. Questions like that. Oh, and one of them, Parvis probably, will ask how all of you intend to be productive members of Mount Weather."

"Will we be vaccinated?" Joe asked.

"It will be encouraged, yes," I answered.

"We've already been told the vaccine is corrupted, or something."

I sighed, wondering who told them, and explained everything. When I was finished, Joe looked somber, as if he was trying to come to a decision.

"Will you be there?" he asked.

"Yes. Believe it or not, I'm part of the operation of Mount Weather."

Joe nodded, like I'd told him something he already knew. "Alright, we'll see you in the morning. Good night."

I watched them disappear around the corner before going back inside. Kelly was waiting for me.

"What did they want?" she asked.

"They wanted to know what was going to happen at the debriefing. I think it's Joe's nature to be prepared. I don't know if I told you, but he used to be a lawyer."

Kelly scoffed. "We sure do have a lot of lawyers around here. You'd think we'd already have people suing each other."

She was right. In fact, there was an issue that happened a couple of years ago. It was a silly dispute over a house and who had the right to live in it. One family moved in immediately after we had fixed it up and another family claimed to have dibs on it. Stark ultimately ruled on it, but then appointed Seth Kitchens as the Mount Weather mediator. Now, with Seth gone, we'd need to appoint someone new. I made a note to discuss it with Parvis.

CHAPTER 24 – MATCHMAKING

"Everyone's in a festive mood," Ruth said. She and I were the first people in the conference room.

"Yeah, Christmas seems to do that," I said. That was the good thing about the Mount Weather community. Nobody was alone. I'd read of suicides increasing during the holidays due to loneliness back before, but that was not a factor here. In fact, Harlan Fosswell Junior was the only suicide in a long time.

"How's junior?" I asked, referring to their son, Justin Smithson Jr. He was almost five years old now and every bit as rambunctious as Frederick.

A big grin crossed her face. "He's excited about the upcoming play."

"How're are you and Justin doing?" I asked.

Her smile faded slightly. "He and I are fine. It's the rest of the nonsense going on that's getting old."

I wasn't sure if she was speaking about the vaccine issue, or if there was something else I was unaware of. "Yeah, I can see that, I suppose. Nothing is ever simple, it seems."

Ruth did not respond, but there was a frown on her face. After a minute, she got up and walked out. She didn't return until the president walked in.

I sat quietly and watched the interview of the Bristol people by our esteemed Mount Weather government infrastructure. Sometimes, their self-perceived importance was overbearing, but Trader Joe handled them well, even when they pressed on personal questions. He surprised them when he informed them he was a graduate of Harvard Law School, and was even personal friends with the late-President Richmond. I met them in the hall after it was all over.

"Is it always like this?" Joe asked.

"I'm afraid so. It's almost like an initiation process but, I'm not totally against it. It's an easy way to identify the crazies and people with possible nefarious motives."

Joe scoffed. "Yeah, I dealt with people like them all the time, back in the day. What time is it?"

I checked my wristwatch. "Almost eleven. You don't think they would've run their dog and pony show past lunch, do you?"

Little Joe laughed. "Speaking of lunch, I'm hungry, let's go eat."

I'd no sooner gotten seated at our table when Kelly spoke my name. I looked at her and saw she was not happy about something. I racked my brain wondering what I'd done as I answered her.

"You need to have a talk with your son," she said.

I frowned and looked over at Frederick, who was paying extra attention to his food and avoiding eye contact with me, his father.

"What did he do?" I asked.

She looked at Frederick briefly, but he was still concentrating on his food.

"Doctor Salisbury was kind enough to give a class to the children today. She'd rigged up a microscope to the projector screen. It allowed the children to look at various slides she had prepared. It was an excellent presentation. She had slides of skin cells, hair follicles, things like that."

"So, what happened?" Rachel asked.

Kelly looked at Rachel and then fixated one of those stares that only mothers could execute. "Frederick was helping change out the slides while Doctor Salisbury stood by the projector screen and spoke to the class." She gave that look again. "He decided to alter one of the slides and then stuck it under the microscope. The next thing you know there's this magnified image on the projector screen. Doctor Salisbury looked at it in confusion and asked what it was. Your son, shouted out it was a booger."

"He put a booger on the slide?" Rachel asked.

"Yes. He had a big one smeared on the slide."

The table burst out in laughter. Even Fred smiled. Kelly, however, was not. Her frown deepened.

"Doctor Salisbury was not amused," she said. "In fact, she walked out of the class."

I fought to get the grin off of my face. Kelly was no doubt embarrassed by the incident.

"Okay, you and I are going to have a long talk about this after lunch," I said to Frederick. "Right?"

"Yes, sir," he muttered.

"I see those folks from Bristol have joined Mount Weather," Fred said, changing the subject.

I looked at him in surprise. "Do you know them?" I asked.

"I bumped into them on my way up here. They seem like decent people," he said.

"How'd it go with Riley?" I asked Cutter. He wiped his mouth and glanced over at the Bristol table before answering.

"Pretty good. I showed her around and she asked me a lot of questions," he said in a low voice, and then lowered it to almost a whisper. "She's a little different though. I can't get a good read on her."

He finished up his breakfast and wiped his face again. "Okay, I'm assigned to the QRF for the next twenty-four hours. See you guys later."

Riley waited until Cutter had walked out before walking over to the table. "Can I sit?" she asked.

"Of course, you can," Kelly said and motioned to the chair Cutter had been sitting in.

She looked over at Fred. "I remember you," she said. Fred responded with a micro. Realizing that was going to be the extent of the conversation, she turned back to the rest of us.

"Some sour-faced woman stopped me in the hall and said I have to clean the women's locker room for the next three days."

"Yeah, that's Lydia," I replied with a smile.

Lydia Creamer recently celebrated her fiftieth birthday in about how you would imagine a spinster turning the big 5-0 would celebrate; with too much wine along with an overabundance of self-pity. She was a plain-looking woman who had a perpetual scowl and spoke in a tight, toneless voice. She loved Kelly and my kids though, so I always went out of my way to be nice to her.

"That's how it works around here. Everyone has to pull their weight," I said and gestured around the table. "All of us have work assignments. We either had guard duty or cleaning assignments for the first six months we were here. Now, Kelly teaches. Janet and Maria help with the daycare. Fred tends the livestock and horses. Cutter is on the Quick Reactionary Force this week. That's why he scooted out of here." I looked at my watch and wondered if he was late reporting, which was not unusual for him.

"I have radio duty for the rest of the week," Rachel said. "Boring as hell, but it beats cleaning the shitters."

Janet rolled her eyes, as she often did when Rachel joked about something, and then patted Grant on the arm. "Grant here is with the medical team. He is often embedded with the missions, which means during nice weather he's gone a lot."

And he does that on purpose, although I did not say it out loud. Grant and I exchanged a knowing look and suppressed a grin.

"And we run the motor pool," Jorge said while nodding at his father.

Josue pointed a fork at me. "Are you working today?"

He'd been pestering me for the past couple of days to give them a hand in the motor pool. It's not that I minded, but it seemed like something else was always getting in the way.

"Yes," I said. "Barring any unforeseen issues, I'll be there."

Josue responded with a grunt and went back to eating.

"So, you guys are going to get stuck with grunt work for a few months," Kelly said to Riley. "Lydia will probably have someone working with you, but she'll also come along behind you and inspect your work."

"Okay, I guess it's to be expected," Riley said. She then leaned closer. "Who are all of those people?" she asked and gestured toward another table.

"Ah, it's the Marines and some of the military teams," I said.

Liam and Logan were sitting with them. Logan saw us looking, grinned and waved.

"Are they all single?" she asked.

"Some of them, yes. The one grinning at you is named Logan O'Malley. He and his brother are recently from Pittsburgh."

"He has lots of muscles," Kelly said. "I'd bet you'd like him."

"He needs a haircut," Riley said, "and a shave."

"I cut Zach's hair," Kelly said. "Logan doesn't have anyone to cut his. Why don't you offer to do it?"

"Could you introduce me to them?" she asked.

"Logan?" I asked. "Sure."

"No, all of them."

This time, Janet and Kelly rolled their eyes.

I checked in with Parvis and informed him I'd be at the motor pool all day. He started to say something, but then leaned back in his chair and gave me a thumbs-up. Josue was waiting for me expectantly when I walked in. He pointed to a line of vehicles.

"Balancing and alignments," he said.

"You're kidding?" I asked.

"You forget how?" he retorted.

I gave him a look. A couple of years ago, we upgraded our garage facilities with a front-end alignment machine and a wheel balancer we found at a Firestone tire dealership. We hauled them back home and put them to use. I had been trained on how to use one by my old friend, Howard Allen, and though both Garcia men were skilled in front-end alignment, Josue seemed to think I was the resident specialist.

"I suppose I need to get started then," I said.

I did not tell Josue, although I'm sure he knew it, but I liked working on cars and trucks. I remembered when I got my first truck, a little Ford Ranger pickup. The front end was badly out of alignment, so the first thing I did was take it to an independent mechanic my buddy's father recommended. He was a rough-looking man with a thick walrus moustache and a lit cigarette perpetually dangling out of his mouth. Even so, I was fascinated watching him fix my truck with practiced ease.

I was working on my third vehicle when Big Joe and Little Joe wandered in. They were accompanied by their friend, Ned.

"How did the physicals go?" I asked.

"The doc said I had a bad case of dermatitis. She said I should use diesel fuel on it, but other than that, we got a clean bill of health," the senior Joe said. "Abby and the kids are having theirs performed as we speak and Riley's is later this afternoon." He looked around the motor pool with an appraising eye.

"This is quite an operation here," he said. Ned and his son nodded in agreement.

"You people have a lot of things going on. I especially love the greenhouses," Ned added. "Where did you get the lemon trees?"

He was referring to four lemon trees we had in one of the greenhouses.

"We found some seeds on a scouting expedition about three years ago. We hope to have them bearing fruit soon."

Ned nodded. "They're in superb shape, a little small though. Fruit trees begin bearing fruit after three years, but those may need an extra year or two."

"That reminds me, did you guys bring any coffee beans with you?" I asked.

Ned shook his head. "We've tried, but we haven't found any."

"Figures," I muttered. "Okay, be sure to let Lydia know you're a horticulturist."

"Oh, we've met," Ned said. "Someone had already told her. When she confirmed it, she assigned us to heating duty, starting tomorrow night. Before I could ask her what heating duty was, she took off chasing someone down the hall. So, what the heck is heating duty?"

I laughed. "I don't know if you noticed, but all of the greenhouses are heated with wood burning stoves. So, during the cold months, someone must sleep in the greenhouses overnight and keep the stoves stoked and the temperature properly regulated. It's not a great job, but it's important." It also made me wonder why Lydia would assign strangers to such an important job.

"That would explain the cots we saw in them," Ned said.

I nodded. "Cots with no blankets. The theory is, even if you're asleep, if it gets too cold, you'll wake up. But, don't worry, whoever has guard duty will check on you every few hours."

"There's one with marijuana growing in it," Ned said with a tone of disapproval.

"Yes, there is," I replied.

"That greenhouse could be put to better use," he contended.

"That's a lot of weed y'all are growing," Little Joe said with a grin. "You guys must be a bunch of stoners."

"That'll do, son," his father admonished.

I nodded. "I must admit, some of our people smoke more than they should, but we also use it as a barter commodity."

When I said the word, barter, the older man's face lit up. "Do you have a bartering team?" he asked.

I smiled. "Do you remember the man that talked you out of those bananas when we met in Bristol?"

"Yeah, is he still around?"

"Yep. His name is Raymond Easting. We half-jokingly call him the director of trade and commerce. He's currently in Marcus Hook."

"Marcus Hook?" he asked.

"It's a borough in southern Pennsylvania. There is a small group of survivors living there who have gotten a refinery operational. They also have a deep-water port, and we've got a wild idea of getting a sea merchant fleet operational."

"A refinery? Is that how you people still have running vehicles?" he asked.

"Yep, they're able to produce diesel fuel."

"And a sea merchant fleet?"

"Right now, it consists of two sixty-three footers, but we're working on it. The biggest problem is a lack of manpower." In fact, I was the one who thought of it, but I wasn't going to toot my own horn. "If everything goes to plan, we'll have an operational fleet by the summer. It will allow us to have easier access to all of the port cities on the eastern coast."

Big Joe nodded. "Impressive. You people think big."

"The weather has hampered travel somewhat, but when Ray gets back home, you two should talk. They have a personnel shortage and I happen to know they don't have a handle on winter crop production."

Both Joes and Ned nodded thoughtfully.

"What are you doing here?" Ned asked, gesturing at the truck I was working on.

"Good tires are scarce these days. So, we rotate, balance, and align the front ends of our vehicles on a regular basis." I pointed at the alignment apparatus.

"All it requires are shims and then wheel weights for balancing the tires. We have plenty of each."

Fifteen minutes after they had left, Riley came wandering in. Logan was with her and trying hard not show the high degree of lust he was currently feeling.

"I see you two have met," I said.

"Yeah," Logan answered. "I was showing her around. Say, Riley says she's got mad sniper skills. Any chance we can sign out some ammo and do some shooting?"

I started to remind Logan we were short of ammo, but then realized he was probably unaware of that particular predicament.

"I'll see what I can do, but if I know Captain Smithson, he'll probably want to save the ammo for the next training class."

Now Logan frowned. "Yeah, I heard about that. We all have to go through it, right?"

"Yep, but with your SWAT training, maybe you can get together with Captain Smithson and review the training. I'm sure he would appreciate your input."

Riley did not look surprised when I mentioned Logan's SWAT experience, so I guess he'd already told her. Obviously, he was interested, but it was hard to tell about Riley. I tried to help him out.

"I don't know if you two have any plans for after dinner, but tonight's movie night. I think they're showing Predator," I said.

"Cool movie," Logan said. "Do you want to watch it with me?" he asked Riley.

Riley shrugged apathetically. "Sure, I guess so."

We talked a little more before they meandered out. I noticed Josue eyeing me. I got back to work.

Kelly and I discussed the best way to handle this minor dilemma with Frederick Zachariah Gunderson and came to the best solution we could think of. I sat my rambunctious son down and had a long, fatherly talk with him. His lower lip was stuck out the whole time, but he listened attentively and didn't talk back.

Once we entered the cafeteria, I took my mischievous son by the hand and walked him over to the table where Parvis, his children, and Doctor Kendra Salisbury were eating dinner.

"Doctor, my son has something he'd like to say to you," I said.

I saw Garret and Grace grinning. They'd obviously already heard the story.

"I'm sorry for putting a booger under the microscope," Frederick said.

"And?" I chided.

"And I won't ever do it again," he finished.

"That was nasty, you understand that, don't you?" Kendra pointedly asked.

"Yes, ma'am," Frederick timidly replied.

"I hoped you learned your lesson," she admonished.

"Yes, ma'am, I did. That was the weirdest-looking thing I've ever seen," Frederick said.

I started to groan, but Grace started giggling, and to my surprise, Kendra cracked a smile.

"Perhaps, in the future, we'll find more pleasant things to look at under the microscope."

Frederick's face lit up in anticipation. "Yeah," he said excitedly.

CHAPTER 25 – XMAS EVE

The next few days went by quickly, and before I knew it, Christmas Eve was here. I finished up a brief journal entry and then I walked to the auditorium. The place was crowded and stirring. We'd not had any type of attack on the compound in years, so people living here had a sense of security, and therefore were more inclined to pursue forms of amusement that had nothing to do with survival. I asked Parvis about it once. I wanted to end all of the amusements, parties, socials, all of it, and force the Mount Weather community to focus only on training and work. Parvis patiently lectured me that humans needed mindless distractions, and if we did not provide them, they'd create their own. And, if people were left to their own devices, they would create their own distractions, and those distractions could be destructive. I hated to admit it, but he was right. He was almost always right.

The festivities tonight was going to be the traditional Christmas play, with the kids playing various roles. Macie was a little too young to recite lines, so she was going to be one of the animals in the manger while Frederick was going to be one of the three magi. I stood in the back, watching everyone. Kelly and Janet were involved with the play, which gave me the freedom not to sit with the rest of the audience. Normally, I wouldn't mind, but I was not in the mood to sit there and listen to people brag on and on about their kids.

"Kind of silly, isn't it?"

I turned to see Parvis. He was looking out at the audience in much the same way I was doing.

"I mean, we do the same thing every year, and every year people behave the same way."

He was right. Mount Weather had every conceivable Christmas movie on file, so they played one or two a night for the entire month of December. Except for the kids, we'd all seen them many times, but we watched them anyway. And then, on Christmas Eve, we had the traditional baby Jesus in the manger play. Not everyone here were Christians, but we did it anyway and it was always a packed house.

"I don't think it matters," I said. "Like you've lectured me before, people need distractions, and I've come to learn, people need symbolic events to help remind them of the past. And, it gives them hope that our lives are getting better."

"Well said," Parvis said with a grin. "I believe I'm going to steal that line from you when I give the toast tomorrow."

I gave a small laugh. Over the years, we had created more than a few Mount Weather traditions. On Christmas Eve, we had the children's play, and then someone would play the role of Santa Claus and pass out presents. Then, after the kids were put to bed, the willing adults adjourned to the adult party room, which was the only indoor location where smoking of marijuana was permitted and the homemade alcohol flowed like water. The next day, Christmas, the cafeteria opened at ten, whereupon brunch was kicked off with a commemorative speech. We did it every year and someone was always nominated to give the speech. This year, it was Parvis.

"I see there's a lot of people who are getting an early start," he commented.

He was referring to several people holding coffee mugs, which were not filled with coffee.

"Yeah, I bet it's going to be a wild party tonight."

Parvis scoffed. "No doubt. Are you going to it?"

"Doubtful. It's up to Kelly. I'd rather be fresh for your profound speech tomorrow."

He scoffed again. "What can I say that hasn't been said every other year? What'd you get your kids?"

"I found a girl's bicycle with training wheels a few months ago, so that's what Macie's getting. My rambunctious son is somewhat of a challenge. I was going to give him a Swiss Army knife, but Kelly nixed that idea immediately."

Parvis laughed. "I wonder why?" he asked facetiously.

"Yeah, too soon I guess. So, Fred and I have rigged him up some cowboy gear, complete with a hat, fake spurs, and a water pistol."

"He'll love it. What about Kelly?"

I shrugged. "That's even harder. She's gotten a shit ton of maternity clothes and baby stuff. All of it's used, of course, but clean and functional. Plus, after our raid on Dayton, she's got all kinds of other stuff that makes women happy."

"Yeah, I'll say. Everyone was ecstatic with that haul. You scored a lot of brownie points on that one," he said with a chuckle. "Especially with Kendra."

About a year after Kendra arrived at Mount Weather, she and Parvis had developed a relationship. This was not uncommon in Mount Weather. New people would arrive and the single people would naturally gravitate toward each other.

I'm not sure what it was, but she and I seemed to have a clash of personalities. Even now, she was sitting on the other side of the auditorium and declined to walk over to socialize the way Parvis did. Shortly after meeting her, I overheard her comment about people from

Tennessee were probably nothing more than rednecks. It was a belief borne from ignorance. I happened to know that back before, Nashville was one of the most culturally diverse cities in the nation.

But, because of Parvis, we had stayed civil with each other over the years.

"Do you know what Kelly is getting you?" he asked.

"I hope it's a blowjob."

Parvis got a good laugh out of my response, but it soon segued into a coughing fit.

"Sorry," I said. I was going to say more, but the lights dimmed, causing everyone to grow quiet. Kelly then walked out on stage, and with a big smile announced the play was beginning.

This was going to be the fifth time for me, and others, but we clapped anyway and watched with rapt attention. It was slightly different this year. Janet and Kelly had put a comic twist on the story, and each kid had one or two humorous one liners. The audience laughed appreciatively and there were several pictures being taken by doting parents. I'll have to admit, I took a few as well.

After the play was over and everyone was milling around, I eased out to go visit Fred.

Guard duty was different these days from when we'd first came to Mount Weather. We'd made many upgrades over the years and hardened our defense works. Now, there was no need to man every guard post. In addition to hardening the defense works, we'd gotten all of the surveillance cameras back online, added several, and even included infrared cameras and motion sensors. The only post that was constantly manned now was the main gate and we had a Quick Reactionary Force in case of attack.

Fred and Rachel had volunteered to man the main gate so others could watch the play and attend the ensuing party. I heard Rachel laughing about something as I walked in. Rachel was smiling, Fred looked, well, like Fred usually does.

"I brought you two some cookies," I said and held out a plastic Tupperware container.

"Wow, thanks, Zach," Rachel said.

Fred looked them over. "Oatmeal?" he asked.

"Yep."

"Good. I need some fiber," he said and took one.

"How was the play?" Rachel asked.

"About the same as last year, but they added a few humorous lines here and there. It spiced it up a little bit."

"Sounds like we missed a good one. Would you like a drink?" Rachel asked as she held up a bottle with a grin. "It's a fine Mount Weather vintage."

I laughed. "No thanks. So, anything going on?"

"Nope," Fred said.

"We were just having a discussion," Rachel said, and I saw the hint of one of her mischievous grins forming. "I think we need your advice. You see, Fred has pointed out more than once that he's old enough to be my father, so, I've started calling him Daddy. He doesn't seem to like it too much. What do you think, Zach?"

I glanced over at Fred, who looked fit to be tied, and started laughing. Rachel started giggling uncontrollably, making me suspect she'd already had more than a few sips of that fine Mount Weather vintage.

"I'll be back at midnight to spell you guys," I said.

"No need for that," Fred said. "We have relief coming at two."

"And don't worry, Daddy will protect me," Rachel said and giggled some more before standing. "Before you leave, I need to go pee."

"Carry your rifle with you," Fred admonished.

"Yes, Daddy," Rachel replied. I heard her giggling as she walked off into the dark.

Fred waited a few seconds before speaking. "We're not sleeping together," he said under his breath. "She's a good person, but I really am old enough to be her father."

"Hey, it's your business," I said. "She really seems to like you though."

"She didn't have it so good, growing up. She never knew her father and her mother had a new boyfriend every month. She more or less grew up on her own."

I nodded in silence. It certainly explained why she'd attached herself to Sarah, an older woman, and then, after Sarah was murdered, Fred.

"How old are you now?" I asked.

Fred's response was a grunt. I figured he was in his late-fifties, but he was still tough as nails.

"Do you feel up to going on a ride in the morning?" he asked, deftly changing the subject.

"Uh, well, sure, I guess. It's a little cold. I don't suppose I can talk you into riding in the truck, can I?"

Fred's response was a silent stare.

"Yeah, okay. They're not going to serve breakfast at the usual time. Brunch starts at ten, so we'll need to fix something for ourselves."

"Yep," Fred replied.

"Yeah, okay. What time?"

"I'm going to need a little bit of sleep, so let's go with six."

I did the mental math. He wasn't going to be relieved until two, so with any luck, and Rachel didn't pester him, he was going to get less than four hours of sleep. I chuckled in appreciation of the man's stamina. Maybe I was getting an inkling why Rachel liked him.

"Six it is," I said. "See you then."

My next stop was the armory. In addition to a Quick Reactionary Force, we kept the armory manned at all times so there would be quick access to the weapons, if needed. Priss was sitting in front of the monitors, feet propped up, reading a book.

She was still a good-looking woman, kept her hair cut short, and worked out regularly. Oh, and she still had a smart mouth, although she'd mellowed her temper toward me and we had become friends. When she saw me walk in, she held her hand over the title.

"Sometimes the Bible in the hand of one man is worse than a whiskey bottle in the hand of another."

"Ah, that one's easy. To Kill a Mockingbird," I said.

We'd started playing this little game a couple of years ago. She was an avid reader, as was I, and she liked to challenge me to see if my memory was as good as I claimed.

"Alright, smarty-pants, which character?" she rejoined.

"Again, a no-brainer. Miss Maudie."

"Are you sure?" she drawled as she eyed me.

"Of course, I am. That quote is classic Miss Maudie. She was full of sayings and witticisms."

She smirked and then looked at the Tupperware container. "What've you got there?"

"Cookies."

"Oh, nice," she replied and took them out of my hands. She took a bite out of one and washed it down with a glass of water.

"I'm surprised you don't have a glass of wine or something," I said.

She gave a slight shrug. "I'll wait 'til the party."

I chuckled. Since hooking up, the two of them got along like fire and ice, but they were still together. I happened to know every once in a while, Priss and Grace would hook up. I only knew because I walked in on them once while they were engaged in a deep, tongue-probing kiss. Priss was amused, but Grace begged me to keep it a secret, which I abided.

"I'm sure Liam is looking forward to it."

"Yeah," she said.

"You don't sound too enthused," I remarked.

"What's the saying, strong as an ox and almost as smart?"

I chuckled and decided to change the subject. "Do you need me to spell you or anything?"

"No, I'm good. Are you and Kelly going to the party?"

"Nah. Kelly doesn't want to be around smoke and I've got an early ride with Fred in the morning."

"Pfft, you're an old fuddy-duddy," she said.

I laughed and scanned the monitors. Priss saw me looking.

"The only thing I've seen moving out there is a coyote who was trying to figure out how to get through the fencing, and you. Oh, and Rachel either doesn't realize cameras are everywhere, or she doesn't care who watches her take a squat."

I laughed again. "I'll let her know. Alright, if you don't need anything, I'm heading back."

Priss suddenly jumped up and gave me a tight hug. "Merry Christmas," she said. "I'm glad we're friends."

"Definitely," I replied, hugging her back.

Before it got awkward, Lawrence Boner walked in and gave us barely a glance as he took his jacket off and hung it up. Boner was a big, beefy man who played football when he was in the Naval Academy. When the outbreak occurred, he was serving as an aide for his uncle, Admiral Jackson Walker, who had become infected shortly after arriving at Weather. Boner made the decision and killed him.

"How's it going?" I asked him.

"Not bad," he replied and looked at the monitors. "Anything?" he asked Priss.

"Nope, all is quiet," she replied.

"Good." He spotted the Tupperware container, looked in, and helped himself to a couple of cookies.

"Those are mine," Priss huffed.

Boner ignored her and walked out.

"Asshole," she muttered.

He and Priss had been occasional friends with benefits over the past few years, that is, until the two Pittsburgh cops showed up. Once Priss latched onto Liam, Boner was cut off. End result, Boner had nowhere to put his boner. I chuckled to myself at my silent pun, wished Priss a Merry Christmas, and went back to the auditorium.

Most everyone lingered in the auditorium after the play. I minded the kids while Kelly and Janet socialized. The two of them had made a point out of having every kid in the play have a line or two to recite. As a result, the parents were overjoyed and filled with pride. As the two women stood there, praises were heaped upon them by the doting parents. Kelly was a natural with people skills. Janet was even worse than me, but tonight she was being gregarious with everyone. I guess Kelly was rubbing off on her.

It was close to midnight before we could get away. The kids were dead tired, and were asleep within seconds of being tucked in. I thought Kelly would be exhausted as well, but after the two of us crawled into bed, she let me know in her own way she was in the mood.

All in all, it was a damn good night.

CHAPTER 26 – STINKY PEGGY

Christmas day was bone-numbing cold. The thermometer was in the single digits and the sky was a dirty gray, but, at least it wasn't snowing and the wind was calm. The kitchen crew was sleeping in, so we helped ourselves to some leftovers from last night's dinner and then saddled up. Parvis and I had no work projects, nor did the president have any meeting planned, so my day was free. Kelly simply rolled her eyes when I told her Fred wanted to go for a morning ride.

"You might want to consider taking Sammy with you," she advised. "You two haven't been paying much attention to him lately."

She was right, as always. Sammy and I had not spent a lot of time together lately.

"He can skip school?" I asked.

"For today only," she replied.

"You are the greatest," I said with a smile.

I sat on the edge of the bed and looked at her lying on her back in what I called the starfish position; arms and legs splayed out, leaving little room for me. She'd only recently started sleeping like that. Before the onset of pregnancy, her favorite position was on her side with her butt stuck up against me.

I didn't mind though. She was mine and I loved her. I think everyone looks for that special someone. The one, the soulmate, whatever you wanted to call them. The first time I fell in love was when I was fifteen. Macie Kingsley; she was a beautiful girl, but if I had met her today instead of back when I was a punk kid, I doubt I would have fallen for her.

Then there was Julie, Janet's daughter and the biological mother of Frederick and Macie. We were good for each other, at first, but before she was killed, we were going through some kind of rough spot. It all started when her little brother was killed in a horrible accident. I don't know if we would have worked out our differences or not, but we never got the chance.

Kelly and I were brought together by fate and the rest is history. She always kept me on an even keel. Her eyes were closed, but she seemed to sense I was still there.

"What?" she mumbled.

"Nothing." I leaned down and kissed her on the cheek. "See you later. Love you."

Sammy jumped at the opportunity, of course. So, it was the three of us, and Zoe, on a butt-cold winter day riding on horses for no apparent reason.

"Where are we going?" Sammy asked.

"You'll know when we get there," Fred responded. And that was that. Even Sammy knew there would be no further explanation until he felt it was necessary.

We turned south after exiting the main gate and were soon deep into the woods. The trees were dense in places, which made it hard to not only navigate the horses, but to also maintain a sense of direction. Even though I'd ridden around this area for five years now, it was still easy to get disoriented. But, that was me. Fred rode casually along, no compass, no map. He seemed to know exactly where he was going with barely a glance at the sky or any other landmarks.

A half an hour later, he paused at the edge of a clearing, turned back to us, and put a finger to his lips before moving his horse forward into the clearing. I should be specific here and say, by a clearing, I only meant there was an area barren of trees about fifty feet square. It was devoid of trees, only some scruff bushes here and there. But, in the middle of this clearing was a mound covered with a little bit of snow. I estimated the dimensions to be six feet long and three feet wide, and I could see rocks peeking out. Sammy voiced what I was thinking.

"That looks like a grave. It is, isn't it?" he asked.

"Yes," Fred answered in a whisper. "Okay, be especially quiet, otherwise, we'll more than likely have some unwanted company." He dismounted and tied off to a tree branch. Sammy and I did the same, and then followed Fred over to the mound of rocks.

"Every time I come here, there's more rocks stacked on top," Fred whispered. He pointed. "Look, there's a couple of fresh ones. They were put here after the last snowfall."

"I wonder who it is," Sammy whispered back.

"It's Peggy," Fred replied.

I frowned. "Peggy? As in, Melvin's ex-wife, Peggy?"

"Yep."

"How do you know?"

"Because I dug it up and had a look," he said.

Sammy's eyes widened. "You dug her up?"

"I did," Fred answered. "She'd decomposed quite a bit and she stunk to high heaven, but it was her. I had a look and then I reburied her."

It took a lot to astonish me these days, but my old buddy Fred was astonishing me now. I think my jaw dropped open as I stared back at the grave. Sammy again voiced what I was thinking.

"The zombies bury their dead?" he asked.

I looked over at Fred, who gave one of his small micro nods.

"How did you find this?"

Fred responded with a casual shrug. I could have pressed him for more specifics, but this was Fred McCoy: nobody pressed him for specifics if he was not inclined to give specifics, not even me. But still, I tried.

"Let me get this right. The zeds are burying their dead now?"

"Remember Melvin's story?" Fred asked, but he didn't need an answer. "I'm thinking it's only people who have some kind of significance to them."

"Significance? What kind of significance?" I asked, hoping he'd clarify what he meant.

"I'm not sure."

I know he didn't do it intentionally, but he had succeeded in confusing the hell out of me. I mean, what the hell? Zombies burying their dead? This was not in the rules. I readjusted my knit cap as multiple explanations ran through my head.

One of the horses snorted. I looked over and saw my horse trying to pull his reins loose. I pointed.

"Go hold on to them. They're skittish."

Sammy nodded and hustled back over to them. I squatted in front of the grave. There were rocks of different types and sizes stacked on, but there was nothing else remarkable about it, nothing more than a rectangular mound. Fred squatted down beside me. I pointed at the rocks.

"None of them are larger than ten pounds. I'm guessing it's because they can't lift much weight. Their muscles aren't what they used to be."

"Yeah."

"Anything else out here?" I asked.

"Nothing I know of," he said. "I hung out here for three days once, never saw a single one of them, but on the third day, as I'm riding off, I noticed a few extra rocks stacked on." He emitted a slight scoff. "It was damned unusual."

"Yeah, for all we know, they're watching us as we speak."

"Could be," Fred said.

I responded with my own micro nod. "Alright, I assume this is why you told me to bring a trail camera."

"Yep," Fred said and pointed at a nearby tree. "I think that's a good place to put it."

I agreed and got the camera out of my backpack. Using some rope, I secured it around the tree approximately five feet off of the ground, the premise being that zeds would have no idea what it was.

"Alright, let's get going," I said after getting the camera in place.

Frankly, I would've been perfectly content to hide out and kill any zombie cocksucker who showed up, but Fred was not so inclined. I asked him about it.

"I need time to figure these rascals out," he replied, and then motioned for us to follow him.

I guess he was right. Over the past few years, they'd done things we couldn't explain and we probably needed to start figuring it all out instead of killing them on sight.

I thought about Peggy as we rode. She was the ex-wife of our resident wild man, Melvin Clark. They'd had a tumultuous relationship back before. It had resulted in him getting kicked out of the Army for domestic assault and subsequently divorced.

After the outbreak, he'd found her in the apartment they'd once shared. She'd become infected, but instead of putting her out of her misery, he took her and strapped her to a chair he'd mounted on the front bumper of his truck. He rode around the countryside with her and introduced her to anyone he happened upon. Most people thought he was crazier than an outhouse rat.

One day, I told him about the dreams I had about her. I'd dreamt she was communicating with other zombies through telepathic means and she was attempting to rally other zombies to attack Mount Weather. I finished by telling him she needed to be killed.

It unsettled Melvin, but one day, he and his girl, Savannah, took her out to the countryside and put a bullet in her brainpan. He started to bury her, but before he could, dozens of zombies emerged from the woods. While Melvin and Savannah sat in the safety of their truck, the zombies picked up the body and carried her off into the woods. We never knew what had happened to her, until now.

Fred could have simply told me about the grave. I would have believed him, but he wanted me to see it firsthand.

"Thanks for showing me that," I said as we rode.

"Yep," he responded.

I cocked my head at him. "Are there others, you think?"

"No idea," he said.

We rode back the way we came for fifteen minutes before turning east. In a couple of minutes, we came into a large valley, still covered in snow. Fred pointed down at the far end of the valley. I could see a vacant house.

"It's still in good shape. I've a notion to move in."

"What'd you have in mind?" I asked.

"I was thinking of a horse farm," Fred answered. "Nothing fancy, maybe a dozen or so. We can put some cows here as well." He pointed again. "There's fencing, no barn though, but I don't think it'd be too difficult to build one. Maybe a greenhouse as well. We're only fifteen minutes from Weather by horseback."

I nodded thoughtfully. "What about those zeds? Peggy's grave isn't all that far from here."

"I suppose I'll need to hunt them down," he said.

"Well, we can certainly take care of that. But, what then? You'll need some help with those horses, it's not a one-man job, and honestly, you shouldn't be out here by yourself."

Fred frowned slightly. "I showed it to Rachel. She wants to move in."

"If you do that, I'll bet she'll require you to service her two or three times a week."

Sammy laughed. Fred frowned. I chuckled as well and looked at my watch.

"Alright, I don't know about you guys, but I need to head back and meet my family for brunch."

We'd only gotten fifty yards down the trail when Zoe started growling. I unslung my AR-15 and brought it up, searching for a target. Fred had his Duster buttoned-up tight, but he kept a pistol in the pocket. He had it out now, and after a moment, he pointed to a thick copse of pine trees fifty yards to the north of us.

"Watch Bunky," Fred said to me. "He's skittish to gunfire."

Fred nudged his horse. He moved slowly but deliberately toward the trees, stopping when he got to within ten feet. I spotted them when we were twenty-five yards out. They were standing in the trees, no more than three feet apart, and they had not moved the entire time.

"Are they frozen?" Sammy asked in a hushed whisper.

"I believe so," I answered.

Fred motioned for Sammy to join him. I stayed mounted and provided backup. Sammy dismounted and tentatively walked over to Fred.

"What do you see?" Fred asked as he pointed to one of the three zeds. It was once a man, who could've been twenty or fifty.

"His skin is old and leathery and his clothes are all raggedy." He paused and looked down. "His boots are worn out too. He's an old one."

"Yep," Fred said and gestured at the other two. "Are there any differences with these two?"

Sammy cautiously stepped closer and looked them over. "No, not really," he said. "Why are they out here in the woods?"

"Any number of reasons," Fred said. "Do you have your knife on you?"

Sammy nodded. On his fourteenth birthday, Fred had given him a nine-inch drop-point knife. Sammy had sharpened it to a razor edge, but I happened to know the only thing he'd used it for was to skin a couple of deer. He unbuttoned his Duster and pulled it from the leather sheath on his waist.

Fred pointed. "You got three zeds. Show us three different ways to kill them with your knife."

"Are you serious?" Sammy asked.

Fred gave him a micro and stared, waiting. Sammy tentatively walked up to the first one. He looked at each of us again, wondering if we were playing a cruel joke on him, and then he took his knife and halfheartedly poked the first zed in the left eye.

"Harder," Fred admonished. Sammy adjusted his feet, drew his hand back, and put some muscle into it. The blade sunk in to the hilt, and the force of the stab knocked the zed off of his feet, carrying Sammy with him.

"I hope you don't make that mistake again," Fred said. "Otherwise, you're a dead man."

Sammy hurriedly rolled off of the now dead zed and scrambled back to his feet. Fred deftly nodded to the other two zeds. "Do it like I showed you," he said.

Sammy approached the second zed, and putting his second hand on the hilt of the knife, shoved it up through the zed's chin, through the mouth, and into the brain. He then jerked the knife out before being dragged to the ground. He stepped back and looked at Fred expectantly.

"Stop fooling around and kill that last one before he gets you," Fred said, even though it too was frozen solid.

Sammy understood. Fred was giving him a practical training exercise. He faced off with the third zed, reared back and stabbed it in the ear. He used his free hand to brace against the zed's head and jerked his knife out with the other. Once again, he looked at Fred expectantly.

"Not bad. Clean your blade," he said and began walking back to his horse.

"How'd I do?" Sammy asked me as we rode back to Weather.

"Pretty good for your first time," I said. "When we get back, be sure to run your knife under some scalding hot water. Oh, and absolutely do not mention this little training exercise to anyone. If Kelly hears about it, she'll give us all a rash of shit."

"Yes, sir," he said.

I glanced over at him to give him a grin. I noticed his hands were shaking, and it wasn't because of the cold. I gestured at them. "It's the adrenalin."

He looked over. "You two aren't shaking."

"It happens," I said. "The only difference is this isn't our first rodeo."

He nodded, but he was still nervous.

"Don't worry, with Fred training you, you'll be hardcore in no time. Now don't forget what I said about Kelly."

"Okay," he replied with a grin.

The cafeteria was full and noisy. I saw more than a few who looked hung over, but mostly there were a lot of smiles and laughter. The three of us stood in line and got full plates. I looked around and everybody had full plates.

"Look at them," I said to Sammy under his breath. "Do you see?"

"See what?" he asked.

"The people. Their bellies are full and they live in a safe domain. Some of them don't even know what it's like to live out there. Others are aware though, and they value the hard work that goes into making sure this place stays safe and there's plenty to eat. This is what it takes to rebuild a society, Sam. You have to keep them fed, sheltered, and protected. Almost everything else falls into place. Societies then grow into greatness. Big things happen. Hell, we might even put a man on the moon again." We walked toward our table and I leaned closer.

"Then you know what happens?"

"What?" he asked.

"People grow complacent, lazy, arrogant. They adopt a mindset of greed and entitlement. Instead of remembering how it was, they grow to believe they are owed. They lose perspective, Sammy. A civilization may last a thousand years, but eventually, it'll always implode on itself."

I sat down beside Kelly, who was frowning at me. Sammy sat across from me, also frowning.

"I bet they don't teach that in history class," I said with a wink.

Kelly leaned over and whispered. "Stop that. This is a happy occasion."

I stifled a sarcastic grunt with a drink of water. She'd heard my rants a time or two and only tolerated them when nobody else was listening. But, she was right. Christmas is supposed to be a happy occasion. I put on a friendly Christmas air and let myself join in the festive mood. Everyone had an enjoyable brunch and everyone clapped and cheered when Parvis gave the traditional Christmas speech.

"Everyone is festive," I said to Kelly, wondering if she detected any sarcasm. "Yep, everyone loves everyone, it seems."

"Quit being sarcastic. By the way, have you spoken with Justin lately?" she asked.

"Not lately," I replied. I caught a sidelong look from her. "Why, is something up?"

She glanced around to see if anyone was listening before speaking under her breath. "I've been talking to Ruth. She and Justin feel like they're being mistreated."

"By whom?" I asked.

"Ruth believes Parvis and President Stark have relegated her status to nothing more than a gopher and Justin believes you don't respect his rank."

I was about to call bullshit, but the look she gave stopped me. She knew what I was about to say, and I knew how she was going to respond. So, I kept my mouth shut and looked around. I spotted Justin and Ruth. They were sitting at a table with Jeremiah and his family.

"Okay, let me go say hello," I said, stood, and walked over. As I approached, they looked up.

"Merry Christmas," I said.

"To you as well," Justin replied. Jeremiah only gave me a nod.

I looked down at Junior, Ruth, and Justin's son. "You were awesome in the play."

"What do you say?" Ruth asked him.

"Thank you," Justin Junior replied. I gave him a smile and refrained the urge to tussle his hair.

"Your face is all rosy," Ruth said. "Have you been outside?"

"Yeah, Fred, Sammy, and I went on a morning horseback ride." I thought of Peggy's grave. "Which reminds me, I want to have a meeting with you guys and the scout teams and compare notes, would this afternoon be good for you?"

"We were planning on spending the day with our respective families," Justin said.

"Unless you plan on pulling rank on us," Jeremiah said. The two men exchanged glances.

"Oh, no, nothing like that. We'll talk about it later. You guys have a Merry Christmas."

"I think I see what you mean," I said to Kelly after I'd sat back down at our table.

CHAPTER 27 – RECONCILIATION

Back before, when I was a punk kid, if I got into an argument with a friend, I had a simple method of patching things up; we'd do something like play Xbox together. If a grown man needed to patch things up with a friend, he'd take him out to somewhere like Hooters, or Twin Peaks. You'd drink beer, eat wings, and ogle the waitresses. A night of camaraderie was usually all it took to smooth things over. But, that was then. Things were different now. No Hooters, no strip bar, nothing like that. One had to find another way to smooth things over.

Kelly and I discussed my options. We came up with a lot of ideas and discarded all of them. We talked about inviting them over for dinner, but we had a cafeteria where food inventory was closely managed and skipping meals resulted in wasted food. We discussed inviting them over for a night of cards, but Mount Weather had its own card league. We had a lot of organized amusements; chess tournaments, trivia night, movie night, you name it.

Fred had listened in silence as we bandied about different things before speaking.

"Country boys used to go fishing," he said. "It was a good way of going somewhere quiet where you could talk things out, or maybe not talk at all and just enjoy the activity."

"It's as good an idea as any," she said.

So, it was decided. I found Jeremiah and Justin in the armory, reloading ammo.

"Good morning," I greeted.

"Good morning, Zach," Justin replied. "Are you here to help out?"

I started to tell them about the meeting I was headed to, but realized it might not be received well. I pulled up a chair and started helping them sort brass.

"What brings you here this morning?" Jeremiah asked me.

"I came here to invite you guys to go fishing tomorrow."

The two men eyed me and exchanged a glance before Justin spoke. "It'll be a little cold, don't you think?"

"Well, if Marines are put out by a little cold weather, I suppose we can pack some hot water bottles or something."

Jeremiah chuckled, which I took as a good sign. We spent the next fifteen minutes working on the reloads in silence. I was going to wait and talk to them while we were fishing, but since I wasn't getting a definitive answer, I decided to go ahead and get on with it.

"I have an ulterior motive for the invite," I said. "I have seemed to have gotten on the wrong side of two men I consider friends. I'd like to talk it over and clear the air. Any thoughts?"

The two men exchanged another glance.

"You've changed, Zach," Justin said. "Lately, you've been throwing out orders like you're the one running the place."

Jeremiah jumped in. "There've been times when you've undermined our authority, in front of our Marines and the other people, and behind our back."

I gave Jeremiah a long hard look. "I know there are times, Dayton for example, when I have countermanded orders, but you're going to have to explain what you think I've done behind your backs."

"There've been times where things were going to be done one way, but then you go into one of those meetings with the president, and when you come out, things get changed," he said. "Things get changed frequently without talking it over with either of us."

"Dayton is a good example," Justin said. "You put out the order to capture a zed without my say-so and then you give the order to go to Detrick."

"I thought we worked that out," I said.

"It should have been worked out from the get-go," he replied. "Not after the fact, and not without our input."

I pursed my lips. "I've never been in the military, as you both know, but isn't there a phrase called a fragmentary order, or a FRAGO? It's my understanding a FRAGO is used to make a change in the mission when the tactical situation dictates it. Am I right?"

There was no response to this.

"Alright, I'll come back to Dayton in a minute. As for going behind your backs, when I walk into those damn meetings, I am not the only voice there." I gestured at Justin. "Your wife is in every meeting, she knows what goes on. She records the minutes, for Christ's sake."

"She says the president listens to you," he said.

"He does, but he doesn't always agree with me. In fact, he mostly listens to Parvis, along with a few other people. He listens to Ruth too."

He shook his head. "He might have, once, but between him, Parvis, Rhinehart, Duckworth, and Nelson, she's been relegated to nothing more than a gopher who keeps him supplied with tea."

There was a lull in conversation now, and I watched the reloading machine do its magic. The cartridges moved along like little brass soldiers getting primed and then capped with the bullet.

"We're down to our last hundred rounds of 308," Jeremiah said offhandedly. "You might want to bring that up in one of those meetings."

"I will, thank you."

I waited to see if either of them had any comments, but the only thing I got was a solitary grunt from Jeremiah. Justin said nothing and instead made a point of fastidiously inspecting the finished bullets. He had two boxes. Most of them were going into one box. The rejects would be used for target practice or recycled. I sighed and stood.

"I apologize for this…" I paused, searching for the right words. "For this misunderstanding between us. I consider the two of you friends, but perhaps I'm wrong. I try to keep a proper perspective of who I am and my role in this community, but it's not easy. In fact, it's hard as hell. I also try my best to fill a role and do the right thing, but I often find myself in Catch-22 situations."

I paused a moment. "Here's an example. Apparently, the two of you believe I was wrong about the decision to take that infected woman to Fort Detrick."

"We never said that," Justin said while still not making eye contact.

"But you two haven't said it was the right decision, now have you?"

Neither answered.

"Well, okay then." I looked at my watch and stood. "I've missed one of those pesky little meetings where I get to go behind people's backs. So, Parvis will expect me to join him in our office, whereupon he'll tell me everything I missed and then quiz me to see what my input would've been."

I looked at my watch again. "We're leaving in the morning at six. We're going to try our hand with the catfish in the Shenandoah. Harold believes there will be so many they'll simply jump up on the bank for us. I hope you two join us. If you don't, I'll understand."

The next morning, four of us enjoyed a light breakfast and made small talk. I knew Sammy and Fred would go, no matter what the weather. I was surprised to see Rachel walk in.

"You're going with us?" I asked.

She nodded. "Fred might fall in and somebody will need to give him mouth-to-mouth."

Sammy laughed. Fred frowned. I glanced at my watch a couple of times. Fred noticed.

"Let's get moving," he said.

I nodded, believing the two Marines had declined the invitation, but to my surprise, when we walked outside, First Sergeant Jeremiah Crumby and Captain Justin Smithson were waiting on us in two idling Humvees.

"Good morning," I said. "Sorry we took so long."

Justin cleared his throat. "Oh, you're not late. Fred suggested we should be early."

Fred had no comment as he walked past us and began loading up the gear, leaving me to wonder what exactly he had said to them.

"Good morning, Jarheads," Rachel said cheerily as she got in the backseat of Jeremiah's Humvee.

"Alright, we can chitchat on the ride, everyone load up," Fred directed and looked at Sammy. "We're riding with the first sergeant."

Justin watched as I put the gear and fishing poles in the back of the Humvee he was driving and got in the front with him.

"I've got the heater on, but I hope the weather warms up," he said as he put the vehicle in drive. "Otherwise, it's going to be cold down there on the river."

"Yeah, I hope so too."

As we exited the gate, I pointed down the road. "Head to Harold's and we'll pick up some fish bait."

"Roger that," Justin replied.

"I appreciate you two coming," I said after we'd signed out with the guards.

"We appreciate the invite," he replied.

Harold and Maude were waiting for us when we arrived. To my surprise, they wanted to join us. The two of them had freshly scrubbed faces and were wearing identical bib overalls with thermal underwear and lumberjack caps. Maude had some fishing poles and Harold was carrying a couple of five-gallon plastic buckets. They both had some foul-smelling concoction in them.

"Good God, what is that?" Justin asked with a disgusted scowl.

"Chitlins," Harold said with a grin. "Hog guts. Catfish will eat this stuff like candy."

Despite the frigid morning air, Justin hastily rolled down his window. Zoe took a cautious sniff and snorted. The closest river to Mount Weather was the Shenandoah, only ten miles away, and we were there in no time.

"I've been fishing this river ever since I was a boy," Harold said, "and it ain't been fished by nobody but me in years. I tell ya', it's gonna be plumb full of catfish."

Maude agreed with a giggle. When I looked over at her, she held her fist up with a thumb slightly stuck out and shook it. I assumed she was giving me a thumbs up, or something. Harold decided he was the master fishing guide and placed us in groups along the bank.

"Okay, we're going for catfish, but don't throw anything back, we'll feed all of the leftovers to the hogs." He then tossed some of the vile-smelling guts into the water before scooping up handfuls and dumping gobs in front of each of us.

"Them fish are gonna love this stuff. Start out at about four feet, and if you don't get any bites, start going deeper."

Fred and Rachel had walked fifty yards down the bank. Jeremiah looked over at Sammy.

"Come on, son. We're going to find us a good spot." They walked in the opposite direction and picked a spot twenty yards away. Justin and I picked a spot between Fred and Rachel.

"You fish much?" I asked Justin.

"Honestly, this is probably my third time. I remember fishing with my grandfather once when I was a kid. I think I caught a brim that was about the size of a tadpole."

"I didn't have a grandfather, but an old man from my grandmother's church took a few of the boys fishing sometimes."

We heard a squeal of joy and looked over to see Maude fighting with her fishing rod.

"It's a big 'un," Harold exclaimed and helped her reel the fish in. He waded down into the cold water, grabbed the fish with his bare hands, and hauled it up onto the river bank.

"Oh Lordy, it's a twenty pounder for sure," he said with a big grin. Maude giggled with glee.

Harold was right. The river was full of fish and the seven of us did a good job of catching them while Harold jogged back and forth grabbing the fish. His job was gutting and skinning them, which he performed expertly with a razor-sharp fillet knife.

"Y'all are doing good," he would say encouragingly as he walked up and down the river bank. "Keep it up."

I waited until Harold walked off before speaking in a low tone, "From the conversation we had yesterday, you two Marines think I've lost respect for you and that I've become too big for my britches, would that be an accurate assessment?"

"Over the past year, there's been a change in you," he said. "It's almost like you have the idea you're running things."

"I can see how it would appear that way," I said.

"Is there an explanation?" he asked.

"It's a little complex, and I think I need to use an anecdotal story to fully explain."

Now Justin gave me a look as if to say, nothing's ever simple with you.

"Alright, I'm all ears," he said.

"Do you remember way back when there were all of those reality shows on TV?"

Justin glanced at me as he wiggled his line slightly. "Yeah, I guess."

"There was one show where a man would take on failing bars. He'd yell and scream at everyone and get them straightened out and they'd start making a profit."

"Yeah, I remember that show," Justin said, wondering where I was going with my story.

"So, there were a lot of episodes where he would jump all over the manager because he was too friendly with the employees to properly supervise them. The manager would piss and moan about how hard it was to boss people around who he considered friends. That dude would shut them down and tell them, welcome to management."

"And the point of this story?" he asked.

"Both Parvis and President Stark have emphasized I need to be more of a manager, even to my friends."

"Why?" he asked. "I mean, why is he telling you to be more of a manager?"

"Because Parvis is dying of cancer and I'm being groomed to take over his job after he's gone."

That revelation stunned Justin into momentary silence. "No shit?" he finally asked.

"He recently had surgery in secret. They removed his prostate, but the cancer metastasized. I'm sure you know, we don't have the equipment or the means for chemotherapy, and, without chemo, he's doomed."

"So, the rumors are true," he remarked. "That's why he's lost so much weight lately."

"Yes."

"Are you going to do it? Take over his job?" Justin asked.

"That's the plan, but it's not common knowledge. That's why I haven't said anything to you sooner."

He stared at me curiously. "That will make you the number two man around here."

"You're forgetting, most issues are voted on," I reminded him.

We still had our senators. When Stark took over, he redefined the roles of the politicians. No longer were they immune from the labor pool, but they were still representatives of what was once our country and therefore, they still had a vote in the major issues of Mount Weather.

"When does this take place?" he asked quietly. "When is he going to die?"

"Kendra, Doctor Salisbury, thinks he has six months, give or take," I answered. "His health is steadily deteriorating. Soon, he'll be bedridden. When that happens, I'll be taking his place, barring any unforeseen circumstances."

I saw him look pointedly at me and we locked eyes. "Are you up to it?" he asked.

I emitted a slight scoff. "That's the question of the day. This thing going on lately where I'm being more authoritative? They're evaluating me."

"So, what's your answer?" Justin pressed.

"I'm not sure I have the correct answer. Parvis has been a terrific mentor and I've learned so much from him. When he learned his cancer had spread, he changed everything with tutoring me. Now, he's focused only on teaching me how to manage. If and when I'm promoted, my effectiveness and competency are going to be repeatedly challenged. I'd like to think I'm up to the challenge, but the question is, is it worth losing friends over."

"How do you think us lowly Marines will fit in this equation?"

"Ah, that's an easy answer. We need to rebuild a standing military, and it needs to be sooner rather than later. I foresee you being the commanding officer of the military."

"You're forgetting a few people, like General Fosswell and Captain Kitchens, and, for that matter, Ensign Boner."

"Captain Seth Kitchens is currently head-over-heels in love with a woman down in Lynchburg and he's going to live there. He'll jump in when we need him, but he has no desire to run the military. Ensign Boner is, as you know, currently in Marcus Hook. We didn't make it commonly known, but his mission is to put together a semblance of a navy."

"You didn't mention Fosswell," he said.

"Yes, he'll be in charge, on paper, but when it comes to boots on the ground, it will be you."

"Honestly, Zach, I'm nothing more than a noncommissioned officer."

"I'm pretty sure General Chesty Puller started off as a private," I said.

Justin groaned. "Zach, I'm no Chesty Puller. He was a living legend and the most decorated Marine in history."

"You get the point though," I said. "You know that adapt, improvise, and overcome stuff. You have the intellect to learn how to run a military."

I hesitated a moment before continuing. "What if I were to tell you we are going to need a standing army within the next year? At least a battalion size, maybe larger?"

"For what? The zeds?"

"Yeah, zeds, and the Russians."

Justin turned and stared in confusion. "What the hell are you talking about?"

"As you are aware, there's a reason why Grace and Garret are only topside occasionally. They spend hours down in the TOC monitoring and analyzing satellite feeds."

Justin was suddenly tense. "What have they spotted?"

"I'll have the full report available for you, but right now, I'll give you the short answer. Two weeks ago, they spotted a significant amount of activity from a port city in Russia named Beringovsky."

"And?" he asked.

"And, nine days ago, they observed a fleet of fifteen ships leave the port. Two days ago, they watched the fleet land in various ports along the coast of British Columbia. We don't know of the exact number of personnel on each ship, and we have no idea what they're up to, but it can't be good."

He stared at me a long minute before speaking. "When, exactly, was the ruling party going to tell the rest of us this information?"

I thought a moment, thinking of the appropriate words. "A couple of them believed the best course of action was to keep this information secret until the appropriate time."

"You sound more and more like one of those politicians every day," Justin said.

"Yeah, I spend too much time with them," I replied. "So, I agreed with them, for the most part. There were only six of us who know about it; Parvis and myself, Stark, Grace, and Garret."

"Who is the sixth?" he asked.

"You."

"Why was it kept a secret?"

"Because the Mount Weather society loves to gossip, and you know how that goes."

Justin gave a slow nod. "Every time it's retold, the facts are distorted and embellished. Point taken."

I watched as his line went taught and he pulled in a decent-sized fish.

"Looks like ten pounds, at least," I said as Harold came jogging up.

"Yep, that's a tenner for sure," he said as he pulled it off Justin's hook.

"So, the brain trust believes a threat is imminent?" he asked after Harold had walked away.

"Eventually," I said. "It is more than likely they'll attempt to establish a stronghold on the west coast and then, eventually, move east. We'll need to eject them, which, in plain talk means, kill them. Parvis and I have done the math and believe we have a year to prepare before they cross the Mississippi. President Stark agrees with our assessment."

"Speaking of President Stark, I have a question."

"Let me guess, you want to know when will there be the next election?" I asked.

"Yeah, and don't think I'm the only one who is asking that."

I paused a moment and glanced down the riverbank at the others. Rachel had snagged one and Fred was helping her with her line. I watched as Fred wrangled the fish in and Rachel took advantage and pinched his butt. He looked at her like he was dealing with a wayward child while she, in turn, grinned playfully.

"Short answer, I don't see Stark allowing a presidential election anytime soon, but it will happen, one day."

"Yeah, I can see that, but, I have to say, and again, I'm not the only one saying it, we're living under a dictatorship."

I didn't answer, but I could not disagree.

"Alright, I guess I understand. So, what's next?"

"Continue with our present mission," I said.

"Sure, I get it, but there's other shit going on, wouldn't you agree? Like, what the hell happened with the vaccines?"

I gave him a cold stare. "You can be certain of one thing: I'm going to find out who sabotaged those batches of vaccinations."

"And then what?" he asked.

I didn't answer. Justin picked up on it.

"Okay, I understand. I know you well enough to know what you have in mind. Count me in if you need help."

"I appreciate that," I said. "Hopefully, it won't come to that."

"You know, we've been through a lot," Justin said after we had fished in silence for several minutes.

"Yes, we have," I said in agreement. "There is no reason for us to be at odds with each other."

He glanced at me. "We're on the same side and all of that shit?"

"Yep."

He gestured down the riverbank at Fred. "Does he know?"

"Probably," I said.

"You've got to admit, he's an odd dude."

"I know him better than anyone, I'd say. Not only do I trust him with my life, I trust him with my kids' lives."

"Yeah, no doubt. So, how does this all work out?"

"I'd like to think I have you on my side, just as you have me on yours. I hope you feel the same. You know everything we're doing is not for us, but for our kids."

He paused a moment before answering. "Of course."

"I have a lot of ideas, Justin. Ideas I've not shared with Parvis or Stark. I think they could work."

Justin lowered his fishing rod and now stared at me thoughtfully. "You have aspirations of replacing Stark one day, don't you?"

I reeled in my line and waited a long minute before answering. "Yes, yes I do. But, make no mistake, I'm in agreement with his mission. I'm as committed to rebuilding America as he is."

"Jeremiah and a couple others don't think it's possible," he said.

"What do you think?" I asked.

He shrugged. "That's a question far out of my pay grade."

"What does Ruth think?"

He gave me a questioning look.

"Your wife is a hell of a lot smarter than everyone gives her credit for."

"Everyone except you and me," he said.

"Yep. I got to know her pretty good back when you people were holding me against my will. By the way, don't think I've forgotten about that."

He glanced at me. "We'd like to have more input," he said. "That being the OMs."

That was the term he referred to when referencing the original Marines.

"All I can say is, when the time comes for me to take over as director of ops, you'll have my ear."

"Do you think it's possible?" he asked. "To rebuild America?"

"Yes, one day," I replied. "It won't be easy though."

We talked throughout the day while we caught fish. Harold would jog up and grab them as we pulled them in and kept gleefully repeating, "I told you it's full of fish!"

It seemed like we'd worked out our differences. At least, I hoped so. Between the two of us, we caught two dozen catfish, and I think we caught the least number. We spent the time talking about everything under the sun. It seemed like old times. While we fished, I'd been absently watching Zoe. She was having a great time wandering up and down the riverbank, occasionally eating some of the catfish guts that Harold had thrown on the ground. Suddenly, she stopped and started sniffing the air before emitting a low growl.

"She smells zeds," I said. I stuck my arm up and waved it back and forth until I got everyone's attention. Once everyone understood, we hurriedly secured our fishing rods and formed up.

It seemed like every river in every state had a road alongside it named River Road. The Shenandoah River was no exception. We moved quietly through the trees up to where we'd parked the Humvees. Jeremiah led the way, suddenly held up a fist, and then pointed down River Road where it intersected with Route Seven.

I counted seven of them. Normally, it would've been a no-brainer. We would've simply moved in on them and hacked their heads off or put a bayonet in an eye socket. But, today there was a difference. I saw Fred looking at me and he cut his eyes to Sammy. He then motioned for us to follow him. He made Sammy get into the Humvee before slapping on the hood of the vehicle. The zeds instantly broke into a jog, coming at us.

They were more agile these days, but still no match for us. It was a simple matter to jam a forearm into their faces. They'd try to bite down through our jackets, which made the knife work easy. Nobody played around. We killed them all within seconds. I was about to give Justin a high-five when I glanced back. Sammy had gotten out of the Humvee and was squared off with two zeds.

"Shit," I growled as I began running toward him. We were all over a hundred yards away from him. I heard a gunshot ring out. A burst of crimson came out of a hole in the middle of the forehead of one of the zeds. I instantly knew it was Fred who made the shot. Before he could shoot the other one, Sammy had tackled it. When I got to him, he was on top of the zed, yelling and stabbing him repeatedly.

My first impulse was to grab him and pull him off, but, Sammy was on a tear. The zed was a male with a stocky build. He struggled for the first few seconds before the life was torn out of him by Sammy's repeated stabs to the head. After several more seconds, Sammy realized it too and stopped. He looked up to see all of us staring at him.

"They were sneaking up on you guys, but I got the sonofabitch," he said excitedly, and then looked at Fred. "You should've let me kill the other one too."

We headed back home two hours before sundown, the back of both Humvees stocked full of fish. Justin was silent all the way back to Harold and Maude's.

"Alright, you boys, take those directly to the cafeteria," Harold said after he'd unloaded all of the fish guts. "There ain't nothing better than freshly fried catfish." He helped himself to a couple of the big ones.

"Momma, we're going to eat good tonight," he said. Maude giggled. Harold bid us goodbye and the two of them walked down the raised walkway to their house.

We arrived back at Weather within minutes. All of our fish were piled up in the back, so we finally figured using a wheelbarrow would be the best way to haul them to the kitchen.

"Sammy and I will take care of it," Fred said. "Get those vehicles washed out so they don't stink."

"You two go ahead," Justin said to Jeremiah and Rachel. "Zach will give me a hand with these."

I nodded in agreement.

"I've been thinking about what you said," Justin said as we hosed down the vehicles.

"Oh, yeah?"

"I believe I understand now and you can count on me. Me and Ruth. I'll explain it to Jeremiah and the rest of them. They'll be on your side. Hell, Joker has always been on your side."

"I appreciate that," I said.

I helped him wash and then park the vehicles in the motor pool. We stood in front of the bay doors in a moment of awkward silence. Finally, I stuck my hand out.

"I hope we're square," I said.

Justin took my hand and we shook. "Roger that," he said.

I told Kelly everything after we'd gotten the kids to bed.

"Sammy killed him?" she asked.

"Yeah."

"I'm not sure what to think about that," she said.

"I know we don't want our kids to go through this, but, you know, he reminded me of the first time I had to kill one of them with a knife."

"He's too young for that," Kelly said.

I sighed. "I'd like to agree with you, but it's time. He's what, sixteen now? That's how old I was when all of this stuff happened. He needs to know how to be able to protect himself and others when nobody else is around, like Fred or me."

"I don't like it," she said with a hint of anger in her tone. I got the impression I should leave it alone and changed the subject.

"In other news, I think I've cleared things up with Justin and Jeremiah." I then proceeded to tell her of our conversation.

"You told him about Parvis?" she asked.

"Yeah."

"It's supposed to be a secret."

"Yeah, but I figured he needed to know."

"I talked to Ruth earlier," she said.

"How'd that go?"

"She said Stark treats her like a servant. That probably has a little bit to do with Justin's behavior."

"Yeah, it could be. He said the same thing."

"Maybe you could have a word with him," Kelly suggested.

I grunted in response and wondered how in the hell was I going to tell President Stark how to behave.

"Well?" she asked.

"Yeah, I'll figure something out."

CHAPTER 28 – FROG ANATOMY

"It's colder than a bullfrog's ball sack," Joker grumbled.

There was some light laughter at his comment. He was right. February arrived with a bluster of icy cold wind and the temperature plummeted into the single digits the entire first week. But, we'd had a brief warm spell with lots of sun, a false spring, and the ice had mostly melted before another cold front moved in. This cold snap was dry though, so that meant we could travel. I looked over at Joker and a small smile crossed my face.

"Did you know, there are some frogs that can freeze solid and when they thaw out, they come back to life?"

"How in the hell can they do that?" Joker asked.

"They have cryoprotectants in their blood," I said.

"What is that?" he asked.

"You mean, you don't know?" I asked. He smirked at me. "It's kind of like antifreeze. Someone like Doctor Kincaid can probably explain it better." I started to say more, but I was suddenly hit with a memory of several years ago, back when I was talking to the Allen family. We talked about zombies freezing solid and then coming back to life after they had thawed. I wondered if that black, oozing blood flowing through zombies had some kind of cryoprotectant. I made a mental note to either send an email or talk to Doctor Kincaid about it.

"The good thing about this below-freezing weather, any zeds we encounter will be moving too slow to be much of a threat," I said.

"Even those new zeds?" Sammy asked tentatively.

Joker gave him a light bop on the back of the head. "We'll find out, won't we," he said with a grin.

"Alright," Justin said. "Let's load up and move out."

We filed our mission plan the night before and exited the main gate at 0600 hours. The route was ninety-two miles, but in spite of the warm spell, there were still sporadic spots of black ice, so we proceeded carefully. As a result, it took four hours to reach Letterkenny Army Depot and we arrived at a few minutes before 1000 hours.

We'd been to Letterkenny a couple of other times. It was a combination of a storage, maintenance, modification, and demilitarization facility focusing mostly on missiles and ammunition. However, the place was also had a plethora of military vehicles, Humvees and MRAPS mostly, and parts for those vehicles. The first time we visited, it was devoid of any ammunition and there were only a dozen vehicles left. We could only get one vehicle running, so the next time we visited, we brought a tow truck.

There were twenty of us in six vehicles, including Sammy, which was going to be his first away mission. Three of the vehicles were tow trucks. Any vehicle we wanted, we were going to hook up and tow back. The plan was to find suitable vehicles to take back with us. We also had the semi and a deuce-and-a-half pulling a five-hundred-gallon tanker.

I drove the semi, with a trailer hooked up this time. We were going to load it up. Bob, Fred, and Sam were with me. There were some, Kelly included, who balked at the notion of Sammy coming along, but Fred and I talked it over. It was time to start treating him like a man and teaching him about these operations.

The deuce was being driven by the new guy, Troy the truck driver. He was a likeable, humorous man, but was given to long bouts of silence. He looked like the kind of guy who was a hundred pounds overweight, back before. He'd long since lost it, but he still had the look. In the debriefing, he told us he was from Kentucky but had mostly lived out of a semi as a long-haul trucker most of his adult life. His only living relative was his mother, who he'd found half eaten one day. Logan rode with him while Liam and Priss drove one of the tow trucks.

It was only ninety-two miles to the depot. The roads were still mostly intact, but we had to be mindful of the ice. After four hours of travel, we stopped in the middle of Coffey Avenue, with a snow-covered golf course on one side of the street and a large metal building on the other. We stared at it in puzzlement. The word "Letterkenny" was written in big block letters, and underneath it was a smaller inscription, "Supporting the Joint Warfighter." But, what puzzled us was some sloppily written words in black spray paint off to the side. More specifically, it was a poem. Someone, it sounded like Kirby Jenkins, decided to read it over the radio.

"To all of you politicians with your vanilla smiles and obsidian wit, you've turned this world into a pile of shit. Now the world's gone crazy, we're all barking at the moon, but one day, politician, you'll meet your doom."

"Holy zombie balls, I think it's a message for you, Senator," Joker said on the radio and roared in laughter.

"Out of all the people in this world who perished, some wiseass poet has survived," Bob grumbled. Clearly, he was not amused.

"They're just messing with you, Bob," I said. "They know you're the only politician who volunteers for these missions."

"Thank you, Zach," he said.

Justin's voice chimed in on the radio. "All Teams, this is Team One, rally around me," he said.

He had stopped in a large parking lot. The rest of us formed a defensive perimeter with our vehicles. Sammy grabbed the binoculars without having to be told to and started scanning our sector of fire.

"Nothing," he said after a minute of scanning.

"Alright, get on the radio to Captain Smithson," I said. "But, be sure to wait your turn. We're the second to the last team."

Sammy got on the radio and relayed the information. Other teams did the same, and then Justin gave the order to dismount. We did so and formed another perimeter of people around the vehicles.

"Get a drone up!" Justin shouted.

Kirby and Erin wasted no time. In fact, I think they'd already anticipated Justin's command and had a drone airborne within a minute.

As I watched the drone go airborne, my line of sight went to a series of utility poles. They were bare of wires. I made a mental note of it; if we were going to put people here, we had a lot of line work to do to restore power. As I shifted my focus back to the horizon, I caught sight of movement across an empty field from Coffey Avenue.

"Shit," I exclaimed under my breath and then spoke up. "Contact, nine o'clock!"

There was a large group of them, easily over a hundred. Two hundred, maybe. I hurriedly stuck my ear plugs in as I heard Justin ordering everyone back to their vehicles and to hold their fire until they got to within fifty yards.

I did not fire for the first minute. Instead, I watched and was pleased to see everyone had adhered to their training and were killing with controlled accuracy. We were mowing them down, and yet they continued coming toward us at a full run. I caught Fred looking at me out of the corner of his eye. I got the message and began shooting.

When the shooting was done, Justin gave the all clear and we exited our vehicles.

"Teams, give me an up!" he shouted. Each team replied in succession indicating nobody had been injured or killed. The drone confirmed there were no other hordes lurking nearby, but we still had two teams act as cover while the rest of us carefully inspected the zeds to ensure they were indeed dead. I deviated from the SOP and walked among the dead zeds, looking them over.

"How many?"

I looked up. It was Bob. He pointed around. "You're the quick counter, how many?"

"Two hundred and eleven," I answered and pointed. "Most of them are old school, but a few of them look fresh."

"Old school?" Bob asked.

"The ones who've been infected for a while." I pointed. "When their skin is blackened from the healed decomposition and it's all leathery looking, they've been infected for over a year. Old school."

"Ah," Bob replied in understanding.

"Holy hell," Flash muttered. He had walked up and stood there looking over the carnage. "Man, they stink. It don't ever get any better." He hocked up some phlegm and spit.

"Yep," I said.

"You know, I saw one of them turn around and run back down the road," Flash said. "I've never seen any of them do that before."

I glanced at Fred. "They're thinking again, to a small extent. Fight or flight, it's a primordial instinct."

"Damn," Flash said. "It won't be too long before they're back on Facebook."

I fought hard to hide a grin as Fred gave him a withering look.

Once we had cleared the area, we spent the rest of the day loading up equipment and vehicle parts. One of the nice things was that there were multiple buildings full of all kinds of goodies, including over a hundred unused tires that were the proper size for the MRAPS. We also found three MRAPS that looked virtually unused. The tires were flat, but that was no problem; we brought spares, and we knew the fuel lines would have to be flushed out before they could run properly, but that's why we brought the tow trucks.

When it was fifteen hundred hours, I walked over to Justin, who was in the middle of a conversation with the two Pittsburgh cops. The three of them stopped talking and the brothers fixed me with stares as I walked up.

"We need to make a decision on whether to stay the night or head back. The sun's been out all day, so a lot of ice has undoubtedly melted, but we're still looking at two hours of nighttime driving, and that means black ice."

Justin pointed at our vehicles. "Every one of them is crammed full. We can't haul anything else if we tried."

I glanced over at Fred, who gave one of his subtle nods.

It was decided. Unfortunately for us, there were others who felt otherwise.

CHAPTER 29 – CONTACT

I heard the bullet whiz by and strike the building behind me followed by the crack of a gunshot.

"Sniper!" I yelled. Everyone took cover. Joke ran and jumped in the Stryker before a second gunshot rang out.

"Contact!" he yelled out of the open hatch. "One o'clock, three subjects, about five hundred meters. They're crouching by a car. I see two long guns."

"Do you have a clear target?" Justin yelled back.

"Aye, sir!" Joker yelled.

"Light 'em up!"

Joker responded by firing the M2 machine gun in four, three-round bursts. A moment later, he stuck his head out of the hatch.

"Dead," he said simply.

"Give us a scan, Sergeant," Justin directed. "The rest of you, hold your positions."

Everyone had found cover after the first gunshot and stayed in place while Joker slowly rotated the turret, utilizing the Stryker's optics to find any additional threats. He worked it slowly, methodically, pausing once or twice to inspect something. The turret rotated around three complete times before Joker stuck his head out of the hatch.

"All clear," he said.

"Alright, everyone, mount up," Justin ordered. Everyone complied without comment. Once everyone was inside their vehicles, Justin got on the radio.

"All teams, follow me to phase line Sunset."

Once we arrived at phase line Sunset, which was at the intersection of Sunset Pike and Cumberland Highway, Justin directed everyone to stop and standby. He jumped out of the Stryker and ran back to our semi.

"Let's go look over who was trying to kill us," he said.

I looked at Fred, who nodded.

"Come on," he said to Sammy and then looked at Bob. "Stay with the semi and don't let anyone steal it."

Bob didn't like being relegated to wait in the truck, but Justin didn't care. We waited for Justin to jog down to Kirby and tell him to send an update to Mount Weather then he hustled back to us. The three of us jogged over and jumped into the Stryker. The three attackers, what was left of them, were lying on the side of Coffee Avenue beside an abandoned car.

"Alright, don't tell Kelly or Janet, but you need to see this," I said to Sammy.

While Joker manned the fifty, the rest of us got out and walked over to the bodies. The kinetic energy of the fifty caliber bullets all but obliterated them. One of them had attempted to hide behind the abandoned car, but it didn't work. Joker simply fired through the car.

"Wow," Sammy muttered.

"They made some tactical errors," I said. "Do you know what they were?"

"Um, they shouldn't have messed with us," Sammy said.

"Sure, but why not?"

"Um…"

"If they had performed a proper recon, they would have seen we were heavily armed, including an armored vehicle with an M2 heavy machine gun mounted on it."

"But, they waited until we were dismounted," Sammy contended.

"That they did, but how would you describe the sniper's accuracy?" I asked.

"It sucked."

Flash, who had joined us, chuckled. "Lucky for us," he said.

Fred had walked over to the mutilated body that used to be the sniper, crouched, and looked it over. He then picked up the rifle and inspected it thoughtfully, before standing.

"The stock is damaged, but the rest seems intact," he said. "I believe I can fix it." He then pointed. "This sniper was a young lady."

"How can you tell?" Flash asked.

Fred ignored him and picked up two other weapons; a semiautomatic handgun and a Ruger Mini-14. Once he collected them, he walked back to the Stryker and got in. It was his way of saying it was time to leave. Justin seemed to agree.

"Alright, I was kind of hoping to be able to identify them, or maybe they'd have a radio with them, but they don't. Let's get on the road."

We had identified shady areas of the roadways, which is where the black ice was hiding, so we were making good time heading back, until after the sun went down. We slowed our speed considerably then.

"Fred?" Sammy asked. Fred looked over at him. "How did you know that sniper was a young woman? I mean, her body was unrecognizable."

"Her lower torso was mostly intact," Fred replied. "First, she was wearing small women's shoes, and if you looked carefully, you would have seen her groin area. She was definitely a lady."

"I'm not sure I'd call her a lady," Bob said. "After all, she was trying to kill us."

"But, she was a terrible shot," Sammy said. "I can shoot better than that."

"Perhaps she hit everything she was shooting at," Fred said.

I looked at him sharply before focusing back on the road. Could it be true? Were those three people simply trying to scare us off? If that was what they were attempting, it was stupid and it cost them their lives. I often thought the apocalypse was a sort of a manifestation of Darwinian evolution in that it quickly killed off stupid people.

"I wonder if they had any people. You know, perhaps they were part of a larger group," Bob mused.

"If there are, and we come into contact with them, I doubt they'll understand our rationale for killing their friends," I said.

"Nope," Fred added.

"So, what do we do?" Sammy asked.

"What can you do?" I countered. "Should we have allowed those people to continue shooting at us? This is the way of the world now, Sammy. You have to make split-second decisions. It might not always be the correct decision, but when you're out here, all of your decisions must have the underlying principle of survival. Self-survival and the survival of your people."

"Um, okay," Sammy said.

"Let me make it short and simple. Someone was shooting at us, we perceived our lives were in jeopardy, and we reacted accordingly." I looked over at him pointedly. "Better to err on the side of caution."

Sammy nodded.

We rode south on I-81 in silence for a few miles. Fred and Bob crashed out in the sleeper while Sammy rode in front with me. At one point, he sighed. Rounding a slight bend in the interstate, our headlights washed over some abandoned cars on both sides.

"Let's play a game," I said and pointed.

"Look at the arrangement of those abandoned cars."

He looked out the window, wondering what I was talking about. "Do you see how they act as impediments? The cars are keeping us from spreading out, or even veering off of the interstate if we need to."

"We should clear all of them out," he said.

"Yeah, but in the meantime, I'm going to throw a hypothetical scenario at you. What if, it's only you driving down the road? You haven't been down this road before. As you travel along, you come upon some derelict cars all stacked together, blocking off the roadway. What do you do?"

"I stop immediately," he said.

"Why?"

"Because it might be an ambush."

"Good, but now you're stopped and you're stationary, which means what?"

"I'm an easy target," he said.

"Yep. So, what do you do?" I asked.

"Find an escape route. Back up and get out of there."

"Good," I said. "Now, I'm going to change it up a little. You're in a town scavenging. You're going to one of the roads and there is what appears to be an old multi-car pileup ahead of you, but you can see an opening. As you slow and wind your way through the opening, a woman suddenly steps out from behind a car, right in front of you. She's holding what appears to be a baby swaddled in a blanket. There is only one proper course of action. What do you do?"

"Slam on my brakes," he said.

"No," I responded harshly, causing Sammy to flinch. "Never slam on your brakes. Don't you see? It's an ambush."

"You mean, I should run her over?" he asked nervously.

"Hell-fucking-yes," I growled. "As soon as you stop, that little fake baby doll she's holding will be dropped and she'll be pointing a gun at you, and her friends will suddenly be surrounding you. If you're lucky, they'll only take your vehicle and everything in it."

I found myself reliving the memory of that time when I encountered the exact situation outside of a small community known as College Grove. I was driving my little Ford Ranger truck. The woman had been hiding behind a derelict car and stepped right in front of me. I instantly stomped on the gas. My little truck did not have a great deal of power. Nevertheless, the woman had no time to jump out of the way. I still remembered the front of my truck striking her with a painful thump and then watched as she went airborne. I remembered the look of horror on her face microseconds before it smacked and shattered my windshield.

"What is it, Zach?" Sammy asked.

I looked over at him and realized I was gripping the steering wheel tightly. "What?"

"Is something wrong?" he pressed.

"Oh, no. Why do you ask?"

"You kind of zoned out for a minute," he said.

"Oh, sorry, bud. I was just thinking."

"Did that happen to you once?" he tentatively asked.

I glanced over at him. "Sammy, you're a good man. You know right from wrong and you know the value of honor and integrity, but understand this; if you have to kill someone to save your own life or the life of someone you love, you do it and you don't apologize for it. Ever."

I took a deep breath. "This is a hard world, and you've got to be a hard man sometimes."

"Yes, sir," he said quietly.

We drove up to the front gate at 2200 hours and lined up at the decontamination station. We weren't sure the procedure was needed anymore, but since we had it in place and operational, we took no chances. We'd disassembled a car wash, one of those types that sprayed water only, no brushes, and reassembled it twenty yards from the main gate. It was heated, so there was no fear of freezing pipes.

We ran each vehicle through it. We had no chemicals anymore, but we substituted with scalding hot water. Each vehicle went through and then drove directly to the warehouse. Two of our bean counters, Lois and Norman Marnix, emerged from the main building with their computer tablets, whereupon they immediately began taking inventory as we unloaded the equipment. It took a couple of hours to unload and neatly stack everything. There wasn't any complaining, but it was obvious everyone was fatigued. Justin took pity.

"Alright, everyone. Let's head to the armory. If we have a hundred percent accountability, you'll be dismissed for the evening. We'll clean them up tomorrow."

There were some murmurs of appreciation at that statement. Even though Justin had let everyone off of the hook, I helped him check in weapons.

"We picked up some good stuff," I said as I helped him check in the weapons.

"Yes, we did. It was a successful mission, all things considered."

"Fred seems to think the girl wasn't trying to kill anyone, she was trying to scare us off," I said as I checked a serial number and put it in the appropriate slot on the rack.

Justin looked at me briefly in puzzlement. "That doesn't make any sense," he said.

"I know. If he's right, those people had no type of proper training. Makes you wonder how they managed to stay alive so long."

When the last person turned their weapon in, we locked up the armory and made our way to our suites.

"See you in the morning," I said.

"You too, brother."

CHAPTER 30 – MARCUS HOOK

February's weather stayed cold but dry, which allowed us to travel. I kissed Kelly and my kids before heading to the motor pool. We were going to be traveling in a Jeep Grand Cherokee, which was pulling a trailer. Ensign Lawrence Boner was going to be driving another Cherokee, both of which had 3-liter turbo-diesels in them. Riley and Little Joe rode with him, and the rest of them rode with me.

"Alright, has everyone gone to the restroom?" I asked while pointedly looking at Little Joe's children. "Once we get going, we're not stopping."

Nobody decided they better go, so I directed them to load up.

Two days ago, we sat down with Trader Joe and his family and discussed Marcus Hook.

"It was a relatively small township south of Philadelphia back before," I told them. "Mostly comprised of industry. The positives of it; they have a good operation set up. They have power and fuel, and the people who live there are a tight-knit, friendly group. They were all working class people, back before. Not a single politician among them," I said and winked at Bob, who smiled graciously.

"What are the negatives?" Joe asked.

"I'll be honest, the accommodations are a little on the spartan side. A lack of manpower is the main reason," I said. "On occasion, the zeds wander out of Philadelphia, and because the entire area is industry, there were a few factories that were not shut down properly and there've been ongoing problems with explosions, but that was mostly during the first year." I thought a moment. "There is a nuclear power plant nearby, but Roscoe said it was shut down properly and isn't a threat. Oh, I almost forgot, during the summer, they make treks to Atlantic City and frolic on the boardwalk. It's only eighty miles away."

"I bet it's filthy," Little Joe grumbled.

I remained quiet. I actually did not know what kind of shape Atlantic City was in. I'd never been there, but Melvin had. He said there was a brothel and a race track there. Somebody asked him what the women looked like. Melvin's response was, if you take all of the women at Mount Weather under the age of forty, found the ugliest one, she'd be a homecoming queen compared to those whores. I figured Boner wouldn't care and he'd go visit at the first opportunity.

It had taken a lot of talking and promises to get the Bristol people to agree to relocate to Marcus Hook. They reluctantly agreed, but only after Parvis told them staying at Mount Weather was not an option.

We finally agreed if they would stay at Marcus Hook, we would have a fortified and powered house waiting for them in September. Parvis and I met with a cacophony of resistance when we presented it at the next meeting. Their argument was we were under no obligation to cater to newcomers in this manner, but they were not yet aware of the Russians and that we were going to need as many personnel as we could get to fight this possible threat. President Stark approved our proposal without comment and moved on to the next topic. I met Joe and his family in the cafeteria after the meeting and told them.

The next recruitment pitch was to Ensign Lawrence Boner. It fell upon Bob Duckworth and myself. He was an easy sell. We told him we'd already discussed it with Roscoe Sidebottom and he was all in favor of Boner taking over the fledging naval operations. He only asked one question.

"And I only answer to Sidebottom, right?" he asked.

"And the president," Bob answered.

He agreed. We left immediately after breakfast.

"Tell me what you really think about this, Zach," Joe urged after we'd traveled forty miles while engaging in idle chatter about farming.

"I spoke with Johnny G on the radio last night and filled him in. He's the number two man, so they are expecting us. He assured me they'd have living quarters ready for all of you. I have no doubt you guys are going to be putting in hard work days, but you're used to that. Roscoe and Johnny G have all kinds of work projects going, much like us.

"There are only thirty people living there, and that includes six kids, so I imagine they are going to be welcoming you with open arms."

I thought about Riley. Sixteen of the twenty-four adults were single men. Seventeen if you included Boner. Unfortunately for Boner, I don't think there was a single woman available.

I looked in the sideview mirror. It looked like Boner was chatting it up, probably making a play for Riley. I can't say I blamed him. She was a good-looking woman. It was my understanding, learned through the Mount Weather gossip hotline, of which my lovely wife was a charter member, Riley had asked Logan to go with her, but he had politely declined. The rumor was, Logan had confided in his brother that he and Riley had a sexual encounter that did not go well. Liam promptly told his new girlfriend, Priss, who was also an active member of the gossip network.

I'd probably never learn the whole story, and although it was probably amusing, I didn't care. I had many other things on my mind, including getting them settled in Marcus Hook and convincing all of them to stay. It wasn't going to be easy. Marcus Hook was not a pristine place to live. It was an industrial town, back before, with little aesthetic scenery, and the apocalypse had not helped much.

As we drove down Philadelphia Pike, we saw the first signs of life in the form of a barricade. An old sign hung over the road welcoming people to Marcus Hook and a sign off to the side identified a big industrial complex as once belonging to Sunoco.

"Welcome to Marcus Hook," I said.

"Shit-hole of America," Abby added.

"And yet, it is the most important place in America at the moment," I said. "I want you all to consider something. A hundred years from now, the history books are going to be full of references about Marcus Hook and Mount Weather. A farmhouse in Bristol or rural Virginia won't even receive a mention. You don't realize it, but you'll be a part of history."

"Oh, boy," Abby muttered. I didn't say it, but her sour disposition was beginning to annoy me. Hell, if she didn't like it, she could always leave.

I could see two guards posted at the barricade as we approached. When they recognized me, both of them gave a big grin. I stopped and rolled down my window.

"Hello, guys," I said.

"Welcome back, Zach. Hello everyone," one of them said. He was a man in his forties who had a long, full beard and a few missing teeth. "You're right on time. Any troubles?"

"None whatsoever," I said. "I didn't even see a single zed."

"That's good news. Okay, all of them are waiting on you guys at the main building."

"I appreciate it," I said and drove forward, stopping at a concrete building with four Greek columns. "They converted this building to their base of operations and living facilities," I said. "It used to be the Marcus Hook Municipal Building. There are also houses back behind there on Green Street. One of them has been prepped for you guys to live in."

Roscoe and several others walked out of the front door as we parked and got out. Everyone was all smiles and gave Trader Joe's family a warm welcome. Raymond Easting was standing there as well. The two of us shook and then gave each other a warm embrace. He then shook hands with Boner, but no embrace.

"Come inside everyone," Roscoe said. "Lunch is almost ready."

I started to unload the trailer, which was full of supplies, but a man stopped me.

"No, sir," he admonished. "Go on in and have some lunch; me and Jimbo will take care of this."

"I appreciate it," I said and pointed at the trailer. "It's full of provisions, but I also brought a few jerry cans I was hoping to get filled."

He grinned. "Don't worry, I'll have them all filled before you leave."

I thanked him and walked inside. It had been a year since I'd been here. Back then, they only had a rudimentary cafeteria, and although they'd made some improvements, it was nowhere near the caliber of Mount Weather's cafeteria. They sat us all down at one of the tables and introductions were made. Roscoe and Johnny G paid extra attention to Joe senior.

"We can't tell you how happy we are that you're here," Roscoe said.

"Well, it's certainly going to be interesting," Joe replied.

"How many boats do you have?" Boner asked.

Johnny G's smile faltered slightly. "Two that are operational. We have others that are still floating, but we've not had the chance to ensure they're seaworthy."

Boner nodded thoughtfully. "Well, it's a good thing I'm here then," he said smugly and glanced at Riley, who seemed not to be paying attention.

We talked through lunch, and after, Roscoe and Johnny G gave the grand tour, ending at a park on the waterfront.

"There you have it," Roscoe said. "We have a large area and a lot of potential, but we probably need a hundred more people to make it a reality."

"There is a lot of work to be done here," Joe senior mused.

"Yes, there is," Roscoe replied.

Joe seemed to ponder this for a moment and then looked at Little Joe. "The Fitzgerald's have never backed down from hard work, isn't that right, son?"

"Damn right," Little Joe replied, but not with much eagerness. The others remained silent. Finally, Ned raised his hand.

"Yes, sir?" Roscoe asked.

"I only saw two greenhouses," he said questioningly.

"Zach said you three are horticulturists, is that right?" he asked. Ned nodded.

"We have plans of creating additional greenhouses, and we have most of the materials, but we haven't had time to build them," Roscoe said. "Now that you three are here, we'll make it a priority. In fact, I think we can start on it immediately, right, Johnny?"

"Absolutely," Johnny G said. "If you don't mind working in the cold, we'll start on one tomorrow morning."

"You know we're only here until September, correct?" Joe asked as he glanced at me. "We have been promised a fortified farmhouse back near Mount Weather."

"That is my understanding," Roscoe said. "I hope by the time September rolls around you people will consider this home." He gestured around. "We all look a little rough around the edges, I'll grant you that, but we're good people."

"Perhaps we will," Joe said without much conviction, but he smiled agreeably.

"I think your Bristol people are not happy to be here," Raymond said to me.

After the grand tour, all of us went back to the municipal building, chatted, went over the operations, had dinner, and then Joe and his family excused themselves to retire to their new house for the evening.

"They can always leave, I suppose," Johnny G said, and looked over at Boner. "What about you?"

Boner shrugged apathetically. "I'm good, for now. I can get you squared away on boats and teach a few of you how to navigate on the waterways, but unless you can get some women or some friendly sheep, I don't know how long I can hold out."

Johnny G laughed. "You're preaching to the choir, brother. I'll tell you what, once we get some things done, let's get on one of those boats and wander around. Maybe we'll find some mermaids."

Boner actually chuckled, which I took as a good sign.

"But, I'm afraid those other people are going to come up to us one day soon and tell us they've had enough."

"If it comes to that, you'll need to loan them a vehicle," I said.

"Bullshit," Johnny G retorted.

"They left their horses with us, so they don't have any means of transportation. I'll see to it you get a replacement vehicle."

Johnny G emitted a long sigh. "I know you will, Zach. I'm just a little frustrated. We welcomed them with open arms and they acted like this was the last place they wanted to be."

I caught myself from letting out my own sigh and looked over at Boner. "Did they say anything during the ride over here?" I asked.

He shrugged. "Not much. When we drove up, the first word out of Riley's mouth was, ugh." He looked pointedly at Roscoe and Johnny G. "No offense, but this place doesn't hold a candle to Mount Weather."

"None taken," Johnny G replied. "There were several places we all could have landed that were nicer than Marcus Hook, but Roscoe had a vision. Oil has powered this world for over a hundred years, and now it's more valuable than gold. We want fishing boats, sure, but we also want a tanker operational. Imagine, if you will, having a tanker going up and down the eastern seaboard. We'll be able to trade for all kinds of commodities."

"You'll need an escort ship," Boner said. "Like a patrol boat, or something similar. Otherwise, I foresee someone deciding they'll just take it from us by force."

"Sounds like a job for a naval officer," Johnny G said with a grin.

Ensign Lawrence Boner nodded at the compliment.

"Okay, getting back to the Bristol people," Roscoe said.

"I'll stay here another month and work with them," Raymond said. "They seem like reasonable people, they're just out of their element."

Roscoe leaned back in his chair. "It is what it is, I guess." He let out a long yawn. "It's past my bedtime," he said, slid his chair back and stood. Johnny G did as well.

"Come on, you two, I'll show you to your rooms."

I followed and found all of my gear lying on the bed, including my rifle and machete. The room might have been a coat room at one time, or maybe a one-person office. It was really small, but that was okay. There was heat and clean sheets on the bed. I moved my stuff, stripped and was asleep before I knew it.

I was up at my usual time the next morning. They had no tea, even though I knew we'd given them plenty of ginseng. Breakfast consisted of two hardboiled eggs and three slices of hard bread.

Nope, this place was definitely not Mount Weather, but I anticipated it getting better, especially since we'd given Ned several different types of seeds he could grow in their new greenhouses.

After breakfast, I made my rounds, saying goodbye to everyone. Jimbo informed me the truck was gassed up and ready to go, and he'd filled all of the jerry cans. Roscoe practically begged me to stay for a day or two, but I told him I needed to get back on the road while the weather permitted.

When I walked outside to my SUV, the engine was running and Riley was sitting in the passenger seat. I paused in confusion. I heard someone behind me clearing their throat. I turned to see both Joes.

"Zach, I must ask this favor of you," Joe said.

"I assume you want me to take Riley back to Mount Weather," I said.

"It would mean a lot to her. She is convinced she would be unhappy here."

Little Joe leaned forward. "She thinks all of the dudes here are," he paused and looked at his dad. "Unappealing. I think that's the word she used. Or, maybe it was butt ugly. Not sure."

Raymond was standing off to the side, and when I looked over, he shrugged and motioned me off to the side.

"Whatever you decide," he said. "But if we make her stay here, I don't think it'll work. The rest of them I can work with. She's another story. When I tried to talk to her, she told me to fuck off and rolled up the window."

I grunted. It sounded like Riley. I thought it over. The fact was, it was a no-brainer. We had a shortage of single women back at Weather, and I could sell her marksmanship skills as a needed asset, even though I'd never seen her shoot.

"Okay. You explain it to Roscoe," I said to Raymond. We gave each other a bro hug and I shook hands with the rest of them.

"Alright, I'm getting out of here," I said, already wondering what Kelly was going to think when I showed up back at Weather with Riley in tow.

"Thanks, Zach," Joe senior said. "We'll see you in September."

"Oh, I'll be around some when the weather warms up," I said and glanced at Riley. "Okay, I better get going."

"Did Dad explain?" Riley asked when I got in.

"Yeah, pretty much. You don't like it here." I waved again at everyone, put the truck in gear, and took off.

"Not at all, and none of the men here do anything for me."

"What about Boner – I mean Lawrence? I thought you two were hitting it off?"

She scoffed. "All he did the whole trip was talk about himself."

"Oh."

"Is anyone going to be pissed?" she asked.

"No, I'll take care of it," I said. "But, you need to stop being so preoccupied with this manhunt quest."

"Easy for you to say," she said. "You have someone. I haven't been laid in over a year."

I glanced at her, but did not respond.

Roscoe had found a good alternate route on fairly rural roads which avoided the big cities. It added several miles to the trip, but it worked. For the first thirty minutes, we drove in silence before Riley spoke.

"Why did you and Kelly decide to have another kid?" she asked. "You already have two."

"Frederick and Macie are from my first wife," I said. "Kelly decided her biological clock was ticking and she wanted to have one before she got old and regretted it."

"Oh," she replied, and after a minute spoke again. "You were married before?"

"Yeah," I replied. I gave her the Reader's Digest version of how I met, fell in love with, and married Julie. I then told her of the events leading up to her death, the confinement of my kids and myself, and the ultimate reunion. I finished by telling her how Kelly and I ended up falling in love. I left out a lot of the more intimate details though.

"Wow, you've been through a lot," she said. "So, you and Kelly started off as friends with benefits?"

I glanced over at her. Like I'd observed earlier, she was blunt. "I'm not sure I'd describe it like that."

"How else would you look at it? You were fucking her, but you weren't in love with her, at least, not at first. Isn't that what you said?"

"That's true, but I don't need our relationship dissected. We're happy together, that's what counts."

"Well, I envy you two," she said after a moment. "I don't seem to have any luck at all."

"What happened to the husband?" I asked.

"His name was Ben. There wasn't any preacher or judge to marry us, so we had our own private little ceremony. He was a lot older than me, but that didn't matter. We loved each other. One day, a few of us rode into downtown Bristol on bicycles to scavenge. We'd done it dozens of times before with no problems."

"I take it there are still a lot of zeds there?"

She shrugged. "They used to blindly chase us, but they started hiding, so I don't really know how many are left. That's what happened to Ben. We'd split up and took some buildings we'd been in before. Three of them jumped him. By the time we got to him, it was too late. That was over a year ago and I haven't been laid since."

I chuckled. "Okay, I've got to ask, what happened between you and Logan?"

She groaned. "Are you sure you want to know?"

I backtracked quickly. "I'm sorry, I'm prying. It's none of my business."

She only waited a moment. "He had a premature ejaculation."

Before I could stop myself, I burst out in laughter.

"I know, right?" she said. "I couldn't decide if I was into him or not, but he was laying it on hot and heavy. It happened that night we went to the movie. We'd been drinking that god-awful moonshine, and as soon as the lights went down, he started getting handsy. I didn't mind though, and after the movie was over, he suggested we go back to his room. His brother was gone, so we started getting frisky. As soon as I touched him, he exploded. Then it got awkward."

"Yeah, I bet," I said.

"Has that ever happened to you?" she asked.

"Uh, no." I wasn't lying.

"He apologized and said it'd been a long time since he'd been with a woman. But, no matter what I tried, he couldn't get it up again. The next morning at breakfast, he wouldn't even look at me."

"Oh. Ouch," I said. It was the only response I could come up with. "I'm sure he was embarrassed. When we get back, you should go talk to him," I suggested.

Riley shook her head. "I don't know. I mean, he's nice enough, and he's buff, but he doesn't seem that smart. My husband owned several businesses and was rich as everything. He was really smart."

I guess that's why she said she didn't mind older men back when they first arrived at Weather. I wondered what her father thought about that.

"There are other single men back at Mount Weather," I said. "For example, there's Flash and Slim. Both of them are decent guys about your age. Both of them are tall and lanky and they act a lot alike. They could pass for brothers, except for one is black and the other is white. And, there's a group of eight or nine people living..." I stopped talking and slammed on the brakes.

Riley looked out and gasped. "Oh, shit."

CHAPTER 31 – THE HORDE

I don't know where they came from. Out of Baltimore or D.C., maybe. I hurriedly put the SUV in park and killed the engine.

"Why'd you do that?" Riley asked.

"So, they won't hear the engine," I said.

We were currently on Conowingo Road near an old Harley Davidson dealership. I think the only thing that kept them from spotting us immediately was eight or nine abandoned cars on the side of the road. I'd stopped a few feet behind one of them and it helped us blend in.

"There's a lot of them," Riley whispered.

"Yeah, several hundred," I whispered back. I slowly reclined my seat until I could barely see over the dashboard. Riley did the same.

"What now?" she whispered.

"If they don't spot us, we wait until they walk off, and then go home," I said.

"And, if they spot us?"

"That's a good question. We've driven over them before. Sometimes it works, sometimes you get hung up on them. I've seen it happen, and I'm starting to believe they will sometimes intentionally get themselves hung up around the wheels so their buddies have a better chance to get at us."

"That would suck," she said. "I thought they didn't travel when it's really cold."

"They don't, normally. They're either starving and in search of food or something has displaced them."

We spoke some more in whispers until they got to within thirty feet. As quietly as I could, I lowered my seat back all the way and Riley followed suit. I looked over at Riley, who had come up with her handgun.

"We don't have enough ammo to kill them all," I warned. It was true. I had two hundred rounds for my assault rifle and four magazines for my 45. It wasn't enough.

She nodded, but I could see the growing concern on her face. I hoped they would walk past without spotting us, but no luck. One of them looked over, saw me, and attacked our SUV with a rabid aggression. That set off the rest of them. They surrounded the SUV and attacked in a rage. They were actually ramming the SUV and trying to claw their way in.

"I should've made a U-turn and got the hell out of here when we had the chance," I said. No need for whispering now.

"Why didn't you?" Riley asked.

"I wanted to get back home before dark, so I took a chance. Sorry, it was stupid of me."

One of them slapped the passenger door, causing Riley to jump.

"Don't worry, I put the caging on myself. They can't get to us," I said, referring to the heavy caging material that covered every window. It hindered visibility a little when driving, but it was well worth it. Right now was a good example.

"Well, what the hell are we going to do then? Sit here all day?" she asked.

"That's exactly what we're going to do," I said. When I looked at her, I could see she was getting frantic.

"Let me explain. If we start shooting, we'll undoubtedly run out of ammo and the noise may attract other zeds in the area. If we try to drive off right now, there's a possibility we'll get a few hung up in the wheel wells."

"Is there a third option?" she asked.

"I think so. We're going to sit here until nightfall and wait for it to get really good and cold. Last night, it got down to four degrees in Marcus Hook. Now, granted, it's on the waterfront, but rest assured, once the sun goes down, it'll get down into the single digits here."

I reached into the backseat where there were a couple of wool blankets. I handed her one.

"Alright, it's going to get cold for us too, but those zeds are going to freeze up. Then, we're going to start up the car and slowly drive over them. They'll be frozen and all they'll do is fall to the ground."

"We can run the engine and keep warm, can't we?" she asked.

I pointed. "See the ones on the hood? They're keeping warm from the residual engine heat. We've got to let them freeze too."

"Do you think it will work?" she asked after a moment.

"I hope so. I've done it before, but I had a four-by-four truck with big off-road tires, and then another time I was in an armored military vehicle." I waved a hand at the Cherokee. "This doesn't have as much ground clearance or big redneck tires, so, we'll see. I think that's why it's imperative we make sure they're good and frozen, so they don't intentionally get themselves tangled up."

"I hope you're right," she said.

"Me too."

We sat there for the next four hours. It was difficult to carry on a conversation with all of the ravenous zeds snarling, slapping, head-butting, and clawing at the metal screens, trying in vain to pull them off. Riley tried to nap, but the zeds wouldn't allow it. She finally sat up and twisted around in her seat, looking at the zeds. I could tell it was getting to her, so I tried to get her talking.

"Tell me about your husband. Ben was his name, right?"

"Yeah," she said. "He was a lot older than me, but he was handsome, and kind, and treated me wonderfully. Back before, he was financially well off and had a two-hundred-acre farm. That's where we lived."

"Sounds like he was a good man," I said.

"He was a wonderful man."

One of the zeds suddenly slapped the roof of the Jeep, causing us both to flinch.

"You know, one or both of us are going to need to answer the call of nature at some point," she said.

"Do you have to go?" I asked.

"Not yet. You?"

"Not yet." I'd been casually watching the zeds until it got too dark, and then I listened to their antics. It was then I noticed something.

"I think they're freezing up," I said. "They don't seem to be attacking the car with as much aggression anymore."

"Yeah," Riley said after listening a moment. "They've settled down. Are you sure they're frozen?"

"I think so. I know I'm colder than a bullfrog's ball sack right about now."

Riley giggled before she could help herself.

"I believe that's the first time I've ever heard you laugh," I said. "We don't know each other all that well, do we?"

"I guess not, but I like talking to you," she said. "I'd never tell anyone about what happened with Logan, but you're different."

"Thanks, I guess," I said.

"I mean, I know Kelly, so I feel comfortable around you."

"Yeah, that makes sense," I said.

"How much longer?" she asked. "My ball sack is freezing too."

I laughed. "Let's go ahead and try it."

Only a couple of them tried to attack the Jeep when I started it, the rest were too lethargic, which was a good sign.

"Okay, while we've been sitting here, I've thought about the best way to do this, let's put it to the test."

I turned the headlights on and watched them. They gave me some dirty looks, well, I mean, zeds don't give warm smiles, but that was about it. I backed up, knocking a few of them down. They didn't get up, so I continued backing, hearing the satisfying crunch of bones as I rolled over them. It would have been nice to back over all of them, but I had that trailer attached, so I put it in drive, jerked it forward for a few feet, and then slammed on the brakes. The ones on top of the hood slid off. Before they could stand, I ran over them. I then continued forward at a slow roll, knocking them over them easily.

"It's working," Riley said.

"Yeah, seems to be," I said and continued forward. They were all crowded together, so it did not take long before we were free of them. I sped up, but only a little, and put distance between us and them. I kept an eye on my rearview mirror and the trailer looked different.

"Hey, crawl into the back and look at the trailer. I think we have an unwanted passenger."

Riley did so and I watched her in the mirror.

"Yep," she said. "One of them is holding on for dear life."

I slowed to a stop and looked around. We were in a rather rural area, and with the exception of the headlights, it was pitch black. I grabbed my machete and got out. Riley got out as well with her handgun.

"Watch my back," I directed and approached the trailer.

The zed appeared to be a teenage boy. He was on the top of the trailer and as we drove along, the wind chill seemed to have frozen him into a death grip. I stood on the trailer hitch and gave the top of his head a good, solid chop. That put him out of commission, but it was hard as hell pulling him off. I finally chopped some of his fingers off, and with a little effort, managed to pull him off. He dropped to the ground with a thud. I hurriedly walked around the trailer and Jeep to make sure there were no other problems before motioning for Riley to get back in.

"Not yet," she said. "I've got to pee."

I agreed. She took one side of the SUV and I took the other side. We were on the road a moment later.

"I used to be more tactically minded, but I'm getting sloppy," I said.

"Like how?" Riley asked.

"First, before we even left, I should have gone over every contingency plan with you. For instance, if I had gotten killed just now, what would you have done?"

"I guess I would have driven back to Hook, I have no idea how to get back to Weather."

"Exactly," I said and pointed at some red spray paint in the road. "I'd like to take credit, but it was Roscoe's idea. He's painted a marker every mile. The H stands for Marcus Hook, and the W is for Mount Weather."

"Oh, and the arrows give the direction for each," she said in understanding.

"Yes. It's not a straight shot, there are several turns you have to make, but every intersection is clearly marked."

"Okay."

"Now, I also should have thought about what my reaction was going to be if I suddenly drove up on a horde. I honestly did not believe we'd see any in this cold weather, but it just goes to show you they're hard to predict these days."

"What should you have done?"

"The safest course of action would've been to beat it back to Hook and come back with people and guns."

"It worked out though," Riley said.

"Yes, it did," I agreed. "It's so cold now, I think we'll be alright if we encounter another horde. By the way, did you notice anything while we were outside peeing?"

She looked at me in the dark and was silent for several seconds, and then she gasped. "I smelled smoke."

"Yeah, I did too," I said. "I thought it was my imagination, but it was definitely wood smoke. There was somebody nearby. We don't have a record of any survivors living in this area, so it's something we'll need to check out later."

"How do you do that?" she asked.

"We'll send out a scout team. People are paranoid these days, but our teams have gotten pretty good about making contact with survivors without any bloodshed."

We continued talking and finally arrived at the main gate well after midnight. Surprisingly, Fred was inside the guardhouse.

"I was about to come looking for you," he said and then glanced at Riley. "Everything okay?"

"We ran into a horde," I said and quickly explained. He walked over and looked the Jeep over.

"They've dented and scratched the hell out of it. Jorge will be upset," he mused. "Hard to tell if there's any undercarriage damage."

"Nobody needs to be touching it," I said. "We'll spray it down tomorrow and then inspect it."

Fred nodded and looked over at Riley. "Welcome back to Mount Weather."

"Thanks. I didn't want to stay at that place and Zach said I could come back."

"Well, that's mighty nice of him," he said. "Let's go inside."

We walked Riley to the dorms. "Get some sleep and we'll see you at breakfast," I said.

"What happens next?" she asked.

"I'm expected to meet with the president after breakfast and update him on the status of Marcus Hook."

"Will he kick me out?" she asked.

"I wouldn't worry about that. After all, he's well aware we have a shortage of single women around here. But, don't be surprised if Lydia has a work assignment waiting for you after breakfast."

She gave a slight scoff. "Yeah, I have no doubt." She looked inside the dorm. "It looks like I've got the place to myself," she said. "Okay, good night."

Fred walked with me back to my room.

"She was giving you the eye a little bit," he said.

"It's not like that," I said. "She didn't like it there and talked her dad into asking me to bring her back here."

Fred had no response, and soon we were standing in front of the door to my suite.

"Now I get to explain to my lovely wife what I was doing for the last twelve hours alone with a woman on a trip that only takes four hours."

Fred grunted. "Good luck with that. See you in the morning."

I nodded and walked in my suite.

"Honey, I'm home," I whispered.

CHAPTER 32 – GRACE'S SECRET

"Anything?" Fred asked as I scanned the pictures. The three of us, Fred, Sammy, and our faithful companion, Zoe, were out riding our string of trail cameras. It goes without saying it was cold as all get out. We were used to it though and had dressed appropriately.

"Looks like four zeds. They're wandering around this area." I looked closer at one of the pictures. It was surprisingly clear. "Females. Humph."

"Why are we putting cameras out here?" Sammy asked.

I started to answer, but stopped myself. Fred seemed not to be paying any attention, but I knew he was listening as he scanned for threats.

"Alright, Mister Sam, I think you need to answer your own question. Why do *you* think we put these cameras out here?"

Sammy looked at me in puzzlement as he bit his lip in puzzlement.

"Think it through," I suggested.

"Um, to watch out for zeds?" he said tentatively.

"That's one reason. We want to monitor zombie movement for what reason?" I asked.

"So, they won't be sneaking up on us?"

"Sure, that's part of it. Right now, we're not seeing large hordes in this area, but that doesn't mean it'll always be like that. What if we download some pictures that are full of zombies?"

"We'd hunt them down, right?"

"Yes," I said. "Okay, what are some other reasons?"

He looked to Fred for a hint, but Fred was having none of it and continued staring down the road.

"Well, I guess we want to watch out for people too," he finally said.

"That's a good guess. Historically, strong governments always have strong intelligence gathering processes. This is just a small part. If we download photos and we start seeing people and vehicles we don't recognize, what do we do?"

"We find out who they are and what they're up to," he said with confidence.

"Yes, correct," I said. "You're getting the hang of this. Fred and I want you to learn all of this forward and backward, okay?"

Sam nodded. He and I looked at the photos. All we had were a bunch of pictures of deer and coyotes, but, the last two still photos were the four female zombies.

We watched as Sammy replaced the data card in the camera and put fresh batteries in it. Fred waited for him to finish before speaking

"Remember, intelligence gathering is always a necessity," he said. "We're not spying on people because we're nosy, we spy to make sure nobody's pulling shenanigans on us. And, by the way, the locations of the cameras are a secret, right? You don't even tell your girlfriend where they are."

"Yes, sir," he replied.

"All's quiet," Fred said, and then gave me a slight nod. There was an issue we needed to address, and it could only be done with a man-to-man talk with young Sam Hunter.

"Speaking of your girlfriend, how's it going with her?" I asked. "What's her name, Serena, isn't it?"

Sam gave a nervous smile. "Serena Abbott."

"Yeah, that's it. Serena's mom is Susan Abbott. She was Senator Polacek's aide at one time. I believe she's a little upset with the two of you at the moment, would I be right?"

Sammy dropped his head. "Yes, sir. How did you find out?"

"Because Susan went to Kelly, and Kelly came to me, and I thought I'd discuss it with Fred before talking to you."

"I guess everybody knows now," he lamented, his head still hanging. A couple of nights ago, Susan had caught her daughter and Sammy having sex. She reacted about how you'd expect a protective mother to react and chased Sammy out of their room while he was still in his underwear.

"I don't know if everyone knows, but Serena's mom is definitely not pleased."

"It's not like we're the only ones around here doing it," Sam said defensively.

"I'm sure you're right," I answered. "But, let's concentrate on you and Serena. Are you two practicing safe sex?"

I waited for an answer, but did not get one. I pushed on.

"Are either of you sleeping with other people?"

"No," Sam answered quickly, his head snapping up. "We love each other."

"Are you ready to get married and become a father?" I asked. I gestured at Fred. "You know, your mentor over there is an old-fashioned Christian man. He'd be extremely upset if you got Serena pregnant and then didn't marry her."

Sam worked his mouth but did not answer.

"Your reluctance to answer indicates you're not ready."

"No, it's not that," Sam said.

"Is it because you haven't thought this through?" I didn't wait this time for him to answer. "No, you haven't. This is why we're concerned. We don't want you to get entangled in a mess. Let me ask you this, what does Serena think about it? Have you spoken to her since you two got caught?"

"Not really," he admitted.

I gave a small smile. "Well, you're in luck, because after dinner, Susan and Kelly have decided to sit you two down and talk about the birds and the bees."

Sammy's face paled. My inclination was to chuckle at his discomfort, but I managed to keep a serious expression.

"So, think about what you are going to say and what your long-term intentions are with Serena. It's extremely important."

He looked up. "Why?"

"Because, if her mother says the two of you can't see each other anymore, that'll be the end of it."

A mixture of anger and fear quickly came over his face. "She can't do that," he cried.

"Yes, she can," I said. "Don't think for a minute she can't. So, think that one over when you talk to her this evening."

"Why?" he asked with a little bit of defiance in his voice.

"Because, you're still a kid, Sam," I explained.

"But you weren't any older than me when you and Julie were together," he contended.

"That's true," I said. "But, this isn't Nolensville. This is Mount Weather, a structured society, and a structured society has mores, you know what those are, right?"

"Umm," he said.

"Mores are the customs and rules of a society."

"I know that," he said glumly.

"So, here's how this goes. If Serena's mom doesn't want the two of you to see each other anymore, that's the end of it. Now, I know how it will go. You two will defy that order and continue to see each other on the sly. Do you know what'll happen then?"

He looked at me but didn't answer.

"I can't simply say, sorry Susan, kids will be kids. We'll have to send you away. Put you up with a family in one of the nearby communities or move you to Fort Detrick. You think about that."

Sam wanted to argue. He looked over to Fred for help. A highly spirited debate ensued. It went something like this —

"Let's ride," Fred said.

That was the end of the discussion.

Fred led and followed tracks that were all but invisible to me. We only went a short distance to an old, dilapidated barn located five hundred yards east of Fred's future house. At Fred's signal, we stopped the horses fifty yards out, tethered them, and then silently converged on the barn. We approached the opening where the barn door used to be and separated to each side, weapons at the ready. I looked at Fred who gave a micro.

I was eager to kill some zeds and fully expected them to put up a fight. However, I was not expecting four pitiful-looking zombies who used to be women, sitting on the cold ground in the corner, huddled together and clinging to each other in sheer terror.

The oldest one looked like she was in her fifties, the youngest was a teenager. Judging from the amount of blackened scar tissue, I guess they'd been infected for at least a couple of years, maybe longer. There were the remains of birds and rodents piled to one side.

I glanced at Fred. "They're scared to death."

He did not even bother with a micro nod this time. Instead, he holstered his pistol, walked closer, and squatted down in front of them. A regular zed would have attacked immediately. These four continued to cower in fear. After a moment, he spoke.

"I believe they are going to need some blankets and maybe some raw meat to eat."

"You're kidding, right?" I asked.

We ended our morning ride with a full-out run for the last mile. It was fun and invigorating, although my face was numb by the time we got back to the horse barn.

"What are you going to do with those zombie women, Fred?" Sam asked as we walked the horses around the perimeter to cool them down.

"Those girls," he said. "Can you imagine the suffering they've gone through?"

I noted he referred to them as girls instead of zeds. "You're feeling compassion," I said. "Do you think they're capable of the same emotion?"

"They feel fear," he replied. "Fear is an emotion, right?"

We rode into the barn before I responded. "You're going to start caring for them, aren't you?"

"Thinking about it," he replied.

Kelly and I filled the role of Sammy's surrogate parents and met with Susan Abbott after dinner. It was almost comical. I mean, Susan was all upset and ranted on in mock outrage about the defilement committed upon her sweet innocent little girl. Serena sat in a chair and if she could have shrunk up and disappeared, she certainly would have. Sam sat staring at his lap, in which he held his hands tightly.

Honestly, I wasn't all that concerned, although I did not say it out loud. When Susan was through with her diatribe, I reminded her that the two of them had been sweet on each other since both were eleven years old. Susan dramatically voiced her concern about an unwanted pregnancy and sexually transmitted diseases. Sammy turned red when I told her he was just as much a virgin as her little girl when they did the deed and there was no possible way he had an STD. The pregnancy issue was another matter, and frankly, it was the only thing Kelly and I were concerned about. In the end, she gave in and said the two of them could continue seeing each other, but only when chaperoned.

We'd gotten the kids put down and were lying in bed snuggling when I told her about the zombie women.

"And you two didn't kill them?" Kelly asked in surprise.

"It's hard to explain, but they looked downright pitiful. I probably should have killed them outright, but there was something about them sitting there, cowering in fear, it was almost unnerving."

"What was Fred doing?" she asked.

"About what I was doing. He's the one who said we should bring them food and blankets."

"Fred said that?"

"Yep."

Our conversation was interrupted by a soft knocking at the door. I looked over at Kelly.

"Are you expecting anyone?" I asked.

She shook her head. "Maybe Susan isn't through expressing her moral outrage."

I got up, put some jeans on, got a handgun out of my lockbox, and peeked out of the door. It was Grace.

"Oh, hey," I said and opened the door. When she saw my naked chest, she immediately turned beet red and fixated on the floor.

"Uh, hi, Zach. Can I come in?" she asked and then hastened a glance up and down the hall.

"Yeah sure," I said and motioned her inside. She clutched her laptop tightly to her chest and walked in. She was notoriously shy when I first met her and even though she was in her late-twenties now, the shyness was still there.

"Hang on, I'll be right back," I said and hurried into the bedroom.

"What's Grace doing here?" Kelly whispered.

"I'm not sure," I said as I put a T-shirt on and locked up my handgun. "She has her laptop, so it may be work-related."

"She always has her laptop," Kelly huffed. "Maybe she wants to show you some pictures of her."

"Yeah, right," I replied with a chuckle. Everyone knew she had a crush on Melvin. Hell, even her twin brother had a crush on Melvin. "Are you coming out?"

She adjusted her head on her pillow and closed her eyes. "Nope, if your unborn child will allow it, I'm going to try to sleep."

I nodded in understanding, gave her a kiss, and closed the door behind me.

I motioned for Grace to sit on the couch and I sat on the opposite end. "So, what's up?"

She cast a quick glance at me. "I'm sorry for coming over so late. I've been worrying over this for hours and I couldn't sleep."

"Worrying over what?" I asked.

She fretted a moment and gave her laptop another squeeze with her slender arms. "I have something to show you."

"Um, okay."

"I found it a while ago. I wasn't sure what to do," she said, opened her laptop, punched a few buttons, and handed it over to me.

I read over the first couple of paragraphs and looked up. She was having a hard time maintaining eye contact.

"Why did you wait so long to show this to me?" I asked.

"I was afraid," she said, and it looked like she might start crying.

Grace was a sweet, sensitive woman who was perpetually afraid of offending anyone, and the tone in my voice probably made her think I was upset with her. I'd suspected for a while both her and her brother had some form of autism, but I never asked and it was never discussed.

"It's okay," I said. "You brought it to me, that's what counts."

I spent the rest of the night reading approximately a thousand pages of documents and emails, stopping only long enough to get a glass of water. Grace watched me in silence for the first hour before stretching out on the couch, pulling Macie's baby blanket over her, and falling asleep.

When I had approached Grace about Fosswell's password, she'd gone a step further and hacked the general's account and the doctors' accounts. A lot of it was mundane, but there were also some interesting documents.

Kelly walked in the next morning, and saw me on one end of the couch and Grace curled up in a ball on the other end.

"Must have been important," she said as she bent down and kissed me on the head. She paused a moment, reading the document on the screen.

"I'll get the kids ready," she said.

I nodded gratefully and closed the laptop before gently nudging Grace. Her eyes opened in fright momentarily, until she recognized me. She then smiled shyly and sat up.

"What time is it?" she asked.

"Almost six," I said.

She looked at me in surprise for a moment before stretching and rubbing her eyes. "Have you been up all night?"

"Yes, I wanted to read it all."

"What do you think?" she asked.

"Who else knows about this?" I asked, ignoring her question.

"Only Garret."

"What about your father?"

She shook her head slowly. I understood. The verbiage of some of those emails could be interpreted in a couple of ways, some of which implied not only his knowledge, but also his complicity.

"Alright, I understand," I said and handed her laptop back to her. "Let's keep this between us. I want to think it over and then we'll talk about it later."

"Zach, I'm scared," she said.

"Don't worry, we're going to figure this out."

She looked at me, the worry in her face plain to see, but she gave me a tentative nod and left a moment later.

Little Frederick came running out of the bathroom, freshly scrubbed, and wearing nothing but underwear with SpongeBob and SquarePants on them.

"I'm hungry, Daddy," he said.

"Me too. Let's get some clothes on you and we'll go to breakfast."

I helped pick out some clothes for him, although, at seven years old, he did not need help to get dressed anymore. However, Macie was six and she still loved being doted on.

"It must have been important if it kept you up all night," Kelly said as she brushed Macie's hair.

"Yeah," I said without elaborating.

Kelly gave me a questioning gaze, but didn't push it. I was going to tell her everything, but not yet. No, this information was too sensitive. If Kelly mentioned something to someone in a casual conversation, it would spread like, well, like wildfire.

No, I couldn't tell her. Not yet. I loved Kelly dearly, but she was a social person and liked to talk. Nope, there was only one person I knew I could share this secret in confidence and he wouldn't tell a soul. That's because the old cuss didn't hardly talk to anyone anyway.

CHAPTER 33 – FRED'S ADVICE

There were the usual conversations at breakfast, and after we'd finished, I used a slight head motion to lure Fred out of the cafeteria. We took Zoe with us and let her run off some steam before we went to the horse barn. When we walked in, I checked out each individual stall to ensure we were alone. Fred watched with his usual stoic bearing. He had a couple of folding chairs in the far corner where we would occasionally sit and talk. I walked over to them and motioned for him to join me. Zoe continued sniffing around in the barn, and at one point, she startled a mouse, which jumped out of the hay and took off at a run. Zoe gave a startled bark and the chase was on. She eventually caught it and clamped down with her teeth, killing it. When she was through chewing on it, she dropped it at my feet.

"What's on your mind, son?" Fred asked.

"I'm not sure where to start," I said. "There is a man who has, how do I put it, gone rogue."

"Who?"

"General Fosswell."

Fred seemed both astonished and outraged. I mean, he was so torn up he blinked twice in ten seconds.

"Yeah?" he finally asked.

"Apparently, he's the one behind most, if not all of the major malfunctions that've been happening around here for the past few years."

Fred was so upset, he looked at some dirt on his boot.

"Any idea why he's doing it?" he asked.

"According to his son's writings, ever since his wife died, he's become somewhat of a religious fanatic. Somehow, he's got it in his head that we are interfering with God's will to eliminate the world of sinners, or something like that."

"What about that pedophile?" he asked.

"You mean Brumley?" I asked. Fred nodded. I shook my head.

"Brumley refused to be vaccinated, which ultimately worked to his advantage. He didn't get infected, but I don't think he and Fosswell were colluding together."

"What happened with him?"

"We left him in Dayton."

"You should've killed him," he said.

I shook my head. "Don't think I didn't consider it, but it didn't seem prudent. Besides, there were too many witnesses. Alright, so, there we are in Dayton and the Pittsburgh cops, Logan and Liam, capture an infected woman and wrapped her up in duct tape. No muss, no fuss."

"From what I've heard, I kind of like those two boys," he remarked.

"Yeah, I like them too. So, now, we have a freshly infected zed."

"And that's why you went to Fort Detrick."

"Yeah. At that time, nobody seemed to know what went wrong and I figured a fresh specimen might help those scientists."

He nodded slightly. 'You never said when you first suspected sabotage."

I frowned in thought. "Probably in Dayton when Brumley told me he had not been vaccinated and he was the only one who wasn't infected. When the docs started going round and round about the possible cause, it made me more suspicious. After some pressuring by yours truly, Kincaid reluctantly conceded both batches of vaccines were bad, but he refused to speculate on the cause."

"Mmm," he said.

"Yeah. So now, we have a problem. Hypothetically speaking, we find a group of survivors and they agree to be vaccinated. Eventually, they'll hear about Ohio and will become angry that we vaccinated them with what they perceive to be bad serums. Instead of them becoming allies, they're now antagonists."

I waited for Fred to say something, but he instead pulled his hat off and casually inspected it.

"Yeah, I'll come back to that. So, we're at Detrick and the Stryker breaks down. That's three Strykers out of commission now, which is yet another issue we'll have to resolve, but that's a discussion for another time. So, we could have borrowed a truck and left that day, but we used it as an excuse to stick around, which allowed me to do a little snooping."

"Did you learn anything?" he asked.

I frowned. "I don't know. We talked to Andre, you remember him, and Stretch. They didn't have any inside scoop. They confirmed both of the Fosswell men had been acting strangely, but they don't know why."

"And those scientists wouldn't call it sabotage," Fred remarked.

I shook my head.

"Mmm."

He liked that word. It was an expressive word full of meaning, connotation, and emotion. He used it often. I pushed on.

"So, we decided to leave the next day and imagine my surprise when Junior met us at the motor pool. I mean, I've never exactly been friends with him. You neither."

That was an understatement. In fact, he got smart with Fred one day, which was a grave error. Fred jabbed him in the throat with two of his calloused fingers. I must admit, it was funny watching Junior frolic around on the floor like he was having a seizure. Ever since then, our relationship with him had been on the frosty side and we only spoke to each other when necessary.

"Mmm," Fred said again, a little overwhelmed by the memory.

"So, to confound my puzzlement, Junior acted all friendly and chatted like we were old friends."

"Why?" he asked.

"At the time, I had no idea. He went on for a few minutes about pets and tells me about his childhood dog. He said its name was Roggenwolf 1199. He repeated the name more than once, which seemed a little odd, but I didn't give it much thought. Then, he set us up with a military deuce-and-a-half. It was a good thing, because the roads were awful."

Fred sat quietly, listening. I knew I was being a little long-winded with the backstory, so I tried to get to the point.

"So, like I said, it was odd, but I'd forgotten all about it. A couple of days later, we find out he stuck a gun in his mouth and I kept thinking about our last conversation. It wasn't until I was in bed one night, about to drift off to sleep when I realized he was trying to tell me something."

"Tell you what?" Fred asked.

"His dog's name. It was his password," I said.

Fred was no longer looking at his hat; I had his undivided attention now. "For what?"

"His Mount Weather intranet account."

Fred gave a slow, somber nod.

"Here is where it gets serious. In order to even see other people's accounts, you have to have administrative rights, which I don't have. Only Parvis has them. At first, I was going to go to him, but I chose Grace instead."

"Why did you do that?"

I thought about it a moment. "I'm not sure. Call it intuition, maybe. Parvis is a good man. He's been good to me, but he's also a close friend to both Stark and Fosswell. I trust Grace," I said. "She's had a sheltered life, but she's trustworthy."

"That she is," Fred said in agreement.

"So, I gave her Junior's password and she ran with it. Once she read the documents and emails in his account, she went further. She somehow figured out how to get admin rights and then proceeded to hack almost everyone's account whom Junior had shared emails with."

Now, Fred looked mildly surprised. "Grace did that?" he asked. I nodded. "Why, that little stinker."

"Yeah, she found all kinds of stuff."

"Like what?"

"For one, Junior's own personal journal in which he memorialized all his father's dirty little secrets. He corroborated some of it with copies of documents from his father's account. He also had a lot of emails." I took a deep breath. "Senior is the one who tipped off Earl Hunter that his wife was having an affair with President Richmond. But, before that, before I got here, a contingent of Marines had gone to Fort Detrick to secure it for the doctors and scientists. One of them was a man by the name of Mayo Craddock. He was a virologist and apparently a good friend of the Fosswells. Senior cooked up a plan to sabotage the mission and somehow talked Craddock into implementing the plan. There weren't a lot of specific details, but long story short, they all mysteriously died."

"Weren't they found?" he asked.

"Yeah. When they went back up to Detrick, they found some of them dead in the labs. There are a couple of them that are MIA. If I had to guess, I'd say they turned."

Fred had picked up a bridle while I spoke and was fidgeting with it, but now looked at me.

"Yeah, and in case you haven't figured it out, he purposely sabotaged all of the vaccines earmarked for Ohio. His son helped him do it. There is a detailed explanation, but in a nutshell, they caught a live one, extracted its blood, and injected it in each batch."

"We need to kill the sonofabitch," Fred said when I finished.

"I've thought about it, but if we do that, I stand a good chance of being banished, and that would include Kelly and the kids."

"No problem, I'll do it and tell them I acted on my own," he said.

I thought about it, but found myself shaking my head. "I don't want that to happen."

"You're limiting our options," Fred said. "I've looked around Detrick once or twice. I'm pretty sure I can get in there without anyone spotting me. Nobody will know who did it."

I sighed. "There are certain people who will be suspected from the get-go, and one of them is you. If you did it, and someone started investigating, well, what can I say?"

He was quiet for a moment. "You're limiting our options," he said again, this time under his breath.

A three-year-old sorrel wandered into the barn and nuzzled Fred. He gave her nose a friendly rub. Fred had named her Priss. When the human Priss found out, she was flattered until I told her Fred named the horse after her because it was as obstinate as she was. She didn't like that too much.

Fred fished into his pocket and came out with a piece of carrot. Priss did not hesitate and nibbled it from his hand. We were quiet for several minutes before Fred spoke.

"So, you've asked for my advice and you don't like it. What are you going to do?"

"I'm thinking the best course of action is to build a case against him and then present it in a formal meeting."

Fred digested what I said as he fished another piece of carrot out of his pocket. Priss took it from his hand immediately.

"So, you're going to build a case, present it to the politicians, and they'll banish him," he said.

"Something like that."

"It won't matter, son, not to those politicians. Let's say they banish him. I have a feeling he's got Fort Detrick all fixed up for his own domain. You already know that, right?"

I reluctantly nodded.

"So, banishment won't work. We need to kill him," he said again in a low voice. "Have you told Kelly?"

"Not yet," I said. "But, I'll have to eventually."

The two of us were silent for a time as we each gave Priss a scratch. She figured out there were no more carrots and wandered back out of the barn, leaving us to our thoughts. Well, I think Zoe was thinking of finding another mouse, while Fred and I were thinking of Fosswell.

"You know what I think?" Fred suddenly asked.

"What's that?"

"I think you need to get a private meeting with our esteemed president and present your evidence to him. Forget about the other people, just him."

"And then what?" I asked.

"Simple," Fred replied. "If I know that man the way I think I know him, he'll give the green light. That is, if he's not in cahoots with him."

I found myself frowning. "Normally, I'd agree, but Fosswell is one of his closest friends. I mean, Fosswell is undermining his mission, so I can't see how he'd go along with any of it, but like I said, they're good friends. I don't see how he'd give the green light."

Fred adjusted his hat before speaking. "Abraham Stark is only interested in his name going down in history as the man who rebuilt America. When you prove to him Fosswell has been trying to undermine his efforts, he'll give it. Trust me on this one."

I leaned back in my chair, digesting Fred's thoughts. What *was* President Stark's reaction going to be when he learned the truth? Would he give the go-ahead to kill General Fosswell?

There was one other issue which was bothering me, and I purposely did not say anything to Fred. That was Parvis.

There were two emails between Parvis and the general which were subjective in their interpretation. Each was written in such a way where one could possibly interpret it in which Parvis knew all about the contaminated vaccines.

CHAPTER 34 – HARLAN FOSSWELL SR.

"Why do you continue to get up so early when everyone else sleeps in?" Kelly mumbled groggily.

I chuckled and sat on the edge of the bed. "You should be used to it by now. Fred is probably already up, and if I don't help him, he'll go feed the cows by himself."

"You've got enough work to do," she said into her pillow.

"Go back to sleep," I whispered, then gave her behind a playful squeeze before leaving.

Besides the kitchen crew, I was the first one in the cafeteria. I fixed a pot of tea while awaiting the other early risers. They began filtering in, a couple at a time. Captain Seth Kitchens was back from the dams and gave me a grin when he saw me. I poured him a cup and we chatted for a few minutes.

"The work is hard, but it's proceeding nicely. As of now, we can power the entire city of Lynchburg, if we need to." He looked around and lowered his voice. "I'm going to move back there permanently," he said. "I'm here to get a tooth looked at and gather all of my personal belongings. After the meeting, I'm gone."

"I understand," I said with a smile.

When Seth and his team went to the Reusen Dam in order to restore power in that area, he came across a group of people living there, including a buxom blonde by the name of Wendy Stover. He tried to get Wendy and her people to come live at Mount Weather, or at least in a house nearby, but they wouldn't have any of it. So, Seth made the decision. I smiled in understanding.

"I'll miss you, but that doesn't mean we have to stop our Morse code conversations," I said.

He grinned and nodded. "If you don't mind, keep it under your hat until I make the announcement."

"You got it."

We worked our way to a table and continued chatting as Josue ambled in and pointed at me like he did every morning before walking to the tea table. Sammy wandered in, still looking a little sleepy. He was probably sneaking out with his girlfriend again, but I couldn't blame him, he was in love and young boys in love never listened to reason. Parvis came in and gave me a nod as he walked over to the president's table. From the expression on his face, I don't believe Grace had told him anything, but it'll only be a matter of time. She was close to her father; there were few secrets between them.

And, finally, Fred came in. He was usually one of the first here, but Rachel was with him this morning. She grinned and walked over to the table while Fred separated himself and made a beeline to the tea table.

"Good morning, Rachel," I said.

"Good morning yourself, handsome," she replied, gave me a peck on the side of the head and sat down. She said hello to Seth as well, but no kiss.

"You don't usually come in this early," I remarked.

"I'm helping Fred today," she said with a grin.

"Oh, yeah, why?"

"Because you have too much on your plate," Fred answered as he sat down.

"I do?"

"Yep," he said and made a subtle glance toward the double doors. Fred wasn't a person who played word games, so I guess he was trying to clue me in on something without spelling it out in front of everyone else.

I acted like I was enjoying my tea while keeping an eye on the doors. Within seconds, I figured out what Fred was telling me when General Harlan Fosswell walked through the doors. He ignored everyone and headed toward the president's table. Shooter, who was now Fosswell's bodyguard and assistant, went to the tea table and began preparing a cup, like a dutiful lackey should. Parvis caught my eye and made a head gesture, indicating he wanted me at the table with him.

"He showed up last night," Rachel whispered.

"Looks like you're right," I said to Fred and stood. "Excuse me."

I walked over and sat beside Parvis. He gave me a pat on the shoulder as I bid everyone good morning.

"How are you, General?" I asked.

He gave me a cool look. "As well as can be expected," he said.

"How are the tests coming with the female?"

"We will be discussing it in detail during this morning's meeting," he answered.

"Excellent," Parvis said with an easygoing smile. "I'm looking forward to it. Let's get some breakfast."

I knew Parvis was intervening, but I went along with it and followed him to the breakfast line.

"Supposedly, he has solved the mystery of the tainted vaccines and will be presenting his findings at the meeting," he said under his breath.

I nodded in understanding. When the subject matter was important, it was not discussed in the cafeteria, but in a more formal environment. This rule was instituted after many heated arguments broke out during the meal breaks in the past, some of which had escalated to shoving and fist fights. So, I excused myself and had an enjoyable breakfast with my family. I ate quickly though and was the first to arrive in the conference room. I chitchatted with people as they came in and found their usual seats, but there seemed to be a palpable tension in the air.

General Fosswell walked in with President Stark. I'd watched them during breakfast and the two of them were chatting like old friends who had not seen each other in a while, which I suppose was true enough. After all, the general had not been to Mount Weather in several months.

"Ruth, would you be kind enough to read the minutes of the last six months in order to bring the general up to speed?" Stark asked.

"Of course," she replied. She already had the file open, which led me to believe she already had gotten a heads up as well.

I sat back and absently listened as I watched the general. For the next thirty minutes, Ruth ticked off the minutes, and the entire time his attention was fixed on her. I did not know why we were going through with this dog and pony show. I happened to know Ruth emailed him the minutes of every meeting.

Ruth finally finished, sat down, and sipped some water.

"Thank you, Ruth. Do we have any new business to discuss?" Stark asked.

In fact, we did, but it was going to wait. Everyone remained quiet and waited for the real purpose of the meeting. Stark knew there was new business as well but also went along.

"Excellent. Next on the agenda is General Fosswell's report. General?"

General Fosswell stood and gazed around the room, pointedly making eye contact with each individual. Even me.

"To briefly recap, on November twenty-fourth, a team was dispatched to Ohio for the purpose of administering vaccinations. They first traveled to the Eastgate Shopping Mall, and then to Dayton. Personnel with the team report there were no problems, no issues, and vaccination protocol was strictly adhered to. The team was led by my son, Captain Harlan Fosswell Junior." Fosswell waited for the hushed murmuring, which lasted maybe a second, before continuing.

"As you all know, both groups ceased radio communications one day after the inoculations. Personnel with Mount Weather proceeded to both encampments and discovered the Ohio people had become infected. I myself was made aware of this catastrophe when Mister Gunderson arrived at Fort Detrick with an infected female in his possession."

He paused and took a sip of water from a plastic glass.

"What I have to tell you next is troubling for me. In fact, I have debated with myself on multiple occasions whether or not I should share this information or take it to the grave. However, after much trepidation, I feel it is in the best interests of our society that the truth be made known."

Another pause, one might even say a dramatic pause, and another sip of water.

"Once I was made aware of the situation, I immediately began an investigation. One of the first people I interviewed was my son. During my interview, he portrayed a tense and nervous demeanor. When I pressed him on specific details, he stumbled in his facts and frankly, contradicted himself several times. I did not want to believe my son would be capable of doing something like this, and for several weeks after his death, I was in denial. But, I am here today to announce to all of you that Harlan Fosswell Junior is responsible for the sabotage of the Ohio vaccinations. Further, I have no indication, nor evidence, to show anyone else was involved."

The general sat down heavily among the renewed murmuring. At one point, he realized I was staring at him and locked eyes with me. I knew he was lying. The perfect scapegoat was his son, no doubt about it, but still, I could not believe he'd do that to his son's memory.

Bob Duckworth was the first person to raise his hand. Fosswell recognized him with a terse nod.

"Do you know why he did it?" he asked.

"Unfortunately, the answer to that question went to the grave with him," Fosswell said, apparently forgetting that he had his son cremated. There was more talk, but I'd tuned it out. Instead, I started thinking about how I was going to proceed from here.

The rest of the meeting was more or less a blur. When it was over, I was the first one out of the door and found myself wandering the grounds, even though it was cold enough to freeze snot. I ended up in the horse barn. The potbelly stove in the corner was lukewarm. I put some kindling in and stoked it before sitting in one of the chairs. I needed time alone to think, and this was the only place I knew of that was only visited by Fred and Sammy. Sammy was currently in school and I knew that Fred had saddled up after breakfast and rode out. I hadn't asked, but I strongly suspected he was making regular visits to that barn where those female zeds were living.

Bunky, one of our horses, wandered in and nuzzled me. He liked me and I usually rode him whenever I went out. Surprisingly, Riley wandered in right behind the horse.

"What's going on with you?" she asked. "You're not in here jacking-off, are you?"

I laughed. "Nope," I answered. "You know, you remind me of a girl who used to be part of our group back in Tennessee. Her name was Andie."

"Tell me about her," Riley said.

"She was a tomboy. Small framed, but tough as nails. We were never romantic, but she was a good friend and I miss her terribly. She saved my life once."

She was quiet for a moment. "I'd like to think of you as a friend," she said quietly. "I hope you know that."

"Of course," I said. "What are you up to?"

"I have guard duty tonight, so my day is mostly free. I saw you walk in here and followed."

I worriedly wondered how many other people had seen the two of us walk in here.

"I've just remembered, I need to check over the chickens," I said and subtly led her back out of the barn.

"Have you spoken to Logan?" I asked as we walked toward the chicken coop.

"Yeah, but it was awkward. I saw him hanging out with a pale nerdy girl last night."

I looked at her in surprise. "You mean Grace?" I asked.

She nodded. "Yeah, I think that's her name."

"Hmm," I said. "Interesting."

"How is it interesting?" she asked.

"Grace is a sweet girl, extremely intelligent, but also extremely introverted. I would not have thought those two would be interested in each other."

"They were sitting awfully close together," she huffed. "And, he had a fresh haircut."

I grunted again and reminded myself to ask Kelly about it later. She'd have the inside info. Riley helped me refill one of the homemade waterers and collect eggs. We carried them into the kitchen and was mildly surprised to see Charlie Mac in the kitchen.

"Hello, Zach," he said, with maybe a little tenseness in his voice.

"You're on the kitchen crew again?" I asked.

"Yep," he said and gestured at the others. "Same crew." He then pointed over at the food waste barrels. "We've already carried last night's barrels to Harold's. These don't go until tomorrow."

"I hope Harold was pleased," I said as Becky took the eggs from us.

"Oh yeah," he replied. "He said we were the best kitchen crew as far as getting the food waste to him on time." He finished that sentence with a chuckle.

"Say, about that smokehouse he wants built. I've been thinking about it and we've discussed it amongst ourselves. We'd like to build it."

I was surprised again. That's three times already and it wasn't even lunchtime yet. "You would?"

"Yeah," Charlie Mac said and turned to one of the men. "Hey, Kass, show him what you've drawn up."

Kass walked over and pulled a folded-up piece of paper out of his pocket. He unfolded and smoothed it out before handing it to me. It was a highly detailed design of a smokehouse, complete with dimension lines.

"I like it," I said.

"Harold likes it too," Charlie Mac said.

"I get the feeling you've done stuff like this before," I said to Kass.

"In a manner of speaking," he said. "I've always been a bit of a handyman and back home I had a wood shop."

"I don't recall that aspect of you coming out in the debriefing interview," I said. "I would have remembered something like that."

His only response was a shrug. Charlie Mac spoke up.

"If you could put in a good word with Lydia, we'd be glad to build it. The four of us would like to get out of kitchen duty for a while."

I looked at the four of them, who were looking back hopefully.

I looked at the drawing again. It was hand drawn and meticulous. I kept any emotion out of my face. Charlie Mac was nothing more than manual labor, as was Becky and Starr, the two women in this work crew. I don't know if Lydia did it on purpose, but she put the four of them together on any type of work detail they were assigned to. If she had an ulterior motive, it worked splendidly because they paired off rather quickly and had been together for over a year now.

"This is a good drawing, Kass," I said.

"Thank you," he replied.

"Okay, the weather is warming up. Let's give it a week and then I'll get you four assigned to this project," I said while gesturing at the drawing. The four of them broke out in smiles.

"Thanks, Zach," Charlie Mac said. "Don't get me wrong, working in the kitchen during the winter is fine, but if we get through early, Lydia assigns us extra work. We're ready for a change of scenery."

"I understand." I then turned to Kass. "Can you train these three how to build stuff?" I asked.

"You bet your ass I can," he replied with a grin.

"Good. In the library is an apiary book. Go check it out and have a look at the beehive boxes. We need at least fifteen built. Work up a drawing and we'll go from there."

His eyes lit up. "Really?"

We spoke some more before Riley and I walked out of the kitchen.

"Is that your job?" she asked.

"Yeah, among other things."

The reason I went to the horse barn was to be alone and think. So far, it wasn't working. I was about to head to my office, but I realized Riley was bored and wanted someone to hang out with. She'd no doubt want to tag along. I thought carefully and came up with an idea.

"Say, have you seen the school where Kelly works?" I asked. She shook her head.

"Why don't I show you? Oh, by the way, always wash your hands after handling chickens and chicken eggs. You know that, right?"

"Salmonella infection?" she said.

"Yeah, that's one possibility. There's others, but I won't bore you. Let's get cleaned up."

We were soon standing in the doorway of the daycare where Maria was. She was sitting with a group of kids playing some type of game. She looked up and waved. I introduced Riley to the kids and it didn't take much for them to talk Riley into joining in. Satisfied with my cleverness, I eased out and went back to my office.

CHAPTER 35 – CONFRONTING PARVIS

I'd been sitting in our office for an hour when Parvis walked in. He was a man of habits, and headed directly to the hotplate.

"Oh, you've already got the kettle on," he exclaimed.

"Yep."

"Excellent."

I watched him as he sat and watched the kettle. I'd almost timed it accurately. The kettle started whistling within a minute. A look of delight crossed his face as he poured two mugs and put the tea balls in. He sat a mug in front of me before sitting back down. Suddenly, he was hit with a coughing fit. He found his handkerchief and coughed into it.

"Do you need anything?" I asked in concern.

He shook his head as he continued coughing for almost a full minute before regaining control. He then took several sips of tea and gave me a rueful smile. I didn't say anything, but he seemed to be having a lot of coughing fits lately.

"You'd think I have lung cancer instead of prostate cancer," he lamented.

I gave him a slow nod. There wasn't anything I could say. We'd already talked about it at length. Unfortunately, removing his prostate did not help. The cancer had spread throughout his body and was starting to show now. He'd been steadily losing weight and if one looked closely, you could see a hint of jaundice in his sclera.

"The general has gone back to Fort Detrick," he said. "He took a substantial amount of food supplies with him."

I nodded and for some reason started thinking about all of the different types of food we didn't have. Back when Felix and I were best friends, we loved Nashville hot chicken and ate it almost every weekend. Those were good memories. Of course, it didn't stop me from putting a bullet in his head a few years later.

"Did you have anything special you want to tackle today?" Parvis asked, breaking me from my reverie.

I stood up and walked over to the wall where we had a map hanging of the continental United States, Canada, and most of Mexico. There were three circles around Mount Weather, each one depicting the one hundred, two hundred, and three-hundred-mile radius. We had little green dots and code numbers of each location our scouts had visited. The code numbers had a corresponding data file on Mount Weather's intranet. The scout teams collected information from each site they visited, including still photos and videos.

"What are you thinking?" Parvis asked. I gestured at the map.

"Even though we're now into the three-hundred-mile ring, there are still many areas we have not yet explored," I said, looking at all of the blank areas without green dots. Green meant friendly contact with survivors. Red meant contact with hostile survivors. Orange signified a large presence of zeds. We made the marks with dry erase markers, and I noted Parvis had removed the green dots from Dayton and Eastgate. They had been replaced with black dots, which meant abandoned or lost. I pointed to the spot where Riley and I encountered the zeds.

"This is the spot where we smelled wood smoke, but we don't have any notation of people living here. We need to explore this area further and make sure this is a safe route to and from the Hook."

"Yes, a lot of unexplored areas, but I think our primary focus should be on helping Marcus Hook at this time," he said.

I knew what he was thinking, but I asked anyway.

"How so?"

"Raymond has agreed to stay there for the next three months, and the Bristol people are certainly helping, but they need another dozen people. We should limit scouting activity and instead divert all of that manpower to Hook."

I stared at him levelly. "What about Fort Detrick?"

"What about it?" he asked without making eye contact.

I continued. "It's going to be up to you and I to find out who all was involved in sabotaging those vaccinations."

"I'm sure General Fosswell's investigation and subsequent conclusions are adequate," he said. "Is there something that leads you to believe otherwise?"

"You don't think it's a little too cut and dry?" I asked. "I mean, he has laid the entire blame on his son. His dead son. It's a little too convenient, don't you think?"

He gazed at me pointedly. "Do you have any evidence which would prove otherwise?" he asked.

"What if I did?" I countered.

He stared at me a long moment. "Do you?" he finally asked.

"Yes, I have something," I answered.

"So, do you want to tell me or should I guess?"

I did not answer. There were a lot of things I could have said, but I chose to remain silent.

Parvis gently set his cup down. "Zach, you've come a long way since we first met, but sometimes you're like a bull in a china shop. A raging bull."

He had another coughing fit for a moment, and then wiped his mouth with a handkerchief before continuing.

"You've obviously come upon some information which makes you suspicious, and yet you are disinclined to share it with me. It begs the question, Zach, why won't you share it with me?"

"I believe there are more people involved in this," I said. "And there is more going on than sabotaging a batch of vaccines."

"So, what do you suggest? Dragging in the suspects and giving them an old-fashioned interrogation, like cops with lead saps and a harsh light pointed in their face?"

"Parvis, over a hundred people were infected. Whoever sabotaged those vaccines committed the equivalent of mass murder, and whoever assisted or aided them is every bit as culpable."

Instead of answering, Parvis went to the restroom. After a moment, I heard the toilet flushing and then water running in the sink before he came back out. He gathered up his cup and made a point of thoroughly washing and drying it.

Parvis and I were friends, close friends. We'd spent many hours together over the past five years. There were several minutes of silence while Parvis read something on his laptop.

"Yes, the more I think about it, the more I am convinced we need to divert manpower from the scout teams to Marcus Hook," he said. "But, not only that, we need to convince at least ten more people to live there permanently. We can present a sales pitch, maybe give some kind of incentives, like personally assigned vehicles with motor pool privileges or something."

When I didn't answer, he looked up. He must have seen the consternation on my face. "Is there something else bothering you, Zach?"

"I need to ask you something," I finally said.

"Yes?"

"The vaccines."

"We're still on that?" he asked with a sigh.

"Do you have any inside information about the sabotage?" I asked.

"No more than you," he answered. "Why?"

"Did you ever know Mayo Craddock?" I asked suddenly.

"Of course I did. He was a little squirrelly, but a good man. Why do you ask?"

"Tell me about him," I said.

"Well, not a whole lot to tell. He was a virologist working as a civilian contractor at Fort Detrick. He was rescued along with Kincaid and Smeltzer."

"He was good friends with General Fosswell, wasn't he?"

"Yes, I believe he was. They went to high school together and were altar boys in the same church, if memory serves me correctly." He eyed me a moment before he took his glasses off and began cleaning them with the tail of his shirt. "I'm sensing you believe there is some kind of nexus between Doctor Craddock and the current situation with the vaccines."

"A task force was created to go back to Detrick and attempt to secure the facility."

"That's right." He picked up his mug and tried a sip, forgetting it was empty.

"It's my understanding Doctor Craddock insisted on going with the task force."

"Yes, he did. He stated his expertise would be a valuable asset. And, yes, in answer to your unasked question, they somehow met a violent death up there."

"Nobody knows what happened to them," I stated. "Not even you."

"Correct," he replied. "And that was a little over five years ago now. We may never know what really happened at Detrick. So, your turn. Why are you concerned about Doctor Craddock?"

"So, he was a Catholic man?"

"Yes, why?"

"Devout? Fanatical?"

"I have no idea, why?"

"Would he be the type of person to do something drastic, martyr himself maybe?" I asked.

Parvis frowned. "What an odd question." He waited for me to react, but I merely stared at him. "I didn't see that in him," he finally said.

I hesitated. Parvis continued staring at me with a steady gaze. He often did that when he knew I was thinking something through. He'd always been a patient man with me.

"Say what you're thinking, Zach." His voice was quiet now.

"Alright, I believe General Fosswell conspired with Craddock, and possibly others, to somehow sabotage the mission. His scheme was probably not intended to lead to Craddock's demise, but somehow it happened. And, I believe General Fosswell sabotaged the two individual batches of vaccine destined for Ohio. And, I believe General Fosswell, for reasons I'm unsure of, orchestrated those two events, among other acts which were designed to undermine the fundamental mission of Mount Weather."

Now he was giving me a solemn look while I stared back. I was looking for anything in his behavior or demeanor which gave any type of indication of deception. He placed his hands under his chin and formed a steeple with his fingers. I'd seen him do this before. He did it when someone, usually one of his kids or me, threw him a curve ball.

"Were you involved?" I asked.

His eyes widened when he realized what I was asking. "Zach? Do you really think that?"

I maintained eye contact with him and waited.

"The answer is no, Zach. I am not, nor have I ever been, complicit in any nefarious activity you suspect General Fosswell of. Furthermore, President Stark has no knowledge of this either. What makes you think Fosswell is behind all of this?" He stopped to address another coughing fit.

"Alright, Zach, tell me what your evidence is. I know you wouldn't be wasting my time pursuing this line of questioning unless you had some kind of compelling evidence. So, what is it?"

"I'd rather not say," I said. He eyed me shrewdly.

"Grace," he suddenly said. "She's been acting peculiar lately. You two found something."

I didn't answer. He dipped his chin down when I didn't respond. I'd seen this mannerism before as well. In spite of the innuendo in the tone of his emails to Fosswell, I was now convinced he knew nothing.

Parvis was a brilliant man. One would think his level of intellect would make him arrogant and condescending, but he wasn't. He was the opposite; humble and unassuming. He had taken me under his wing when I first got here, and I'd spent five years under the tutelage of a MIT professor who was arguably one of the smartest men in the world. I'd learned a lot from him. And what's more, I learned what kind of man he was. I knew he was honest, forthright, and there wasn't an evil bone in his body.

"I don't yet know why he's doing what he's doing, but I've been put off long enough. I'm going to find out, with or without your consent. And, I believe he is not acting alone."

At some point during this conversation, he no longer felt the need to maintain eye contact with me and instead stared at the map on the far wall. After a while, he spoke softly.

"I'm tired, Zach. So tired."

He rubbed his chin in thought a moment before reaching for the phone.

"An important matter has come up. I believe we need to talk to you right away. I think it'd be better if we discuss it in person." There was a pause before he spoke again. "Thank you, sir, we'll be right there."

He hung up and motioned at the door. "Let's go speak with President Stark. You can plead your case to him."

The meeting lasted two hours. When it ended, I walked around Mount Weather until I found Captain Justin Smithson. He was in the warehouse, looking over our inventory, trying in vain to find replacement parts for a baby carriage. He spotted me as I walked in.

"What's up?" he asked.

"Remember that day we went fishing and we had a discussion about some things?" I asked.

"Yes, of course."

"And we talked about the sabotaged vaccinations?"

"And I said I'd help you out if you needed it," Justin said. "Yeah, I remember."

"Were you serious?" I asked. Justin nodded somberly.

"Alright. You, me, and Fred are going on a little trip tomorrow," I said and explained.

CHAPTER 36 – CONFRONTING FOSSWELL

I drove the deuce. Justin was in the passenger seat. We'd dropped Fred off a few miles away from Fort Detrick and watched him as he jumped out and ambled off into a nearby wood line.

"Why drop him off this far out?" Justin asked as I put the deuce in gear.

"If you were running Fort Detrick, wouldn't you have active patrols?" I asked.

"Okay, point taken, but will you explain to me once again how he's going to be our backup?"

"He didn't really say. He only said he'd be there when we needed him," I said.

"He believes he's going to sneak on base without anyone seeing him," Justin said.

"Yep. He's going to have a look around and gather some intel, but when the time comes, he'll be there for us."

"How?" Justin asked.

I shrugged. "He didn't say."

"He's only wearing that jacket and hat. It's going to be cold tonight."

"The jacket is called a duster, and he's wearing his winter hat. It's made of felt, or maybe wool. Anyway, it's a Resistol, which is a damn good hat. He found it on a dead truck driver. He loves that hat. He'll be fine."

Justin stared at me like I was creating some kind of elaborate joke.

"What about the duster?" he asked sarcastically.

I glanced at him. "Well, you didn't hear it from me, but I think he found it at a gay clothing boutique, but I'm not sure. He got Sammy one just like it. It's a great jacket to wear if you're riding a horse. I'll have to admit, I was a little jealous when he gave that coat to Sammy and he didn't have one for me."

Now, Justin scoffed.

"So, he's going to stay out all night and sneak into Fort Detrick without anyone knowing about it," he said.

"Yep."

"And he didn't say how?" he asked.

"Nope."

Suddenly, I saw two zeds walking down the middle of the road. "Well, would you look at this," I said. I hit the gas in an attempt to run them over, but the zeds deftly jogged out of the way.

"Well, that was interesting," I said as I slammed on the brakes and parked. I grabbed my machete before jumping out and giving chase.

"Damn it, Zach!" I heard Justin shout as I ran toward the zeds.

They weren't your normal, old school zeds. If they were old zeds, they would've only been able to run at a loping gate. These two charged me at a full sprint, and even spread out so they'd hit me from two sides. I charged at the one on the left. He lunged at me with his arms outstretched. It prevented me from chopping at his head, but I ducked, sidestepped, and swung the machete across one of his legs. The machete cut deep, severing muscle and tendon. It wasn't a killing blow, but it slowed him down.

I ran in a wide circle and worked my way back to the second zed, who was trying to chase me down. A quick swipe with the machete severed the left side of his neck. I worked the machete out as he tried to reach for me and hit again. The second strike severed his spinal cord. He dropped to the ground, but wasn't finished. He continued to gnash at me as I struck the death blow, decapitating him.

The first zed I attacked was undaunted and made his way toward me while dragging his injured leg. I executed the old classic tomahawk chop. My machete buried itself in his skull, coming to rest between his eyebrows. I hastily looked around for any other zeds as I worked the machete free, but the only thing I saw was Justin, standing there with his arms crossed, staring at me like I was crazy.

"Was that really necessary?" he asked.

I looked at the two dead zeds before looking at him. "I believe it was."

"I really wonder about you sometimes," he said as we walked back to the deuce. "You and Joker get off on this shit."

I shrugged. I couldn't disagree with him.

"If you're through, why don't we get going," he suggested.

"Yep, sounds good," I said.

We drove up to the front gate of Fort Detrick ten minutes later. The guard post was actually manned, which surprised me. It was Stretch. I killed the engine and rolled down the window as Stretch walked up.

"This is unexpected," Stretch said.

"Yeah, I imagine so," I said. "We wanted it to be a surprise." I expected her to open the gate immediately, but she didn't do it.

"I have to call it in," she said.

I gave her a look. "Is there a reason why I'm not allowed admittance to a facility which Captain Smithson and I personally helped secure?" I asked. I pointed at the line of Gabion barriers. "You know who helped assemble and fill those up don't you?" I asked and pointed at Justin and myself.

"I'm only following orders, Zach," she replied. "Nobody is allowed entry without General Fosswell's okay."

I sighed and waited for her to get on the phone, the same phone system I helped get operational. After a long couple of minutes, we were graciously allowed to enter.

"Sorry, Zach," Stretch said as I drove past. As an afterthought, she saluted Justin.

I parked the deuce at the loading docks of their main building. Shooter and a couple of others walked out and greeted me.

"Why are you two here?" he asked.

"Because we've missed you," I replied.

Shooter scoffed. "Yeah, right. Really, why are you here? General Fosswell just called and is asking."

"I told Stretch why we're here," I said and gestured at the back of the truck. "We brought supplies."

"Yeah, well, he thinks y'all have some kind of other motive and insisted I follow up. Help a brother out here," he said.

"I had some follow-up questions for the scientists. The weather was pleasant enough, so Captain Smithson and I thought we'd drive up and deliver some supplies. That's a good thing, right?"

"Yeah, I guess so," he replied.

"Is there a problem with us being here?" I asked. "There never used to be. Is something going on?"

Shooter involuntarily looked behind him, as if he were being spied on or something. "No, it's just, well, the general is, well, you know."

No, I didn't know, but I nodded as if I did. "Alright, tell the general we have supplies and I wanted to get an update from the doctors about the infected woman they have. Nothing more."

"Okay. How long will you two be staying?" he asked.

"Overnight," I said. "We're heading back first thing in the morning."

I waited until Shooter walked back to the little office in the motor pool and got on the landline before looking over at Justin. "If you have this, I want to hustle over to the labs and talk with the docs before Fosswell intervenes."

"Yeah, I got it. How long do you need?" he asked.

"Hmm, two hours. I'll meet you in their cafeteria."

I left him and headed to the labs. When I walked in, all four of the docs were sitting in their office. They were chatting and laughing about something, but immediately became silent when they spotted me. Doctor Smeltzer was the only one who actually smiled in greeting.

"Hello," I said.

"Ah, Zach, what brings you to Fort Detrick?" Smeltzer asked.

"You guys," I said with a placating smile. "How about an update on the infected woman?"

I proceeded to have a long conversation with the four of them. They enthusiastically told me of their testing and observations of the infected woman. Their experimentations were limited, nothing invasive, and nothing dire. They'd trained her to change out her smock every day, but occasionally, she still took a crap in the corner of her cell rather than in the toilet.

The conversation was relaxed, casual. There was no harsh language, no subterfuge. It was like old friends gathering together. I guess it helped that I did not once mention the sabotaged vaccines.

After spending the day with them, Justin and I ate dinner with the Detrick populace and updated them on the current gossip and goings on of Mount Weather. We even engaged in a poker tournament in which the winner was awarded a baked chicken. Neither of us won. It wasn't our intention to. Of all people, Shooter was the ultimate winner. I congratulated him wholeheartedly.

After, I bid goodnight and went to the dorm room. I waited until after midnight, when I was certain everyone had gone to bed, before exiting the dorms and making my way down the hall. I gave a quiet, reluctant knock on his door. After a moment, there was a response.

"Who the hell is it?" came his gruff voice through the door.

"It's Zach Gunderson," I replied.

After a moment, I heard the deadbolt turn. He opened the door a couple of inches and peered out. I could see pillow marks on his face, but he was awake and alert. I could also clearly see a Beretta in his hand. If he was surprised to see me, he didn't show it. Instead of surprise, there was a look of suspicion.

"Sorry to disturb you so late, sir, but I have something important here that's been causing me no small amount of anxiety," I said as I gestured with the laptop in my hands.

"Can't this wait until morning?" he asked.

I looked down at the floor with my best dejected expression. "I suppose it can. Sorry, sir." I turned away and got five steps down the hall when he stopped me, like I knew he would.

"Just a moment, Gunderson," he said.

I stopped and turned. He spent a moment looking me over, his military instincts performing a threat assessment. I was wearing a plain white T-shirt and baggy shorts. I completed the ensemble with a blanket draped around my shoulders. The blanket looked natural because the man still insisted on keeping the temperature uncomfortably low. I looked about as nonthreatening as I could.

"This better be good," he said and motioned me inside. I walked in and stood, holding my laptop, waiting on him. His room was a spartan suite, except for an expensive-looking leather chair in front of a standard government-issue desk. He sat in the chair, not bothering to invite me to sit, and put the sidearm in his lap. I guess he thought I was not going to be here long enough for it to necessitate any formalities.

"Alright, out with it," he directed.

I opened the laptop and punched a few buttons. I then placed the laptop on his desk and slid it across to him.

"Check this out," I said.

He glared at me a moment before putting a pair of reading glasses on and peering closer.

"What am I supposed to be looking at?" he asked.

"It's the results of the DNA test from that infected woman we picked up in Ohio, the real results, not the ones given to President Stark."

He scowled at me. "And it was so important you wanted me to see it now?"

"Yes, sir, that's part of it, but the most important thing is this." I reached over and simultaneously hit the alt and tab buttons. The screen changed over to a Word document Grace had shown me.

"What is this?" he asked.

"A journal of your sins," I said.

He looked at me in slight confusion before glancing back down at the laptop's screen for a long minute. His scowl deepened as he read. It took another minute before he trained the scowl back at me.

"Where did you get this nonsense?" he demanded.

"A sweet computer nerd located it for me at my request," I said.

He scoffed and slammed the computer shut. "Well, maybe you should fire her. I've never stored a journal in a confounded computer."

"I didn't say it was *your* journal," I replied. "It belongs to your son. He'd documented everything you've done over the years, including your latest act, which was sabotaging the Ohio vaccines." I scrutinized him with my own harsh expression. "You blamed him, but it was you who was the person behind all of it."

His expression changed ever so slightly now and he pointed to a steel folding chair. I pulled it over to where I was directly across from him and sat. In his mind, I'm sure he thought he was in control. After all, we were in his domain. And, more importantly, he was armed and I wasn't. What he did not realize is he'd already given me what I needed, a tacit confession. If he told me any details, so much the better, but I now knew the documents the late Harlan Fosswell Junior had in his file were factual, and not made up in an attempt to besmirch his father. The general leaned forward in his chair.

"What the hell are you after, Gunderson?"

I matched his stare. "I want to know why."

"Why?" he asked in a demanding tone. "Why what?"

"Why did you do it? Why did you purposely infect all of those people? Why do you think everyone should die?"

"Not everyone," he replied. "The righteous shall survive, but the unworthy deserve to die."

"Please explain. I want to understand."

He stared a moment. I guess he was deciding whether I was worthy of an explanation.

"Let me ask you, have you read the Bible?"

"I have."

"But, do you understand it?" he asked.

"Somewhat," I answered. "I admit there are parts that are confusing, there are parts I may have misinterpreted, and there are parts which I'm convinced are nothing more than tall tales."

"And the Book of Revelations?" he asked, but did not wait for an answer. "We are living in the apocalypse. God's apocalypse."

He gave a grim, furrowed smile. "You are interfering with God's plan. You are all interfering with God's plan."

"How? By creating a vaccine and saving lives?"

"Yes, Gunderson, by creating a vaccine and saving the lives of people whom God intended should die."

"Tell me, General, how do you determine who gets to live and who is condemned to die?"

Fosswell chuckled. "Oh, you naïve young man. What makes you think I make the decisions? I don't make the decisions, only God makes the decisions."

"How do you know that? Does he talk to you or something?" I asked.

"Oh yes, he speaks to me in many ways. Ways in which you would not understand. Ways in which you would never understand."

I sneered. "Yeah, you're not making any sense, but I didn't expect you to."

"I had mixed feelings about you, Gunderson. God truly intended for you to live, this is obvious, and yet, you have repeatedly chosen to go against his will. I cannot allow this to continue."

He started to reach for his gun, but he encountered a problem. In the blink of an eye, I was holding my own gun on him. I'd had it all along, hidden by my blanket in the waistband of my pants. He probably should have searched me.

"The next thing I want to see is your hand slowly coming up from behind that desk, empty. You have one second."

He complied with a smirk and placed both of his hands on the desk. I smiled back, made a show of visibly relaxing, and held my gun casually.

"I was told to never underestimate you, Gunderson. I should have heeded that advice," he said.

"And I never underestimated you," I replied. "But, what I can't understand is you."

"How so?" he asked.

"I've read your personnel file. Top of your class at West Point, highly decorated, one of the youngest one-star generals in the last fifty years. You were damn near perfect. How and why you turned into a total religious nutjob?"

His smile turned to a smirk. "It's called enlightenment, Gunderson. You said you've read the Bible, but you don't even realize you have no understanding of it. I've read it many times throughout my life and have immersed myself in theology. All of the answers are in the Bible."

"You mention the Bible and God. Let me remind you what King Solomon said. Righteousness exalts a nation, but sin is a disgrace to any people."

His eyes narrowed and he started to surreptitiously slide his right hand off of the desk.

"What do you think you're going to do now, Gunderson, kill me?" he asked. He started gesticulating with his left hand while he inched his hand slightly more toward his lap. I maintained eye contact with him.

"Yes," I said. "Because of our past history, and the respect I once had for you, I was going to put you in the brig and let President Stark figure out what to do with you, but I can see you'd never go for that."

He barked out a laugh. "You are correct, Gunderson. Besides, do you really think President Stark will abide by this nonsense?"

He laughed again and his hand moved again.

"There is something you should know, General," I said.

"What might that be, Gunderson?"

"Stark is the one who gave the order."

His eyes widened as he realized what I meant. Then, a change came over him and his eyes glazed over.

"And when he had opened the fifth seal, I saw under the altar the souls of them that were slain for the word of God, and for the testimony which they held, and they cried with a loud voice, saying, how long, O Lord, holy and true, dost thou not judge and avenge our blood on them that dwell on the earth?"

He was practically shouting now. And then, his right hand ducked down into his lap.

He'd forgotten, or never knew, that I'd been trained by the best. The first bullet struck him on the bridge of the nose, causing it to burst in a spray of crimson. The second bullet, which was perhaps a hundredth of a second after the first bullet, was a mere fraction of an inch higher. Like I said, I was trained by the best.

I stared at him in silence for a couple of minutes before standing and searching his room. He had no computer, but there were several files in his desk drawer of printed reports. Interestingly, one file had my name on it. I held off reading it and found an empty olive drab canvass satchel sitting beside his desk. I scooped up the files and stuffed them into the satchel before giving him one, final last look.

He had not moved from his chair. His left hand was still on the desk and the right hand was in his lap, clutching the Beretta. His head was leaning back, causing his lifeless eyes to stare heavenward. Like I said, I once had a deep respect for the man.

When I emerged from the general's room, Fred was standing a few feet down the hallway, casually leaning against the wall. I had no idea how he had gotten into Fort Detrick without being spotted, but he did. When we made eye contact, he gave me a micro.

CHAPTER 37 – CHANGE OF COMMAND

Justin was sawing logs in the dorm room when I walked in. I gently shook his foot and he instantly bolted upright. It took him a second to recognize Fred and me.

"It's done," I said.

"He's in custody?" he asked as he rubbed his eyes.

I shook my head slowly. "We knew he wouldn't go along with that."

He stared at me a moment and then nodded somberly.

Justin dressed and then the three of us went back to General Fosswell's room. Everything was as I had left it. We laid out his blanketing on the floor and rolled the body up in it. The only guard on duty never woke up as we carried Fosswell outside and dumped him in the back of the deuce. When we were finished, the three of us went to the cafeteria.

Fred fixed us tea, but I found myself drifting off to sleep before even taking a sip. Fred nudged me an hour or two later as people started coming into the cafeteria. We sat at the back and waited patiently.

"The breakfast atmosphere here is a lot different from Weather," Justin said under his breath.

He was right. Breakfast time at Mount Weather was a noisy affair because everyone was engaging in breezy conversation. Here at Fort Detrick, it was quiet, subdued. Nobody was smiling and only conversed in hushed voices.

Breakfast consisted of one egg and sausage patty each, and as much wheat porridge as you wanted. It wasn't all that tasty, some butter or honey would have certainly helped, but it was better than starving.

I kept a running head count, and when everyone but two people were present, I nodded at Justin. He stood and walked to the front of the cafeteria. A few people noticed him, and there were some nudges and fingers pointed in his direction. Soon, the entire cafeteria became silent.

"Good morning, everyone," Justin said. "As of now, I am taking charge of Fort Detrick. General Fosswell has been relieved of command."

"I want to hear that from the general," Shooter instantly said. There was a singular murmur of agreement.

"Then load your ass up on the deuce and ride back with us," Justin retorted. "You can ride in the back with his body."

Shooter paled when he realized what Justin said, looked around wildly, and then pointed in our direction.

"They did it!" he shouted.

All eyes turned toward us. I stood slowly and walked to the front of the cafeteria. This was on purpose. Now, most of the people were focused on Justin and me, not Fred, who was armed to the teeth with two pistols and multiple speed loaders. I think the quickest I ever reloaded a revolver with a speed loader was about three seconds. Fred could do it in the blink of an eye. So, I wasn't worried about my personal safety, but I hoped to avoid any further bloodshed. When I got to the front, I stopped, turned, and spoke calmly, yet clearly, so everyone could hear me.

"I killed the general," I said. "I'll explain, if anyone is interested."

There was a stunned silence and a long moment before anyone spoke.

"I would like an explanation," Doctor Kincaid said, his voice cracking.

"As you know, the general claimed to have uncovered evidence that his son, Captain Harlan Fosswell Junior, was solely responsible for sabotaging the vaccines that infected the Ohio people. That was a false accusation. Through our investigation, we found that in fact it was General Fosswell who perpetrated the sabotage. His son assisted him, but it was definitely the general who was behind all of it. President Stark sent me up here for the purpose of informing General Fosswell with the findings of our investigation and to get his input. Last night, I was having a frank conversation with him when he retrieved a Beretta handgun. I had no option but to fire in self-defense."

"So, you killed him," Shooter stated.

"That is correct, Simon," I replied.

"That's bullshit," he said.

"Your statement seems to imply that I should have offered to give him a manicure or something rather than defend myself. The man posed a threat to my life, and I reacted. I remember a time, let's see, a few years ago back in Nolensville. You shot a man and made the same assertion of self-defense, correct?"

He stared hard at me a moment before looking away. A few years back, a gang confronted us while we were trying to retrieve medical equipment out of a hospital located in south Nashville. One of the gang members stated he recognized Shooter and his brother, and was about to tell us something when Shooter shot him. He later claimed the man had made a threatening move and shot him in self-defense. We went as far as to put Shooter on trial, but he was found not guilty. I think it was a story he wished everyone would forget about.

"What happens now?"

I looked around and found it was Andre who asked the question.

"Business as usual," Justin said. "There will be some changes, like in a minute or two I'm going to change the thermostat settings to sixty-five degrees. But, for the most part, there will be nothing different in day-to-day operations. Are there any questions?"

An hour-long discussion ensued. As I suspected, the people living here were not happy. The death of Fosswell opened the spigot and there was a torrent of questions and criticisms. Justin handled it well, promising changes for the better. I also made a few promises, including increasing the amount of provisions, which was going to put a strain on our resources. While I listened, Fred made eye contact with me and gestured at the door. I gave him a micro and we made a silent exit.

"Look," Fred said as we walked outside. He pointed toward Doctor Kincaid fast walking away from us. It wasn't any problem for me to run and stop in front of him.

"I'm so glad I bumped into you," I said as I stood in front of him and waited for Fred to amble up to us. He nervously looked over his shoulder at Fred's approach. Fred seemed to have that effect on people.

"What do you want, Zach?" he asked.

"Let's take a walk to the lab," I answered and grabbed his forearm.

"Why?" he asked. "We answered all of your questions yesterday."

"Yeah, well, we believe it would be for the best if we kill that zed you're experimenting on," I said.

He stopped suddenly. "We can't kill her, Zach. It is imperative we keep her alive."

I could tell by the look in his eye Fred was about to yank a knot in his ass, so I quickly spoke up.

"Alright, tell me why," I demanded.

"Because, she's pregnant."

Both Fred and I fixed him with a hard, puzzled stare. "Are you sure?"

"Oh, yes, definitely," Kincaid answered.

"Show us," I demanded.

Kincaid swallowed. "Promise you won't hurt her."

"I'm not promising anything. Now, show us."

Smeltzer had walked outside during this and watched tentatively while standing in the doorway, as if he were contemplating running back inside. At my beckoning, he reluctantly walked up to us, and the two of them led us to a section of the NBACC building I'd not visited before. It was similar to the other labs, but this one had a room that looked exactly like a jail cell. The room was a smaller version as one of the containment labs, but there was a concrete platform that served as a bed with one of those thin, foam mattresses on it, and a stainless-steel combination toilet with a sink.

The infected woman was sitting on the mattress. She was wearing a hospital gown, and they'd even put slippers on her feet. She sat silently, staring at us through lidded eyes.

"It is a bit difficult to notice, but she is in her second trimester. She won't eat regular food, only raw meat, and she's relearned how to drink from the sink."

I looked over and saw a turd on the floor in the corner. I pointed at it. "She doesn't seem to be potty trained."

"Yes, we've been debating on how to teach her. We've not come up with an adequate solution yet," Smeltzer said with a frown, but then he pointed. "Do you gentlemen notice anything unusual about her?"

Both Fred and I looked her over as she stared back.

"She seems calm," I observed.

"We have her sedated," Smeltzer answered. "We sneak it into the raw meat."

"Does it work?" I asked.

"Somewhat," he responded. "She'll gnash at us sometimes, but we use welder's gloves when handling her. We limit the dosage though, so we won't harm the fetus. After she gives birth, we plan on trying different types of opioids and other psychotropic drugs and testing her reaction."

Kincaid read the expression on my face as I glanced at Fred. "I believe I know what you're thinking."

"You do, huh? Is your telepathy telling you there is no reason to find a way to treat these things?"

"I'm sure the both of you believe the only option is to kill anyone who is infected," Kincaid replied. "But, what if we could find a way to manage their condition?"

"And then what? Do you guys think they could once again become functioning, productive members of society?" I waved a hand. "Don't get me wrong, it's a noble effort, but this isn't like AIDS or polio, or hepatitis, or some other viral infection. Once you become infected with this virus, it's game over."

"There may be evidence to indicate otherwise," Doctor Smeltzer contended. I got the impression he wanted us to ask him what the so-called evidence was so he could launch into a long diatribe.

"Gentlemen," I said, holding back a smart-assed retort, "you should be concentrating on the production of the vaccine, not some type of care plan once someone becomes infected. And, for the record, there is nothing you doctors have shown me that proves you can cure someone who has become infected." I pointed at the woman. "She's proof you have no such cure, otherwise, she wouldn't be crapping on the floor."

Doctor Kincaid eyed the both of us, his eyes lingering on Fred's pistols. "Gentlemen, we have been, and are continuing to successfully produce the vaccine. Now, it is time for us to explore the possible creation of a cure. Allowing this woman to give birth may advance our research by leaps and bounds."

The other three readily nodded in agreement.

Justin and Stretch met us at the truck. There were a couple of others there, looking at Fosswell's body, even though it was rolled up in a bedspread and you couldn't see him.

"We're done here, for now," I said.

Justin nodded. "Everything is in place. Sergeant Siegenthaler here is going to be my number two. I'm not foreseeing any major problems. How are the doctors?"

"I think they're fine," I said. "We had a little talk with them and I think we've come to a tentative understanding."

He nodded. "I'm heading over there now to have a little chat with them."

We spoke for a few more minutes before shaking hands.

"Alright. I'll see you in a few days," I said.

He waved and walked away. I started to get in the truck, but Stretch stopped me.

"Have you talked to Cutter?" she asked.

"Sure, we talk frequently," I said.

"I mean, has he said anything about the letter? You did give it to him, right?"

"Yeah, almost immediately after I got back. He took it, but he never said anything to me about it," I said.

"Did he read it?" she asked.

"Not in front of me."

"Did you read it?" she asked.

"No, ma'am," I said. "It was none of my business."

She was fighting hard to hold it in, but I could see her eyes watering up. She nodded her head and then turned to catch up with Justin. Fred caught my attention and nodded toward the truck.

CHAPTER 38 – BACK TO WEATHER

We'd driven ten miles in utter silence, which was not unusual in the company of Fred McCoy. Even so, I felt like I needed to talk.

"None of those doctors seemed too terribly upset about Fosswell's death, did they?"

"Nope."

"Maybe they're masters of controlling their emotions, like Vulcans," I said.

That one elicited a slight smile. "Maybe," he said.

"I don't think they were in on it, but I think they knew more than they're letting on. Especially Kincaid and Smeltzer. Those other two are just happy to be here."

"Could be."

"Do you think we should've killed her?" I asked, referring to the pregnant zombie woman.

"Probably."

"Kincaid made a good point though. If that baby is born normal, it might be immune, and maybe actually lead to them finding a cure."

I glanced at him and waited, but he offered no response now.

"You know, those four are kooky enough to have an ulterior motive."

He glanced over at me. "Like what?" he asked.

"They might be allowing the birth to go through simply to see how that infected woman would react. You know, will she act like a mother or will she sink her teeth into her newborn child and eat it?"

Fred nodded slightly. "Hadn't thought of that one."

I waited for him to say more, but he lapsed again into silence.

"Well, your input has given me a lot to think about," I deadpanned.

He glanced over at me again. "They knew what he did," Fred said. "They had it figured out as soon as you brought that infected woman to them."

"If that's true, why did they not tell anyone?"

"Fosswell catered to them," he replied. "Think about it. They had access to one of the best labs in the world and could do any kind of testing and experimenting they wanted. No oversight, no micromanaging, no regulations, no red tape. Three hots, cots, and bodyguards. They're in heaven. The only thing they're lacking is a couple of busty hookers visiting them every Saturday night."

"Yeah, but I'm not going to forget it," I declared. "There will be a reckoning."

236

"We'll all have a reckoning one day," Fred said quietly.

I didn't agree out loud, but he was right. It seemed like he was always right. Fred lapsed into silence again, but I wasn't through.

"How's that harem of zombie women you have?"

He waited several long seconds before responding. "I killed them."

I looked at him incredulously. "You did?"

"I was fooling myself. They weren't ever going to have a normal life. It was the best thing for them." Another pause. "I killed the oldest one last. The look on her face…" He paused and cleared his throat. "I'd never seen such a look of heartbreak and sorrow."

"Melvin told me he once saw a zed being chased by people and it looked to him like it was scared to death."

"Mmm," Fred said.

"Fear comes from the amygdala. I wonder if their brain is somehow healing."

I started to say more, but I caught a look at Fred's face before he turned his head and stared pointedly out of the window. I suddenly realized killing those zed women bothered him a lot more than he let on. I waited a few minutes before speaking.

"Well, I guess it's a good thing we never told anyone about them. Those docs would have probably insisted you impregnate them or something," I said, hoping to lighten the mood.

Fred turned back to me with a frown.

"I'm curious about what the docs think about these zeds becoming afraid," I said. "When we get back, I'm going send them an email and see what they think."

"That pregnant woman, it isn't going to matter," Fred suddenly said. "I mean, I don't know a whole lot about this zombie virus stuff, but I don't think it's going to matter if that baby is infected or normal."

"We can always go back and kill it," I suggested.

"Your call."

I glanced over at him. "You don't give a shit, do you?"

"Nope. Not anymore."

He turned and focused out of the passenger window again. We'd traveled almost five miles and I thought he was done talking, but he spoke again. "Priss is pregnant."

I glanced at him before focusing back on the road. "Which one?"

"The horse." A long pause. "And Serena."

"Serena?" I asked. Fred gave a micro. I sighed. "Well, shit, that figures. Does her mother know yet?"

"Don't know. Sammy told me just before we left yesterday. They might have broken the news by now."

"So, Sammy's going to be a father before he turns seventeen. Kelly's pregnant, the zombie's pregnant, Serena's pregnant, and a horse is pregnant. Maybe we should throw a great big baby shower for all of them," I said.

Fred's only response was a grunt.

That was the extent of our conversation for the rest of the trip.

CHAPTER 39 – TRUE'S REVENGE

I spent two days watching them. I wanted to get to know their habits, figure a way to get them all at once, if I could. Otherwise, I was going to have to sneak around and pick them off one by one, and that could take months.

They ambushed us about a week ago, or more. I'm not sure exactly, the days have kind of been a blur for me. They got us good; they even had some hand grenades, or dynamite, or something. We probably deserved it. I had no doubt they were associated with someone we'd raided or killed in the past and they were out for revenge.

I was out of the fight before it even started. One of those grenades knocked me for a loop. I remembered walking from the docks to my RV, when suddenly I was being tossed in the air and then everything went dark.

When I came to, it was well past sundown, but the night was lit up because all our campers and RVs were on fire. I don't know how long I was out, but I regained consciousness by the sound of someone screaming in agony. There was blood in my eyes, and although everything was still blurry, it didn't take much to see a person being held down and getting their head cut off. The man doing the cutting held the head up with a big, evil grin. His companions cheered, and in the firelight, I could see it was Shane, Sandy's brother. He was an arrogant, loudmouthed prick and I didn't like him too much, but he was Sandy's brother and Prairie's uncle. The sight of him like that made me sick to my stomach.

Suddenly, someone shouted. "Hey, we got another live one!"

I saw other people turn toward me, including the man who'd decapitated Shane. He was a big dude, and the lighting from the fires made him look like an apparition. He was holding a large Bowie knife and he'd been sprayed with blood when he'd cut into Shane's jugular. Looking up from the muddy ground, I saw the one who had discovered me. He was a punk-looking teenager with a face full of acne. He got to me first and started kicking me. I tried to block them, but he got a few headshots and almost knocked me unconscious again. I knew I had to do something or I was the next one who was going to lose their head.

Somehow, I got to my feet, pushed acne face away, and began running. It was more stumbling than running and I even heard them laughing at me. I tried running faster, but even with the ringing in my ears, I could hear at least one of them gaining on me. He tackled me as I reached the edge of a bluff overlooking the Tennessee River. It was a long drop straight down, maybe twenty or thirty feet. I fought and kicked. When I got away from him, I ran and jumped. It seemed like I fell forever before hitting the cold water.

The smack of the water hurt like hell and it was so cold it took my breath away. I sank like a rock. Fortunately, I guess, I only went down maybe ten feet before hitting the soft, muddy river bottom. I pushed up with my feet, losing my shoes in the effort, and struggled upward. When my head broke the surface, I gasped for air, taking in a fair amount of water before I went under again.

I'd never been a good swimmer. Hell, there wasn't any fancy Olympic pool in those government housing projects I grew up in. But, there was one summer when I was about nine or ten. I got to spend two weeks at an FOP youth camp. They had a pool at that camp and a couple of those cops taught us to swim. The first thing they taught us was how to hold our breath when we went underwater and how to push off of the bottom and come back to the surface. The second thing they taught us was how tread water, and the third thing they taught us was how to dog paddle. It seems like there was some other stuff they taught us, but that's the only things I remembered at the moment.

All of my splashing around drew their attention, and even though it was dark, gave them an idea where I was. Some gunshots rang out and I could actually hear the zips of the bullets as they entered the water around me.

"This is what you get when you mess with Big Sandy!" one of them shouted in between gunfire.

I took a deep breath, went under, and stayed under until I thought my lungs were about to burst. When I broke the surface, I tread water and tried to be as quiet as I could. I could see the beams of flashlights pointed down at the water from the bank, but the current had carried me far enough downstream where they couldn't see me.

I continued treading water and let the current carry me, but I was colder than I had ever been in my life and quickly losing strength. Eventually, I saw the dim outline of dry land. As I got closer, I could see it was one of the many islands in the area. I dogpaddled as best I could to it and crawled up the muddy bank, whereupon I puked up all of that river water I'd swallowed.

I had to do something. If they realized our fishing boats had electric trolling motors on them, they could come looking for me. I crawled further up the bank, wondering if I was going to crawl on top of a snake, and tried to hide myself among the reeds and bush. I was so cold I was shaking uncontrollably, but the moon was out now, and as my eyes became accustomed to the darkness, I saw some cattails. My brain was working in slow motion, but I knew if my body lost its ability to heat, my heart was going to stop and I was going to die. I grabbed a couple and chewed on them. It tasted awful, but I forced it down and started on the second one.

As I chewed on them, I spotted something at my feet, and although it was dark out, I could see enough to tell it looked out of the ordinary. I put out a shaking hand and tentatively touched it. After feeling it for a few seconds, I realized it was a tarp. Part of it was buried in the muddy bank, but there was enough to grab ahold of. It probably had a nest of copperheads living under it, but I pulled it out of the water and the mud and gathered it around me. It was foul-smelling and muddy, but if I wrapped myself in it, I figured I might be able to warm myself up a little.

And then, as if things couldn't get worse, it started raining again. I worked the tarp over my head, and sat there, shivering like one of those religious nuts who was feeling the spirit.

I was all done in, helpless. If they found me now, they had me. I was utterly exhausted, cold as hell, tired beyond belief, and my eyelids were damn near impossible to keep open. But, I'd had cold weather training, back when I was active duty, and I knew my core body temperature had dropped to dangerous levels. If I fell asleep, I would certainly die of hypothermia.

I pulled my knees toward me, which caused a shooting pain to my side. That acne-faced asshole probably broke a rib or two when he was kicking me. I was having a hard time thinking. I forced myself to think and take stock of my situation. In addition to the pain in my side, my ears were ringing and my head hurt like hell. I had a spark in my brain. It told me when I puked earlier, it was a sign I had a concussion. There was only one way I was going to live through this and that was by sheer willpower.

"Stay awake and live," I whispered to myself. I repeated it over and over throughout the night as I constantly rubbed my hands up and down my arms.

I have no idea what time it was when I crawled up on the island and wrapped myself in that tarp. All I know is I kept repeating that mantra over and over, maybe a million times, until at some point I realized I was hearing the morning birds happily chirping away. I stuck my head out and saw the sky was gray. My brain was having a hard time deciphering what that bit of information meant at first, but then I realized the sun was coming up. I warily looked around, but I didn't see any people or boats. I kept listening. A casual conversation, the lap of a water against the bow of a boat, sounds like those traveled across the water and were easily heard, but I didn't hear anything, other than the birds.

"Stand up and live," I whispered. Easier said than done. Standing was sheer agony. Every muscle in my body ached and it felt like somebody was thumping on my head. I was still cold down to my bones and I seemed to be hurting worse than last night. I started softly kneading the cramps out of my muscles while I tried to figure out what I was going to do next.

The first order of business was to look for snakes. I didn't like snakes. I'd sooner fight with a horde of zombies than come across one single water moccasin. I didn't see any, but that didn't mean anything. Those evil bastards were experts at hiding.

The second order of business was try to figure out exactly where the hell I was. It wasn't until the sky started turning a pumpkin orange that I saw the old earthen embankments for the Civil War era railroad tracks. I almost smiled to myself then. I'd run many a trot line in this area with Lee and Jinni. I was on an island in the middle of the channel. On the east bank was Old Johnsonville State Park. That was a good thing. Back when my three buddies were still alive, we'd made up several caches in old rusty barrels and stored them in the area. One of them was in the park.

All I had to do was swim across the channel, but that wasn't going to be easy. It was almost a hundred yards wide with another thirty yards or so of shallow water. The rain was gone, and the sun was warming things up, but it didn't help my state of mind much. Getting back in the river was going to plunge my core body temperature down again and I wasn't sure my body could take it.

"Damn," I muttered to myself as I stared at the far bank. Back behind me on the west side, I could wade through some backwater to a larger island that extended south. If I took that route, it'd eventually lead to the Highway 70 Bridge, but it'd take hours of slogging through muddy marshland that I knew from personal experience was filled with snakes. I hated snakes.

"Damn it all to hell," I muttered again.

I might've said it four times or forty times, I wasn't sure. I took my muddy clothes off and tied them in a ball. Getting back in the water was pure sack-shrinking torture. I would've cussed again, but I was too busy gasping for air and trying not to drown. I kept pushing my ball of clothes along as I dogpaddled, but they became waterlogged and I soon lost them.

It seemed to take an eternity and there were a couple of times when I almost went under, but I finally made it to the shallows. I slogged along until I got to the bank, crawled up, collapsed, and stayed that way for a long time. The aches, pains, the pounding in my head, the hunger, all of it had intensified, and once again, I was shaking uncontrollably. But, the sun was up and I could feel the warmth on my back.

I eventually rolled over and let the sun warm the front of me, and after several minutes, forced myself to stand. I was stiff and ached all over, but I was warmer now. I ran my hands all over my body, trying to rub some more warmth into the muscles. Looking around, I nodded to myself.

"Yeah," I muttered. I recognized familiar landmarks and once my slow-moving brain worked it out, I knew exactly where I was; the old Johnsonville State Park. It was a small town once, back before they put in Kentucky Dam. I seemed to recall that man they called the Devil Forrest blowing up the town or something during the war and they never rebuilt it.

I wasn't far from the cache now, but the problem was, my bare feet had been wet for several hours. The soles looked like shriveled prunes. Walking was going to be painful.

"The journey of a thousand miles begins with one step," I whispered to myself. Ole Mister Johnson liked to quote dead people, and he liked to use that one. Some Chinese dude said it, I think. So, there I was, buck naked, barefoot, beat all to hell, and shaking like an alcoholic in need of a drink. I got my bearings and started off, taking one gentle step at a time.

I got disoriented a few times before I found the replica Army garrison, which only consisted of some small, cheaply made log cabins that were barely large enough to hold two people. The old barrel was over by the fake outhouse. I would've run to it, but my feet hurt too much.

The lid had to be pried off, but that wasn't a problem. When we put the barrels out here and there, we hid a screwdriver near each one of them. The one I hid at this location was inside the outhouse. I found it and worked the lid open as quietly as I could and dug in.

There was a poncho on top. I pulled it out and spread it on the ground. Then I found a gallon jug of water. I set it aside for the moment, pulled out the musty-smelling clothing, and began putting them on. Pulling the socks over my feet was painful, but I suffered through it and put three pairs on. It was an old set of my combat utilities, but I'd lost so much weight the past few weeks, they hung loosely. I finished by donning a wool-knit cap and then helped myself to some water.

After drinking a couple of swallows, I found a Tupperware container sealed with duct tape. I used the edge of the barrel lid to hack at the tape and was soon rewarded with some salty hardtack.

Hardtack was kind of plain-tasting normally, but under these circumstances, it was like manna from heaven. I sat on the poncho and chewed on it slowly and washed it down with water. When I'd finished everything, I even licked the sides of the container, getting as many calories as I could inside me. I then took stock of the rest of the contents. There was a schoolbook-sized backpack, two more Tupperware containers, another gallon jug of water, and a 38-caliber revolver with six bullets. I put everything into the backpack and lay back, enjoying the morning sun and a full belly.

I still hurt, but I'd finally warmed up and the shakes had stopped. Even so, I was exhausted. I picked up the poncho and backpack, and headed to one of the little replica cabins. They had wooden bunks inside, no mattress or pillow, but I was so tired it didn't matter. I closed the door and lay down, wrapping myself in the poncho.

I didn't even remember falling asleep, but I awoke sometime during the night to the sound of something walking along the road. I cautiously peeked through the cracks between the wood slats. It was dark, but there was no mistaking the smell and raspy breathing. It was a small group of zeds, six or seven of them. Too many for me to take on.

I stayed quiet as a church mouse. If any of them opened the door, I'd have to get the revolver out of the backpack before they could get to me. Thankfully, they never sensed me and kept walking. I think I lay there for two hours, wondering if they were going to come back, but exhaustion took over and I fell back asleep.

The next morning, I enjoyed another gourmet meal of hardtack before making the trek back to the marina. It was slow going, because even though I had on three pairs of socks, I still didn't have any shoes. I kept the revolver in one hand, just in case.

The boat marina and campers weren't far, maybe five hundred yards. Nevertheless, I walked slowly, and when I got close, I hid behind a large oak tree and scouted things out. There was no movement. No sounds. The only things of note were the smoldering RVs.

Seeing nobody, I walked in. It was then I saw the bodies. All of them had been lined up and all of them had been decapitated. I found a chair, turned it upright, and sat there, staring at what was left of my pseudo-family. A cold rage coursed through my soul as I stared at Sandy's head.

"Y'all are gonna pay for that," I mumbled.

I sat there for I don't know how long, thinking about how I'd gotten myself into this mess. I guess it had to do with the women. We were three lonely men, and the women attached themselves to Blake and BC immediately. BC hooked up with Kathy Ann. She wasn't a bad-looking gal, but Lee once told me she was an easy lay, back before. He said she'd spread her legs for anyone with free drugs. Since I knew he was a meth cook, I asked him if he had ever taken a turn with her. He refused to answer, but the big shit-eating grin said it all.

Sandy latched herself onto Blake on the second day, and I thought I was going to be all alone until one night she knocked softly on the door to my RV and made a pass at me.

After that, it didn't take much for the three of us to be sucked into their lifestyle of raiding and marauding. We'd blindly, maybe even willingly, accepted Gavin as our leader. He was mean as a snake, cold, cunning, and ruthless. He loved to go out, find other survivors, and steal what they had. If they resisted, we killed them. He loved that part. He often bragged about spending time in prison for murder, like it was a badge of honor.

Like I said, we probably deserved this. It was only a matter of time before someone we'd wronged came looking for revenge. I might've understood better, but there was one thing they shouldn't have done. Prairie was missing. She had either burned up or they had taken her. Either way, I was going to pay them back.

Before I realized it, the sun was setting. I stood stiffly and made my way over to the boat docks. They had set them on fire too. Several of the boats had burned, but one of them, a houseboat, had broken free and had somehow lodged itself on a mooring.

It was Gavin's boat. We didn't have gas anymore, but he kept it up and during the summer he and Leslie lived on it. I took my clothes off, waded out to it, and crawled on board. As I suspected, there were some mason jars of food, some toiletries, and some shoes. They were a size larger than my feet, but that was okay. All I had to do was wear extra socks.

I got a rope and secured the boat on the bank before drying off and putting my clothes back on. I stayed the night in the cabin. As I lay there in the musty-smelling bed, I knew what I was going to do. I was going to find those people. If they had Prairie, I was going to get her back. In spite of the circumstances, I'd come to love her like she was my own daughter. She was a beautiful little girl who looked at the world in wide-eyed wonder and would grin and giggle at the drop of a hat.

Ultimately, Prairie was the reason Sandy and I stopped sneaking around. Or, maybe it the final reason Sandy needed to break it off with me. It hurt like hell, but I accepted it.

I lay there, thinking about Sandy's body and her decapitated head. I wondered what happened to Prairie. There were only two possibilities really; she burned up or she was taken. I didn't know which, but I knew I was going to hunt those sons of bitches down and take out as many as I could before they got me.

I woke up early the next morning and helped myself to a jar of applesauce I found in the cupboard. As I ate, I remembered back to the time when Leslie and Sandy spent the day mashing up apples and then using the pressure cooker to can a dozen jars. It seemed like a lifetime ago.

I finished the jar, used a toothbrush that I really hoped belonged to Leslie instead of Gavin, and then walked over to my burned-out RV. The RV was nothing but a shell of burned and warped metal, but the round behind it was undisturbed.

"Y'all missed something," I muttered.

I couldn't find a shovel anywhere, but I found a small garden spade. It took a while, but I finally got the footlocker dug up. Opening the lid, I looked in and gave myself a nod.

It was the M60 that Zach had given us, a little over five years ago now. We'd never used it and I still had the five hundred rounds of ammunition. I had put grease all over it before hiding it. Breaking it down, I used a piece of somebody's shirt to clean off the excess grease before reassembling it and storing it all in a musty-smelling canvass bag.

I took one final look around before heading out. I didn't bother burying the bodies. Didn't see any point.

Our cars and trucks didn't work no more because the gas was all bad, and none of these west Tennessee people had ever learned how to ride a horse, which I thought was strange. We rode bicycles or used a sailboat whenever we traveled, but I guess they took the bikes because I couldn't find a single one.

So, I loaded up the M60, put some mason jars in my cargo pockets, and walked. The ribs were still tender, but I could handle it.

It wasn't hard to find them. When that knucklehead yelled out about messing with Big Sandy, he wasn't talking about a person; he was talking about a small, rural town that was a little over twenty miles north of Johnsonville.

It took me two days of walking to get there, and then it was only a matter of remembering how to get to where they lived. We'd raided them a few months previous. They lived in a big farmhouse nestled in a valley near the Big Sandy River. There were two additional house trailers, all of which was encircled by barbed-wire fences and tanglefoot.

I found a spot on the side of a small hill five hundred yards away from them and dug out a spider hole under cover of darkness. Then I started watching them. Tactically speaking, it was stupid. From my vantage point, I had a clear target.

I watched them for the next three days, learning their habits. The weather had been pleasant, which led them to eat their meals at picnic tables in the backyard. I was too far away to hear their conversations, but as I watched them with the little pair of binoculars, I could see them laughing and carrying on. The big dude was obviously the leader and everyone deferred to him. I was going to need to kill him first.

As I watched, I thought back to the time we'd raided them. We spotted two of them in town, riding bicycles. We kept our distance, and followed them from a distance. That was back last fall, and it was cool enough at night that they built fires, so it wasn't hard following the smell of wood smoke that evening.

It was Gavin, BC, and me. We watched them from a spot not too far from where I currently was. One morning, a bunch of them left, leaving only two people at the house. Gavin wanted to kill them, but BC talked him out of it. Amazingly, they had some good fuel and a diesel truck. We loaded up with as much as we could and took off.

I relived the memory of that day while I lay there in my spider hole, watching them go about their daily lives.

They didn't seem much different from us. I'd see a couple of them go hunting and come back at the end of the day with a deer. I watched the big man hang the deer and butcher it with expert efficiency. I watched them plant their spring gardens, which was probably a little early, but that didn't stop them. I watched them gather buckets of water from a well. I watched them wash laundry and hang it out to dry.

Like I said, not much different from us. But, even though we didn't kill that man and woman, they felt the need to retaliate. I might've understood, and while I lay there in that spider hole, I started having second thoughts, but then, on the second morning, I saw little Prairie. She walked outside carrying a pitcher of water or something, and dropped it. One of the women walked over to her. I couldn't hear, but it was obvious she was scolding Prairie, and then she hauled off and slapped her so hard Prairie fell to the ground.

"You gonna pay for that," I whispered.

On the third morning, I woke up before daylight and got ready. I couldn't spend any more time in this little hole. I was out of food, almost out of water, and even though they didn't have roaming patrols, they were eventually going to find me.

I assembled the M60 in the dark and fed the linked ammo into the tray. I then waited for sunup and for them to gather at the picnic tables for breakfast, like they had the previous two mornings. I watched them with the little binoculars I'd taken from Gavin's houseboat and did a headcount. They were all there. All I needed was for Prairie to leave the picnic tables, and then I was going to light 'em up.

The old lady who'd slapped Prairie suddenly grabbed her arm. It looked like she was once again scolding Prairie, who stood there, her head hanging and looking at the ground. The old woman pointed back toward the house and Prairie dutifully began walking toward it.

I looked around and found acne face. He was the only guard on duty, and currently, he was sitting at the table, shoving food in his ugly mug, his shotgun propped up at the end of the table. None of the others were armed, except for the big man, who had a pistol holstered on his side. They felt safe. Why shouldn't they? They'd killed all of their enemies, or so they believed.

The big man was sitting by the woman who had been mistreating Prairie. I decided I was going to kill him first and then spray in a left-to-right pattern, saving acne face for last. I doubted he'd run off. He'd grab that shotgun and look for a target, but a shotgun couldn't get anywhere close to me.

I took one final look with the binocs, confirmed the headcount, and confirmed Prairie had not wandered back outside.

It was time.

I checked the ammo tray again, gently closed the cover, and pulled the charging handle. Flipping up the rear sight, I took aim and squeezed the trigger. The intermittent tracer rounds confirmed I was on target as I sprayed the area. Some tried to run. It didn't do no good. Some tried to hide under the wooden tables. The 7.62 hardball ammo had no problems penetrating the soft wood.

There was a dozen of them and only one of me, but I had the high ground and five hundred rounds of agony. The odds were against them. I kept firing and firing until I had no bullets left, which maybe lasted a minute. The barrel had an angry red glow and steam was coming off it. I'd probably seized it up. No matter. A slow scan with my binoculars confirmed I'd inflicted death and destruction. There were bodies everywhere.

I crawled out of the spider hole and began jogging down the hill. I'd left the M60 behind and was now only armed with the .38. This was when I was the most vulnerable. Someone could've been in the house the whole time and I'd never seen them. All they had to do was wait for me to walk into range and pump me full of lead.

But, there wasn't anyone hiding in wait. Most of them were dead. The old woman, Prairie's tormentor, had a couple of bullets in her midsection, but she was still alive. She was trying to hold her guts in with her hands and watched me walk up to her with a mixture of fear and hatred in her eyes. I took a knife off of the nearest picnic table, walked over, and stabbed her in the side of her neck. The blood squirted out like water coming out of a garden hose.

There was one other person still alive: acne face. He caught a stitching of four bullets across his torso, but somehow, he was still alive.

"Remember me?" I asked, and waited until recognition dawned in his eyes before I did the same thing to him as I did the old woman.

The rest of them were dead, even the big mean-looking one. My hands were shaking a little bit from the adrenaline, but I felt no emotion for them. They'd massacred my people and cut their heads off. They got what they deserved. In the end, we all get what we deserve.

I got the shotgun, checked to make sure it was loaded, and then cautiously searched the house. I found her hiding under a little dirty cot, which I assumed was her bed. She stared out at me apprehensively with her big blue eyes.

"Hi, Lil' Bit," I said.

"Uncle True?" she questioned.

"Yep, it's me. Come on out from under there."

It took a little bit of coaxing, but she finally wiggled out and stood. Other than some dust bunnies on her clothes, she was unscathed.

"You're dirty," she said. "And you smell bad."

I smiled at her. "I'm sure I do."

She was right. I could've done with a bath and some clean clothes, so could she, but there wasn't time. The gunfire was either going to attract zombies, people, or both, and I didn't want to have any contact with any of them.

"Do you want to go on a trip with me?" I asked her.

"Where?"

"It's a place a long way from here. There's lots of nice people and there's kids you can play with all day long if you want to."

"Is that where Mommy and Daddy are?" she asked.

"No, sweetie. Your mommy and daddy are in heaven now."

"Oh."

She never answered my question. I knew her young mind was having difficulty processing everything at the moment, so I pushed ahead.

"Okay, you wait right here. We'll get going in a few minutes."

"Okay, Uncle True."

The car I had my eye on was one of two Toyota Land Cruisers. They had a biodiesel setup on them, and I believe that's what they used to travel to Johnsonville to pay us a visit. I started walking over to them, but then I glanced over at the picnic tables. Some of the plates had eggs and venison on them, which all of a sudden made me ravenous. I grabbed a plate, cleaned it off quickly, and did the same to another plate. Washing it down with somebody's glass of water, I refocused and walked over to the Toyotas. My heart sunk when I got closer to them. Both of them had multiple bullet holes in them. There was a mixture of antifreeze and oil forming under both of them. I was so fixated on killing everyone I hadn't paid attention to these two vehicles. I knew it was going to be useless, but I tried to start them anyway. The results were about what one would imagine.

Gas was no good anymore, and unless you had some kind of special rigging, anything with an internal combustion engine didn't work, like the two Toyotas. There weren't any horses around here that I saw, so that left only one other mode of transportation: bicycles. The trouble was going to be how to accommodate Prairie. I looked around in a barn and found a kid's bicycle, along with a well-used mountain bike.

Unfortunately, Prairie didn't know how to ride a bicycle, but leaving her behind was out of the question. After a little bit of figuring, I found a large rucksack she could sit in and loaded her up. It was a little awkward and I couldn't fill it up with food and water now, so I found a smaller bag that I was able to strap on the handlebars. It didn't hold much, so I was going to have to figure out something along the way.

When I walked Prairie outside, she acted like the bodies were invisible and said nothing. I knew one day I was going to have to explain everything to her, but not right now. I strapped up the ruck, squatted down where she could step into it, and mounted the bike. I had some rough directions in my head, but I had no idea of how arduous a journey it was going to be. It took us all day before we even made it to I-40, and we were still in Tennessee, several hundred miles from Mount Weather.

CHAPTER 40 – TRUE AND PRAIRIE'S BIG ADVENTURE

I took a detour. There was no way we were going to make it to Mount Weather like this, so I detoured to the school on Concord Road, a little bit between Nolensville and Brentwood.

I expected people to be there, and I hoped they'd help us out, but the school was a burnt-out shell and there wasn't anyone around. Same thing with the radio tower. I rode back over the bridge crossing I-65 and turned into the parking lot of a large church. It wasn't burnt, but it too was empty. I walked in warily, my rifle at the ready, but there were no signs of life. The air inside was tired and stale. Nobody had been in here for a while.

They'd had get-togethers and socials and stuff, back when people lived here. The back wall had been made into a bulletin board. It was filled with notes and pictures. People used it to try to reconnect to lost loved ones. I wondered if there had been any success stories.

"Why are we here?" Prairie asked me.

"Some people used to live here, but I guess they're gone now," I said. I looked around. "Alright, let's see if I can round us up some food."

The church's pantry was empty, but, there were rabbits running around everywhere outside. I managed to kill one with one shot and boiled some water from the nearby creek. Amazingly, one of the old tree houses that they'd used as a lookout was still intact, so we slept in it before heading out the next morning.

It was going to take us several days, I knew that. I didn't have a map, but I vaguely remembered the route. It was over three hundred miles, I knew that well enough. We were making thirty to forty miles a day, which wasn't bad, until the bicycle's chain broke somewhere north of Bristol. Try as I might, I couldn't fix it. When I finally gave up on it, I wiped my grimy hands as best as I could on the thick Johnson grass along the side of the interstate and looked down at Prairie.

"Looks like we're going to be walking for a little while."

She looked up at me with her big blue eyes and nodded, like it was no big deal. That was three days ago. She simply was not strong enough, nor were her feet tough enough to walk a long distance. So, when she got tired, I'd put her on my shoulders. Her little legs dangled over my shoulder and sometimes she'd softly hum to herself. We must have looked quite the sight; a pretty little white girl being carried by a filthy black man.

Our situation wasn't looking good. I believe a good word would be bleak. We had no transportation, no water, no food. All I could do was put one foot in front of another. One foot in front of another. At some point, I'd zoned out. I don't know how long I'd been like that until I bumped into an abandoned car. It scared the hell out of me when I realized I could've walked the two of us right into some zombies.

I stopped and rubbed my face with a grimy hand. I was thirsty. And tired. And my feet hurt. My shoulders hurt. My ribs hurt. Hell, I hurt all over. But, what hurt most is what I knew. I knew I was failing, and my failure was going to kill the little girl sitting on my shoulders.

"True," Prairie said from her perch.

"Yeah?" I asked, my voice raspy with thirst.

"I need to pee."

"Yeah, okay."

I stopped, and with a little difficulty, dropped to one knee and helped her off of my shoulders. She started to squat down beside me, but I stopped her.

"Hang on a second," I said and scanned the area. I saw no zombies or any other signs of life, only a couple of crows flying overhead and maybe a blue jay chirping somewhere nearby.

"Yeah, okay," I said quietly. "Go ahead."

I walked up the interstate for a few yards, giving her some privacy, and worked the rucksack off of my shoulders. I dropped beside it, worked myself into a sitting position, and set the AR-15 in my lap. I leaned my back against a guardrail post and wondered if I had the strength to go much further. Prairie finished, then walked up and sat beside me.

"I'm thirsty," Prairie said.

"Me too, Lil' Bit."

"And hungry."

I sighed. I was hungry too and I only had four bullets left. I had more at one time, but we kept running into zeds. Outrunning them was out of the question; the combination of the ribs and utter exhaustion prevented it. So, I had to shoot them, and use up my precious ammo. I'd shot up all of the .38 ammo too. The gun was currently sitting useless in my rucksack and I was seriously considering dumping all of the gear to shed weight.

I pulled the AR-15 to me and checked the magazine. In my exhausted state, I was hoping I'd miscounted and the magazine was still full. No such luck. I tried to shift my weight to find a more comfortable sitting position, but that was always impossible when it came to broken ribs. I glanced over at Prairie, who was looking at me expectantly.

"Prairie?"

She looked up at me.

"I'm sorry I got you into this. I'm sorry for everything."

"It's okay, True," she said.

"Let's rest a spell and then I'll find us some water," I told her.

I hated making such a promise, but I didn't want to upset her. The sun was going down. We could spend the night in one of the abandoned cars, like we'd been doing, but, that wasn't going to get us any food or water. And, I could feel a nip in the evening breeze. It was going to be a chilly night. She was oblivious, a naïve little girl. She'd go to sleep and wake up believing there would be a hot breakfast waiting on her.

"Are we going to rest here?" she asked.

"Just for a little bit," I answered.

She nodded, plopped down, and snuggled up beside me. Within a minute, she had fallen into a fitful asleep. Just as well. We weren't going to be traveling anymore today.

"I'll just rest myself a few minutes," I mumbled and leaned my head back against the guardrail.

That was a mistake. I must have dozed off into a deep slumber within seconds. The next thing I know, I felt someone wiggling my foot. When I finally opened my eyes, there was a white dude squatting down in front of me, and he had my rifle in his hands.

"Howdy," he said. "You were sleeping so good I thought you might've been dead."

He was older than me, more meat on his bones, clean shaven, and a fresh haircut. He was clean too, unlike me and Prairie. He stared curiously, not smiling or nothing, but curious.

My eyes looked over at the rucksack where I had the pistol. If I could get it out, maybe I could bluff him down. A slight smile crossed his face.

"I see you looking over at your rucksack, so I'm thinking maybe you have another weapon in there. I'd appreciate it if you'd just leave it be. We're friendly enough and I'd hate for things to get ugly before we even get to know each other."

"We ain't got anything worth taking," I said, which was mostly true. Besides the pistol, the only thing I had in there was a blanket, poncho, and two empty canteens.

"And we aren't looking to steal anything from you," the man said as he continued inspecting my rifle. He then looked back at me with a steady gaze.

"My name's Melvin and that's Savannah," he said as he gestured over his right shoulder.

I looked over and for the first time saw a woman standing beside a big redneck truck, rifle in hand. She was a few years younger than the man, cute, with hard brown eyes, making me think she'd seen some rough times. She was wearing a short-sleeved shirt revealing slender but muscular arms. She was a little on the skinny side, but who wasn't these days. Well, this dude wasn't skinny, but he wasn't fat neither. He looked like all muscle. I was waiting for her to say something, but she didn't, she only stared.

"Alright," I said, my voice a little hoarser than it was before.

"You sound thirsty," Melvin said.

He didn't wait for me to answer. He made a head nod at the girl, who reached into the cab of the truck and came out with a canteen. She walked over and tossed it to me. I watched her for a second or two, noticing a large knife sheathed on her hip, and then woke up Prairie.

"Here, Lil' Bit," I said.

Prairie stirred and rubbed her eyes. When she saw Melvin, her eyes widened in a mixture of surprise and fright.

"Who are you?" she asked.

The man gave a friendly grin now. I couldn't help but notice he had pearly white teeth and there weren't any that were missing. You didn't see that too often these days.

"My name's Melvin," he said again. "Where'd you two come from?"

"Does it matter?" I asked. I was reluctant to answer. After all, I had no idea if he was friends with the people I'd killed.

His smile didn't falter. In fact, if anything, he looked like he was amused.

"No, I don't suppose it does. I was just curious." He looked back at Prairie. "Hey, sweetie, why don't you have a drink of that water?"

I helped her unscrew the top and then the three of us watched her slurp it down.

"Don't gulp it down, or else you'll get stomach cramps," he admonished while still smiling.

I looked over and gently pulled the canteen out of her hands before wiping off the water running down her chin with my sleeve.

"Like the man say, drink it slow."

"You drink some too," Melvin said. "Go ahead, we've got enough for all of us."

I stared at him warily a moment and handed the canteen back to Prairie. When she had enough, I took it back and drank down several gulps. The water tasted wonderful. It had a clean, filtered taste. I was sure of it. Melvin waited patiently while I drank several swallows.

"I appreciate it," I said. "My name's True."

"I'm pleased to meet you, Mister True," he said and looked down at Prairie. "And what's your name, sweetie?" he asked.

"I'm Prairie," Prairie said. "I'm hungry."

"Well, now we can't have that," Melvin said and nodded at Savannah again, who went back to the truck and came out a moment later with something wrapped in an off-white cloth. She brought it over and opened it up. I caught a whiff and my mouth started watering, like that dog Ms. Stewart talked about back in science class.

"That there is what's left of some damn good sourdough biscuits," Melvin said. "I must admit I ate more than my fair share, but I couldn't help myself."

Savannah handed Prairie a biscuit. "You sure are pretty," she said as Prairie took the biscuit.

"What's your name?" Prairie asked.

"My name is Savannah," she said and smiled at her as she brushed some hair out of Prairie's face. She then turned to me and held her hand out. I tentatively took one of the biscuits, trying to hide how hungry I was.

"Take a couple," she urged me. I gratefully took an extra one.

"Thanks," I said and before I knew it, I'd eaten both of them and helped myself to some more water before handing the canteen back to Prairie.

"I appreciate this, I really do, but are you going to keep my rifle?" I asked.

He didn't answer, even when he saw me giving him a hard stare. I had a lock blade knife on my side. It wasn't my trusty bayonet, but it was sharp. From his angle, I don't think he could see it. I continued looking him over, sizing him up and weighing my odds of being able to stab him and not getting shot by the girl. For some reason, despite his friendliness, he gave me the impression he was a fighter. I guess his skinned-up knuckles might've been a clue. He'd been in a recent fight and his face was unmarked. That told me a little something.

"If you're going to spring on me, you should stand up first and get the muscles loosened up a little," he casually said. "Maybe even wait a few minutes for your meal to settle."

He didn't seem too worried on whether or not I was going to jump on him. I chose to stay seated for the moment. He stood, took the magazine out, and racked the action back. After counting the bullets, he inspected the bore closely.

"You've fired some rounds out of it recently, but you've got a nice coat of oil on it. That tells me you know the value of keeping your weapon in good shape," he said. He then handed the rifle back to me.

"If you don't mind, I'm going to hang onto these bullets for the time being until I get to know you a little better."

I shrugged nonchalantly. "I got more."

The amused smile was back. "No, my friend, you don't." He waved a finger toward me. "Those are some well-worn combat utilities you're wearing. I got a feeling you earned them the old-fashioned way, the same way I earned mine, and no decent soldier I ever knew would go around loaded with only four rounds if they had more bullets."

I didn't say anything. There wasn't no need to. He had me mostly figured out.

"What're you two doing around these parts?" I asked. "Do you live here?"

"We live a few miles from here," he answered. "We travel around on occasion. You know, scavenging and what not."

"Are you marauders?" I asked.

His easygoing grin faltered now. "No, sir, we're not marauders. Never have been. Since you're not going to tell us where you're from, do you mind telling me where you're going?"

I thought about it a moment and figured, what could it hurt? "A place called Mount Weather."

As soon as I said it, the girl gasped. Melvin then arched an eyebrow.

"You know of Mount Weather?" he asked.

"Never been there," I answered. "But some friends of mine went up there a few years back. I'm hoping they still there."

"Oh yeah? We know a few people who live there. Maybe I know your friends. What's their names?"

I almost told him it was none of his business, but if I kept being belligerent, they'd either kill us or just leave us here to rot. Besides, I was trying to figure out how to get him to give us directions.

"One of 'em is a dude by the name of Zach. He's tall, got some muscle on him, and he don't smile much except when he's playing with his kids. Oh, and when he do smile, he has teeth as white as yours."

Melvin glanced over at his girl, Savannah, and there was a kind of silent communication that passed between them. He then stood, held out his hand, and pulled me to my feet.

"True, I think the two of us are going to be friends. Would you and your little buddy like a ride?"

"It depends on where you're going," I said.

He let out a belly laugh now and handed me back my bullets. "Here," he said. "We've got some more in the truck and you can top off your magazine. Alright, who's ready to go to Mount Weather?"

CHAPTER 41 - JOURNAL ENTRY, MARCH 25TH, 8 A.Z.

It's late and I'm exhausted, but I'm too keyed up to sleep. Several hours ago, my beautiful wife gave birth to a handsome baby boy. His name is Hardy Gunderson, named after Kelly's father. It goes without saying I've been bouncing off the walls with joy. Even Fred cracked a smile when he saw the little fella.

Kelly is understandably exhausted and at the moment, she's sound asleep. The kids wanted to sleep with their new baby brother, and when they couldn't, they insisted on sleeping with their mother. I started to protest, but Kelly said she wouldn't have it any other way. I tried to squeeze in, but the three of them were sprawled out, leaving little room for yours truly, but that's okay. In the past, I'd slept on the cold hard ground, on a concrete slab in a jail cell, in cramped vehicles, pretty much everywhere. So, riding the couch so my family could sleep peacefully was a no-brainer.

Besides, like I said, I was too worked up to sleep, so I thought I'd do a little writing.

I started with the great news, but now I have to write about some bad news. Parvis died last week. His health had gotten progressively worse. We knew it was going to happen, but even so, we were all understandably saddened by his death. We cremated his remains, in accordance with his wishes, and held a memorial service in the form of a party, which was also what he wanted. Garret and Grace were devastated, but they'll be okay. Kendra handled it with the professionalism of a doctor who had seen many people die when she was an ER doc, but even so, she shed a tear or two during the eulogies.

The freezing weather broke in early March. Several days of sunshine melted the roads of ice. Our first visitor was good old Roscoe Sidebottom with another tanker full of diesel and our old friend Raymond Easting. We responded with enough food to feed his people for a couple of months, along with several Proctor and Gamble products. Joe Fitzgerald Senior had ridden with Roscoe and spent the day with his daughter, Riley.

Our second group of arrivals this month was Melvin and Savannah. They'd been gone all winter, and I think it's safe to say everyone had missed them both. Surprisingly, they brought people with them; Nimrod True and a cute little blonde-headed girl by the name of Prairie. They had found them nearly starving to death outside of Stephens City.

During the debriefing, True told of the trek to west Tennessee with Blake Mann and Brandon Casswell, whereupon they encountered BC's aunt and uncle and their small group of survivors. They lived together near Kentucky Lake before getting ambushed one evening. True said he and Prairie were the only survivors.

I got the sense he did not tell us everything during the debriefing, but I wasn't concerned. He'd tell us when he was ready. After the debriefing ended, he surprised me by asking to be reinstated in the rank and file of the military. The last time I had spoken with him, he said he was done taking orders. I asked him why the change in attitude, but his response was only a vague shrug.

The warmer weather has also allowed us to mobilize our scout teams. We're being bold this year and are sending most of the teams west of the Mississippi. Despite the president's trepidations, we broke the news and told everyone about the fleet of ships landing on the west coast last winter. The bottom line is, we needed to find out, somehow, what their intentions are.

Of course, their primary mission is to find survivors. It is hoped we can create outposts where we can stage and resupply. Once they start compiling census counts, I strongly suspect our population projections are going to multiply exponentially.

Our goal has not changed; reestablish a formal government and reunite our nation. This sounds easy, but rebuilding the infrastructure of America goes along with this goal. It is a monumental task to say the least, but I think I can safely say the survivors we've brought into our fold are onboard with this.

Now, for a final note of bad news. A couple of weeks ago we discovered a traitor in our midst, General Harlan Fosswell Senior. Surprisingly, nobody knew about his nefarious activities until his son gave him up. He had become a religious zealot and somehow decided people needed to die. He'd conducted several acts of sabotage within our community, culminating with intentionally tampering with the batch of vaccines earmarked for the survivors of Ohio.

The result of that act is we now have a new strain of the plague. They display the same symptoms of hyper-aggression, but even more alarming, their bodies don't immediately begin decomposing. Therefore, a freshly infected individual is extremely dangerous.

Both Harlan Fosswell Senior and Junior are now deceased. Junior committed suicide. Senior met an untimely end and was cremated. We are convinced more parties were involved in his crazy scheme, but unfortunately, any direct evidence died with the general and his son. I have my suspicions of the complicity of two particular scientists, but believe it or not, I am not going to act only on suspicions. I'll wait and do something when the time is right.

CHAPTER 42 – LISANDRA

Fred sat in Parvis' chair, sipping tea and looking around as he stroked Zoe's head.

"I don't think you've ever been in my office," I remarked.

"Nope," Fred replied. "I don't see how you can spend hours in this windowless room."

"You never really get used to it, but I'm doing the job of two people now, so I seem to spend more time than normal in here," I said as I struggled to finish typing a report.

After Parvis died, a meeting was held to discuss the merits of whether I was going to take over the position of Director of Operations. While I sat in the hall outside of the conference room, they had a long-winded debate on whether or not I was qualified for such an important position. One would have thought it would have been a simple decision; either promote me or don't and put someone else in the position. But, nothing is ever simple with politicians. Somehow, the job opening was the impetus for old, festering issues to resurface.

President Stark was uncharacteristically magnanimous and made several concessions, one of which was the appointment of William Rhinehart as vice president. There were other administrative changes made, including the declaration that an election would be held within four years, along with minor trivial matters. A vote was finally put forth and I was formally appointed the position of Director of Ops, but, as of yet, I had no assistant. So, now I was doing the work of two men.

Fred was in a talkative mood this morning and continued his diatribe.

"I never liked any room without windows," he said. "Offices, computers, staff meetings, I never cared much for them."

I shook my head. "You know, you're turning into a grumpy old man." Before I could say anything further, my phone rang.

"Never liked phones either," he muttered.

I ignored him and answered. After a brief conversation, I hung up and stared at Fred.

"What?" he asked.

"We have new arrivals at the front gate," I said. "And one of them is saying she's my sister."

I thought I saw a slight arch of Fred's right eyebrow. He was obviously dumbfounded.

"Aren't you an only child?" he asked.

"Yeah, I am. Let's go check it out."

We stood together and made the walk to the front gate. We bumped into Grant in the hallway carrying his medical bag.

"We have new arrivals," he said.

"Yeah, we heard. I take it you're the one who is going to check them out?"

He held up his bag and smiled pleasantly. "Are you two going out to meet them?"

"Yes, we are. One of them said she was my sister," I said as we walked.

Grant frowned. "I didn't think you had a sister."

"I don't."

There were four people sitting at one of the picnic tables; three men and a woman who had her back to me. They were all dirty; an indication they'd been on the road for a while.

One of the men spotted us and said something under his breath. The woman stood and turned toward us. Grant stopped walking and grabbed my arm, causing me to stop suddenly.

"Zach, I know that woman," he whispered.

"Okay, who is she?" I whispered back.

He took a deep breath. "Do you remember me telling you about another subject who had antigens in her blood similar to yours?"

I remembered. When he was a member of the CBIRF, they had kidnapped my kids and me, massacred several people in my group, including Julie, and held us captive at Fort Campbell. While under confinement, Grant had told me of a woman whose blood had similar properties to mine.

I stared at him. "That's her? Are you sure?"

Grant responded with a nod. "I mean, it's been a few years, and she's got some mileage on her, but that's her. Her people told us she'd been killed. I guess they were protecting her."

We resumed walking, exited the gate, and stopped before them. She was tall for a woman, maybe six feet, and I guessed her to be a couple of years older than me. She was thin, but had broad shoulders, like a onetime athlete. All of them were rough-looking, dirty and unkempt. Their clothing, jeans, and various types of shirts, looked like they'd not been washed in several days.

"Welcome to Mount Weather," I said.

One of the men, the oldest one of the group, offered a nod while the other two men stared silently. The woman offered a smile, revealing crooked teeth that'd never been seen by an orthodontist. Zoe walked up and stood beside me. She stared at me without emotion. I noticed her nose was a little bent to one side, like it had been broken once and not reset properly.

"Are you Zach?" she asked.

"I am. Who might you be?"

"My name's Lisandra, but everyone calls me Lisa."

I nodded. I'd get the rest of their names later, but right now it was time to get right to the point.

"The guards said you told them you're my sister."

"Yeah," she answered matter-of-factly, like it was common knowledge, or no big deal.

"I think I would remember if I had a sister," I said.

"We've never met, but we have the same father. I guess that makes me your half-sister," she said.

I glanced at Fred and Grant, and then back at her. She returned my gaze, looking me over the same way I was doing her. I gave her a slow, solemn nod.

"Well then, I suppose we have a lot to talk about."

THE END

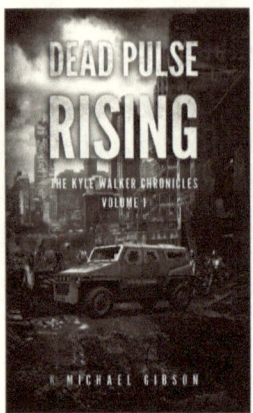

CHECK OUT OTHER GREAT ZOMBIE NOVELS

DEAD ASCENT
by Jason McPhearson

The dead have risen and they are hungry...

Grizzled war veteran turned game warden, Brayden James and a small group of survivors, fight their way through the rugged wilderness of southern Appalachia to an isolated cabin in the hope of finding sanctuary. Every terrifying step they make they are stalked by a growing mass of staggering corpses, and a raging forest fire, set by the government in hopes of containing the virus.

As all logical routes off the mountain are cut off from them, they seek the higher ground, but they soon realize there is little hope of escape when the dead walk and the world burns.

CHAOS THEORY
by Rich Restucci

The world has fallen to a relentless enemy beyond reason or mercy. With no remorse they rend the planet with tooth and nail.

One man stands against the scourge of death that consumes all.

Teamed with a genius survivalist and a teenage girl, he must flee the teeming dead, the evils of humans left unchecked, and those that would seek to use him. His best weapon to stave off the horrors of this new world? His wit.

CHECK OUT OTHER GREAT ZOMBIE NOVELS

RUN
by Rich Restucci

The dead have risen, and they are hungry.

Slow and plodding, they are Legion. The undead hunt the living. Stop and they will catch you. Hide and they will find you. If you have a heartbeat you do the only thing you can: You run.

Survivors escape to an island stronghold: A cop and his daughter, a computer nerd, a garbage man with a piece of rebar, and an escapee from a mental hospital with a life-saving secret. After reaching Alcatraz, the ever expanding group of survivors realize that the infected are not the only threat.

Caught between the viciousness of the undead, and the heartlessness of the living, what choice is there? Run.

THE DEAD WALK THE EARTH
by Luke Duffy

As the flames of war threaten to engulf the globe, a new threat emerges.

A 'deadly flu', the like of which no one has ever seen or imagined, relentlessly spreads, gripping the world by the throat and slowly squeezing the life from humanity.

Eight soldiers, accustomed to operating below the radar, carrying out the dirty work of a modern democracy, become trapped within the carnage of a new and terrifying world.

Deniable and completely expendable. That is how their government considers them, and as the dead begin to walk, Stan and his men must fight to survive.